UNDISCLOSED
Desire

INTERNATIONAL BESTSELLING AUTHOR
seven rue

SCAN THIS CODE FOR MORE SEVEN RUE BOOKS

Chapter One

Rooney

Breakups meant heartbreak, tears, and many, many fights.

Luckily, those weren't words I would describe my first breakup with.

I'd say mine was...calm, eye-opening, and relieving.

Thankfully, AJ made it easy for both of us.

We met two years ago on my first day of college, and at first, I had thought he would be that kind of guy I could call a friend and hang out with whenever my best friend, Evie, didn't have time for me.

But the more time I spent with AJ, the closer we got, and I realized that maybe he was that kind of friend who could show me a good time whenever I needed it.

Turned out we never got to the good time part.

Instead, we hung out a lot, even kissed whenever we felt like it, but I never let him get further than that.

It also turned out that keeping my heart locked up while I let him get close to me wasn't such a good idea, as he was starting to catch feelings for me.

We never talked about it.

About what we were and what we wanted to be in the near future.

It was always clear to me that AJ was someone I could trust and spend time with when I was bored, then send home whenever I needed some alone time.

He, on the other hand, thought we were dating, and I was just playing hard to get.

Not sure how that was what it seemed like to him, but I wouldn't call it dating.

Somehow, things ended up with me slipping into this weird relationship with him, where we would kiss whenever we saw each other on campus, or hold hands and dance together at parties, but we would never say what we felt for each other.

I loved him.

I really did...but not like *that*.

AJ's a nice guy, maybe even too nice.

Especially for a girl like me who doesn't know shit about love.

At twenty, I shouldn't have life all figured out and be in a stable relationship though, right?

I should be having fun, which I did have, and I shouldn't be thinking about marriage and children.

Anyway, back to the relationship I had with AJ.

This morning, we sat down and talked.

We *finally* talked.

And although we were both quiet at first, we quickly picked up a nice, easy-going conversation.

It was obvious that we had different ideas of where this was going, but in the end, we agreed on staying friends since we still attended the same college and would cross paths every day.

Not to mention all the friends we had in common.

And after agreeing on staying friends, and never going back to what we had before, I happily walked out of the frat house he lived in to head back to my dorm.

I was in the middle of moving out of it.

Evie, whose parents owned an apartment complex close to campus, had a spare room after her roommate moved out.

Instead of looking for someone, she offered me the room without hesitation.

I didn't think it would be such a good idea to live with your best friend, but I couldn't say no as my dorm was insanely small and hard to stay in.

It was dark, and the sun never shone into the window, which was depressing.

Evie's apartment complex had a nice view over the fields of Riverton, Wyoming.

We both grew up around here, and decided that Central College was where we wanted to go after high school.

It's our home, and neither of us wanted to leave town.

I loved being close to my family, even if they now moved onto the country side, a few hours away from Riverton.

I still saw them at least twice a month, but it was nice having a little distance between us to not get on each other's nerves.

When I arrived in my dorm, I grabbed my phone and checked my messages, but I didn't see anything other than Evie's calls I missed.

I tapped the screen and tucked my phone between my shoulder and ear to continue packing my suitcases.

"How did he take it?" Evie asked first thing after picking up.

"Good, I think. We're friends now," I told her, puckering my lips.

"We'll see how long that'll last." I could *hear* her roll her eyes. "When will you be here? I grabbed a few things for tonight to make pizza. And I also put a few movies onto my list to watch."

"I need a few more hours. I have to clean the dorm once I've finished packing," I explained.

"Want me to pick up some of your stuff?" she asked.

"Uh, no, I can fit it all into my car. By the way, are you sure I can park in front of the complex?"

"Yeah. One of my neighbors moved out and the parking spot is free. Don't worry about it. God, I feel like you're dreading coming here."

I laughed at that. "A little. But only because I know we'll stay up far too late and never get anything done. My grades are gonna suffer because of you."

"Hey, you agreed on moving in. Don't blame me if I'll be the best roommate you'll ever have."

"All right, all right. I'll text you when I'm done."

We hung up the phone, and before I set it onto my bed, I received a message from AJ.

Glad we talked things out. Let me know if there's something you need. Good luck living with Evie.

AJ and Evie had a love-hate relationship.

They acted like brother and sister, and it often times was a pain in the ass going out with them.

Safe to say they knew how college life worked, whereas I wished I had already graduated.

Me too. Thank you for understanding. And I think I'll survive somehow.

Thanks to AJ, I realized that relationships weren't really my thing.

Not sure if he was the reason why I didn't want one, or if I just wasn't capable of being in one.

Either way, I loved being single.

I wasn't a major flirt, but if a guy caught my attention, I surely wouldn't just stand there and wait until he noticed me.

I was open for whatever came my way.

Anything besides an actual relationship.

***

"Finally!" I heard Evie's voice shout from the top floor of the apartment complex.

It was a nice, industrial looking building, and I knew the inside was just as nice.

Evie threw a few parties here already, and I also slept over whenever I was too tired to get back to my dorm.

"I'll be right with you!" she shouted.

I gave her a thumbs up as I got out of my car, and while she walked down the stairs, I got out all of my suitcases and bags.

I looked around the parking lot and noticed three other cars, one of which was Evie's.

Her Porsche didn't fit into this part of town, but she grew up in a gated community on the other side of Riverton, where her parents not only owned the country club, but also a few car dealerships around the state.

As rich as her parents were, she wasn't too stuck up.

She did have her moments, but knowing her since we were four, she never acted up around me.

I remembered meeting her the first time in kindergarten.

She made me cry because she said the dog on my shirt was ugly, that I would never get my own dog, and that her chihuahua was so much prettier.

Weirdly enough, we found our way to each other after realizing we had one thing in common.

We both loved to draw.

And we were pretty damn good at it too.

That's why we took the same classes, and art was a big part of our lives.

If things worked out right, we would open our own gallery to sell our paintings, but neither of us were ready to go there yet.

We still had to graduate and create a plan on how we would run a business surrounding our art.

"I'm so excited! We'll have a party tonight. Just us two, with lots of snacks and wine."

She hugged me tight.

"Wine? Are you sure you wanna drink tonight?"

After she let go of me, she raised her brows at me. "It's Saturday. We're usually out at a party on Saturday," she pointed out.

"Right. But you partied last night, and I can still smell the vodka on your breath, Evie."

She rolled her eyes at me and reached for one of the suitcases.

"Stop acting like my mother or I will kick you out even before you made it up the stairs," she warned, not meaning one word of what she just said.

"You wouldn't dare," I muttered. "You need me."

"Yes, probably. I just don't know it yet," she said with a shrug.

As we arrived upstairs with all of my things, we entered her apartment and put everything into my new room.

"We can put your things away tomorrow. Let's eat, I'm too tired to do anything tonight."

Evie's apartment took up the whole upper floor, which was a little extra considered the other six people living in this complex had far smaller apartments.

I knew about a family that lived here once.

Their three kids had to share one bedroom, and Evie was up here partying and living her best life without worrying about anyone else.

I blamed it on her parents.

They were filthy rich and arrogant.

So damn arrogant.

But, hey...I didn't have to deal with them.

I got lucky with my parents.

Mom and Dad supported me with everything I did, but they gave me enough space to breathe and explore the world by myself.

Mom still sent me money each month for food and other necessities, and Dad liked to check in and ask when I was going to visit them.

I loved them, but college was great, and I had fun doing whatever I wanted to without them monitoring everything I did.

"How about some music?" Evie asked, holding up the speaker in one hand, and her phone in the other.

"Sure."

I didn't mind doing nothing for the night.

After all those weekends we spent at frat houses and bars, both of us could use a little time off.

Wells

"Too loud!" Ira whined.

I've been trying to get him to sleep for almost an hour now, and I was slowly losing my mind.

I wasn't an impatient man, but if that brat upstairs kept that music so loud for one more minute, I would head upstairs myself and tell her to turn it the fuck off.

Ira wasn't the only one who needed his sleep.

I had to get up early to get him ready, feed him, and then drive him to my mother so I could head to work.

Shit.

Why was this the only affordable apartment close enough to both my mom's and work?

The owners of this complex were arrogant pieces of shit, and their daughter acted like the princess of this town.

If it weren't for work, I would've never moved here.

Never in a million years.

My life was perfect before I came here, and adjusting in a new town with a three-year-old wasn't easy.

And this girl was not being a good neighbor.

Not sure if anyone else in this building had a problem with her being so damn loud almost every evening, but I couldn't let her keep this shit up.

"Daddy!" Ira's cry was what I needed to pick him up and head straight out of my apartment.

"We're gonna turn the music off," I told him with a heavy sigh.

I loved my son.

He was what was left from my past life, and I'd do anything to make him happy.

To keep him safe and raise him to be the greatest man ever.

He was like a copy of myself when I was his age.

Same dirty blond, wavy hair, dark green eyes, and same facial structure.

Ira's my world, and I'd do anything for him.

"Bell?" Ira asked as we stopped at the front door leading to the penthouse.

That was the only appropriate name for what was up there.

Why would a college student need an apartment that big?

"Yes, ring the bell, buddy," I told him, letting him lean down to press it with his small finger.

He grinned as he heard the sharp sound of the bell, then he wrapped his arms around my neck again.

"Let's see if she heard it."

I hoped so.

If not, I'd stand here until she did.

I breathed in deeply and rubbed Ira's back, then kissed his head.

Surprisingly, the door swung open sooner than expected, but instead of the bleach blonde barbie doll opening the door, a natural brunette with the prettiest hazel eyes stood in front of me.

The music in the back was still playing, louder now that the door was open.

The girl looked at me, then at Ira and smiled sweetly.

"Hi, can I help you?"

How was I supposed to stay mad?

"Uh, yes, actually. Is Evie around?" I asked.

Saying her name left a bad taste in my mouth.

I wasn't an angry person in general, but she was good at not letting us sleep at night, and she also didn't care about anyone else in this complex.

Evie was just as ignorant as her parents at times.

"She's taking a shower. Is everything okay?" she asked, worry showing in her eyes.

Ira, the social butterfly he was, reached out to grab a fistful of the girl's long hair.

She didn't seem to mind and let him touch her hair as much as he wanted to.

"I live downstairs. The music's a little too loud, and it's not the first time he's had trouble falling asleep."

"Oh! I'm so sorry!" she said, the worry growing stronger. "I'll turn it off. If I had known I would've turned it off earlier."

"Thank you. Could you also let her know I was here? I don't wanna be *that* neighbor, but Ira's three and he needs his sleep. I do too as I work all week long."

I also worked every night at home when Ira was down, and on the weekends when I was supposed to relax with a beer in hand, but she didn't need to know that.

"I'll make sure we're not too loud from now on. I'm so sorry once again."

From now on?

"Did you move in?"

I saw Evie's roommate move out a few days ago, which I at first thought would make her stop with all the parties she threw weekly, but I guess she already found a new friend.

She nodded, but before she replied, she lifted her finger. "Let me go turn off the music."

I made Ira let go of her hair, and after a quick disappearance, she was back again without the music playing in the background.

"Evie's my best friend. I know she can be a little...irritating at times. It won't happen again, I promise. You need to visit dreamland, hm?" she asked, poking Ira's chest gently.

He scrunched up his nose and giggled.

Well, *shit*.

She's just who I needed in this building.

I smiled at her, then held out my hand while keeping my other arm around Ira. "I'm Wells, this is Ira," I told her.

"Rooney," she replied with a beautiful smile stuck in place. "Nice to meet you."

"You too. I'd love to stay and talk, but I gotta get him to bed. Thank you again, Rooney."

"Anytime! If there's anything you need, just let me know." She looked at me with an apologetic look, then turned to Ira and smiled again. "Goodnight, Ira. Sleep tight," she told him sweetly.

"Night night!" Ira replied happily, waving at her.

"Goodnight," I told her, and after staring into her eyes for far too long like an idiot, I walked back down the stairs to finally head to bed.

Rooney, maybe life's gonna get easier from now on because of you.

Chapter Two

Rooney

"You're a horrible neighbor," I told Evie as she walked out of her bedroom with her hair still damp.

She raised a brow, waiting for me to explain myself.

"Wells came upstairs to ask if we could turn down the music because his son couldn't fall asleep. I can only imagine how many times he came upstairs to ask you to turn it down," I said with a sigh.

Although I understood Wells, it didn't occur to me to turn down the volume while I was waiting for Evie to come out of the shower.

Stupid me.

Evie rolled her eyes. "He complains all the time. Is it my problem? There are things called headphones."

"Evie, he has a three-year-old son. Is he supposed to put headphones on him as well?" I asked with raised brows.

She shrugged.

"The music wasn't even that loud. He's just looking for reasons to be annoying."

It was impossible to have a normal conversation with her when it came to things like this.

She was always in the right, and whoever had a problem with it, just had to deal with it.

It was best for me to let it go, but I'd make sure we weren't too loud from now on.

Poor Ira.

It was already past eight, and kids his age shouldn't be up that late.

"It's Saturday. The evening has just begun, Rooney. Get the snacks and wine out while I get dressed."

Evie disappeared in her room again, and after letting out a heavy sigh, I headed back to the kitchen.

Living with her was going to be a nightmare, but it was still better than living in that sad, sad dorm.

We would have classes most days anyway, and I could now control the volume level in this apartment to not bother any of the neighbors.

I didn't understand how someone could be so self-centered and careless about the people living around you, but Evie was difficult to begin with, and telling her to not bother anyone around her wasn't gonna help.

I brought the wine and snacks into the living room and sat on the couch to wait on her, and while she took her time to dry her hair and get dressed, I pulled out my phone to check on the messages I got while we were eating our self-made pizzas.

AJ's name lit up the screen, and I tapped the message to read what he had written.

No partying tonight?

I knew they were having a party at the frat house, but even without moving here and having to clean my dorm, I wouldn't have gone anyway.

I'm exhausted. I'll see you Monday.

His quick reply was a simple thumbs up emoji, and I was lucky that everything we talked about this morning was put behind us so quickly.

Now that I thought of what we had, it felt weird and almost cringeworthy.

We made out a lot, held hands, and acted like a couple.

But I never let him take off my clothes, and that one time I slept in his bed was the most awkward night of my life.

He wanted to cuddle, but once I felt his boner, I pushed him away and told him that I didn't like being cuddled.

It was a lie of course, and he knew.

And I shouldn't have kept going with whatever thing there was between us.

"I have picked five movies. Which one do you wanna watch first?" Evie asked as she walked outside the bedroom.

"You choose," I told her, reaching for the bottle of wine and filling my glass, then hers.

I wasn't a big drinker, and I stayed away from alcohol at parties, but a glass of wine to make my head stop hurting and to relax wasn't so bad.

"Love Actually it is."

Before she would disappear in her own little world while watching a movie, I had to try one more time to see if she would agree on a few things now that I lived here too.

"Evie, we won't have parties every week up here, right?"

She frowned while she opened the list with all the movies she had saved. "Why not? We finally live together. Isn't that what we always wanted?"

I shrugged. "Sure, but we still have to study and I can't do that if we keep throwing parties."

"Is this about Wells? God, Rooney...he's an adult. Probably in his forties. He pretty much *has* to complain about every little thing. Don't let that get to you."

"It's not just because of him, Evie. I need some weekends off from partying to study. But also, you should have a little more respect for the people who live here."

She rolled her eyes at me, but for some reason it seemed that she actually thought about the things I said.

"Fine. Two weekends party, two weekends off. Deal?"

I thought about that for a while, then nodded.

"Deal. But the music can't be too loud. Not like today."

"You are literally the worst best friend ever. Remind me again why we decided to hang out in kindergarten?"

I laughed. "Because you were rude to every other kid and I was kind enough to volunteer as your friend."

I wished that was a joke, and luckily, she wasn't hurt by that.

Wells

"Daddy?"

Ira's small voice made me move my gaze from my computer to him, and with a soft sigh, I held out my hands to him.

"Can't sleep?" I asked, pulling him onto my lap as he reached me.

He shook his head and rubbed his eyes with both fists, then he leaned against my chest and stuck his thumb into his mouth while his other hand moved into his hair to twirl it around his finger.

That was his way of calming himself down.

I rubbed his back and kissed his head.

He has only been in bed for two hours, but him waking up was usual even without Evie blasting music in the middle of the night.

I looked back at the screen and saved the open documents, then put the computer to sleep to get up with Ira in my arms.

"Wanna sleep in my bed tonight?"

That happened about once a month.

I didn't want him to get used to sleeping with me in my bed, but every once in a while, it helped me relax, knowing he would sleep well with me by his side.

He nodded, and I turned right into my bedroom to tuck him under my covers.

"I'll be right with you, okay? Do you want me to get Hulk?"

Another nod.

My kid loved every single superhero there was, but Hulk was definitely his favorite.

He had a few posters, two pajama sets, and more than ten Hulk action figures in his room.

I spoiled him when it came to toys, but that was okay because I knew he played with every single thing I got him.

Luckily, my son wasn't already addicted to an iPad or my phone like other kids his age already were.

Sure, I let him watch cartoons on TV some mornings while I got dressed and ready for work, but that was it with screen time.

He never really asked for it anyway, and as long as he had his Hulk, he was the happiest and most satisfied kid on the planet.

I leaned down to kiss his forehead, and after grabbing his plush from his room, I tucked it next to him under the covers.

"Try to sleep. I'll be right back," I assured him.

I walked out of the room and left the door open and light on while I went to brush my teeth and get ready for bed.

If it weren't for Ira, I would sit there in front of my computer until the sun came back up in the morning.

I was overworking, putting too much effort into work although I wasn't much appreciated at my job.

It's the same company I worked as a civil engineer for, but ever since I moved here, the branch I was at never really welcomed me.

Not that it mattered as I had my own office and didn't interact much with the others, but it would be nice to at least have normal conversations and no one looking at me with raised brows if I had to present my newest projects.

It was a pain in the ass to do those things, but I somehow managed, and in the end, it was Ira I got to come home to.

I was lucky enough to have my mother close by, and she took care of him every single day that I couldn't.

Ever since Dad left, Ira was her happiness and motivation.

Besides, Ira loved his grandmother, and I knew he was safe with her.

Once I was done, I walked back into my bedroom and turned off the light, then got into bed and let Ira crawl over me to make himself comfortable on me.

He wasn't so little anymore, but I was over six feet, and when he was a baby, he used to sleep on my chest almost every night.

It was a pain getting him off and hoping he wouldn't cry, but he wouldn't sleep anywhere else other than my chest.

This time, at three years old, only half of his body was on me, and his legs spread out next to me on the mattress.

I made sure to cover him fully so he wouldn't get cold at night, and once we were both comfortable, a relieved sigh escaped me.

"Goodnight, Ira. Daddy loves you."

"Okay," was his response.

The concept of love wasn't what a three-year-old should know, and I took his okay as a confirmation that he at least heard what I said.

He had only just turned three, but for his age, he had a wide vocabulary which he put to use daily.

Not when he was tired, but I could have full-on conversations with him, even if not everything was comprehendible on either side.

At least he did speak.

Chapter Three

Rooney

I was up way too early the next morning.

Normally, I tried to sleep in so I would be energized to study all day, but something told me to get up and head to the closest bakery and get Wells and Ira some freshly baked croissants as an apology for last night.

I still had this bad feeling inside of me and I wanted to show him that I wasn't like Evie.

Not to make her look even more annoying than she already was, but one of us had to be the nice neighbor, right?

Besides, I couldn't stop thinking about Wells last night.

As tired as he looked, he was still insanely handsome, and the fact that he was a single dad made him more attractive.

Not just his looks, but his character was great too.

After taking a quick shower, getting dressed, and driving to the nearest bakery to grab a few baked goods, I headed up the stairs to his apartment at exactly eight a.m.

I could hear footsteps coming from inside, and I hoped I wasn't too late to get them breakfast.

I knocked on the door just in case one of them was still sleeping, and after waiting a few seconds, the door opened.

Wells stood there in his sweatpants but with no shirt on, and I had to take a look at his upper body because I was still just a twenty-year-old college student who enjoyed looking at men.

Sue me.

"Rooney," he said, surprised to see me this early in the morning.

"Hi! I hope you didn't have breakfast yet. I got you and Ira something from the bakery. I wanted to say sorry once again for last night," I told him, giving him an apologetic smile.

He looked at the box in my hands, then he smiled and shook his head. "You shouldn't have. That's very kind of you. Thank you, Rooney."

I let him take the box even if he was a little hesitant at first, but once he got over my little present, he tilted his head to the side and pointed inside.

"Would you like to come in? I'm sure you haven't had breakfast either," he offered.

"Oh, actually..."

Yes. You should go inside, Rooney. It's just breakfast, and he's a nice guy.

My subconscious was deciding for me, and there was no way I could do the opposite of what it said.

"Sure, sounds good."

I smiled at him as he stepped aside to let me in, and when I saw his apartment for the first time, it was clear that a toddler lived here.

"Sorry for all the toys. Ira likes to wake up early and pull out every single one of his toys on weekends."

"Don't worry, I'd do the same if I were his age," I assured him, smirking.

"The kitchen is down the hall to the right," he told me, nodding in that direction.

Like our apartment upstairs, there were exposed brick walls and old, creaky wooden floors, but thanks to the renovation that had been done three years ago, the kitchen and bathrooms were modern.

Still, Wells's apartment looked far livelier thanks to the few plants around and the paintings all over the walls drawn by Ira.

I liked it.

"Ira, come say hi to Rooney," Wells said as we reached the kitchen.

The floorplans were a little confusing, but the kitchen opened up into the living room, where on the other side of it the bedrooms and bathroom were.

Not sure who designed this building, but the apartments weren't laid out like usual.

I watched as Ira turned his blond curl covered gaze to me, and once he recognized me, he pushed himself off the floor where he was playing with action figures and walked over to us.

He stopped next to Wells's legs, wrapping an arm around one of them and pushing his thumb into his mouth.

I squatted down to be on his level.

"Good morning, Ira. I brought you something yummy," I told him with a smile.

His eyes grew wide, but seconds later, he frowned at me.

"What is it?" he asked with his thumb still in his mouth.

"A donut with sprinkles on top. Have you ever had one?" I asked.

He nodded, but for a three-year-old who should be obsessed with sweets, he didn't seem too fazed by what I brought.

Ira turned his head to look up at his dad, and it looked like he was questioning something.

For a toddler, Ira sure knew how to express himself.

"You can get a little bit of the donut," Wells said.

I looked up at him, and when I stood back up, I scrunched my nose. "Not big on sugar?"

"Uh, not really. Ira's diabetic."

Well, shit.

Now I felt like an idiot.

"I'm sorry...if I had known I would've picked out something—"

"You couldn't have known, Rooney. It's all good." He smiled at me, then nodded to the table.

"Sit. I'll get everything else out."

"Wanna see my Hulk?" Ira asked, tilting his head back to look up at me with the biggest and greenest eyes.

"Of course! I see you have so many action figures," I told him.

Instead of sitting down like Wells told me to, I let Ira pull me into the living room.

"Hulk is my favorite," he said, picking him up and holding it out to me.

For his age, his speech was clear and understandable which was astonishing.

He did have a slight lisp, but that didn't stop him from talking a lot.

"You take him," he told me, and I took Hulk out of his little hand.

Then he reached back to the other figures and picked up The Flash and Wonder Woman.

After turning back to me, he looked at Hulk, then at the two figures he held in his hands with a frown.

"No, I want Hulk," he said.

I switched with him, but there was no time to play.

"Ira, come wash your hands," Wells called out, and without making a fuss, Ira ran to his dad.

I followed him after placing the figures onto the coffee table, and when I reached the kitchen, Wells nodded to the now set table.

"Take a seat. Those croissants look incredible. I've never been to that bakery," he told me as he helped Ira wash his hands.

"It's great! They also make sandwiches for lunch. Now that I live close by, I'll definitely head over there every day."

While they sat down at the table, I looked at the box.

"I feel bad for bringing all these things," I told Wells.

But even if I had known that Ira was diabetic, I wouldn't have a clue on what I could get him that he was allowed to eat.

"Don't," Wells said. "It's not that he can't eat any of this. We might have some leftovers though."

I watched him cut up the donut into thirds, and since it wasn't a big one after all, the piece Ira received was small.

Then Wells reached for the cup next to Ira's plate and put a straw inside.

"Hulk juice?" Ira asked, eyeing the thick, green smoothie in his red cup.

"That's it, buddy. Drink up so you'll get as strong as him," Wells replied.

And just like that, Ira started drinking it.

"It's broccoli mixed with carrots, avocado, and spinach," he said to me as he noticed my intrigued gaze.

"Is it hard? I mean, monitoring what he eats?"

"Not anymore. I learned a lot, and thankfully, Ira never really noticed a change in his diet."

"When did you know he was diabetic?" I asked.

"One year ago. It was harder watching him get adjusted to the insulin pump than the food."

I didn't know what that was, but he quickly continued to explain it.

"It's a little device that delivers small doses of insulin continuously into his body thanks to a sensor on his stomach. It also automatically checks his blood sugar so we don't always have to poke his finger to check. It's a nice device, and it makes life a little easier."

I nodded, smiling at Ira who was now reaching for one of the croissants.

Wells grabbed it and cut it in half in case he wouldn't eat the whole thing, then he smeared a little bit of butter on it which seemed to be enough for Ira.

"Are there any disadvantages with that device?" I asked.

Wells was very attentive and calm, which made me hate Evie and myself even more for disturbing him last night.

"For Ira, it's the device itself which he has to carry around all the time. It's clipped to the hem of his pants right now, but whenever we go out, he can hang it around his neck if he wants to. For me, it's the cost. But I'd rather have him carry that device every day instead of having to inject him with the insulin myself."

I nodded, understanding his point, and while I watched him help Ira get to his milk, I made a mental note to someday make a nice meal for both of them.

I wondered how long he has been a single dad, or since when Ira lived with him, but that was none of my business, and I didn't want to be too intrusive.

At least not yet.

"You're in college," Wells pointed out, changing the subject.

"Yes, I'm a Junior," I told him. "Evie and I are both majoring in art and art history."

"Oh, so you draw and paint? If Ira wasn't so far gone and focused on his croissant, he would ask you to draw with him. You have no idea how many crayons and colored pencils we go through every month," Wells said with a chuckle.

"I saw the paintings in the hallway. They're pretty good for a kid his age."

"He's good at everything. Sometimes he overwhelms me with everything he does and I can't even start to appreciate one thing before he picks up the next and impresses me."

Seems like Wells was an amazing father.

Ira was calm and gentle, but it was clear that he had a lot on his mind which he put to good use.

"What do you do?" I asked, grabbing the cup of coffee and drinking a few sips.

"I'm a civil engineer. I'm responsible for the city's environment, buildings, and streets."

"Have you always wanted to do that?"

Wells was an interesting man, and although we hadn't talked about much yet, I liked getting to know him.

We were neighbors after all, and I liked to make new friends.

"It was clear to me from a young age that I wanted to be one of the people to decide what goes and what doesn't in a city. Politics was never my thing, so the closest thing to being someone who runs a city was to become that one guy who changed and improved it."

"Is there a project I might know of?" I asked.

We were both spreading butter and then honey on our croissants while the conversation flowed.

"When I first moved here, I got a green light to change up the park next to the two ponds. It wasn't a big project, but I added a few trees and hedges for more privacy, changed the gravel paths to pavement, and added a big playground and dog park."

"Oh, yes! I remember when they started working on it. It looks great. If I ever have a dog, I told myself I would go to that dog park every single day," I told him with a chuckle.

"Ever had one?"

"A dog? No, sadly. But I'm not ready to have one yet either. Maybe someday when I have my own apartment."

He nodded with a soft smile on his lips. "Ira loves it there. I try to take him as often as I can, but it's his grandma who takes him there most times."

This was going great.

Our conversation was going well, and although we were practically strangers, he trusted me in his apartment and most importantly around Ira.

"Grandma is coming?" Ira asked, looking at Wells with hopeful eyes.

"Not today, buddy. We'll spend some time together today and tomorrow."

"Can I have the donut now?"

Ira was quick to change the subject.

He had eaten half of his croissant, but the milk and smoothie were gone as well.

"Yes, you can."

Wells placed one third of it onto his plate, and after a sweet *thank you,* we watched as he started to nibble on the frosting.

"He's adorable. He looks just like you," I pointed out, quickly realizing I complimented Wells too.

A soft chuckle left him as a smug grin appeared on his face. "Would you believe me when I say that he's more liked by women my age then I am?"

"Yes. One hundred percent. He looks like a little prince charming."

"I can't wait until he's old enough to date. Hope he doesn't turn into one of those teenage boys who sleep around with every girl that looks at him."

I puckered my lips and grabbed my cup of coffee again. "Possible that you were one of those boys?" I challenged.

He laughed, crossing his arms over his naked chest.

Props to myself for not looking down while we sat at the table.

His handsome face was enough to distract me from his chiseled chest.

"I had my moments in high school, but after that, I was a real gentleman."

I nodded slowly, studying his face closely with narrowed eyes.

But no matter how big of a player he was years back, he most definitely wasn't one now.

Not sure how old he was, but with a toddler and a full-time job, I was positive there was not much time left to date.

Chapter Four

Wells

"Let me check the number, then you're free to go play," I told Ira after helping him down from the chair he stood on to wash his hands.

I knelt in front of him and pushed up his little sweater to get to the pump.

"Okay, you're all set. After I've cleaned up the kitchen, we'll get ready to head to the park," I assured him, and after kissing his forehead, I let him run into the living room.

When I got back up, Rooney was already stacking our plates and then carrying them over to the sink.

"You don't have to. I'll handle it," I said, but she didn't listen.

"It's the least I can do. Besides, I'm dreading going upstairs to study," she replied, chuckling.

"You should come with us to the park then. It's nice outside."

It was too early to ask her to come with us.

But then again...we just had breakfast together.

"As much as I'd love to, I can't. I have a few assignments I still have to write, but after the next week, I'll have a little more time."

"We'll find some time to spend together," I added, smiling at her.

Although we had a few years between us, she didn't seem taken aback by my offer of spending time together.

I liked her, and Ira did too.

She's the first person who tried to talk to us, and in this goddamn town, I could use a friend.

Even if I could easily be her father.

"How old are you, Rooney?"

I stood by the sink and started to wash the dishes while she put away the leftover fruit and the jars of honey and jam.

"Twenty. My birthday's coming up in a few months though."

Her smile grew as she realized all the things she could do becoming an adult.

Though, she surely has broken a few rules before.

"What about you?"

I puckered my lips.

I could've lied.

Tell her I was ten or even fifteen years younger than I actually was.

My dirty blond hair and beard showed no sign of my age, but if I wanted her to be my friend, I needed to be honest.

"Forty-two."

"You don't look it," she said with a gentle smile.

"Thanks. Hard to believe my life has mostly been stressful, huh?" I chuckled.

"Why stressful?"

She didn't seem to be in a hurry, and I didn't mind having her for a little while longer.

"Because work has always been a lot. Even before Ira, there wasn't much time for me to spend doing things I liked. Right after college, I put work first, which was a mistake. I shouldn't have said yes to every little thing my co-workers asked me to do, even if it wasn't my job."

"Why did you do it then?"

Good question.

I shrugged, puckering my lips and studying the plate in my hands.

"I guess I wanted to impress others."

"And have things changed a little regarding always saying yes?"

"Yes, but as soon as that changed, Ira came into my life. But he made things so much better," I told her with a smile.

"That's great! I can tell you raised him right." She was quiet for a while, and after thinking intensely about what to say next, she finally spoke again. "Do you mind me asking where his mother is?"

I didn't mind her asking, but I didn't like talking about it.

"That's a story for another time. It's a little bit of a long one."

Luckily, she didn't get offended by me not telling her.

"No worries. I didn't mean to..." she said, not finishing her sentence.

"It's fine, Rooney. It's a rightful question to ask, but I haven't spoken about it in a while."

"I understand," she told me, smiling again. "As much as I don't want to, I really should head back upstairs."

I nodded and placed the last plate into the dishwasher, then dried my hands and looked over to the living room.

"Ira, come say bye to Rooney," I called out.

When he walked toward us, she squatted down in front of him to be on his level and placed her hands on both his sides.

"I'll see you soon, okay? I'm sure we'll have plenty of time to play with your action figures another day," she promised him.

"Okay," he replied. "Thank you for the yummy food," he then added, surprising me just as much as Rooney.

Ira was a sweet kid, but sometimes he even fascinated me with his kindness.

Did he really learn that from me?

"You're so welcome! Thank you for showing me your toys. And hey, your dad told me you like to draw. Maybe next time I can bring a few brushes and colors so we can paint together. Would that be fun?"

Ira's eyes grew wide. "Yes!" he called out.

To make this whole interaction even sweeter, Ira wrapped his arms around Rooney, and after a quick but tight hug, he ran back into the living room.

"I think he's my new favorite person," Rooney said as she stood back up, holding her hand over her heart and pushing her bottom lip out to show her adoration.

I chuckled and agreed. "He's incredible. So...I'll see you soon?" I asked, walking to the front door with her.

"Definitely. I'm sure we'll cross paths around here, and if you need anything, just knock on my door."

"Likewise. Thank you for breakfast."

"My pleasure. Have a good day at the park. I'll see you around, Wells."

Her voice got softer by the end of the sentence, and after looking into my eyes for a few seconds, she lifted her hand to wave, and like an idiot I let her go without even hugging her goodbye.

What. A. Dick.

Rooney

"You ate breakfast with him?" Evie asked with her brows raised up to the roof.

"I did, and it was nice. In fact, it was so nice that I wished I had said yes to going to the park with him and Ira instead of studying."

I was pouring myself a cup of coffee to get me through the first half of the day while Evie was standing there in her gym clothes with her arms crossed over her chest.

"He's, what, forty-five?"

"Forty-two," I corrected her. "And what does it matter anyway? He's a nice guy and Ira's a sweet kid. I could use some distraction from everything that's going on in my life."

"There is something going on?" Evie's brows pushed even higher.

"No, but that's the problem. I don't wanna hang out with guys my age right now. That thing between AJ and I made me realize that college guys are all the same. Sure, I was able to have conversations with AJ, but not like the ones I had with Wells this morning. He's smart, and although he's a little introverted, he's great."

"He's forty-two," Evie pointed out.

She probably didn't even listen to what I said.

"I don't care," I shot back, then grabbed my cup of coffee and walked past her and into my bedroom.

"It's not like I'm gonna date him or anything. I like spending time with him, and if that's what makes me happy, then no one can stop me."

Evie followed me into my bedroom and sat on my bed while I got out my laptop.

"So you're friends with an older guy and a toddler now. Anything you want me to know? Am I not enough anymore?"

She wasn't taking this too seriously, and it was quite funny how she tried to act all hurt and confused.

"You are too much, E. That's why I need someone who can calm me down. Wells is good at that. I realized when I sat at the table with him and Ira that all my worries about the assignments and homework were gone, and the second I stepped into our apartment, the worries were back."

"I think you just need to get fucked by some random, horny college guy. Maybe that's what you're lacking."

"Can't lack anything I never really had in the first place, Evie."

Or could I?

Either way, sex wasn't what I needed.

Or wanted.

At least not yet.

"Whatever you say. I'm going out for a run. Don't die of boredom while I'm gone," she said, already walking out of my room.

"I'll try not to."

***

Six hours into studying and writing my first assignment and it was finally time for me to eat something.

Often times I was too focused to get up and eat, but this time, my stomach couldn't stop growling.

In the kitchen, I opened the freezer to check if there was anything I could quickly push into the oven, and to my luck, there was a frozen pizza lying inside which I knew Evie wouldn't eat unless she was drunk.

But since parties would only occur twice a month, I chose to eat the pizza myself.

As I waited for the oven to preheat, I checked my phone for messages.

I turned on night shift to not get disturbed while studying, so I missed all of AJ's messages he sent me hours ago.

After reading through them, I sighed and decided to call him instead of typing a reply.

Not five seconds after calling him, he picked up.

"Studying?" he asked without greeting me.

"Yes, and I intend on continuing until late tonight," I told him, answering the question he asked me via text.

"Sucks. What about Evie?"

He wasn't asking for himself, but more so for all his frat brothers who enjoyed Evie's wildness.

AJ, whose real name was Aiden James, wasn't into girls like Evie.

Not talking about her looks, because Evie was most definitely one of the prettiest girls on campus.

AJ was easygoing and calm, had a strange sense of humor, but it was one I got along with well. Still, he needed a girl that didn't sleep with the whole football team.

"She's out on a run, but I'll let her know you guys are having a party at the house. I'm sure she'll be there though."

"All right."

After a quick pause, he let out a sigh. "You okay, Rooney? I have a feeling there's still a few things we need to talk about."

I frowned. "I don't think so. We've talked it out and agreed to never talk about it again. Let's not tear up wounds we want to be closed."

"You're right, I'm sorry. I guess I had hoped it would turn out a little differently," he said with a smile audible in his voice.

"Guess so," I whispered. "I'll see you around, AJ. Have a good weekend."

"You too. Bye."

A relieved breath left my chest.

AJ really was a nice guy, but not even he could get me to fall in love with him.

I knew it was me that had issues of opening up about my feelings, or letting someone in, which is why I never even imagined myself being in a relationship.

Maybe it was because I've never been in one or because I never found a man who I knew was worth it all, but I still had time.

At twenty, I didn't need to find love.

Chapter Five

Wells

"Wait a second, Ira," I told him as we entered the apartment after a long day at the park.

I knelt down in front of him and lifted his shirt, then checked the number on his insulin pump.

He's had his afternoon snack already, but his insulin level needed to be raised again, even after an active day on the playground.

"I'm not cooking until later tonight. Would you like to have another apple or a peach?" I asked, straightening his shirt again and then taking off his shoes.

"Peach, please! With peanut butter!"

A bit random, but he could have some of that as well.

"All right. And what do you think? Should we invite Rooney over for dinner?"

I wasn't moving too quickly.

She was my neighbor, and since she's the only person I had a real and normal conversation with in years, I wanted to make sure I showed her my appreciation.

She's a new friend, but I couldn't be too pushy and intrusive.

"Okay!" Ira replied, holding up his little thumb. "Can I play now?"

I leaned in to kiss his forehead, then nodded down the hall.

"Go get your toys and bring them into my office. Dad has to work a little."

I watched him run to the living room, and while he relocated all his toys into my office, I prepared his snack and filled his bottle with water.

"All done!" he called out, and I carried the plate and water over to him and set in onto the small table I put into my office for situations like these.

Ira sat down on his chair and started eating the peach, dipping it into the peanut butter next to the slices.

"Is it good?" I asked.

That's something he never asked for, but he seemed to enjoy it.

"It's good," he replied.

Perfect.

I sat down in my chair and turned on my computer to check if I received any emails from either of my co-workers who liked to send me shit even when it was my day off, but if I handled their requests now, I could leave earlier on the weekdays and spend more time with Ira.

That's what I always aimed for.

Strangely enough, there weren't as many emails as I had thought there'd be, so I quickly worked through them and spent another hour on the new project while Ira played with his toys after having eaten his snack.

It was getting dark outside, and when Ira walked up to me with his hand covering his stomach, I knew it was time for me to stop working and get to the kitchen.

"You're hungry again, hm?"

After getting up from my chair, I picked him up and walked over to the kitchen to check what we had left in the fridge.

"How about I make tacos tonight? You think Rooney would like that?"

Ira nodded and pointed to the chicken breast in the fridge. "With chicken inside?"

"Chicken, avocado, tomatoes. Whatever you wanna put in it. Sound good?"

"Yes!"

"Great. Let's go see if she wants to come down to eat with us."

We headed out and walked up the stairs to get to her door, and once Ira rang the bell, we waited a few seconds before the door opened.

It wasn't who I wanted to see, but if I wanted to get to Rooney, I had to talk to her.

"Hey, Evie," I greeted.

As annoyed as I was because of her most of the time, I wasn't a dick.

"Going out?" I asked, looking down at her skin-tight dress and high heels.

"Yes. Is there something you need?"

Her brows were raised, and with that much make up on, she was slightly scaring Ira as he stepped behind me with his arm around my leg.

"Is Rooney home?"

Evie sighed and turned to walk back into the apartment.

I looked down at Ira and brushed through his curls, then looked back up as she came back.

"She'll be right with you."

Evie grabbed her bag and walked past us, and with a quick *bye*, she walked down the stairs to head out.

Perfect.

So no loud music or people dancing tonight.

"Hi!" Ira squealed and waved as he saw Rooney come down the hallway, and I smiled at her after taking in the comfortable looking loungewear she was wearing.

"Hi, Ira. Did you have a good day at the park?" she asked, reaching out to caress his cheek gently.

"It was fun! I played with Benny," he explained.

"That's amazing! I wish I had the time to play with my friends," she said with a sigh, then looked up at me with a smile. "Hi."

"Hey, Rooney. Ira and I wanted to invite you over for dinner. We're making tacos. Wanna join?"

"Please?" Ira said.

"Well, I can't say no to you." She chuckled, looking back at Ira. "Sounds great! I'll have to change into something more appropriate though," she added.

"Oh, don't bother. We'll change into our pajamas before dinner anyway. You look great," I told her, taking another look at her body.

Even in a sweatshirt and messy bun she looked pretty.

I'd take her over any other girl every time.

"Okay, but give me a moment to put away my things and I'll be right down."

I gave her a nod and picked Ira up, then pointed toward the stairs. "We'll see you in a few then."

She smiled and quickly waved at Ira before she walked back into the apartment, and I headed down the stairs to start preparing for dinner.

I had a feeling it was going to be a great evening, and for once in my life I was excited to put Ira to bed and hope he would sleep in it all through the night.

Rooney

I'd be lying if I said I wasn't nervous to eat at his place once again.

I enjoyed breakfast, and after a long day of studying, homework, and writing assignments, a nice dinner with Wells and Ira was what I needed.

I put away my things and headed over to the kitchen to grab the bottle of wine Evie never opened and thought it would be a nice little dessert for Wells and me.

Not sure what he had planned exactly, but I wouldn't mind spending more than just dinner with him.

No, sex wasn't what I wanted, but I liked our talk this morning, and I could use someone who was capable of keeping a conversation going.

I wouldn't have anything better to do anyway.

When I arrived at his apartment, I noticed that the door was open, and after pushing on it, I looked inside.

"May I?" I called out.

"Oh, yeah, come in! We're in the kitchen!" I heard Wells say.

I closed the door behind me and walked down the hall and to the kitchen where Wells was standing by the fridge and Ira on a chair at the table.

"Hi," I greeted, smiling at both of them.

"Hi!" Ira said with a wave, then he held up half of an avocado. "I make guacamole!" he announced before continuing to mash the avocado in a bowl with a kid's fork.

"Hey. You eat meat, right?" Wells asked.

I nodded, then held the bottle of wine out to him.

"I brought you something. Maybe we can have a little later tonight?"

Flirting.

No.

No, I wasn't flirting, right?

The way Wells smirked at me told a whole other story though.

He looked pleased but surprised.

"Sounds like a plan."

He grabbed the bottle and placed it onto the counter, then nodded to the table. "Wanna help Ira cut up the vegetables? I'm cooking some chicken."

"Yeah, of course."

"Look!" Ira said, his sweet voice full of joy as he pointed to the bowl. "It's Hulk color!"

I sat down next to him and reached for the kid-safe knife to start cutting up the bell pepper.

Wells definitely knew how to cook healthy and it was a good thing he invited me over or else I would've simply put another pizza in the oven.

"Is green your favorite color?" I asked Ira, and like I had imagined, he nodded.

"And I like blue because it's daddy's favorite color," he explained.

"I see. Those are both pretty colors. And what's your favorite food?" I asked, keeping the conversation going while Wells listened.

"Everything," Ira replied.

"That's a really good answer. I like everything too."

"Lucky me," I heard Wells mutter.

I chuckled and turned to look at him. "Easier to cook that way, right?"

"Oh, so much easier. He even likes spicy food. I don't let him have too much of it because it can cause stomach aches, but he enjoys some drops of hot sauce with his meals."

That was surprising.

I didn't like spicy things until I was sixteen, and this kid was already eating full meals with hot sauce.

"That's amazing," I chuckled.

We continued to prepare all the vegetables while Wells cooked the chicken, and once we were all done, he came to the table and sat down next to Ira.

"Wanna put together your own taco, buddy?" he asked.

"Yes, please!"

We watched him grab one of the soft taco shells and place it into his plate, then he put the guacamole he made on it, then some vegetables, and at the end he tried to roll it up.

"You do it, Daddy."

Wells helped, and once he was done and Ira was ready to eat, we assembled our own tacos.

"Thanks for inviting me again, by the way. I'm really starting to like spending time with you two. It's a nice distraction from everything going on upstairs."

"You mean Evie and her shenanigans? Still not sure why you'd move in with her in the first place. Where did you live before?" he asked.

"On campus. I had a dorm, but that was so much worse than having an actual apartment. Besides, there won't be much noise in the future thanks to me. You can count on that."

He let out a soft laugh. "You're heaven-sent. And you can come over whenever you feel like it. We're here every night anyway, and you promised to draw with Ira sometime. Kids never forget promises. He'll hold it against you if you don't come over with your brushes and colors soon," he said with a smug grin.

"I always keep my promises," I told him with a smile.

"Good. Because I think I'd like to have you around more often as well."

I felt my cheeks heat up.

Shit.

And I thought he wasn't interested in me that way?

Not that I would deny my attraction toward him, but I wasn't really looking for a guy to date.

Much less one who was as kind and attractive as Wells.

I also had to consider our age difference.

It excited me to spend time with a man twice my age, who happened to be a dad, but the second I thought it was okay, I remembered Evie's reaction concerning the age difference.

So many people had something to say about that topic, and although I didn't look at it as a bad thing, he had much more experience in so many fields than I did.

The biggest being the sex part.

I was taking it too far already.

We were just having dinner.

There was never a mention of this being a date, and I didn't want to overthink it, because that would only disappoint me or ruin things.

He was just being nice, and me being only twenty and never really having talked to actual grown-ups other than my parents and professors, I had never engaged into adult conversations.

"So...you said your mom lives close by?"

"Yes. Just a few streets away," Wells replied.

"Does she live on her own?"

"Occasionally. She met a guy at a bar a few months ago. Nice man, and Ira likes him too. My dad moved to Vegas a few years ago. He loves to gamble, and his growing addiction was what made my mom get a divorce. We don't see him very often, but we keep in touch via phone. What about your parents?"

I puckered my lips and wondered if I should tell the actual story, or just find a way to skip over the awkward parts.

But since he was being honest with me, I decided to go down that route as well.

"My parents both grew up riding horses and bulls, so right after I went off to college, they moved back to the country side. They bought a ranch and since they're still so passionate about bull riding, they decided to make a business out of it."

"Sounds great to me! Why are you using that hesitant tone of voice?"

He definitely was a good listener.

"Because they don't do traditional bull riding. Well, the riding is the same, but instead of wearing normal outfits other bull riders wear, they dress up as clowns to give the crowds, especially the kids, some entertainment before the actual competitions start."

Not something a college girl was proudly going to flaunt.

It was weird, but I still loved my mom and dad.

Wells chuckled. "I need to meet your parents."

"Moving a little too quickly there, cowboy," I said with a laugh.

He grinned and winked at me, then our conversation kept going until we were all full and satisfied.

One thing I knew for sure: I wanted to spend more time with him tonight.

Chapter Six

Wells

Her laugh lit up the whole room, and I wondered how no guy has ever noticed that.

She was single, that much I knew.

But has any guy ever tried to make her his?

Rooney was an interesting girl who loved to have honest and deep conversations.

She was great with Ira, which started to worry me because I knew Ira was already starting to get attached to her.

He knew a good person when he met one, and Rooney was definitely one of them.

But worse than that was the fact that I was starting to like her a little too much as well, seeing the sweet and caring woman she was.

I never had much time to date, and after everything that went down with Ira and his mother, he was the only one I wanted to give my love to.

"Can you play with me now?" Ira asked Rooney after I helped him down from the chair which he pushed up to the sink to wash his hands.

"That's a great idea, buddy. Show her your room. I'll start cleaning up here," I told him, looking over at Rooney.

"Sure you don't want me to help?" she asked.

"I'll manage. You can keep me company once he's in bed," I told her.

You could say that I was definitely flirting, but I didn't do it on purpose.

Not at all.

"Okay." She placed her hand on my upper arm, then let Ira take her toward his room by pulling at her hand.

"I have more Hulks!" he announced happily.

"Oh, you sure do! I like the big one on your bed," I heard Rooney say.

For reasons like these I didn't mind not having soundproof walls.

Eavesdropping into my son's conversation with our new neighbor pretty much made my whole night.

They were adorable together, and I was glad there was now one more person Ira could share all his favorite things with.

I washed the dishes and placed the left overs into the fridge to eat the next day, and once the table was cleaned, I walked over to Ira's bedroom to find them both sitting on the floor with action figures in their hands.

"Come play too, Daddy!" Ira urged.

"I'd say it's time for you to go to bed, bud. It's way past your bedtime."

He frowned for a second, then looked at his toys and tried to figure out what to think of that.

"If your daddy's okay with it, I can bring my brushes and colors with me tomorrow so we can draw and paint together. What do you think?" Rooney asked him, caressing his cheek gently with her fingers.

Ira's eyes lit up and looked at me.

"Sounds like a plan. Now, let's go brush your teeth and wash your face."

I held out my hand and he quickly got up to grab it.

"Say goodnight to Rooney," I told him.

"Night night!" Ira said, waving at Rooney.

"Sleep tight, little man. I'll see you tomorrow," she replied, smiling.

"Make yourself at home. I'll be right with you," I told her and nodded toward the living room.

I walked over to the bathroom to help Ira brush his teeth, and once we were done with that, I carried him back to his bedroom and tucked him in.

"Who's gonna sleep with you and Hulk tonight?" I asked, already picking up a few more of his stuffed animals.

"Teddy," Ira told me, reaching for the teddy bear I used to sleep with as a kid.

Strange how long stuffed animals lived.

"Anyone else?"

"Woody," he replied, pointing over to his little desk.

I got up and picked him up to place him next to Ira under the covers. "Getting crowded in here," I said, smiling at him.

"Daddy?"

"Yes, buddy?"

"Can I have a sleepover too with Benny?"

I puckered my lips.

Kids were smart, and he knew Rooney was going to stay a little while.

But what he didn't know was that she wasn't going to stay for the night.

"I'll ask his mom the next time we see him at the park, okay? A sleepover sounds like a fun idea."

I guess it was time for me to start inviting his little friends over so he wouldn't have to play with his old man all the time.

Must be getting boring.

"Goodnight, Ira. I'll see you in the morning," I told him, and before leaning in to kiss his forehead, I moved his pajamas up to check his insulin level.

"I love you," I whispered, and after giving me a kiss on the cheek, I got up and walked out of the room, leaving the door cracked open.

As I got to the kitchen and grabbed the wine bottle she brought, I glanced over to Rooney and watched her stand by the large bookshelves, admiring the books I owned.

"Do you read?" I asked as I walked over to the couch.

She turned around and smiled. "Occasionally. I have a few books in my room, but not as many as you have. You've quite the collection going on."

"Yeah, well, I loved to read as a kid, and I still do whenever I get a moment to myself. I hope I can soon get Ira into reading as well."

"I'm sure he'll love it. I can see so many resemblances to you in him."

She walked over to me and sat down on the couch while I poured us both a glass of wine.

"You shouldn't be drinking," I pointed out, yet I kept pouring the wine.

"You know, I always thought I'd be that one girl who'd have her very first alcoholic drink on her twenty-first birthday, but it's impossible to avoid it with a friend like Evie," she explained with a chuckle.

"As long as you don't drink until you pass out, a glass of wine once in a while is all right," I said, sounding like one of those dads who wanted to act all cool in front of their kid's friends.

"Got it," she said, grinning. "Does Ira always go to bed that easily?"

"Yes, but he likes to wake up in the middle of the night and crawl into my bed often times."

I held one glass to her, and once she took it, I held mine up to make a toast which I thought was necessary for the night.

"To you. For bringing a little quietness into this apartment complex and making us all sleep."

"My pleasure. Thank you for dinner. It was amazing."

Our glasses clinked, and we both took a sip before I leaned back and stretched out my arm on the back of the couch.

"I've been wondering this all evening long but you don't have to answer the question. But how come you don't have a boyfriend?"

Straight forward.

And if she answered, I'd at least know how I should act around her in the future.

She didn't react much to my flirting, but she also didn't look too taken aback by it.

"I'm not sure I want one. I mean, there is a guy I had...*something* with. But I don't think I'm made for relationships. At least not now."

Her eyes moved from her glass to mine.

"I think I'm just letting it all happen naturally. I'm not looking for love. Not sure that's something people can do anyway without getting hurt too many times, but I'm also not saying that I wouldn't let love in."

Her words made sense.

So much so that a smile spread across my face.

"I'm with you on that. You're quite the deep thinker, huh? I'm surprised you can talk about these things so easily, using the right words."

I should've stopped complimenting her, but at least I wasn't flirting anymore.

Truthfully, I didn't think a relationship was what I needed either.

Not right now.

"I guess I reflect on things before I talk. One of my professors once told me that she saw her ninety-eight-year-old grandmother in me. Because of the way I talk or express myself. Not sure if I should take that as a compliment," she said with a laugh.

"I'd say it's definitely a good trait. I remember when I was in college and all those girls trying hard to get the guys's attention. I'm not saying it didn't work, but most times I let them get closer just to make them stop talking."

"Understandable." She smirked and took another sip of her wine.

"It was different back then," I said, shrugging. "I can't imagine how this whole thing with online dating and all that works. Looks like too much pressure of always having to look good, always have nice pictures ready to post on whatever social media platform there is, and I can't stand those kids with their eyes glued on those screens."

The puckered lips and amused gleam in her eyes told me that she was enjoying this conversation.

"You're definitely a few generations older than I am," she said. "Which isn't a bad thing at all. I think it's great how you're raising Ira and that he's not asking for a phone or TV all the time."

"And I'll try to keep it that way for a little while longer. He loves his toys, and I don't wanna ruin his childhood. I want him to see how great life can be even without all those electronics. Sure, one day it'll be impossible to avoid it, but for now, I want him to see how much fun it can be to play with the things I played with when I was his age."

Rooney

"I think that's amazing," I told him with a smile. "I can tell he's happy. That's all that matters."

I pulled my legs up and got more comfortable on the couch next to him.

Didn't plan on leaving anytime soon.

"I thought it would be difficult to raise him on my own, but he knows he's loved," he told me.

That made me immediately think about Ira's mother.

I knew I shouldn't be that nosy, but since we were being honest and open with each other, I couldn't stop myself from asking.

"Does he ever see his mother?"

A soft smiled appeared on his face, but unlike his positive expression, he shook his head.

"Ira has never met his mother. It's a little bit of a complicated story." He paused and looked down at his glass, then he took a few sips before he continued to speak.

"His mother, Leah, and I dated a few years back, but it didn't turn into something serious. She was a great woman, loving and sweet, but we stopped seeing each other after she met another man. I didn't think much of it as I didn't feel as if we'd ever turn into something more than just two people who liked to spend time with each other, but a little more than a year after we stopped talking, her new man stood in front of my door with Ira in a carrier."

I had no idea where this story was headed, but for some reason the thought of Ira not being his real son crossed my mind.

"She never told me she was pregnant, but that day he stood there with a six-months old baby, telling me it wasn't his, I knew I had to take responsibility in that very moment. Leah passed away giving birth to Ira, and she never got to be a mother."

His words were like a sharp knife burying deep inside my chest.

"I'm so sorry. I can't imagine how many thoughts and feelings you had," I said quietly.

"It was a lot to take in, but I was glad he brought Ira to me. He was exactly who I needed in my life, and ever since I signed the papers to claim him as mine, my world had never been the same since."

There were tears stinging Wells's eyes, and when he noticed, he laughed softly and shook his head. "I'm sorry. I've never talked about this other than with my parents."

I reached out to touch his arm, rubbing my thumb along it to show him my affection.

"Don't be. You're strong and I can see that Ira's your world. Thank you for telling me your story," I said.

"I sometimes wish she was still with us. For Ira. He never asked about his mother, but that's because

I never talked to him about her. I'm not sure he even knows that he has a mother."

That was heartbreaking, but it wasn't his fault.

Talking about a parent who wasn't around anymore was hard, and if it was difficult for Wells to deal with, it would definitely be hard for Ira to comprehend.

"Maybe when he's a little bit older you'll get to tell him about her. I'm not a parent and I don't want to intervene in something I have no clue about, but I know you'll do great things."

My hand was still on his arm, but I moved it up to cup the side of his neck and brush my thumb along his stubbled jawline.

"You're really making it hard not to like you," he said quietly and with a small grin on his lips.

I pressed my lips into a thin line and pulled my hand away to get some distance between us, but he quickly reached out to grab my hand to pull it into his lap.

"I'll be good, I swear. I could use a friend, and you seem like the perfect fit."

Friend.

Jesus, Rooney. Don't try and manipulate your own damn mind.

I took a deep breath and nodded. "I can be your friend."

Maybe it was my way of being affectionate and touchy when it came to situations like these, but even if my touch wasn't meant to provoke anything in either of us, deep down I knew damn well that I liked to touch him.

Not denying that.

He squeezed my hand and then wrapped his fingers around it to keep on holding it in his lap.

"So you'll come over tomorrow? I don't wanna use you to babysit Ira, but you'd be a great help so I can work on my project for a few hours before the week starts."

"I'll be here. It'll be fun. Besides, I could use a break from studying."

"Do you get up early on weekends too?" he asked.

"Most times. I got up at seven this morning. Will do the same tomorrow and if you'd like I can come over after lunch."

He nodded and smiled. "Sounds like a plan."

My excitement grew.

Wells was an incredibly nice guy who I sure wanted to spend more time with, plus Ira, of course.

Chapter Seven

Wells

"You sure you don't want another glass?" I asked, pouring myself one.

"Oh, no, I'm good. I don't think I can handle another one without falling asleep right here on the couch."

I wouldn't mind.

"It's getting late anyway. I should head upstairs and get into bed," she said, her voice low and raspy.

She was tired and I didn't want to hold her back any longer.

"All right. Let me walk you to the door."

I set my glass down and got up from the couch, then reached out my hand for her to take.

"Thank you," she said as she pulled herself up with her hand in mine.

We walked past the kitchen and down the hall to get to the front door, and once we were there, I opened it and stepped aside.

The light in the staircase turned on, making it easier for us to see one another.

"I had a great time tonight. Thank you for inviting me," Rooney said.

I smiled at her and nodded. "I had a great time too. I'll see you tomorrow afternoon then?" I asked, leaning against the doorframe and crossing my arms.

I wasn't ready to let her go yet, but if this friendship had to work without weird things happening between us, I had to let go once it was enough.

And right now, we had already spent half of the weekend together, which was more than enough being friends.

"Yes, I'll be here tomorrow afternoon. I can't wait."

She fidgeted with her fingers in front of her belly, and for a second there was unsureness flashing through her eyes.

I could tell she wanted to take a step forward, and since I was the older one here, I took it into my own hands to say goodnight first.

I loosened my arms over my chest again and reached out to place on hand on her waist, then leaned forward to kiss her cheek and pull her closer into a quick but tight hug.

Her arms came around me and her hands moved to my shoulders before stepping back again to put distance between us.

"Good night, Rooney."

"Good night," she whispered, then quickly spun around to walk up the stairs.

I took a deep breath and waited until her door closed, then I walked back inside and locked the door myself.

A breath of fresh air.

That's how I'd describe Rooney.

After I collected all my thoughts, I walked back into the living room to put away the wine and two glasses, then headed over to Ira's room to check if he was still asleep.

I smiled at the sight of his closed eyes and parted lips, and the sound of his soft breathing added to the cuteness.

As much as I wanted him to learn to sleep in his own bed at night, I had moments in which I wanted to just pick him up and take him to my bedroom to cuddle him.

Often times I felt like I was the child, and he the one who protected me.

In a way he did, because without him I had no idea where I'd be.

Probably lost, working all day with no clue what my life would become.

Ira was my purpose, for now and forever.

***

"It's Rooney!" Ira called out as the doorbell rang.

It was too early for it to be Rooney.

Not even eight a.m., and we hadn't even started on breakfast yet.

"I don't think it's Rooney, buddy. Let's go check."

He grabbed my hand and pulled me off the couch we were sitting on while looking through a comic book.

When we reached the door, I lifted him up to let him look through the peephole.

"It's Grandma!"

I frowned, then stepped back a little to open the door.

"You're up early," I told my mother.

"I knew you'd be up, so I thought I'd come visit you two. Oh, look at you! You've already grown since I last saw you!" she said, holding out her hands to Ira.

I let him cling to my mom and walked back inside. "We haven't had breakfast yet. Wanna join?"

"Of course! Rob won't be up until later and he stopped eating breakfast a while ago. Not sure how that would help his health."

"I am healthy," Ira called out, pointing at his chest.

"I know you are, sweetie." She let him down so he could run back to the couch and continue looking through the comic book while I started to brew some coffee.

"How are you doing?" Mom asked, sitting down at the table.

"Good. Had a stressful week at work but the weekend's treating us right."

"I see. And you had a visitor?" she asked.

I raised a brow and turned to look at her, and when I followed her gaze, I sighed at the bottle of wine on the counter.

"Uh, yes, I did. Last night."

"Is she still here?"

"Mom," I muttered, turning to look at her again. "No woman slept over last night. She's our new neighbor. Sweet girl, but nothing happened between us."

"Too bad. I was hoping you finally found a woman."

I rolled my eyes and turned back to the stove. "Mom, let's please not talk about this."

"Why not? It's been years since you had a date and I don't think just having someone over without wanting more is what you need right now."

"You don't know what I need. She's a friend and Ira likes her too. Besides, she's twenty. Don't think there could ever be anything more than a friendship between us."

"Oh, don't make it about age, Wells."

I couldn't start fighting with her about this.

Hell, I didn't need a relationship to be happy.

I *was* happy.

Luckily, Ira came to my rescue and changed the subject from Rooney to comics.

"Can you read this to me, Grandma?" he asked as he walked up to her with the comic book in his hands.

"Of course, sweetie. Come here."

In the time she read him a few pages of the book, I set the table and got everything that we needed out for breakfast.

I also made some more of Ira's Hulk juice, and once that was poured into a cup, I sat down to finally start breakfast.

"Drink up, buddy," I told him, pushing his cup toward him and sticking his favorite straw inside.

"Thank you!" he said, making my heart melt every damn time when he was polite without me having to tell him to be.

I was raising a real gentleman, that much I knew.

"If you want, I can come pick up Ira tomorrow morning since my yoga classes got canceled for the next few weeks."

"Yeah, that would be great. I'm trying to get into work earlier than usual from now on so I can leave before five. Ira's up at six most mornings anyway, and instead of him not letting me sleep, I'd rather get up and go in early."

My mother nodded and mixed herself a bowl of muesli. "So you can have breakfast at grandma's house tomorrow. How does that sound, Ira?"

"Sounds good!" Ira replied, holding up a thumb and then continuing to drink his Hulk juice.

Good.

Going into work early meant not having coworkers bothering me for a few hours, and I would have half of the afternoon to spend more time with Ira.

Rooney

"Don't tell me you're going back downstairs to him," Evie said with a deep frown between her brows.

"You're up already. That's new."

She rolled her eyes and grabbed a cup from the cupboard to pour coffee I made into it.

"The party last night was lame. Good thing you didn't come. AJ made out with some freshman. Wasn't fun to look at."

Why would I care?

Looked like he moved on, just what I hoped would happen after our talk.

"I promised Ira I would paint with him this afternoon while Wells gets some work done. I'll be home later tonight so we can have dinner together," I suggested.

"So you're babysitting him now?" she asked. "Is he at least paying you?"

"Evie, as much as I love you, can you please not pick at every little thing I'm doing in my life? Wells is a nice guy, and Ira is a sweet kid. They're a great distraction from studying, which you should do today by the way. That assignment we had in art history isn't easy, and it should be done by Wednesday."

"I know, I know. I'll start working on it today, don't worry. And maybe I'm picking at everything you do because I'd want to have an older guy-friend myself. Minus the child."

I raised a brow at her and chuckled. "Older friend or lover? I know you. You'd try the man out, have an opinion about him, then throw him away like you do with all the other guys you ever had sex with."

"No, I'm being serious. You're not the only one having daddy issues, you know? Mine doesn't really love me," she said with a shrug.

"I don't have daddy issues. But I do enjoy Wells's company a lot. He's easy to talk to and he doesn't pressure me into doing things I don't wanna do."

Evie puckered her lips and leaned against the counter with her arms crossed over her chest.

"If you really wanna keep him at a distance, I might just come downstairs with you and apologize to him personally for being a brat."

"You can apologize, but you won't stay. I really like him, and I think you two should get along. He's a hard-working man and I can only imagine how hard it was for him to have trouble falling asleep with you blasting loud music up here."

"All right! I'll apologize. But if he ever makes a move on me because he realizes how good I look, I won't hold back."

I doubted he would ever try and get Evie's attention, but them being on good terms was a start.

I didn't like people who disliked each other for the stupidest reasons, although Wells had a good one.

"Wanna come apologize right now so you get it out of the way?" I asked.

"Sure, why not."

Surprised, I grabbed the supplies we'd need to draw and paint, then we headed downstairs to knock on Wells's door.

I let Evie stand in front of me, and once the door opened, I smiled at Wells and nodded toward Evie so he would listen to her.

"Hello, neighbor. I understand my best friend here is really starting to enjoy spending time with you and your son, so to do her a favor, I am here to apologize for being loud most evenings. I'm sorry I didn't let you or your son sleep, but I promise you from now on, and since my loving best friend is a literal mood killer, I won't turn up the volume at future parties."

Wells was unsure what to respond for a second, but after taking in everything Evie just said, he smiled at her and nodded.

"Apology accepted. That's very kind of you, Evie."

"Great! I'll let you two get on with flirting now. Have a nice day!" she called out as she started walking back to the stairs.

A low chuckle escaped Wells, and I pressed my lips together to keep myself from grinning like an idiot.

"Hey," he greeted, stepping aside so I could walk inside.

"Hi," I said back, walking into his apartment and turning to look at him. "I didn't think she would actually apologize that easily."

"Honestly? Me neither. But I'm glad she did. Got quite the collection there," he said, nodding to the brushes sticking out of a coffee cup.

"Oh, well...us art students go through too many of these. My parents got me a life-long supply when I started college," I told him, laughing.

"Wouldn't say that's a bad thing."

"It definitely isn't. How was your morning?" I asked.

"Calm. My mother came by and took Ira on a little walk, so I got to clean the apartment and wash some clothes. He's in the living room. I set up a little painting station for you guys. He's very excited and has been asking for you all morning long."

That little boy was slowly melting my heart.

We arrived in the living room, and the second Ira saw me he jumped up and ran to me to check out what I had brought.

"Paint!" he squealed, reaching for one of the tubes.

"Lots of it as well," Wells added, placing a hand on my lower back. "I'll leave you two to it. And, Rooney?"

"Yes?"

"Thank you for doing this. I promise you this won't turn into a weekly thing. I know you have enough to do for college."

"Don't worry about it, Wells. I actually have to paint a little something for one of my classes, so this is a great opportunity to get it done. And I'm sure Ira can help me choose the colors and brushes I need, hm?"

"I'm good at colors," Ira stated with a big nod.

"See? I got my little helper. You go do what you have to do, and we'll be right here having some fun with paint."

Wells smiled at me, and after a quick brush through Ira's hair, he leaned in closer to me.

"I owe you one," he whispered, and after a long, deep stare into my eyes he left.

I had to take a deep breath before I shifted my mind back to normal to concentrate on Ira and our fun afternoon.

"Can you draw Hulk so I can color it?" Ira asked with hopeful eyes.

"I can definitely try!"

We sat down on the already stained table cloth spread out on the floor, and I set everything up to start painting.

This was going to be a nice afternoon, and as much as I tried, I couldn't get over the way Wells looked at me before he left to go to his office.

Oh, boy.

Chapter Eight

Rooney

"Look, Daddy!"

Ira held up his painting of Hulk which he colored in better than any other kid his age could.

He fascinated me with his fine motor skills and how calm and focused he was the whole afternoon.

"Wow! That's amazing, bud! We're gonna hang this one up in your room, what do you think?"

Ira nodded and went straight back to coloring another picture, and I sat up straight to look at Wells.

"Done with work?" I asked, smiling at him.

"Yeah, I think I've done enough for today. You two had a fun time, huh?" He moved his gaze to all the paintings we laid out on the floor to dry.

"There were so many things he wanted to draw and I think they all turned out perfect," I said.

"They look great. And which one is for your class?"

I reached for the small, rectangular canvas and held it toward him. "The assignment was to paint a scene that tells a story, and since I now know why that park in this town got renovated a few years ago, I decided to take it as my inspiration."

He eyed the painting, then smiled as he noticed all the little details that I painted onto it to recreate the park he had built.

"This is incredible. And you did this in four hours?"

I smiled and shrugged. "It wasn't too much work. Once I turn it in to get it graded, I want you to have it."

Wells smiled back at me. "That's sweet. Thank you, Rooney."

"Daddy?"

"Yes, buddy?"

"Can we eat?"

"I'll start making dinner in a few. Wanna stay?" he asked me after answering Ira's question.

"Oh, I'd love to, but I promised Evie we'd have dinner together. But another time for sure," I told him.

I couldn't spend every hour of the day with them, even if I'd love to.

"I have to get back to studying anyway," I added.

"All right. Are you leaving right now?" he asked.

I puckered my lips and thought about my answer for a while, then nodded and guessed that it would be best if I got some of the studying in before having dinner with Evie.

"Yes. I had a really great time with you today, Ira. I love all your artwork," I told him.

He smiled up at me and quickly got back to his sixteenth painting.

"If it's okay with you, he can have these paints and brushes. I have enough upstairs," I told Wells.

"That's nice of you, thank you. Say goodbye to Rooney, Ira."

Once I got up, Ira waved at me, too focused on his painting to say a word.

"Bye, Ira," I said with a smile, then followed Wells down the hallway.

"How about dinner next week?" he asked as we stopped at the door.

"I definitely have time on the weekend. Just let me know," I told him.

"All right. I'll see you around then."

I smiled and nodded, then leaned in to give him a quick hug before opening the door and stepping outside.

"Have a good night," I said, smiling.

"You too. Good night."

His eyes were just as intense as they were before, and I wished he didn't have such an effect on me.

"Night," I whispered, finally finding my strength to move my legs up the stairs.

As much as I loved to spend time with them, I knew a few days apart would let me think clearer.

I spent most of the weekend with Wells and Ira, and it was a nice distraction from college, but I knew I soon would miss being around them.

They lit up something in me I never knew existed, and although I had no idea what it was, I knew it was something special.

"How was your play date?" Evie asked as I walked into the apartment.

I laughed softly.

It pretty much was a play date.

"It was fun. Did you study at all today?"

She rolled her eyes at me and sighed. "Yes, *Mom*. I'm hungry. Wanna get takeout? We don't have anything in the fridge."

"Order whatever. I'm going to take a quick shower."

"'Kay. By the way, I invited Jonathan over."

"Who's Jonathan?" I asked, frowning.

"Some senior I met last night. Never seen him around campus before, but he's hot," she explained.

Right.

"Is he coming over as a one-night-stand? Or to actually hang out with you?"

"We'll see. We didn't talk much last night, but he got my number and we've been texting all day. He might bring a friend."

No need for that.

"I will lock myself into my room and get some more studying done, then I'll go to bed. Tell Jonathan to not bring a friend. He'll only be disappointed."

"I can take both," Evie said with a smug grin on her face.

I knew she could, and before she could say any more, I headed straight to my bathroom.

For some reason, college guys really didn't appeal to me anymore.

They were young and too hyped up.

Too...confusing.

Or confused.

Whatever they were, I wasn't on the look-out to date anyone anyway, but I was already excited to see Wells again soon.

***

The week was moving by fast, which was definitely a good thing.

I had finished all my assignments, got a good grade for the painting I made on Sunday, and successfully passed both tests, one of which was a surprise.

Hard work paid off, but college didn't give much time to relax.

Friday nights were great to sit in the coffee shop on campus without getting bothered by anyone else since everyone was either hanging out at a bar or getting drunk at a frat party.

Here it was quiet, and they were open until late at night.

I could've gone home, but I got sucked into one of the history books and forgot about the time.

The coffee left in my cup was cold, but I wouldn't get another one.

It was getting late, and I still had to eat dinner.

I packed all of my things into my backpack and reached for the cup to bring it to the counter as someone stepped up to the table, standing in my way.

"Leaving already?"

As I looked up, AJ was who was blocking my way.

"Hey. Yeah, I haven't eaten yet. Need to get home," I explained.

His gentle smile and tilt of his head made me look at him for a little too long, but once I got over his handsome face, I cleared my throat and took a step forward so he would move.

If I were Evie, I'd definitely would've kept lying to myself about what I really felt for AJ just because of his looks.

He was tall, muscular, and his bright, hazel eyes were striking in contrast to his dark, olive skin.

Sadly, looks didn't really do much for me.

Sure, he'd be nice to look at if he was my boyfriend, and girls would definitely be jealous, but who was aiming for that anyway?

"I haven't had dinner yet either. Wanna get something on the way home?" he asked.

I studied his face for a while, then shook my head. "I actually went grocery shopping yesterday, and I got a few things I wanted to cook. But...you're welcome to join."

Why?

God, Rooney, you're not helping yourself if you invite your ex—whatever he was—back to your apartment.

"I'd love to. Here, let me put this back for you."

He grabbed the cup out of my hand and carried it over to the counter, then he came back and reached for my backpack.

"You don't have to carry it, AJ," I said, sighing.

"I want to. Now, stop whining and let's head to your apartment."

We started walking across campus to reach the main street which would lead us to the apartment complex.

I didn't feel like talking, but since we were friends, I couldn't just ignore him and let Evie take over once we reached home.

"How are classes going?" I asked.

"Uh, pretty good. I can take a little bit of a breather next week as we need to train for our first game of the season."

AJ was a football player, but although most of his friends liked to brag about it, AJ most times seemed to not actually enjoy being on the team.

Not sure if he was just trying to impress others, or his family, as they were quite focused on having athletic children.

AJ's brother was still in high school and he was being called one of the best young athletes in history.

And his older sister competed in the Olympics a few years ago, winning a silver medal for whatever it was she did as a gymnast.

It's clear that I had no clue about sports, and they didn't really appeal to me either.

I was happy holding a brush in my hand and getting paint all over my clothes.

"Haven't seen you much around campus the past week and we missed you on quiz night too," he told me, looking at me with concern in his eyes.

"I was busy, that's all. Maybe next week I have a little more time."

"You have time. I think you just schedule your week wrong."

I scrunched up my nose and shook my head. "I don't think that's what it is. There's homework, studying, assignments, laundry, cooking, cleaning, and sleep that I need to all somehow manage to get through in just a week. It's not as easy as you think, frat-boy. Not everyone is lucky enough to have people around you who schedule the week for you."

"Hey, it's not my fault if those freshmen pay to be our personal assistants," he said with a laugh.

"Pretty sure that's illegal anyway," I replied with a grin.

"No, not illegal. Just a little degrading when you look at how other guys treat them. I was thinking of letting Marie go anyway. She's a sweet girl, but she's mostly in it for the parties she gets invited to since she plans most of them with the other girls."

I nodded once, although I also didn't understand why they would ever give up their spare time which they didn't have much of in the first place just to be seen by those guys.

"They'll fall on their faces sooner or later, and then they'll realize they're better off without guys who only waste their time."

"Woah! Are you saying you wasted your time with me?" he asked, covering his chest with one hand to show me just how hurt he was by my words.

I rolled my eyes and laughed. "I wasn't your personal assistant, Aiden."

"No, you were so much more than that. Remind me again why it didn't work out?" he asked.

"Because I don't know what I want when it comes to guys and because I'm not ready to be in a committed relationship. Same as you."

"Don't remember me saying I wasn't ready."

"But you aren't. Or else we would've talked things out much earlier."

We arrived by the apartment complex, and I turned to him and placed my hand on his chest. "We're friends. And I would like to keep it that way."

He lifted both his hands to defend himself from my words. "Friends," he said with a grin.

We walked inside to head upstairs, and when we passed Wells's door, he had to come out right when I walked by with AJ.

"Hello, Rooney," he greeted, his voice not very amused but he didn't seem too bothered by AJ either.

"Hi. Uh, Wells, this is AJ."

"Nice to meet you," Wells said, giving him a quick nod.

"Likewise."

Wells looked back at me, then pressed his lips into a tight line. "I was just about to come upstairs and ask if you'd like to have dessert with Ira and me. But I see you have plans."

Ugh!

I couldn't kick Aiden out after having invited him to dinner.

"We're just gonna have dinner. I spent most of the evening at the coffee shop, studying."

"That's fine. Another time. Have a good night," he told us, giving Aiden a quick glance and then looking back at me with slight disappointment in his eyes.

"You too," I said quietly, hoping he didn't think I was dating AJ again.

After Wells closed his door, I sighed and walked up the stairs to get to my own apartment.

"Dessert, huh? Isn't he a little too old for you?"

"He's forty-two. He's not old, and he's my friend. His son is adorable."

"So you babysit?"

I rolled my eyes at him and wished I could make him disappear so I could head downstairs to eat whatever dessert Wells made.

My heart was aching in a way it never did before, and I felt horrible for having to say no to him and sweet Ira.

My goal was to get dinner over with and then head back downstairs and hope for both of them to still be up.

"Hi, handsome," Evie said with a wide grin as we walked into the kitchen.

"Hey, Evie."

"You two have something going on again?" she asked.

"He's just eating dinner with us, then he'll leave."

"How's the friendzone, AJ?" Evie's laugh filled the whole room.

"Honestly? Quite cozy."

Good.

Because that's where he'll stay forever.

Chapter Nine

Wells

For the first night in a long time, Ira and I were cuddled up on the couch watching the ninja turtles and relaxing without worrying about anything.

It wasn't late, but since spending time with Ira was what I needed, I didn't mind him falling asleep a few hours later than usual.

Seeing Rooney with AJ did something to me that I firstly, wasn't really proud of, and secondly, still bothered me whenever I thought back to it.

She said she wasn't dating him anymore, and there wasn't a problem with her hanging out with him anyway.

Still, seeing her with him bothered me.

There wasn't much she said about him last week, but it was obvious that she didn't wanna date anyone.

I was a damn adult.

I shouldn't be worrying about shit like that.

I brushed along Ira's hair and kept my eyes on the screen as the turtles fought against some bad guys.

Honestly, I wasn't paying much attention to the storyline, but Ira was having a blast watching the movie.

"Want some more water, buddy?" I asked, always trying to keep him hydrated until he went to sleep.

He nodded his head and sat up straight to reach for his bottle, and while he took a few sips, I checked his insulin pump.

The number wasn't too low or too high, but we still had to change the pump since he had this one in for almost a week.

When he was younger, I used to change his pump every day, but thanks to the newer version, it allowed us to keep the pump in for almost six days.

It made life a little easier, and I knew once he was old enough to change it himself, he'd not be annoyed doing it on his own.

He already loved to help me change it, and the needle through which the insulin would be injected into his body didn't hurt him anymore.

He got used to it fast, but for a three-year-old, he was tougher than most teenagers.

Or even some adults.

"Are they winning?" he asked as the fight on the screen got more intense.

Luckily, there was no blood showing in the movie, and after all, it was made for people of all ages.

I even laughed a few times.

"Of course they are. They're the Ninja Turtles! You know, daddy used to watch the cartoon version when he was your age."

"Really?" he asked, his eyes wide with surprise.

"Yes. And the blue one was always my favorite. His name is Leonardo," I explained.

"Because blue is your favorite color?" Ira asked, looking up at me.

"Yeah," I said with a chuckle." Which one's your favorite?"

"The blue one," he replied.

"Great choice."

Even though some characteristics he had resembled Leah's quite a bit, Ira was exactly like me.

He leaned back against my side to cuddle again, but he couldn't stay that comfortable as we heard a knock at our front door.

"Rooney!" he called out, and this time I thought he might be right.

I paused the movie and got up from the couch, then let him grab my hand and walked over to the door with him.

I looked through the peephole, just in case it wasn't Rooney, but there she stood with worry and a hint of sadness in her eyes.

I opened the door, and the second she saw us, she smiled.

"Hi, you two," she greeted, running her fingers through Ira's locks before moving her gaze to mine.

"I hope it's not too late," she asked, her voice filled with hope.

"We're watching a movie!" Ira said happily.

"Oh, really? Sounds like you're having a fun evening."

"We are. Come in," I said, stepping to the side to let her in. "We even have some dessert left. I was really hoping you could join us earlier. I didn't know you'd have a visitor."

Which was okay and nothing I had to be jealous about.

"AJ was at the coffee shop when I was about to leave, so I invited him over for dinner. He went home a while ago. I'm sorry if that was awkward. If I had known, I wouldn't have invited him."

"Don't apologize, Rooney. I have to admit that I didn't react the way I should've reacted. But I'm happy you're here now."

Ira ran back to the living room to sit on the couch and press play, and I opened the fridge to take out the bowl with chocolate mousse in it.

"This looks delicious," she said, her eyes wide and lips smiling.

"Ira and I made it. It's dark chocolate with a little bit of orange zest on top. Try it."

She grabbed the spoon out of my hand and tried the mousse, then her eyes widened with delight.

"It's amazing! You have to give me the recipe!"

"Can't do that. It's Ira's and my secret," I told her with a grin.

"Guess I have to come over more often when you make dessert," she said, shrugging.

I smiled, thinking that wouldn't be such a bad idea.

As we walked over to the couch, I picked Ira up and sat down to place him on my lap so Rooney could sit next to us.

My couch wasn't big enough for two and a toddler.

"The blue one is my favorite," Ira told Rooney with pride. "And Daddy's too!"

"What's his name again?" she asked.

She probably knew, but she was quizzing Ira, and I thought that was the cutest thing ever.

"Leonardo!"

"Oh, right! Leonardo is great," she said, smiling and looking at the TV.

The movie suddenly wasn't so interesting anymore, and I couldn't take my eyes off Rooney.

Strange how someone could change the way you thought about things in only a few days.

Or hours, if we were to be exact.

I hadn't known her for long, but I already felt like spending time with her would change the way I thought about relationships, and if I wanted to try and date again.

How bad could it be?

Rooney's a sweet girl, but she made it more than clear that she wasn't looking for anything more than friendship.

She must've felt me staring at her, but instead of questioning why I couldn't stop looking at her, she smiled sweetly, then continued to eat the mousse and watch the movie.

Unbothered.

Maybe she liked being watched.

Not in a creepy way, of course.

I gave myself a slap against the back of my head mentally to finally tear my gaze off of her.

The movie was almost over, and the way Ira leaned back against me with his one hand twisting his hair and his other thumb in his mouth, I knew he would soon fall asleep.

"We still have to change your pump, buddy," I whispered.

"Do it now?" he asked, his voice sleepy.

"Sure."

As the credits rolled, I stood up with him in my arms, then looked at Rooney. "Mind waiting here for a while? I'll be right back."

She nodded, then reached out her hand to caress Ira's arm. "Sleep tight, Ira. Dream big," she told him.

"Night night!" was his usual response, and I smiled at their cute little interaction before walking to the bathroom to brush his teeth and change the pump.

"Wanna hold up your shirt?"

I set him on the closed toilet seat, and he pulled up his shirt without hesitation.

"Am I healthy?" he asked.

"Of course you are healthy, buddy. You drink your Hulk juice every morning, and you eat lots of fruits and veggies for every meal."

"And I get sweets when I'm good."

"You're always good, Ira."

Sometimes I wondered what it would be like to have him fuss and cry over things for once, but Ira never did.

At first, it was unsettling because every other kid his age had things they didn't like.

But then I told myself that I shouldn't manifest those thoughts, and to just let him be this way forever.

Things could still change.

"Do you wanna pull the needle out?" I asked, carefully pulling the tape around it so it would be easier for him to remove it.

He nodded, then reached for the plastic part where the needle was in to gently pull it out from underneath his skin.

The doctor suggested to connect the pump there so it wouldn't bother him too much.

Once the old needle was out, I threw it into the bin and pulled out a disinfectant wipe to clean the spot where we'd always insert the needle, and once his skin was wiped clean, Ira already pinched the skin with two fingers.

The inserting of the needle was what I still had to do, but once he was ready, I'd let him try and do it himself.

"One, two, three," I counted, and the new needle, or cannula, was already inserted in his skin.

Getting his new pump ready was an easy process, and after making sure the tube injecting the insulin was connected to the pump, Ira pushed his shirt down and wrapped his arms around me to make me carry him to bed.

"Who's sleeping in bed with you tonight?" I asked after tucking him in.

It took a while for him to decide who could sleep with him.

"Now, have a good night, all right? Grandma will come pick you up early tomorrow morning. Are you excited?"

He nodded, too tired to answer me with words.

I leaned in to kiss his forehead. "I love you, buddy," I whispered.

Another nod, and I got up from the bed to get out of his bedroom.

When I got to the kitchen, I grabbed the bottle of wine Rooney brought last week and two glasses to then head over to her still sitting on the couch.

She had her legs pulled up underneath her, and she leaned against the back of the couch sideways, with her hand holding up her head.

Her smile grew as she saw me, and once I sat down next to her, she took both glasses out of my hand and held it close to me so I could fill them with wine.

"I don't think I've ever heard a father talk to his son the way you do. He's a lucky boy," she said, her voice soft.

What was I supposed to say to that?

I knew I did a good job raising him, but I didn't want to come off as arrogant.

But then, how bad was it really to be proud of the way I parent?

"He's got all my love, and I want him to know that."

I set the bottle down and took one glass out of her hand, then smiled at her and touched mine to hers.

"I'm glad you came by," I told her, looking deep into her eyes.

"I'm glad you still let me in. If I had known, I wouldn't have invited AJ over."

I shook my head. "You don't have to push your friends away because of me. That's what he is...right?" I asked, just to make sure.

"He is." Her smile was gentle, and after taking a sip of the wine, she looked down into her lap with a frown between her brows.

"What's wrong?"

I kept my eyes on her face to make sure not to miss anything that flashed through her eyes.

She was so damn expressive, and I liked to think that I was good at reading people.

"Do you think it's possible to change your mind about something you once were so sure about?"

Her gaze lifted and her eyes met mine, worry settling in hers.

"If that happens, then I think it's your heart telling you that your mind was wrong about something."

She studied me for a moment and let her eyes wander all over my face before her gaze dropped again.

"And do you think it's possible to try and hide whatever it is your heart wants to feel because you're scared you'll get hurt?"

"No."

My response came quick, but it was an honest one.

"That's torture. If you keep everything locked up inside of you, and never let your heart feel what it wants to feel, then you'll hurt yourself more than any other person ever could. I don't know much about love, other than the one I have for my son, but I know that what you're asking me isn't something anyone should ever do."

I saw a smile appear on her face, and when she looked up at me, I smiled back at her.

"This is the best advice I can give you. Don't hold it against me if it doesn't work," I told her, chuckling.

She laughed softly and shook her head, "I think that's the best advice I have ever received. Thank you, Wells."

Her hand moved to my shoulder, and she placed it right at the crook of my neck the way she had done before.

I didn't want to interpret anything the wrong way, but it was clear that something was happening between us.

Despite our age difference, we were on the same level mentally.

She was smart and beautiful.

We saw eye to eye, which was rare nowadays as she grew up so much differently than I had.

"How are things at work?" she asked, changing the subject and making me stop staring at her.

"Getting better. I decided to start work earlier than usual so I'd have more time to spend with Ira. I started a new project, and to my luck, I'm not getting bothered by any of my coworkers for once."

"What kind of project?" she asked.

Her fingers moved along the side of my neck, brushing over my beard and then hiding into my curls at the back of my head.

If she kept doing that, I wasn't sure I could let her leave tonight.

It also seemed as if she wasn't doing it on purpose, but more so naturally because touching was her way of showing affection.

I liked that.

A lot.

"There's this diner at the outskirt where a dirt road behind it leads back to town. I need to figure out a way to close that street and build a new one where I'm allowed to put streetlights without interfering with the wildlife out there. It's a dangerous road either way, as many deer have already been killed by cars. But I'm figuring things out and have a meeting with the town's mayor to make sure he's okay with my plan."

"Your job is one I never even thought about existing. I like it. It's different," she said with a smile.

"Yeah, it's not something I ever imagined doing, to be honest. But I'm glad it's what I do. Can get a little tricky sometimes, but I wouldn't change it for anything else."

I took another sip of my wine, then put the glass onto the coffee table and placed one hand on her thigh so we both had something to touch.

"What's your plan after college?" I asked.

"I'm not sure yet, but if things work out right, Evie and I would love to open our own gallery one day where we paint and sell our work. Being an artist is definitely my dream, but it's hard to find people who actually wanna buy your paintings. There are so many amazing artists out there."

"I've seen how good you are just from that little painting of the park you made last week. It's realistic. Detailed. Far better than all those abstract paintings which have lines and splashes of paint all over. Don't really see what's so special about those."

She laughed and nodded. "We talk about abstract paintings all the time, and I can assure you that more than half of the class doesn't get it either. Sure, you can interpret things into each of those works, but in the end, not even the artist had a clue what he was doing."

"Glad you agree with me on that. I was scared we'd start a discussion about this."

Rooney scrunched her nose and shook her head. "Abstract isn't my world. I love spending hours on a painting and perfecting every little detail there is. It's what makes me happy. To know that I have created something so...unique."

I squeezed her thigh and brushed along it with my thumb as her hand fisted at the back of my head.

"You're passionate about it. That's what's most important."

And if we didn't stop touching each other soon, I would show her just how passionate I could be with her.

Fuck.

Chapter Ten

Rooney

We talked late into the night and since we were getting closer to each other anyway, I found myself with my head in his lap and his hand brushing through my hair while he looked down at me with caring eyes.

I liked being this close to him, yet I knew I would say no if he'd ask me to stay over for the night.

I wasn't ready yet, and all those thoughts running through my mind were messing with me.

We hadn't talked for a few minutes, only looking into each other's eyes and trying to figure out what was happening between us.

We hadn't known each other for too long, and the biggest question I had was if things were moving too fast.

Especially because I promised myself to not focus on anything related to men or feelings.

But how could I not when it came to Wells?

He was slowly sneaking into my heart, and I hoped I wouldn't regret it sooner or later.

Not because of him, but because of the exact thing I asked him about earlier.

If my heart wanted something, then why on Earth would I ever keep that thing from it?

Why would I let myself suffer?

But what if I was wrong?

"Tired?" he asked, his fingers curling around my hair.

"A little," I replied.

"Maybe it's time for us to go to bed."

I puckered my lips. "Are you kicking me out?"

"Not unless you wanna stay here," he said.

There it was.

The sentence I knew would be said.

I thought about it, even if I had my answer already locked in and ready.

But before answering, I sat up and turned to look at him. "Do you want me to stay?" I asked.

Maybe hearing his opinion on it would change my mind about my rejection.

He studied me for a while, then cupped my cheek with one hand and smiled. "It's you who's having trouble figuring out where we stand, Rooney. If it were up to me, I'd keep you with me tonight. But it's your decision."

Well, shit.

I lowered my gaze and reached out to grab his shirt in my hand, and after taking in a deep breath, I looked back up into his eyes.

"Another time. I think I have to get my thoughts straight first."

I was being honest, which was what I needed to be if I wanted to be able to open up more.

Showing and talking about my feelings had never been easy, and Wells knew that after I told him what happened between AJ and me.

That's why he wasn't hurt when I answered him.

He accepted it because he knew I was being honest.

"Another time," he repeated with a gentle smile.

I nodded and got up from the couch while he did the same, and with our fingers intertwined, we walked down the hallway to the front door.

"Tonight was great. Thank you for coming," he told me, still keeping my hand in his.

I smiled up at him. "Thank you for letting me come over."

"Anytime. I know you need a little time, but how about we go eat breakfast together with Ira tomorrow morning?"

Sounded like a nice idea.

"I'd love to."

"Perfect. I'll see you in the morning," he said, his voice low and raspy.

Once the door was open, he leaned in and placed a kiss to my cheek, close to the corner of my mouth.

"Goodnight, Rooney," he whispered, sending shivers down my spine.

"Goodnight, Wells," I whispered back.

My cheeks were heating up, and when he moved back again to let me pass him, I kept my head low to not let him see what kind of effect he had on me by doing the simplest things.

My heart was beating fast, but like always, my brain was trying to shut down any possible feeling building inside of me.

"Don't be too hard on yourself," he told me as I started to walk up the stairs.

Oh, how I wish it would be that easy.

***

"You're up early," I said as Evie walked into the kitchen the next morning.

"I'm spending the day at the country club with my parents. They wanna talk finances," she replied with a roll of her eyes.

"Sounds important."

"They wanna build another apartment complex next to this one. Not sure how much help I can be, but Dad might write me another check to buy more art supplies."

The way she smirked when she said the last two words told me that she was probably going to spend that money on clothes and alcohol.

"Why are you up? Another date with the neighbor?"

"Uh, yeah. We're going out for breakfast with Ira."

"So...you like him?"

"I guess so."

She raised a brow at me. "*I guess so?* Rooney, I don't think any twenty-year-old would hang out with an older guy and his son if they didn't like him. Clearly you got the hots for him."

"Okay, okay. I like him. Maybe a little too much for only having known him for a week."

"Then what's making you act so unsure?"

A few things. But mostly the fear of commitment.

I didn't know what held me back.

Sure, I had my reasons, but there were little fragments I still had to find and put into place.

Things that stopped me from putting everything into one piece which would help me realize that catching feelings and falling in love wasn't such a bad thing after all.

"Myself," I replied, shrugging.

"You'll figure it out someday. But if this thing between you and him is serious, don't let him fuck you before you are sure about what you want."

Advise from Evie wasn't what I usually listened to, but this time...she might've had a point.

"I'll see you tonight," she called out, already walking out of the kitchen.

"Bye," I replied, and once she was gone, I let out a heavy sigh and talked myself into being more relaxed.

Breakfast with Wells and Ira would be fun, and even with all my worries, I was excited to see him again.

His kiss still lingered on my cheek, and I could still feel his fingers running through my hair, caressing my head.

"What are you doing to me," I whispered, catching myself smile like a fool.

Wells
Wasn't such a good idea to let him stay up late after all.

Ira was still asleep, and I hated to wake him up when he needed his sleep.

But we still had time, and Rooney wasn't here yet anyway.

I leaned in to kiss Ira's head before letting him sleep for a little longer, then I headed out of his room to go to the kitchen.

But just as I was about to turn left, a knock came from the front door.

It's her.

I opened the door and found Rooney standing there in a sweet outfit, perfect for fall.

Her knitted, dark green sweater was pushed inside her black overalls, and her hair flowed down over her shoulders, almost reaching her hips.

"Hey, gorgeous," I said, smiling at her.

"Hi. Ready for breakfast?" she asked sweetly.

I held out my hand for her to take and waited until she placed hers into mine, then I pulled her closer and put my other hand on her waist.

"We might have to push it back to lunch. Ira's still asleep, and I'd hate to wake him."

"Oh, that's fine. Guess it did get late last night," she said.

"Yeah, a little. Want a coffee? I don't think it will take too long for him to wake up."

She nodded and kept that sweet smile in place, and after I closed the door, I walked with her to the kitchen.

"Take a seat. I have some fruit you could eat so you won't starve until lunch," I told her, pointing to the fruit basket on the table.

"Oh, no, that's fine. Coffee's just fine."

I turned to the counter and started to brew the coffee, and once I filled two cups, I sat down at the table next to her and passed her a cup.

"Did you have a good night?" I asked, taking a sip of the coffee while keeping my eyes on hers.

"I did. I couldn't fall asleep for a while, but once I got you off my mind it was all right."

I grinned at her words.

"Same here. Last night was nice."

Rooney bit her bottom lip before taking a sip of her coffee, then she placed her cup down and sighed. "Maybe I should've stayed," she whispered.

"No, you shouldn't have. As much as I would've wanted you in my bed, I think we should let whatever this is grow the way it wants to. Naturally, without us pushing things."

"Okay," she agreed.

We could make this work if that's what we really wanted.

And I could see it in her eyes that she was trying to open up her heart and let me in, even if I was figuring my own heart out myself.

We kept drinking our coffee while looking into each other's eyes deeply, not saying a word and just taking in each other's presence.

Not too long after, I heard Ira call out to me, and I quickly got up to get to him. "I'll be right back."

When I got to his bedroom, he was already sitting up in his bed with his stuffed animals all around him.

"Hey, buddy. Did you have a good night?" I asked, squatting down next to his bed.

He nodded, rubbing his eyes with both his fists and yawning.

"Rooney's here. Let's go wash your face and get you dressed, hm?"

"Did you have a sleepover with her?" he asked.

This kid was gonna make me regret ever telling him about sleepovers.

Luckily, he had no idea what adults did at sleepovers.

"No, she left after you fell asleep," I explained, helping him out of the bed and walking over to the bathroom with him.

"And now she is back?"

"Exactly. We missed breakfast because you slept so much, but we'll have lunch together, okay?"

He nodded and stepped up onto the little stool which helped him reach the sink, and once I pulled up his sleeves, he held his hands underneath the stream and then splashed water onto his face.

"What do you wanna wear today?" I asked, letting him dry off his face and hands.

"The bear sweater."

"Great choice."

We went back to his room and after I pulled his sweater with bear ears on the hood and a pair of plain jeans out of his dresser, I helped him change into it.

"All set?" I asked, tugging at the fluffy material of his sweater and clipping the pump to his pants to ensure he'd be comfortable for the day.

"I wanna see Rooney!" he announced happily, jumping up and down.

"She's in the kitchen. Go say hi," I told him.

I followed him, and as he reached her, he threw himself at her with joy.

His arms wrapped around her neck and she pulled him up onto her lap to hug him tight.

"Hi, little man. I like your outfit," she told him.

"It's a bear! See?" He leaned back and pulled up the hood, then made a growling sound to imitate a bear.

"That's amazing! I wish I had one of those. Did you have a good sleep? You slept longer than usual, huh?"

Ira nodded, and I watched them having the most adorable conversation ever while smiling brightly.

They were too damn sweet.

"We have lunch together," Ira pointed out.

"That's right, and I'm very excited."

"What do you wanna eat, Ira?" I asked, watching as he pushed himself off Rooney's lap.

"Uh..." I let him think about it for a moment, then he lifted his little finger to let us know he had an idea.

"Pasta!"

"Sounds good to me. Up for some Italian?" I asked Rooney.

"I love Italian," she replied, still smiling.

God, if I kept looking at her, I might change my mind about everything concerning her.

"We can leave now and play at the park a little bit before heading to the restaurant. I don't think they open before eleven."

We grabbed our things and headed outside the apartment.

"Do you like swings?" Ira asked Rooney as they walked down the stairs hand in hand.

"Of course I do. It's my favorite thing at the park," she told him.

"Can you swing high? Daddy always pushes me until I touch the sky!"

I chuckled at his statement.

"That high? Wow! Maybe your daddy can push me that high as well. What do you think?" Rooney said, grinning back at me.

Whatever she wanted me to do, I'd do it.

Chapter Eleven

Rooney

We played on the playground, had a delicious lunch, then we headed back home because it started raining.

Ira was tired anyway, and Wells suggested he'd have some quiet time with his books and toys.

"Wouldn't be surprised if he fell asleep right there on the floor," Wells said, sitting down next to me on his couch.

I looked over at Ira who was looking through a book with his stuffed animals, whispering things to them and pointing at the pictures.

"He's got a lot of energy," I admitted.

I had never seen a toddler run around that much, and although he had lots of fun at the playground, he didn't complain when Wells told him we'd head back home.

"He does. I've been talking to him about what kind of sport he'd like to do once he's old enough to join a club. He told me he liked anything that had to do with running. Guess I'll have to let him join in on a few training days to see which sport he likes best."

"Did you play any sports when you were younger?" I asked.

I leaned my head against my hand, with my elbow propped up on the back of the couch.

"I did competitive swimming and played football for a few years. I found out that I wasn't much of a team player, so I started going on runs by myself."

"Do you still go on runs?"

He shook his head. "Ever since Ira, there wasn't really much time to. I do some home workouts whenever I get the chance to, but other than that, carrying Ira and groceries a few times a day is what keeps me in shape," he explained with a grin.

I laughed softly and let my eyes wander down to his chest, then moved them further down to his shirt-covered abdomen.

"You look great. I liked eating breakfast with you for the first time ever without you wearing a shirt," I admitted, making his grin grow wider.

"Figured. You couldn't take your eyes off me."

I rolled my eyes at him and slapped his chest gently, and before I knew it, he pulled me closer with one hand on my thigh and the other around my shoulders.

Placing my hand on his chest gently this time, I let him keep me close to his side while our faces were closer than ever.

Our eyes met, but as intense as this was, neither of us made another move.

As if we were indecisive about something.

I knew I was, but if I'd kiss him right now, things might not turn out the way I hoped they would.

But just being close to him was enough for me at the moment.

Besides, Ira was right there, probably sneakily watching us with his eyes peeking over the edge of his book.

He had gone quiet the second Wells pulled me to him.

"I think we're being watched," he whispered, a small smirk on his lips and confirming my theory about Ira.

I laughed softly. "Maybe we should get some distance between us," I suggested.

His hand on my thigh tightened, which I took as a harsh *no*.

He moved his gaze to Ira, and I did the same only to find him staring at us with the biggest green eyes so similar to his father's.

We both couldn't hold in a laugh at the sight of him, and when he realized we had caught him, his cheeks turned a bright red and his eyes quickly disappeared behind the book again.

"He has never seen me with a woman before. This is all new to him," Wells explained.

I smiled, looking back at him and placing my right hand at the back of his neck to twist his curls around my fingers.

"Are you worried he won't be okay with...this?"

His eyes moved from mine to my lips, then back up.

"No. He likes you. I think he'd be upset if you would stop showing up," he said with honesty in his voice.

"And you? Would you be upset if I wouldn't show up at your door anymore?" I asked, my voice soft.

He studied my face for a while, and his silence was starting to make me nervous.

But instead of answering with words, he lifted his hand and cupped my cheek gently, then he leaned in and tilted my head to the side to place his lips on my jawline.

I closed my eyes to take in this sweet gesture, and once he leaned back again, his eyes immediately found mine.

"I'd be more than upset, Rooney."

I pressed my lips into a thin line.

As much as I wanted to, I couldn't keep eye contact with him, so I avoided his eyes by looking down into my lap where his hand still touched my thigh.

I reached for it and let my fingers move gently through his until they interlocked, and I squeezed his hand gently before finally being able to talk.

"I don't think I can stay away from you," I whispered.

He smiled and brushed back a few strands of my hair, tucking them behind my ear while his eyes kept wandering over my face.

Words didn't come easy in situations like these, but that was a good thing.

"Good," was his simple response, and as he leaned in again, he placed his lips on my cheek while his thumb brushed along mine.

How bad was this really?

Sure, the age difference was something we—no, *others*—would have to get over, but other than that it seemed as if Wells and I were going in the right direction.

Still, I had no idea what I wanted to happen between us, I just knew it felt right, and that I didn't want this to end anytime soon.

My mind was confused, but that's okay.

At least for now.

His lips moved down to my neck, nibbling and sucking gently on my skin.

I closed my eyes and tightened my grip in his hair to keep him right there close to me, and even if it felt like an eternity, his lips were gone again, and as if it were planned, my phone started to ring.

I gave Wells an apologetic look before reaching for my phone on the coffee table, and when I looked at the screen to see who was calling, I let out a sigh.

"It's Evie."

"Pick up. I'll prepare a snack for Ira," Wells said, squeezing my hand once more before getting up from the couch.

Evie knew how to ruin a perfect and intense moment.

I swiped over the screen to pick up, but it wasn't me talking first.

"You have to come to the club. My parents invited friends from all over the country and you know what a party at the club means," she said, her voice full of excitement.

It meant free drinks until she couldn't stand up straight anymore.

"I'm not really into partying tonight, Evie," I told her, looking over at Wells who was cutting up a few strawberries.

"Oh, come on, loser. It's been a while since you've last been here, and I'm just now realizing that I didn't tell you the best part about tonight yet."

I raised a brow and waited for her to continue talking.

My guess was male strippers, but I couldn't say that out loud.

Not with Ira watching me closely.

God, he's adorable.

"Remember how I told you about the Kristoff's? That crazy rich couple that loves art? Well, they'll be here tonight, and I think that would be a great opportunity to try and get them to invest in our dream of opening our own gallery someday. You can't miss this, Rooney."

She was right.

I couldn't miss out on an opportunity like that.

I looked back at Wells who was filling up Ira's cup with his Hulk juice, and as much as I would've wanted to spend more time with him, I couldn't say no to meeting the Kristoffs.

"Okay, I'll be there. Is a dress necessary?" I asked.

"And high heels. And pretty make up. I'll see you later."

Evie hung up the phone and I smiled at Wells who was now walking back into the living room.

"Can't stay?" he asked.

"Evie's parents are having a little party over at the country club. They invited a couple who's been interested in some of Evie's and my artwork before, but that was two years ago. They might be potential investors, and I can't let Evie talk to them by herself if it's my dream too."

He didn't seem too upset about me having to go.

"Sounds great! Invest in a place for you two to work after college?" he asked.

He was interested, which made me feeling bad for leaving much more relaxed.

"Yes. That time we talked two years ago they said if we were to successfully graduate, they'd help us build something up. They're nice people, immigrated from Russia only about five years ago, but they're really sweet. I should head upstairs and get ready."

He gave me a quick nod and smiled at me. "Let me walk you to the door. Ira, Rooney's leaving."

"Why?"

"Because she has to attend an important party," Wells explained.

Party was right, but I wouldn't do much partying.

"I'll see you soon, Ira. I had fun with you today," I told him, squatting down to meet his eyes.

"Me too," he replied, wrapping his arms around my neck to say goodbye.

Once I was back on my feet, Wells walked me to the front door with his hand on my lower back, and when we reached our destination, I turned to him and smiled.

"Today was perfect."

"Couldn't agree more," he replied, a soft smile lingering on his lips. "I'll see you soon. Ira and I will be spending the day with my mother and her boyfriend tomorrow."

I nodded. "I'll see you around. I'll be upstairs if you need anything," I told him, hoping he would need something.

He pulled me closer with his hands on my waist, and I wrapped my arms around his neck to hug him tight.

I could still feel his kisses on my neck, and so I wasn't the only one to receive that kind of affection, I turned my head to kiss his cheek before taking a step back.

"Have fun tonight," he said quietly.

"Thank you."

With his hands tightening at my waist and then letting go of me, I opened the door and left, not looking back again or else I would already start missing him too much.

And while talking to potential investors, I didn't want my mind to drift off and dream about Wells.

Though, I would definitely dream about him tonight after his gentle touches and kisses.

***

"Finally!"

Evie walked toward me with her heels clicking on the marble floor, making too much noise.

Her dress was white and sparkly, looking almost like a wedding dress.

"When's the last time you dressed up?" she asked with a grin as she looked down to take in my light blue dress and black heels.

"It's been a while. But this just reminded me how much I love pants and wide shirts and sweaters," I said, laughing.

"You look amazing. Come on, my parents are already waiting."

We walked down the large hallway to get to the ballroom located on the west wing of the club, and when we entered, I immediately wanted to turn back around.

Too many people, too much beauty.

Not my world at all, but if I wanted to secure my future as an artist, this was one way I could do just that.

I took a deep breath and let Evie lead me to her parents who were sitting at a large table with the Kristoff's.

I smiled, and Evie's mother got up to greet me with a hug.

"Rooney, it's so good to see you again. Did you settle into the apartment already?" she asked.

"Hello, Fleur. I'm all settled. The apartment is great," I told her, knowing that would make her happy.

She loved every single building they owned and complimenting them would only get me more brownie points.

"Rooney," Evie's father said, holding out his hand for me to shake.

I smiled at him. "Hello, Dan. Good to see you again," I told him.

"Likewise. You remember Morgana and Michail?"

"Of course. It's so good to see you again," I told the couple, smiling sweetly.

"We've been waiting for you to arrive. Have you been studying today?" Michail asked in a thick, Russian accent.

I like it, but then, I was a sucker for any accent a person might have.

"I took a little break from studying today, but I'll get back to it tomorrow," I told him.

For some reason, I felt like having to prove myself to them.

In the end, they would decide whether they wanted to support Evie and me or not.

"If only Evie would study as much as this girl does. Your parents must be so proud of you, Rooney," Fleur said.

It's not that they weren't proud of Evie, and she didn't seem hurt by her mother's words either, but they were so much stricter than my mom and dad that I often felt bad for Evie.

"Evie's doing good in school. Sit, girls. We have a lot to talk about tonight," Dan said.

I prepared myself for what's to come, but I was excited to find out what kinds of plans Morgana and Michail had in mind.

Whatever they would offer, I knew would be a good opportunity for Evie and me, and by looking at their happy faces, I knew things would take a positive turn.

Chapter Twelve

Rooney

"That went so much better than expected," Evie whispered as we walked away from the table.

I nodded, still in shock about what Michail offered us.

It was life-changing.

Well, life hasn't gotten us that far yet, but once we'd graduate, our lives were pretty much settled.

"I can't believe he wants to buy a whole building just for us and our art. Evie, do you realize what that means?" I asked, mostly asking to try and get it into my own head.

"Of course I know that that means, silly. They're rich, have enough money to throw around, and we're the lucky ones who get to live out our dreams thanks to them."

Yes, our dreams of owning a gallery where we could paint and sell our paintings, and with as much space as Michail promised us, we'd also be able to host auctions.

"Good thing you came. I would've fucked it up by myself," she said as we reached the bar.

"Two glasses of champagne, please," she told the bartender, but I quickly shook my head at him.

"I can't drink tonight. I'll have a Coke," I said with a smile.

"God, you're so boring! We should be celebrating! Don't tell me you already wanna leave." Evie raised a brow at me.

"No, I'm not leaving yet, I just don't feel like drinking," I told her.

Once we got our drinks, we walked over to the big balcony and headed outside to catch a breath of fresh air.

I was still processing it all.

I had to tell my parents.

They'd be so excited for us.

"I hate to say it because it sounds arrogant, but having rich parents does come in handy. What they lack in showing their affection for their daughter, they definitely get points for helping out with my future."

No matter how much help we received from her parents, or their friends, I knew once we'd settle into our new gallery, we'd have to work hard to sustain it.

I didn't come from a wealthy family, and working hard for my dreams was important to me.

But even if I had a little bit of issues accepting Michail and Morgana's offer, I was so very grateful for them for giving us this opportunity.

"Your parents seemed a little more relaxed tonight. Is their marriage getting better?"

"They've been going to a therapist to talk about what their relationship lacks, but I've seen some change too. Guess it's a good thing they realized something was wrong before things got out of hand."

I nodded, happy for them to have found a way to fix this.

I took a sip of my coke and looked around the outside area, seeing a few faces I knew from college.

Mostly seniors who grew up here and chose to attend Central College so they didn't have to move away from their rich families.

Understandable.

Then, out of the corner of my eye, I saw AJ walk toward us, and I turned to look at him as he stopped right in front of us.

"Fancy seeing you here," I told him, getting a chuckle from him in return.

"You too. Didn't think I'd see you tonight. You look beautiful," he said, his eyes wandering down along my dress and stopping at my shoes.

"Thank you, Aiden," I replied. "You look great too."

But then, it wasn't hard for men to look good in suits.

I wonder what Wells looks like with a suit and tie.

"Thanks. No champagne tonight?"

He nodded at my glass, noticing my non-alcoholic drink. "Not tonight. I drove here," I pointed out.

"You could stay and sleep in one of the guest rooms on the east wing," Evie suggested.

That's what she would probably do as she drove here herself as well.

"Oh, no, that's fine. I wanna sleep in my bed tonight."

"Mind driving me back to campus? My parents already left, and I told them I'd get an Uber. Driving with you is more fun though."

I smiled at him and nodded. "Of course. Let me know when you're ready to leave."

"It's still early. How about we get on that dancefloor and show off our moves?" he said with a wide grin.

I didn't feel like dancing, but I also didn't wanna seem like a bore.

Besides, at college parties I was always the last one leaving the dancefloor.

"Okay, but only if Evie tells the DJ to play better music."

"Already on it!"

I laughed and finished my drink, then placed it on an empty table and let AJ pull me onto the dancefloor in the middle of the room.

As soon as the music genre changed, we started moving, and sure enough, all eyes were on the three of us.

I wasn't a good dancer, but who the hell cared if it looked good?

I was starting to enjoy myself, and I needed to celebrate my future which was handed to me on a silver platter tonight.

Someday I'd get back to Michail and Morgana, just to make sure they knew how amazing they were.

Music was all I could hear, but the more songs that came on, the more people joined in on the dancefloor.

At some point, I let AJ pull me to him with my back pressing against his chest and his hands around my waist.

As long as he kept them there, I didn't mind dancing this close with him.

We've done this before, but every time we danced at a frat party, he had to show off that he had a girl with him.

His lips moved all over my neck, and back then I even liked it, but if he were to do it today, I'd push him away quick.

To my luck, his hands and upper body were the only things touching me.

No matter what had happened between us, AJ was a gentleman, not pushing any boundaries.

As much fun as I was having, I was starting to get tired, and without having to look at the time, I knew it was late.

I stopped dancing and turned to look at AJ with a tired smile.

"I need something to drink," I told him.

"Me too."

He grabbed my hand and pulled me toward the bar where he ordered a glass of iced water for me and some alcoholic drink for him.

"Are you ready to go home?" he asked, watching me as I drank the water. "You look tired."

"I am. I was up early this morning. Why are you here, by the way?"

"My dad met with his business partners and wanted me to come along. Since I won't have a future playing any sports, he's starting to introduce me to his world of owning a million-dollar business."

I puckered my lips, feeling compassion and hating that there was no way he could decide his own future.

"And how did it go?"

He shrugged, a smug grin appearing on his face. "I'd be lying if I said I knew exactly what they talked about. That shit is boring, but I guess I'll have to please my father somehow, and this is one way."

"Hey, at least you can hang out here with other rich people. Isn't that the dream of most students at Central?" I asked jokingly.

"Can't compare me to those guys. Besides, you're here too."

"Because of Evie," I simply replied.

His eyes were glued to mine, and after a few seconds, he finally spoke again.

"You look happier," he said, his voice low.

"Happier? What makes you think I wasn't this happy before?"

He shrugged. "I don't know what changed, but I can see it in your eyes. They haven't glowed like this when we hung out."

As sweet as his words were, I didn't want to tell him about Wells and what I was starting to develop for him.

Hell, I didn't even know exactly what it was

"I think that's just my tiredness, AJ."

I emptied my glass and sat it down on the bar, then smiled up at him. "Ready to go home?"

He nodded hesitantly, then finished his drink and placed the glass next to my empty one.

"Let's go."

We had lost Evie, but I was sure she was safe with some random guy she happened to meet on the dancefloor.

When we got to my car, Aiden opened my door like the true gentleman he was, but I knew he wasn't trying to impress me.

That's just who he was.

"Thank you," I told him with a smile and got inside the car.

Once my door was closed, he walked around the front while I turned on the engine and waited for him to get in.

The drive to campus was quiet, and in all honesty, I was happy about that.

Thoughts about Wells were running through my mind, and when I checked the time, I knew he wouldn't be up anymore.

It was almost two a.m., and I needed to get sleep myself.

I parked in front of the frat house and looked over at AJ as he loosened his tie. "Thanks for the drive home."

"Of course. I had fun tonight," I told him.

"You did? You seemed a little...distant. At least with your mind. Is there something you wanna talk about, Rooney?"

"No. I'm fine, AJ. I just...have a lot to think about. Have a good night. I'll see you around."

He studied me for a while, then leaned in to kiss my temple before getting out of the car. "Goodnight," he said with a gentle smile, then he closed the door and left.

A sigh of relief escaped me.

As happy as Wells made me, even after only a few days we spent together, I didn't wanna be too open about it.

I was scared that if I talked too much too soon, I would be disappointed if things with him wouldn't work out.

"But for things to work out you have to talk about your feelings," I whispered to myself.

Not now.

I still had time, right?

I drove home and parked my car next to Evie's empty parking spot, and after getting out and locking the car, I walked inside the building to head upstairs.

I missed my bed.

I missed Wells.

God, I missed him so much!

And that's why I stopped in front of his door, standing there like a total fool and wishing he'd suddenly open up the door to let me in.

I wondered what would've happened if I stayed instead of leaving for the club.

He was kissing my neck and squeezing my hand tightly, showing me just how sweet and gentle he could be.

I couldn't get enough of him, but I had to take a few steps back and head upstairs before I actually knocked on his door and woke him and Ira up.

I couldn't be that selfish.

Not if I still had to get my emotions intact.

When I reached the top floor and the lights turned on automatically because of the sensors, I was surprised by the note on the floor in front of the door.

It had my name written on it, and my thoughts immediately went to Wells.

Apart from a handwritten note being incredibly romantic, I found it sweet that he let Ira scribble all over the white paper to make the note look more fun.

Smiling, I unfolded it and was taken aback by the simple words carefully written on it.

You looked beautiful in that dress. – Wells

My cheeks turned red, but how did he know what I had on?

The only possible way he could've seen me was out of the window as I got into my car, but however he got a look at me, this note was what made me smile the most.

He was thoughtful.

After staring at the note for a while, I unlocked the door and headed inside, then quickly headed to my bedroom to change out of my dress and into my pajamas.

I would keep that note close to my bed so I could look at it as often as possible, and once I was all settled and ready to sleep, I turned off all the lights and stared at the note for a little while before putting it onto my nightstand and closing my eyes.

I missed him, and no matter how many times I would repeat those three words, I couldn't get my heart to open up the way I wanted it to.

Maybe time was what I needed, and for Wells and Ira, I would spend as many hours figuring out my feelings until I had a clear vision of what my heart wanted.

Chapter Thirteen

Wells

She was stuck on my mind and I couldn't get her off of it.

I had to admit on doing some stupid things when I started to like someone in the past, and that didn't change with Rooney.

Last night, after she left to get dressed for the dinner at the country club, I listened closely for her footsteps in the hallway, just to get a look at her through the fucking peephole.

When I saw her walk down the stairs, she looked incredible.

Like a princess.

But if she'd hear me say that she'd shake her head and tell me that she wasn't a princess.

Well, to me she looked like one, but I could tell by the look in her eyes that she wasn't too comfortable in those shoes.

Either way, I had to write her a note to let her know how beautiful she looked, so once Ira was in bed, and after I let him decorate the note with his colored pencils, I walked upstairs to put the note in front of her door.

It was the next day, and as much as I wanted to head up there again to see her, I had to walk the other way and take Ira to my mother's.

She invited us for lunch, and I knew she'd keep us there for dinner as well.

Maybe a little distance between Rooney and me wasn't such a bad thing after all.

I didn't want to push her, and even if she enjoyed me kissing her neck yesterday, I had to stay back for her to know what she really wanted.

I put Ira's seatbelt on and made sure he was secure, then gave him back his action figures.

"Ready to go to grandma's?"

"Yes!" he replied happily.

I glanced up to Rooney's bedroom window, knowing she was probably still asleep as she hadn't been home before midnight.

Yes, that much I knew about last night.

"We're gonna have lots of fun and eat a lot of yummy food," I told him as I got into the car myself and put my seatbelt on to start driving.

"I like yummy food," Ira said.

"I know you do. I do too."

The drive to her house was a short one, but I knew once it was time to head back home, Ira would already be tired and not up for walking.

He'd do plenty of that at grandma's, seeing as she had a nice garden and a swing set she bought just for Ira.

We arrived at the house and I got out of the car just as my mother walked out of the front door to greet us.

"Oh, I'm so happy you two are here," she said, giving me a quick hug and kiss to my cheek before she turned to the more important one here.

I wasn't offended.

"Hi, Grandma!" Ira called out with a wave as she opened his door, and even if the straps securing him in the car seat were difficult to open, he somehow always managed to open them before I even got the chance to get out of the car.

Luckily, he never did that when we were still driving.

"Hello, darling. Are you hungry yet?"

It was only eleven in the morning, but I didn't mind eating lunch already.

"We didn't have much for breakfast," I told her as she picked Ira up.

He didn't mind being carried, but right now he didn't feel like it.

He squirmed in her arms and she let him down on his feet, quickly running toward the front door.

"Okay, we'll have lunch in a few then," she said, smiling up at me.

"You didn't bring your date," she pointed out.

She had told me to bring the girl I was seeing so she could finally meet her, but asking Rooney to spend a whole day at my mother's didn't sound like fun.

Mom would ask her a million questions, and I didn't want to scare Rooney off.

"No, I didn't. Another time," I told her.

"If you're trying to hide her from me, I will be mad at you for the rest of my life," she muttered.

"Won't be too long then," I replied with a grin.

Mom hit my chest and murmured a curse at me, rolling her eyes.

She knew I was just joking, and I was lucky she didn't take anything serious that I threw her way.

Being her only child, she tried to make me more of a friend than a son to her.

She succeeded with that, but there were moments where she couldn't stop herself from showing me her motherly side.

We followed Ira into the house and I let him run to the kitchen where a delicious smell came from.

"How is Ira doing?"

"He's good. We have a doctor's appointment in a few weeks just to check on how things are going with the pump."

"He looks happy and healthy to me," Mom said, smiling brightly at me. "I always knew you'd be the best daddy ever. Shame there is no woman who can watch you be one twenty-four-seven," she said, puckering her lips.

I rolled my eyes at her. "I don't need to prove to anyone that I'm a good father."

"No, you don't. But it would be nice having someone close to you who appreciates you for who you are. I can tell you like that neighbor of yours, or else your eyes wouldn't have that happy gleam in them. What's her name again?" she asked.

I couldn't get away from this conversation, so I might as well go along with it.

"Rooney," I told her,

I lifted Ira up to sit him down on the counter next to the sink so he could wash his hands.

"And she's twenty, you said? Is she in college?"

"Yeah, she's studying art. She's really talented."

"I painted with Rooney!" Ira called out with a smile on his face.

"You did? Do you like Rooney?" Mom asked.

She was trying to make a point here even though she never met her before.

"I like Rooney," Ira said, nodding his head and then pointing at me. "Daddy likes her too."

"Oh, does he now?" She looked at me with a raised brow.

"Daddy kissed Rooney."

Guess he kept spying on us while I got closer to her. "I kissed her on the cheek, buddy. That's a different thing."

Why the fuck was I trying to justify this in front of my three-year-old?

"Cheek, lips, what's the difference?" Mom asked. "I wanna meet her soon. Next time I invite you over, I want you to bring her with you."

Starting an argument with her wasn't taking me anywhere, so I gave her a quick nod to hopefully make her change the subject.

To my luck, her boyfriend walked into the house with a newspaper in hand and a sweaty tracksuit on.

I didn't take him as a sporty guy, but even for his age, George was pretty much in shape.

"Visitors," he said as he walked up to the kitchen.

"Good to see you, George," I told him, shaking his hand.

His grumpy and tired face were only a façade. George was a nice guy, caring and loving.

"Good to see you too, Wells."

"I'm here too!" Ira called out.

"Hey, big boy. You having lunch with us today?"

"And dinner. They're spending the day with us today," Mom explained.

"That's great! Let me go take a quick shower and I'll be right back down."

When he left to head upstairs, I looked at Mom as I helped Ira get down from the counter.

"Why hasn't he moved in yet?" I asked.

"Because he likes his space and I like mine."

Understandable, but not what I would wanna go for if I loved someone.

If things worked out between Rooney and me, I for sure would ask her to move in with me.

Maybe not after asking her to be mine, but soon after.

Ira would love having another person around the apartment, but having her as our neighbor was as close as we'd get for now.

Rooney

"These are our potential galleries. Michail wrote in the email that we could choose the one we like best, then get back to him and he'll make sure to contact the building's owner."

I looked at the pictures on Evie's phone she was holding close to my face, but my eyes had yet to adjust to the light she rudely switched on without a warning.

How come she was already up and I had trouble even if I was the one who came home first?

I sat up and reached for her phone, then leaned back against the headboard and rubbed my eyes before taking another look at the two buildings.

I recognized both of them, and I knew one of the buildings was once a club. A strip club, to be exact.

The other one was an old industrial building where they used to have pop-up stores or farmer's markets in it, and I knew the inside looked incredible.

"I like this one better. It's also closer to home," I told her, pointing at the mahogany red building covered in brick.

"Figured. I would've gone for the old strip club in the hopes there would still be poles around, but this one fits better for a gallery."

I raised a brow at her and laughed. "You don't know how to pole dance," I pointed out.

"I could learn," she replied with a shrug. "So, this one?"

I nodded, still unsure if we were just being pranked or if I wasn't actually dreaming.

"Isn't it a little too early to have him buy a building? We still have almost two years of college ahead of us."

"If the building's available, why wait? We could start putting our paintings in there, renovate what's needed, and have parties in there before we turn it into an actual art gallery. Stop overthinking and let that rich, Russian couple invest in a damn building for us, Rooney. Our future is secured. Stop worrying."

I had a few problems with those two things.

First off, as hard as I worked on each and every single one of my paintings, it didn't feel as if I did enough to just get gifted an entire building, and secondly...I worried because there was no way we could be sure about having buyers.

Selling my art was what I had to do to have a stable income.

"You and AJ had fun last night, huh?" Evie asked, changing the subject.

"Uh, yeah. It was nice. Where did you go?"

"Remember Jonathan? I made him pick me up and take me to the frat house. They had a party going, and I figured it would be more fun than at the club."

"I see. Did you have breakfast yet?"

"Breakfast? Sis, it's almost one. I'm ordering Chinese. Want some too?"

Shit, did I sleep that much?

I'd have to start studying the second I finished my lunch.

"Yeah, sure. I'll have whatever you're having."

"Perfect." She got off the bed and headed out of my room, and I still tried to fully wake up and finally start my day.

My thoughts immediately went to Wells and the note he wrote last night.

I reached for it on the nightstand and smiled as I read those words again.

Maybe someday I could wear that dress again for him, or I might buy a new one just for him.

Too many people have seen me in that dress already, and it wouldn't be special if I'd wear it on my next date with Wells.

Because that's exactly what we were doing, right?

Dating.

Getting to know each other better and having a good time while getting closer.

If only I could open up and ask him directly about it instead of keeping my thoughts in the dark.

Chapter Fourteen

Rooney

It's been a week since I have last seen Wells and Ira, and because it was Friday, I thought I'd head downstairs to see if they were home.

Throughout the week I've been busy with classes which I mostly took online this time and painting, so there wasn't much time for me to get out of the apartment.

I let Evie do all the grocery shopping, as she wasn't much interested in focusing on college.

Plus, she made sure we actually got the building Michail and Morgana promised us, and Evie has been emailing back and forth with them all week long.

It still wasn't getting into my head that we could soon move all of our canvases and material in there, though, I probably wouldn't go there to paint just yet.

Evie had planned parties already, and I didn't want anyone to destroy my art.

After packing all my things into my backpack, I went into the bathroom to brush my hair and make sure I wasn't looking too homeless, and once I adjusted my loungewear, I headed to the door to head downstairs.

Hopefully they were home.

As I got to their door, I rang the bell and waited, my heart suddenly picking up speed and making me nervous.

It's only been a week, but I missed Wells close to me.

The door swung open and a surprised, half-naked Wells stood in front of me. "Rooney, hey," he said, smiling at me.

I couldn't stop my eyes from wandering down his chest and muscular abdomen.

He must've been working out in the past few days.

"Hi," I replied, feeling my cheeks suddenly heat up and my breathing hitch. "I, uh...are you free? Right now?"

His smile turned into a grin as he noticed my nervousness, then he stepped aside and nodded. "Come in. Did you have dinner yet?" he asked.

I shook my head and passed him to get inside. "No, I'm not very hungry, actually."

Wells closed the door and turned to look at me, then he placed a hand on my lower back to walk me past the kitchen and into the living room.

"Why not? Did you have a late lunch?"

"Kinda. I've been up since five to get some studying done. Evie came home for a few hours and brought some snacks, and I've been eating those all day long."

He motioned for me to sit down on the couch, and before he could reply, I frowned and spoke again. "Is Ira already asleep?" I asked.

"Uh, no. Ira's spending the weekend with his grandmother. I was actually going to ask you if you'd like to spend some time with me the next two days."

I smiled at him. "That's exactly what I was hoping to do this weekend. I'd love to," I told him.

The corners of his mouth turned up and his hand moved from my shoulder to the back of my head where he fisted my hair gently.

"Perfect. I have a few ideas. If I had known you were coming tonight, I'd have prepared something to eat. I'm not that hungry either, but if you want I can make us something light a little later tonight," he suggested.

"Sounds good," I told him, still smiling at him because it seemed as if I wasn't able to get rid of my joy when he was around.

"Want something to drink?" he then asked, turning around and walking back to the kitchen.

"Please. Whatever you have is fine."

He pulled out two glasses and grabbed a bottle of champagne out of the fridge, then he walked back to me and sat down on the couch.

"How was your week?" he asked, pouring the champagne into both glasses.

"Busy. I had a lot to do for college, but I finished everything I had to finish and now I'm free the whole weekend."

"Smart. Wish I had done it that way when I was in college. I pushed everything back until I had no other choice than to study on weekends," he explained, chuckling.

"But you still attended parties," I guessed.

He laughed and nodded. "Of course. Couldn't miss any of them. I still don't know how I managed to graduate, but I'm glad I did."

He put the bottle onto the coffee table and picked up the glasses to hand me one.

He was still shirtless, and it didn't bother me at all, but I wished my eyes wouldn't move to his chest all the damn time.

"I'm happy you're here tonight," he said, touching his glass to mine.

"Me too."

We both took a few sips, and when the sweet taste of the champagne hit my tongue, shivers moved down my body.

In a good way, of course.

"Do you like it?" he asked as he saw the obvious bliss in my eyes.

"It's delicious. Where did you get this?"

He looked at the bottle and puckered his lips, thinking about his answer. "My coworkers put together a basket filled with things like that for my fortieth birthday. Have had that bottle for two years now, but never had an opportunity to open it," he explained.

I smiled at him. "I'm honored."

"You should be," he grinned, taking another sip and placing the glass on the coffee table. "Speaking of birthdays...Ira's fourth is coming up in a few weeks. He's been asking to have sleepovers for a while now, and I was thinking to let him invite a few of his friends to come over that night. You're invited too, of course," he said.

"I'd love to come! Oh, I have to get him a present and I could make him a cake!"

"You don't have to do that, Rooney. It's hard enough to find a cake with no sugar in it, and I don't want you to stress about a recipe Ira actually can eat lots of."

I puckered my lips and tilted my head. "Hey, have some trust in me. You'll have to stress about enough things that day, so let me take it off you. I'll figure something out."

His smile didn't meet his eyes sometimes, and I wondered what really bothered him. Surely, it wasn't the fact that I wanted to make a cake for Ira.

I reached out my left hand to cup the side of his neck, and with my thumb I brushed along his stubble gently. "Let me take care of the cake," I told him in a serious voice.

He eyed me for a while, then his unsure smile turned into a grin. "All right, fine," he said, chuckling. "No need to growl at me."

His hand squeezed my thigh and then he pulled me closer to his side.

And now that I knew about Ira's birthday coming up, I already had an idea of what to get him.

"How's work?" I asked, looking straight into his eyes and letting his hands move along my leg to pull it over his lap.

I loved knowing he wanted me close and I liked his gentle yet determined touch.

"I went through with my plan of starting early and getting out a few hours earlier in the evening, and it worked pretty well. I got to spend more time with Ira, which is great. I might keep that up for a few more weeks until I'm done with the project."

I nodded and smiled at him, then studied his face for a while before talking again. "Is it hard for you to leave Ira with your mother for a whole weekend?"

"Saying goodbye isn't easy, but I know he's gonna have lots of fun with her, and I don't mind spending some time on my own. Or with a beautiful girl like you," he said, his tongue licking his bottom lip.

His compliment hit hard and right in the chest, leaving me speechless for a few seconds.

I cleared my throat and moved my hand into his hair, gripping it gently and softly pulling at it, knowing he'd like that.

"You said you had a few things planned this weekend. Do I get to know what?"

"Well, first I thought we could head into town and find a nice place to eat lunch together, and after that I was thinking of letting you choose what we'll do. I don't really know much about you other than you like art, so maybe the museum would be a nice place to go."

I didn't wanna tell him that I've been to the museums around town too many times in my life, but they had different exhibitions every other month, and I haven't been in any of them in a while.

"Sounds good to me. Maybe I can teach you a little bit of what I learned in school," I suggested, grinning.

"Perfect. That way I'll know exactly what you'd be happy about getting for Christmas or your birthday."

I laughed and shook my head. "If you wanna make me happy on holidays and birthdays, all you need to do is give me food."

"What about art supplies?"

"As long as it's something I can actually use, or eat, I'll accept the presents."

"Good." He reached for his glass and took a few sips, then he squeezed my thigh again with his other hand and nodded to the kitchen. "Let me go check what I have in the fridge. Now that you mentioned food, I'm starting to get hungry. You don't have any preferences, right?"

"No, I'll eat anything."

Pulling my leg off his lap, I let him get up.

I watched as he walked to the kitchen, taking in every single one of his back muscles as they moved.

He checked for something in the fridge, and after a moment of silence, he pulled out a few vegetables and turned back to look at me.

"How about some pasta with fresh veggies?"

"Sounds good to me. Want me to help?" I already got up from the couch and grabbed both our glasses and the champagne, then walked over to him and set it all onto the counter.

"If you'd like. Let me go put on a shirt. Don't want you to cut yourself handling a knife while you get distracted by my body," he said jokingly.

My cheeks turned red again, and I looked away to hide my embarrassment.

He noticed me staring, but at least he knew I liked what I saw.

He was back in less than a minute, his upper body now covered in a long-sleeved, gray shirt which looked great on him.

"How about we eat outside on the balcony? I got a little table out there and also a lounger. I don't ever go out there," he explained.

"Perfect," I replied, smiling at him and getting the veggies ready to cut them by washing them in the sink.

"What's one thing you don't like?" he asked as he got out the pasta and filled a pot with water.

"In general?"

He nodded.

"That's a good question. Well, there's not really much I dislike. I avoid and ignore the things I don't like, so I guess I can't really name a specific thing," I replied truthfully.

"That's one way to deal with it," Wells said, chuckling. "I'll ask the question differently and more precise. What do you dislike in men?"

Ah, that was a question I sure knew how to answer.

"Arrogance is a huge turn off. And men who think and act like they're superior."

"Don't you think that kind of behavior can be changed if it's a deal-breaker?" he asked.

I frowned, shaking my head and looking up from the bell pepper I was cutting. "No, unless they have an actual change of heart. I find men who are arrogant don't like to show weakness, and when you tell them they're being arrogant, they respond by saying that they're just being honest. Honesty can be expressed differently though. Without acting like a know-it-all who thinks no other opinion matters than their own. But if I ever come across a man like that who does show me it is possible to push that arrogance off, I won't hold it against anyone anymore."

He kept his eyes on mine for a while, then he smiled and nodded. "You really know how to say things without offending anyone."

"That's because you aren't arrogant. If you were, you would have stopped me in the middle of my sentence and told me that I was either overreacting or being rude."

"You're probably right." He turned his gaze back to the tomatoes he was cutting. "I've never thought about it that way."

I smiled. "What about you? What do you dislike about women?"

He had to be very careful here.

Not because I'd get offended easily, but in this day and age, it was hard being respectful and choosing your words right.

I had to do the same.

He thought about it long and hard, but when he had his answer ready, he moved his eyes to me again.

"I'd appreciate certain types of women a little more if they'd respect other people's relationships. Sure, men can be just as bad at this as women, but I've seen so many women throw themselves at men who were happily married or in relationships, yet, they wouldn't stop harassing them. I know this is a difficult topic, I just think some women can't take no for an answer and immediately see things as a challenge. There's nothing they have to prove to anyone to show they have a strong character. Women are amazing for everything they go through, but their beautiful yet intense characteristics can be shown in other, more positive ways at times."

I accepted that as an answer.

And honestly, I had to agree with him.

It's not just women, but some men were the same.

"Good answer," I told him, puckering my lips.

We continued to cut the veggies and then cook the pasta, and once that all was done, I carried our plates over to the balcony where we sat down at the table.

The moon and the stars were shining brightly in the sky, which made it even more romantic than I had anticipated.

"Enjoy," Wells said, pouring both of us another glass of champagne.

"Thank you for having me over tonight. I've had an amazing time so far."

"Me too. Let's see where tonight takes us."

I nodded, unsure of how this night would end.

I wouldn't turn away from staying here for the night, but I also wouldn't be upset if we both decided to skip sleeping over.

Chapter Fifteen

Wells

Tonight was going great, and I loved every single second of having her close to me.

After I put the plates away and poured ourselves yet another glass of champagne, we sat down on the lounger to get more comfortable.

I pulled the blanket from the couch over our legs to keep us a little warm, but the champagne and her presence did it already for me.

"What's the funniest thing Ira has ever said?" Rooney asked, leaning against my side and taking a sip of her drink while I put my arm around her shoulders.

I thought about it for a while, then grinned as I remembered a conversation Ira had with a girl. "We were at the playground one day and I was sitting on a bench next to a teenage girl. She must've been around sixteen, looking after a boy Ira's age. Probably babysitting him. When Ira ran back to me with his new little friend, he greeted the girl and then tilted his head to the side, eyeing her closely. He straight up asked her if she had chickenpox, and then I looked over at her to get a closer look as I didn't notice what Ira had noticed. But as I looked at the girl, she turned bright red, letting him know that those were pimples. I felt bad because I know how difficult it is for teenagers to have acne, or to try and hide it, and I apologized for Ira putting her on the spot like that and invited her and the boy she was watching to get ice cream. I think that made it better."

"Oh, no!" Rooney cried. "Poor girl. But it is a little funny. Kids don't have any filters when they speak, huh?"

I chuckled and nodded. "I'm glad he hasn't picked up any curse words yet."

"Will he start kindergarten next year?" she asked.

"Yeah. He's been asking a lot about it, knowing he can play all day. Not that he's doing anything other than that already," I said, chuckling.

"I'm sure he'll make lots of friends. He's adorable and sweet."

I knew that, but it was always nice hearing someone other than my mother say it.

I turned my head to look at her, and after kissing her temple, I took a deep breath and let out a sigh. "I sometimes try to imagine what he'll be like when he's eighteen. I'm trying my best to raise him to be a great man, but at the same time I don't ever want him to grow up."

Rooney's hand moved up to my chest and it lingered there as she turned her head to look at me.

"Isn't watching your children grow the most special thing about being a parent?" she asked.

"Of course it is but I don't know if I can relive moments I had with Ira in the future."

Our eyes met, and luckily, she didn't take that as a hint for her to someday become the mother of my future children.

It didn't sound too bad, but we were only dating, and talking about having kids together wasn't a topic

I thought anyone should have on their very first, actual date.

"You're an amazing dad, Wells. As long as you know Ira is happy, I think there's nothing you have to worry about."

I smiled at her and gave her a quick nod.

"You're right. I'm happy he likes you too. He's never had issues with new people, but he knows this is something different."

"It is?"

"Yes, Rooney." I moved my hand from her waist up to her cheek, brushing my thumb along her cheekbone and licking my lips as I looked at hers.

I didn't feel like talking anymore.

Whatever was happening between us, I needed her to know that I was attracted to her and that I couldn't keep my distance any longer.

I leaned in and made sure she wasn't backing away from me, and once I felt her fist my shirt in her hand, I knew she wanted to kiss me as well.

It's been too damn long since I've kissed someone, let alone fucked, but I couldn't fully take over and had to let her show me how far this could go.

I was open to whatever she wanted, but for now, I wanted to explore her pretty mouth before I'd go any further.

Our lips touched, and the first thought that ran through my mind was, *fuck...those are the sweetest lips I've ever tasted.*

I moved my lips gently against hers as I pulled her closer and deepened the kiss by tilting her head to the side and leaning in more.

She let me have control over the kiss, but her hands made sure I wouldn't do anything she wasn't ready for yet.

It wasn't her first kiss as she definitely knew what she was doing, but I could feel some sort of tension in her body.

Maybe she was nervous.

I sure was.

As she eased into me a little more, I felt her tongue brush along my bottom lip to ask for permission, and once I parted my lips more, I started to softly explore her tongue with mine.

It was passionate and intense, letting each other take this slow.

As her fist unclenched and she let go of my shirt, she moved her hand down to the hem of my shirt where she then slipped her fingers underneath it to touch my muscles.

Guess she wasn't holding back as much as I thought she would.

"I think I like it better when this is off," she whispered into the kiss, and I chuckled as she tugged at the fabric.

And I thought it would be much more comfortable on my bed rather than on this lounger.

"I wanna take you to my bedroom," I told her, hoping I didn't sound like a creep.

"Okay," she whispered back, still not breaking the kiss.

I picked her up by the waist and as I got up, I pulled her with me to wrap her legs and arms around me.

She clung to me to make sure she wouldn't fall, and while I carried her through the apartment and into my bedroom, I placed kisses all over her shoulder and neck.

Once I let her down onto the bed, I pulled off my shirt and placed it on the dresser next to the bed, then I let her eye me for a moment before she reached for me again to pull me over her.

"You'll let me know if I'm going too far, right?" I asked.

She nodded, smiling at me sweetly and running her hands through my hair before pulling me closer and kissing me again.

This time, I was the first one to push my tongue into her mouth, getting a taste of her sweetness and feeling her tongue against mine.

I was pushing myself up on my elbow while I moved along her side with my other hand.

Her legs were wrapped around me again, keeping me close and making me push my crotch against her.

My dick was already getting hard, but how could it not if I hadn't been this close to a girl in years?

It felt nice, and I pressed against her more while she moved her hips to adjust underneath me.

A soft moan escaped her as she must've felt my hardness press against her middle, but she seemed to like it as she pressed her hips against me harder.

Was she a virgin?

If so, I didn't wanna ruin her first time after hooking up on our first date.

She deserved something special, and frankly, I didn't think I could enjoy sex without knowing what exactly I was feeling.

I liked Rooney a lot, and I knew the feeling was mutual, but that didn't mean shit after hanging out only a few times.

Fuck.

I was thinking about it too much, and would probably ruin this thing we had if I kept trying to figure things out.

Just let it happen, man. If it's meant to be, it will be.

Our kiss turned into a full-on make out session, and I enjoyed every single second of it.

Her hands were in my hair, pulling and fisting tightly as our kiss got deeper and more passionate.

The soft sounds coming out of her made my dick jolt every time, and to stop it from hurting too much because it felt too damn good, I pressed against her and moved my hips in slow circles to ease the tension.

A growl left my throat, and she wasn't the only one showing her pleasure anymore.

I moved my hand from her waist down to the side of her ass, and when she lifted her hips to meet my hips' movement, I cupped her bottom and gently squeezed to feel more of her.

Her body was amazing.

Slightly curvy hips, a thin waist, and all in all a perfect shape.

But then, I would be into her no matter what she looked like.

She had a beautiful soul, and the fact that Ira liked her was a bonus and added to her beauty.

This kept going for a while, but as I moved my hand back to her waist, she broke the kiss and looked at me, trying to catch her breath as her lips swelled and cheeks turned red.

At first, I had thought she was going to say something, but when she kept looking at me with desire and unsureness in her eyes, I knew it was time for me to stop this.

I brushed back a strand of her hair and tucked it behind her ear, then leaned in one last time to kiss her lips and look back into her eyes.

"How about a movie and some more champagne?" I asked, my voice low and raspy.

She studied me for a moment, then nodded and smiled. "Okay."

It was enough for the night.

She clearly wasn't comfortable going any further than that, and to not shy her away, I wasn't going to push her.

I got up from the bed and reached for my shirt again, and while I pulled it over my head, I felt her eyes on me.

"Or should I keep it off?" I asked, jokingly.

She laughed softly and shook her head. "No, you can leave it on now."

She bit her bottom lip as her eyes moved to my crotch, and I knew what she was seeing might've been a little shocking.

At least that's what she looked like.

I reached for my shaft and cupped it over the sweatpants I was wearing, and seconds later it didn't stand out that much anymore.

"It's a compliment," I told her with a smug grin on my face.

Her cheeks turned a brighter red, and I chuckled while reaching for her hand. "Come on. Let's get comfortable on the couch."

She placed her hand in mine, and with our fingers interlocked, we walked back to the living room.

"Sit. I'll get our drinks."

She did as I said. "May I have a glass of water as well?" she asked.

"Of course. Here. Figure out what we're gonna watch." I gave her the remote, then walked outside to get our glasses and the bottle of champagne, which was almost empty, and after I put it all onto the coffee table, I walked back to the kitchen to grab a glass of water.

She looked peaceful, but there was still this unsureness on her face which bothered me a little bit.

Maybe because I was feeling the same but didn't realize it.

As I walked back to the couch, Rooney smiled up at me and pointed to the TV. "How about this?"

I looked at the screen and nodded as I saw the name of one of my favorite movies. "Haven't watched that in a while. Sounds good to me," I told her and sat down next to her.

She drank a few sips of the water before placing it onto the coffee table and then cuddling up to me with her head on my shoulder and her arm around my stomach.

I put my arm around her again to keep her close, and once she pressed play, we both kept quiet and enjoyed each other's company without having to talk.

There was no awkwardness between us, which I was grateful for or else I had no idea how to deal with it, and I was happy she was comfortable enough to stay here even after our make out.

In the middle of the movie, I looked down at her face and brushed back her hair to find her eyes closed.

She had moved her head down into my lap and curled up on the couch in the sweetest way possible.

It had gotten late, and going to bed actually sounded like a good idea.

"Rooney," I whispered.

She pulled her brows together and made a soft noise to let me know she was awake.

"Would you like to sleep here with me?" I asked.

A nod was enough for me to reach for the remote and turn off the TV, then I carefully picked her up and carried her into my bedroom.

Once she was in bed and nicely tucked in, I kissed her forehead and whispered, "I'll be right with you."

"Okay," she whispered, and with one more kiss, I headed into the bathroom to get ready for bed.

Ending the date cuddling her in my bed was exactly what I needed, and once I was done brushing my teeth and taking off my shirt and sweatpants, I got into bed with her and turned off the lights.

She moved closer to me and wrapped her arm tightly around my waist, and I put my arms around her, kissing her head.

"I had a great evening with you, Rooney," I told her softly.

"Me too. Goodnight, Wells," she replied, making me smile.

"Goodnight, gorgeous."

Chapter Sixteen

Rooney

I hadn't slept this good in a very long time.

Lying in Wells's arms and having him pull me closer every time I moved was what I never knew I needed.

He not only made me stay calm and relaxed, but I felt protected. Something I never really felt in AJ's arms.

Wells's manly smell filled my nose as I woke up, and by keeping my eyes closed, I enjoyed his presence before we'd have to get out of bed and start the day.

Though, that could take a while as I figured he was still asleep.

I kept my eyes closed for a while longer, but the sun started to shine right through the window and into my face.

I opened them slowly and adjusted to the light, then looked up at Wells who had his eyes still closed, just like I imagined.

His breathing was slow, and I watched his relaxed face as his chest lifted and fell gently.

How could a person look so beautiful without even trying?

The stubble on his jaw was getting thicker, but I liked it that way, even if he looked just as handsome when he shaved.

There wasn't one thing I didn't like about his looks, which of course wouldn't have made me dislike him if he didn't look like this.

He had a gentle and kind soul and as caring as he was, I don't think anyone could ever dislike him.

I was lucky to be lying here next to him.

Our date last night was incredible, and I could still feel his lips on mine and how his tongue moved against mine passionately.

The last time I kissed someone like that was back when AJ and I had yet to realize that whatever we did or didn't feel while being that close, wasn't what I was feeling with Wells.

My heart pounded just thinking about him, and even with being this close to him, I wanted to get even closer.

It was...different.

I *felt* different.

Yet, I knew there was no way I would ever speak about my feelings.

Wells moved his hand to my lower back and his other hand pulled my leg higher and over his hips.

"Morning," he whispered in a thick, raspy voice, keeping his eyes closed as he turned his head to kiss my forehead.

"Good morning," I replied, letting my hand move from his chest up to the side of his neck.

"You're still here," he said, a small grin appearing on his lips.

"Why wouldn't I be?" I asked, laughing softly. "Did you really think I would disappear after that beautiful date we had last night?"

He moved his head to look into my eyes as his smirk turned into a smile. "I was hoping you wouldn't. You never know what's going on in someone else's head."

Unless they talk about it.

"Our date continues today and I don't feel like leaving your side. Not yet."

There.

That must've been enough for a while, right?

"You're too damn sweet."

His hand moved up to cup my jaw, and by tilting my head back, he got better access to my lips.

His kiss was gentle and quick, but it was enough for now.

"What would you like for breakfast? Now that Ira's not here I can make us whatever you'd like without me feeling bad that he can't have certain things."

"Surprise me," I told him, pressing my lips to his jaw and then pushing myself up on my elbows, looking down at him.

"All right. And heading into town is still on for today?" he asked, eyeing me and brushing my hair back.

"Of course. I'm excited," I said as my excitement grew.

"How about you go get ready for the day upstairs while I do the same and start on breakfast?" he suggested.

I nodded, thinking that was a good idea as I had to figure out what to wear anyway.

Not because I wanted to put together the best outfit, but more because I didn't have actual outfits.

I just threw stuff together without ever thinking about the clothes matching or not, but for a nice date I wanted to look decent.

Evie could surely help me.

"Okay. So you wanna get up already?"

"You don't?" he asked, smirking. "You're quite enjoying this, huh? I wouldn't mind having you back in my bed tonight, but if we stay here any longer, I might fall back asleep."

I didn't want that, because I knew I'd do the same. "I'll be right back," I told him, kissing his lips once more before getting out of bed and grabbing all my things to head upstairs.

A low chuckle came from him. "See you later," he said in a sexy growl, and after giving him a sweet but shy smile, I walked out of his apartment to get upstairs.

I took a deep breath as I entered my apartment, and just like she had been doing lately, Evie surprised me by being awake already.

The wide grin on her face meant there were thousands of thoughts about Wells and me spending the night together on her mind, but I had to disappoint her.

"We kissed, that's all," I said to her as I walked into my bedroom to let the clothes I wore last night fall onto the bed.

"*That's all?* Girl, your face tells a whole other story."

Evie stood in the doorway with her arms crossed and her brows raised. "What happened?"

"We kissed, Evie. We made out. Heavily. And I really liked it."

No chance to hide that from her.

"Shit, and he's forty-two. Maybe I should try older men sometime. You didn't turn bright red when you told me about you and AJ making out. *Heavily.*"

"Maybe because I didn't like it as much as I did last night," I murmured.

"Uh-huh," she voiced, keeping her grin in place. "Then why are you here this early?"

"I'm just gonna take a shower and head downstairs again. We're gonna have breakfast and then head into town," I told her, smiling.

"You're actually dating him. And I always thought I'd be the one to actually start dating first."

I laughed and shook my head. "I don't think that's ever going to happen, Evie. You love being single, and you don't want kids or marriage in the future anyway."

She shrugged. "True. But I guess I never imagined you to actually date someone seriously."

Me neither.

At least not while still in college.

"Would you like to pick out an outfit for me?"

That wasn't even a question. She already walked over to my dresser and started to pick out anything she thought looked good.

I left her to it and went to take a quick shower, and when I got out, I saw the clothes she picked laid out on the bed.

Looked like a skirt and long-sleeved turtleneck shirt.

I could work with that, though, I would've gone for a pair of black pants.

But since I always wore those, I figured changing it up a little wouldn't hurt.

"How was the party last night?" I asked her as she walked back into my room while I got dressed right in front of her.

We were like sisters, and seeing each other naked was never a big deal.

Turned out some girls found it weird though, as Evie and I were the only two changing without trying to hide from the other girls in the changing room at school.

Maybe that changed now though.

"Crazy. I didn't know Cayla had a boyfriend, so that was fun to watch. Other than that, it was the usual shenanigans. Too much alcohol and the music was far too loud."

"Did you leave early that you're up already?" I asked, buttoning up the skirt in the front.

It was a pretty, burnt orange and velvety skirt I bought a while back but never wore.

Perfect for fall and fitting with the gray turtleneck on top.

"Kinda. AJ and Jonathan drove me back because they had to be somewhere."

I nodded, turning around and looking into the mirror to see how I looked.

"Do you like it?" she asked, letting her eyes wander down my body.

I nodded and picked at the skirt a little to adjust it.

"I think it looks nice. What shoes should I wear?"

Evie puckered her lips and thought about it for a while before walking out of my room.

I followed her after grabbing my backpack which I often used instead of a purse, then followed Evie to the front door where we kept all our shoes.

"How about these?" she asked, holding up a pair of light gray sneakers.

"Haven't worn those in a while, but sure."

I put them on and checked myself out one last time before turning to Evie and hugging her tight.

"Thank you. I'll see you soon. Probably tomorrow," I said, smiling at her.

"Have fun! And remember you don't take the pill!"

I rolled my eyes but had to laugh at her comment.

As I reached Wells's apartment, I knocked and then let myself in to see if he was still in the shower or not.

"It's me!" I called out, waiting by the door just in case he wouldn't like me to just come in.

"I'm in the kitchen!" he called back.

After closing the door behind me, I walked down the hallway to the kitchen and saw him fully dressed in black pants and a deep, dark colored gray sweatshirt.

He looked good, even if what he was wearing was simple.

His hair was damp, but it was already starting to curl at the ends which made him look even more handsome.

Shit. I was staring again.

"You look gorgeous," he said, ripping me out of my thoughts and smiling at me with that charming smile.

"Thank you. You look great yourself," I replied.

He nodded to the table, and when I looked at it, I noticed the French toast sprinkled with cinnamon and some fresh fruit on top.

"You made this?" I asked in awe. "It looks delicious!"

"My specialty. But then, I can pretty much cook anything you'd ask me to."

I laughed softly and stepped closer to him to put my arms around his waist while he stirred the scrambled eggs.

"You're amazing. Thank you so much for making me breakfast."

"Don't tell anyone, but I'm doing this to impress you," he whispered and winked at me.

"Well, you had already impressed me that time you made the dark chocolate mousse. But you keep on surprising me."

He smiled and leaned down to kiss my cheek, then he nodded back to the table. "Sit. I'll be right with you."

I couldn't stop myself from kissing his lips before I did what he told me, but instead of it being a quick peck on the lips, he deepened the kiss and turned it into a long, passionate one.

He definitely knew what he was doing, no doubt about that.

But I was slowly starting to think that there was nothing for me to do to impress or surprise him.

Or to show him that he wasn't the only one putting effort into this.

But I wasn't as good of a cook as he was, and I sure as hell wasn't good at expressing my feelings.

Yet, I hoped just being myself and showing him some affection was enough.

If not, I was sure I would notice something didn't sit right with him.

I sat down at the table and looked at all the delicious food he had put on it in a short amount of time, or maybe I didn't realize how long I'd been up there getting ready and talking to Evie.

When he placed the plate with the scrambled eggs onto the table, his phone rang.

"It's probably Ira. He likes to let me know he's okay and having fun at Grandma's," he explained, sitting down at the table and picking up.

"Hi, Daddy!" Ira's sweet voice came through the speaker, and Wells put the phone on the table to lean against his cup of coffee.

I was sitting opposite of him, but I soon figured he was on facetime.

"Hey, buddy! Having fun?" he asked.

"Yes! Grandma and I painted yesterday," Ira said, and I watched as Wells looked at the screen.

"Oh, wow! Did you draw me and you?"

"And Rooney. Look!"

That took me by surprise and my chest immediately warmed.

God, that little boy had already found a place in my heart.

Wells looked up at me with a worried frown, but when he noticed I didn't mind Ira including me in his family portrait, he smiled.

"I see. That's beautiful, bud! What are you up to today?" he asked, pointing at my plate to tell me to start eating.

"I don't know. Grandma wants you," Ira said, then I heard his little footsteps tapping on the floor.

"Here, Grandma," he said, and Wells's expression suddenly changed.

"Did he show you what he painted last night?" a woman's voice asked, and Wells visibly cringed.

Was he uncomfortable with his mother knowing he was dating me?

Probably.

I wouldn't want my parents on the phone either when he was around, because there could be something weird and embarrassing coming out of their mouths.

"He did, yeah. Something you need to tell me?" he asked.

"Yes. Mind bringing over Ira's rain boots? I was thinking of taking him to the zoo and I don't wanna get his white sneakers all dirty and muddy."

"Uh, yeah, of course. I'm having breakfast, but I'll be there right after."

"Okay. Bring your girl with you. Don't try and hide her from me," she said, her voice stern.

Wells looked at me with an apologetic grin, and I smiled back at him to let him know that there was nothing he had to be sorry for.

"I'll see you later, Mom. Bye."

They hung up and Wells put his phone to the side.

"Your mom seems nice," I told him, finally starting with breakfast.

"She can be a little direct at times. You don't mind if we head over to her house before we go to town, do you?"

"No, that's fine with me. I'd love to meet your mom," I said.

"No doubt she'll like you. It'll be like the very first time I brought home a girl."

I smiled at that, feeling good about the fact that I was the first girl in a long while he introduced to his mother.

Chapter Seventeen

Wells

Breakfast didn't take as long as I hoped it would to spend a little more alone time with Rooney, but since Ira needed his rain boots to go to the zoo, I didn't want him to wait for too long.

We finished breakfast and Rooney helped me clean up, which I thought was very sweet of her, and after grabbing Ira's boots we headed downstairs to my car.

I opened the door for her, and with a soft smile she thanked me quietly before getting inside.

"Here, let me take these," she said, reaching for the boots in my hands.

"Thanks. Just another hint for you so it makes buying a present for Ira easier," I said, nodding to the superhero-covered rain boots.

She laughed softly and nodded. "I actually already have something in mind which I think he'll love."

"Really? Wanna tell me?"

"Nope. It's gonna be a surprise and I don't wanna risk you telling him," she said with a grin.

"I would never," I said, covering my chest with my hand as if she had just hurt my feelings.

She chuckled and shook her head, then gently pushed me away from her. "Get in. Ira is waiting for his boots."

I closed the door and walked around the car to get inside myself, and once we both put on our seatbelts, I pulled out of the parking lot and onto the street.

"The zoo. It's been a while since I took him there. Sometimes I feel as if I have no ideas for what Ira and I could do together. There are so many places I could take him to, but it somehow always ends up being the park."

"I'm sure he's not complaining about that. Besides, Grandmas are always more fun," Rooney said.

"You're right about that. But didn't you enjoy your days with your parents while they rode some bulls in clown costumes?" I asked mockingly.

She laughed. "Hey, I was hoping you wouldn't bring that up anymore."

"I think it's great what they do. A little dangerous, but fun. After you meet my mother today, I definitely wanna meet your parents soon."

I felt her eyes on me, and when I turned my head to meet her gaze, she was smiling.

"You wanna meet my parents?"

I shrugged. "Guess we're heading in that direction anyway, aren't we?"

"Yeah, I guess so." She chewed on her bottom lip and I turned to look back at the street ahead of me again.

"What will they think about you seeing a guy that could easily be your dad?"

She was quiet for a while, and when I stopped at a red light, I turned to look at her again and saw her brows furrowed.

"I'm not sure. They're open about most things, but this might be a shock to them as my dad is only a year older than you."

I could see how that would be a little disturbing to her parents, but as long as Rooney didn't have a problem with that, there was nothing I had to worry about.

I reached over to place my hand on her thigh and squeezed it gently to ease her mind. "It's not like we have to go meet them right now. Whenever you're ready," I told her.

She gave me a quick nod and a smile. "Okay."

A few minutes later we arrived at my mother's house, and before getting out of the car I turned to look at Rooney once again.

"She's gonna ask lots of questions, and George is probably gonna frown at you the whole time, but that's just his facial expression. He's not judging, just observing."

She laughed and already opened the door. "It'll be fine, Wells. I'm excited to meet them."

I had to make sure she wouldn't leave me after meeting my mother and realizing how intense she could be, so I leaned in and grabbed her jaw tightly before kissing her lips.

She kissed me back, smiling against my lips and letting the door close again so she could place her hand on my chest.

I wondered if it were any other girl I was taking to my mother's house, if I would've been more nervous.

It felt right taking Rooney here, and I knew Mom would like her.

Besides, Ira would be happy to see her again too after drawing that picture with her next to me.

I broke the kiss and looked into her eyes to see the glow inside of them get brighter.

"Last chance to run and hide," I whispered.

"In your dreams," she replied with a grin.

I watched her step out of the car and wait for me to do the same, and once I got the strength to, I walked over to her.

We reached the door and I knocked before pushing the door open. "It's me!" I called out to make sure they wouldn't get startled by someone just walking into the house.

Ira's footsteps could be heard from a mile away, and when he rounded the corner, he smiled brightly and ran to me with his arms wide open.

"Daddy!"

"Hey, buddy," I said, picking him up and kissing his cheek. "How was your morning?"

"Good. We're going to the zoo!" he announced.

"That's fun! Lucky I brought your rain boots so you can get all dirty today, huh?"

He looked over at Rooney and only now realized she was here too.

"Hi, Rooney!" he said a little too loudly and too close to my ear, waving at her although she stood right next to me.

"Hi, little man. I like your shirt," she said, poking Ira's belly gently.

"It's Flash. He's very fast!" he let her know, and I smiled at their little interaction.

But then, everything they did together made my heart melt, which was for one, a good sign, and two, showing me that Rooney was the right girl to take home to Mom.

"Super fast, huh?" Rooney added, then her eyes moved from Ira to my mother who was walking toward us.

"Ah, you must be Rooney. I'm going to try my best not to make this awkward for you two, but it's a real pleasure to meet you, sweetie. I'm Elsa," she said, and the sweet girl Rooney was, she stepped closer and hugged my mother to greet her.

"It's so nice to meet you, Elsa."

"I could tell by the picture Ira painted that you're pretty, but you are beautiful!"

For once, I agreed with my mother.

"Would you like to have a cup of coffee? You're not in a hurry, are you?"

I looked at Rooney to let her decide if she wanted to spend a little more time here before heading to town, and the smile on her face was enough for me to know that she was okay with staying a while longer.

"Sure," I said, letting Ira back down so he could run back to whatever he was doing before we came.

"Take a seat. I'll be right back," Mom said as we reached the couch.

I sat down with Rooney and smiled at her to ensure her this was okay with me, as I felt like I've given some different vibes in the car.

"Daddy, look!"

Ira came back running to us with one painting in each hand.

He gave Rooney one and me the other.

"It's the zoo and the animals are superheroes."

Some might say he talked a little too much about superheroes, but I loved his admiration and obsession with those figures, so why would I ever stop him from loving them?

"All the animals have capes," Rooney pointed out, making Ira grin.

"These are amazing, buddy. You're a pro at drawing," I told him.

"Like Rooney?"

"Even better!" she replied, knowing just how to make a kid happy. "You have to teach me how to draw these animals someday. How about that?"

Ira nodded and looked at us with wide eyes. "Do you come to the zoo too?"

I looked at Rooney with a questioning look, an she smiled at me and shrugged, telling me that she wouldn't mind spending the day with my family.

"Sure, sounds fun," I told him, brushing my hand through his wild locks.

There was no need to tame his hair as it would never do what I wanted it to.

"Yay! Grandma, Daddy and Rooney are coming to the zoo with us!" he called out, then ran back to the kitchen.

I chuckled and leaned back, then placed a hand on Rooney's back, moving it up to cup the back of her neck.

"Change of plans," I told her.

She turned her head to look at me, smiling and seemingly excited. "I don't mind. It's gonna be great," she said.

I kept my hand buried in Rooney's hair as my mother walked back into the living room with a tray in her hands and cups on it.

"You're coming with us?" she asked.

"Yeah. We were thinking of spending the day in the city, but the zoo sounds fun too," I said.

Mom nodded and sat down on the other couch, and while she gave us our coffee, George waked into the room.

"Oh, George, this is Rooney," Mom said.

He looked at her and nodded, then sat down next to Mom and gave Rooney a quick smile.

"Nice to meet you."

"Likewise," she replied, smiling back at him.

I finally pulled my hand away from her hair and sat up straight again to take a sip of my coffee.

"So, Rooney, you study art?"

"Yes, I do. Art history, to be exact. I've always loved to paint," she explained.

"Ira told me about you two spending a day together and drawing. That's nice of you. You're their neighbor, is that right?"

This was what I meant when I said that she could be a little annoying and intense.

She was asking things she already knew the answer to because either I told her or Ira snitched, but as long as Rooney was okay with it, I'd let them talk.

"Yes, I moved in with my best friend a few weeks ago and that's how I met Wells and Ira."

"How old are you, Rooney?" George asked, changing the subject in an instant.

"I'm twenty," she replied, staying calm and friendly.

"And have you ever dated a guy twice your age before?" he asked.

How was this making me more uncomfortable than her?

"George, don't ask such questions," Mom hissed, giving Rooney an apologetic smile.

"You don't have to answer him. Age is just a number, and I can tell you're happy."

"That's fine. I don't mind Wells being older. I really like him," she said, looking at me with a gentle smile.

I smiled back and squeezed her thigh before looking back at my mother to change the subject once again in case George felt like asking another stupid question.

He was a great guy, but he was a little skeptical at times.

"What did Ira eat?"

I knew she was careful not to give him things that would spike his insulin levels, but I liked to make sure just in case.

"We had a couscous salad last night with some chicken breast and vegetables in it. And this morning he had a slice of bread with butter and a little bit of honey. I also made him a green juice," she said.

"Hulk juice, Grandma!" Ira corrected her, making us all chuckle.

"And did you like the couscous, Ira? I don't think you've had that in a while," I told him, pulling him to me to stand between my legs.

"I liked it a lot," he told me, pressing his hands against my cheeks for his enjoyment.

"You look funny, Daddy," he said, laughing and pressing tighter against my cheeks.

"I do? Let's see if you look funny like that too."

I cupped his jaw with one hand and gently squeezed his cheeks together with my thumb and forefinger. "You look even funnier," I told him with a grin.

He laughed again and pushed my hand away, then he crawled onto my lap and sat down on it.

Rooney was watching us with a sweet smile, and I gave her a quick look to let her know that I appreciated her being here, even if I had yet to adjust to the fact that she had already met my mother.

It wasn't a bad thing at all, I just didn't think this moment would ever come.

"Can we go to the zoo now?" he asked.

"Yes, you need to get your boots on first," I told him, kissing his head and then reaching for his rain boots next to the couch.

"I do it."

He moved off my lap again and sat down on the floor to put them on, and while he did, Rooney and I finished our coffees.

"Are you coming with us, George?" I asked, but he shook his head.

"I'm meeting my brother for lunch later. You guys have a nice day at the zoo."

While he took the tray back into the kitchen, we walked over to the front door where I grabbed Ira's jacket.

"We can take my car then," I told Mom, and she nodded while she put her shoes on.

"Are you excited to see the animals?" Rooney asked, smiling down at Ira.

He nodded with wide eyes.

"What's your favorite?"

It took a while for him to decide, but then he answered, "Lion!"

"Good choice! They're beautiful animals, hm?"

"And strong!" Ira added.

"That's true. I'm sure we'll see some lions today," Rooney said, looking back up at me.

I smiled at her and placed my hand at her lower back to walk her out of the house, and while we stepped down the stairs to get to the car, I kissed her temple.

"I can't wait to get you to myself again tonight," I whispered, pressing one more kiss to the side of her head.

Her cheeks turned a soft shade of pink.

Without even trying too hard, she was making me feel all types of things.

Fuck me.

Chapter Eighteen

Rooney

Going to the zoo wasn't such a bad idea after all.

I've not been here in years, and I liked animals, so it was a bonus.

Ira was all excited and jumpy after we got our tickets and went through the gate, and Elsa already had to start chasing him around to make sure he wouldn't get lost.

"Nice not having to be the one to run after him for once," Wells said with a grin plastered on his face.

I laughed softly and looked up at him. "Poor Grandma," I said.

"Hey, it was her idea to come here."

He reached for my hand and interlocked his fingers with mine, and I leaned against him as we followed Ira and Elsa along the path leading us to the first animals.

"Look, Daddy! Timons!" Ira called out, pointing to the adorable little creatures.

"Someone's seen The Lion King," I pointed out, and Wells chuckled.

"Those are Meerkats, buddy," he told his son, and we watched as Ira stepped up to the glass and placed his forehead against it to get a better look.

"They look funny when they stand up," he told us.

"They do, huh? They're also very mischievous."

Ira turned around and furrowed his brown at us, then he pointed at himself and said, "Not like me. I'm very good."

I smiled at his own recognition, and Wells nodded proudly. "You sure are," he agreed.

I had no idea what it felt like being proud of your child, but I knew it must've felt amazing.

Wells was a great father, and having raised Ira all on his own was incredible.

Single moms and dads deal with so many things, but they overcome any obstacle with strength and greatness.

We continued to walk and occasionally stopped at any cage Ira wanted to stop at, but as fascinated as he was, so were us adults.

"Ever ridden on an elephant?" Wells asked and squeezed my hand gently.

"Yes, actually. When I was little. It was at a different zoo, but I remember it being amazing. You?"

He nodded. "Yeah, me too. I wonder if Ira would wanna go on a ride. He's not so much into heights, but I think if he knows I'm right there behind him it'll be fine."

"I'm sure the fact that he'll be sitting on an elephant is enough to take his mind off the height."

"True. Hey, buddy!" he called out, and Ira stopped in his tracks and turned around to look at his dad.

Wells let go of my hand and picked him up, then we stopped walking and he pointed toward a billboard with elephants on it.

"What do you think? Should we ride on an elephant?" he asked, and Ira's eyes immediately widened.

"On an elephant?" he asked, his fascination growing.

"Yeah, how about that?"

Ira nodded and pointed to the elephants on the billboard. "Can we go now?"

"Of course," Wells said, smiling and kissing his cheek. "Maybe we can get Grandma to ride with us."

"No way," Elsa said, shaking her hand and finger at her son. "You three go do that and I'll take some pictures," she suggested.

"Are you coming too, Rooney?" he asked me.

"I'd love to!"

We headed to where the elephants walked around an area simulating the Indian jungle with lots of trees and muddy grounds.

"Woah!"

Ira noticed how big these animals were, and he couldn't stop staring at them.

"Beautiful, huh? I'm sure you can touch it once we're up there," Wells told him.

"Here, let me take your backpack, sweetie," Elsa said, holding out her hand and I gave it to her with a thankful smile.

"That's kind of you. Thank you, Elsa," I said.

"Of course," she replied, smiling back at me.

We went up the stairs where a line had already formed, and we waited until it was our turn to ride.

"Ready?" Wells asked as he looked at me, and I nodded.

"It's gonna be fun."

It was finally our turn to sit on the elephant's back, and one of the zookeepers instructed Wells to sit in the back, me right in front of him, and Ira in the front.

Ira didn't mind Wells not being right behind him, and I made sure to hold on tight to him while he gripped the blanket we were sitting on tightly.

Wells's arms came around us, and he secured us even more with his strong arms.

It felt great, and I loved how much trust Ira, but also Wells, had in me.

"Here we go, hold on tight, buddy!" Wells told Ira.

He was giggling at the elephant started to move slowly, and before we disappeared in the jungle, Elsa called out for us to wave at the camera.

We did, and Ira was quick to notice the monkey running and climbing freely around the trees.

"Monkeys!"

"Aw, those are amazing, huh?" Wells asked as he pulled me tighter against his chest.

I was comfortable right in that spot and I was enjoying myself while getting to spend the day with his family.

Ira was joyful, which made us adults happy too, and the way his eyes glowed was taking me back to my own childhood.

"See those monkeys all over the trees?" the zookeeper making sure the elephant went the right direction asked us, looking up.

We nodded, then he continued to tell us all about them and the jungle itself.

It was nice to get some knowledge in while having fun, and I was positive a lot of the things he'd learn today would stick with him.

Wells

I wanted to keep my arms around her and hold her tight while she held on to Ira.

The elephant ride was amazing, and once we were back on the ground, we met my mother at a bench she had been waiting on.

"That looked like so much fun, Ira! How was it?" she asked.

"So cool!"

I chuckled and grabbed Rooney's hand again, then nodded toward the sign which indicated the way to the rainforest and all the animals that lived in there.

"How about we go meet some frogs and snakes?" I asked Ira.

He nodded and quickly grabbed my other hand to pull us toward the building.

We spent the afternoon looking at reptiles and then checking out the big cats and how they were fed.

Ira was a little frightened at first, but once he realized there was no way for those lions and tigers to get out of their enclosures, he was right up front against the glass checking every single one of them out and giving them names, as a toddler would.

"Daddy, I'm hungry," he told me once we passed the zebras and kangaroos, and I picked him up after letting go of Rooney's hand.

"We can eat at the zoo's restaurant where we can watch turtles and fish. How does that sound?" I asked him.

"Okay."

I turned to look at my mother and Rooney, and they both agreed on dinner at the zoo.

Since we were here anyway, I wanted Ira to have the best experience.

We got to the restaurant and were taken to a table right next to the big tank surrounding the guests.

The glass was high enough to keep children from falling in or throwing things inside the water, so it was okay for Ira to stand on the chair to get a closer look while I kept my hand on his back to make sure he wouldn't fall.

"It was a nice idea taking him here today, Mom."

"I'm glad you two came with us. He couldn't have done most of the things if he came with me alone."

She meant riding on an elephant and going into the petting zoo and feeding smaller, friendlier animals.

"We had fun too," Rooney told her, smiling at my mother.

They had a few conversations while I was either jogging after Ira or helping him go down the slide on the playground.

I observed them a little bit, and I could tell they liked each other already.

"Rooney's a very sweet girl. I'm glad you two found each other," Mom said, as if Rooney wasn't right there next to her.

Luckily, I wasn't the only one enjoying her company, and often times I saw Ira take Rooney's hand and just hold it while we walked along the paths.

It was adorable.

Shit, I couldn't wait until I had her all to myself again tonight.

As if she had read my mind, she reached out her hand to caress Ira's arm to get his attention. "Are you spending the night at Grandma's tonight again, sweetie?" she asked.

Ira nodded and looked at me with a serious look. "Don't worry, Daddy. I'll be back tomorrow, okay?"

We laughed at how concerned he was for me, and I leaned in to kiss his cheek and assure him it was okay with me.

"That's okay. You have fun at Grandma's tonight and we'll see each other tomorrow."

We didn't have to wait too long on the food, and as it was delicious, it was gone as fast as it was on our table.

We were all full, and Ira was slowly getting tired which was a sign for us to leave the zoo.

At the exit, I turned back to face the zoo and told him to wave goodbye to the animals, and since he gave most of them names, I had to stand there and wait until he said goodbye to at least ten of them.

"He's the cutest," I heard Rooney say to Mom, who happily agreed.

"Wells was the exact same when he was little."

I didn't remember how I was as a kid, but from what Mom always told me, I knew I was similar to how Ira was now.

I was an easy kid, and not having siblings wasn't so bad either, but I've always wondered what it would be like if Ira had a little brother or sister.

"Bye everyone!"

He was finally done saying goodbye to all his new friends, and when I turned around, Rooney was smiling at me sweetly.

Mom was already walking through the exit, and when I stepped closer to Rooney, I pressed a kiss to her forehead before heading out as well.

She sure did something to me, and knowing Ira liked her too was going to be hard if I ever decided to let go of her.

Wasn't my plan though.

We drove back to my mother's house, and since Ira fell asleep in his car seat, I told Rooney that I'd be right back and carried him up the stairs and to his own little bedroom.

"Daddy," he whispered, his eyes opening slightly.

"Yes, buddy?"

I tucked him in after quickly checking his insulin pump.

"Are you having a sleepover with Rooney?"

Damn kids.

Always knew exactly what was going on.

Luckily he had no idea what grownups did at sleepovers.

I smiled and nodded. "Yes, I am. Did you have fun today at the zoo?" I asked to change the subject.

"Yes, I liked the lions," he said, his voice almost a whisper.

"Yeah, those were great, huh? Sleep now. I'll come pick you up whenever you call me tomorrow morning, okay?"

He nodded, and once I placed a kiss to his forehead, he had one last thing to say.

"I like Rooney."

Of course he did.

How couldn't he? She was incredible.

I smiled and brushed through his hair one more time. "I do too. Sleep tight, bud. I love you."

"I love you," he replied, making my heart melt.

That was the first time he actually replied to it without using *okay* as an answer.

He was slowly starting to understand those three words which meant so damn much, and I was already excited to say it to him again just to hear him say it back.

I left the room and walked back downstairs to see Mom talking to Rooney.

As they noticed me, she placed a hand on Rooney's arm and smiled, whispering something to her before turning and walking back to the house.

"Is he asleep?" she asked.

"Yeah, but I'm sure he'll be up for some water anytime soon. Thanks for today, Mom. I'll see you tomorrow."

I leaned in to kiss her cheek, and after she said goodbye to Rooney again, we got into the car and drove off.

I took a deep breath and looked over at Rooney who was smiling down at her hands in her lap.

"Are you happy?" I asked, reaching for her hands and squeezing them tightly.

"Yes, very happy. You?"

She now looked at me, eyeing me closely while I focused on the road.

"Yes, I am happy. I'm glad you came along today. You gained a whole lot more bonus points from Ira."

She laughed softly and turned her hand to interlock her fingers with mine.

"I had a lot of fun today. Wouldn't mind doing it all over again," she told me.

Me neither, and I was secretly planning another fun trip for just the three of us already.

Chapter Nineteen

Rooney

We arrived back at the apartment complex and got out of his car to head inside.

"Mind if I go grab a few things from my room? I'll be right back," I told him as we stopped in front of his door.

"Sure, take your time," he replied, placing a hand on my waist and kissing my cheek gently. "I'll be waiting."

I nodded and ran upstairs to enter my own apartment, and when I realized Evie wasn't the only one inside, I stopped to check the coats on the hanger to see if I recognized one of them.

But just as I got a closer look at all of them, a girl walked out of my bedroom, surprised to see me.

"Oh, you're Rooney, right? I used your bathroom, I hope you don't mind," she said.

"Uh, no, that's fine," I replied with a smile, being too kind as always. "I'm sorry, but what's your name?"

"I'm Dana. We've actually met before at a frat party. You probably don't remember me."

I didn't.

"Sorry," I said with an apologetic smile. "Who else is here?" I asked, looking toward the living room but not seeing much other than the large painting Evie once made and never found a place to hang it.

"Evie, Jonathan, and AJ."

The last name caught my attention.

"Oh, so you're dating Aiden?"

Dana puckered her lips and shrugged, unsure about it herself but obviously into the idea of dating him.

"Dana, what's taking so long?" I heard Aiden call out from the living room, and shortly after he walked around the corner, looking handsome as always.

"Rooney, hey. I was wondering where you've been," he said, smiling at me.

Evie hadn't told him I was out with Wells?

Dana walked over to him and placed a hand on his chest, smiling up at him and tilting her head to the side.

"I hope you didn't start watching the movie without me," she purred, quickly showing me her other side.

"No, we didn't. Go get comfortable, I'll be right with you," he said, keeping his eyes on me.

"Don't be too long," Dana added, giving me one last look and then leaving.

I gave him a quick smile and walked into my room to get a clean pair of underwear and a clean shirt to sleep with.

"Are you two dating?" I asked, wondering why I was even interested.

"Is that okay?"

I frowned at him as he leaned against the doorway with his arms crossed over his chest.

"Why wouldn't it be? She seems nice," I told him, turning back to grab a clean pair of socks.

"She is. She's very nice. But she's nothing compared to you, Rooney."

That made my frown deepen, and I turned around to look at him again. "I thought we were over this, Aiden."

My frustration was slowly creeping up on me, and I hoped he wouldn't make a big deal out of this.

"We are. I'm just stating facts. It seems as if no other girl I meet is as fascinating as you are, and I'm having a slight problem with that. It bothers me that we couldn't make things work."

His words made something in my chest sting, and as much as I appreciated him being honest, I needed him to stop immediately.

We were over.

Hell, things never even took off between us.

"I don't think we should be talking about this anymore, Aiden. Whatever it was that we had...it didn't work out. And I'm not sure it ever will. I'm seeing someone and—"

"And you think with him you'll know exactly what you want?"

He raised a brow at me and started to walk toward me slowly until I had to back up against the dresser and hope he wouldn't come any closer.

He wasn't threatening me, I just didn't feel comfortable with whatever he was trying to say.

"Wasn't that the problem you had? Being unsure about your feelings and not being able to open up to someone? How is he any different than I am? Unless...you lied about us."

I sighed heavily and shook my head. "I didn't lie about us, Aiden. I can't explain it, but we tried. We tried and it didn't work out. Maybe Wells isn't the right one for me either, but at least I'm giving him— us—a try."

AJ studied my face as he stood only one step away from me, towering over me and making my breath hitch with his deep stare.

"So you used me?"

"What? No! Don't be ridiculous, Aiden! We talked about this and we agreed that what we have wouldn't bloom into something deeper. More serious. It's not my fault and it's not yours either. I can't force my heart to love someone, and neither can you. Please...can't you just let it go?"

He clenched his jaw and kept his eyes on me.

"That's gonna be hard," he whispered, reaching out his hand and cupping my cheek.

My heart was racing, but not in a positive way.

He was leaning closer to me, but he wasn't going for my lips.

Instead, he moved closer to my ear.

"He's too old for you, Rooney. Let me make this right. Let me win you back. I'm in love with you," he whispered.

His words took my breath away and were so overwhelming that my whole body went numb.

"Aiden," I whispered, knowing this was going to hurt both of us like hell. "You don't love me. Whatever you're feeling, it's not love you feel for me."

A harsh laugh left him, and he leaned back to look me in the eyes again. "How would you know? You keep your damn heart locked up and don't let anyone in. You don't even try, Rooney. And I'm sorry to tell you this, but whatever you're trying to prove with him, it's not gonna work. You'll lead him on, let him get close to you and leave him like it's nothing. You need to let people in to be loved, Rooney. This shit you're pulling isn't going to work."

My vision was blurry thanks to the tears he was causing, and as much as I wanted to ignore his words, I knew there was some truth in them.

But what was going on between Wells and I was so much different.

I knew that, and I wouldn't let AJ ruin it for me.

"I might need some time to figure things out. To let my heart figure things out, but I know that you can't pull me away from him. I'm sorry if I hurt you. It wasn't my intention and you know it, but I won't let you ruin this for me. I'll make mistakes in my future. Can't avoid them. But you made a big mistake right here, Aiden. I thought we were friends."

I kept my voice low but honest and direct, and from the look in his eyes he knew this conversation shouldn't have happened.

"He's waiting," I said quietly, wiping my tears away and stepping to the side to leave my room.

Without saying another word, I headed downstairs and pushed his door open with my shoulder as my arms and hands were holding on to my clothes.

"That took a while," I heard Wells say, and as he rounded the corner from the kitchen, he was probably seeing my bloodshot eyes from trying not to cry any more.

"What happened?" he asked, worry showing in his eyes.

He walked over to me and pulled me into his arms with no hesitation, and I dropped everything to put my arms around him and lean against his chest.

"What's wrong, Rooney?" he asked, caressing my back and burying his other hand into my hair.

It took me a moment to catch my breath, but once I did, I sighed and fisted his shirt.

"AJ is upstairs and..."

Get your shit together, Rooney.

"Did he touch you?" he asked, his body tensed.

"No. No, he didn't. He just...said things which upset me."

He kept holding me with my clothes covering our feet, and I opened my eyes as he cupped my face with both hands and turned my head to look up at him.

"What did he say?" he asked, studying my face closely.

"That I used him, and that I'll use you too because I don't let anyone too close."

I had to be honest with him, and I needed him to know that this between us wasn't just a game to me.

"I really like you, Wells. I'm not just using you and I don't wanna hurt you."

My words didn't make much sense to my own ears, but Wells was looking at me with the most understanding eyes ever.

"We're taking things slow, Rooney. We're both figuring things out, and I know you're not just using me. I would've felt it if you were."

His thumbs brushed along my cheekbones and his eyes moved down to my lips as he licked his.

"Forget what he said, okay? This is about us and no one else. We're working things out, me and you, Rooney."

I nodded.

That's who I wanted this to be about.

Just Wells and I.

A gentle smile appeared on his face, and he leaned in closer to kiss my forehead. "As much as I hate seeing you cry, you look damn adorable when you do."

I laughed softly and looked back into his eyes. "You're a weirdo," I whispered.

I was happy that he didn't overreact or felt the need to go talk to AJ, which was something AJ would've done if they were in each other's positions.

But Wells wasn't in college anymore, and there was no need for him to show off that he was the one holding me instead of AJ.

As much as I hated what he said, I was sad that things ended this way with Aiden.

He was a friend, but he went too far.

"How about a cup of tea and a good movie to end the night?" he suggested.

I nodded, but before he could pull me into the living room, I pushed myself up on my tiptoes and kissed him gently on the lips, holding on to his shoulders tightly.

His hands were still cupping my face, but when he deepened the kiss, he moved them down to my waist, then further down to cup my ass.

He kept them there, but moved his left hand up to pull me closer by placing it on my lower back.

Our tongues met, and it didn't take too long for a simple kiss to turn into a deep, passionate one.

He held me close and squeezed my ass gently while I buried my hands into his locks, pulling and tugging until a groan made his chest vibrate.

Automatically, I had to press my thighs together to stop the tingling between my legs, but the more he squeezed and touched my body, the more intense the tingles got.

This was another reason why I knew things between Wells and me were different than with AJ.

I didn't feel those things when Aiden touched me, and my heart never pounded this fast in my chest when he kissed me.

Wells had a different effect on me, and I loved every single moment of having him this close.

After his tongue brushed against mine one more time, he pulled back to look at me again with a grin.

"Or we could skip the movie and head straight to bed," he suggested, making me laugh.

I moved my fingers against the back of his head and placed the other at his chest, looking down at it and puckering my lips.

"As inviting as that sounds, I'd love to cuddle up on the couch with you," I told him in a whisper.

"Okay. Get comfortable. I'll be right with you."

He placed a kiss to my forehead, then picked up my clothes and headed into his bedroom to put them on the bed.

I smiled, watching him for a moment before walking to the living room and sitting down on the couch, pulling the blanket over my legs.

"What kind of tea would you like?" he asked.

I turned my head to look at him, and after thinking about it for a second, I replied, "I'll have whatever you're having."

I waited on him to choose a movie to watch tonight, and once he sat down next to me on the couch, he placed both cups on the coffee table.

"What's Aiden doing up there, by the way?" he asked out of curiosity.

"I don't know. I guess Evie invited him and two other friends to watch a movie. He brought a date, so I have no idea what's gotten into him."

I didn't tell him about AJ telling me he had fallen in love with me, because for some reason, I didn't believe he actually did.

Maybe he was defeated, felt bad or hated the thought of not getting a girl so he had to show off his alpha side.

AJ was a good guy, but tonight he had shown me a side of him I never knew existed.

"He's unsure. That's what I get out of this. I don't know him, but when men start to act like assholes, they are unhappy with themselves," Wells said.

I gave him a tight smile and nodded.

Figured so.

"So...if you start acting like an asshole, I know it's not because of me but because of you?" I asked, mocking him.

"Pretty much, yeah. Hold anything against me if that happens, but I promise you'll never have to see that side of me."

I leaned against him and took a deep breath. "I feel good when I'm around you," I whispered.

"Good, because I intend on keeping you right here next to me."

Chapter Twenty

Wells

It didn't take long for Rooney to fall asleep in my arms last night, and once she did, I carried her into my bedroom to put her into bed which was far more comfortable than the couch.

I had taken off the pants she had worn to the zoo, just so she was more comfortable while sleeping.

She didn't wake, and I tried my best not to get too close to a part of her body she didn't want me to get close to.

It was obvious that she trusted me even in her sleep, because if a stranger tried to undress me, I'd definitely wake up from it.

Her eyes were still closed and her breathing flat and calm, but then, it was still early and I had no intention of waking her.

There was no reason to, and watching her sleep was relaxing.

She looked so content, even after what happened with her and AJ before she came downstairs.

I had nothing against AJ, but if he made her cry or got too close to her one more time, I would let him know just how I feel about it.

I buried my hand in her long hair and caressed her head gently.

Her sweet scent filled my nose, and it reminded me of flowers and peaches.

It was a gentle overwhelming scent, but I was afraid if I inhaled too much of it, I would get addicted.

Rooney fit in my life and things didn't become harder when she was around.

No, things were so much easier, felt so much easier, and I knew if it were any other girl, it wouldn't be the same.

One thing I always relied on was Ira's intuition.

He didn't push Rooney away or take little steps to trust her. Instead, he was just as fascinated and happy about her being around as I was.

She was perfect for us without ever having to try too hard or convince me that she was an amazing person.

I kissed her forehead and trailed kisses down to her cheeks, and when my lips reached her jaw, I started nibbling on her skin.

I hated the thought of her waking up from it, but I couldn't stop myself.

Her hand was flat on my naked chest, and when I pulled her closer with my hand on her lower back, she moved hers up to fist my hair in her hand, letting me know that she was slowly waking up.

A sweet mumbling sound escaped her which told me she was liking it.

I continued to kiss her skin until I met the side of her neck where I sucked on her softness gently without leaving a mark.

We weren't teenagers anymore, and as much as I wanted to show everyone that she was seeing me and wasn't available, I didn't think hickeys were appropriate.

I licked along her skin with my tongue and then pushed myself up to lean over her and get better access to the other side of her neck.

Both of her hands were now buried in my hair, and I had to be careful not to press my hardness against her and scare her away.

Though, not two seconds after I had that thought, she moved her hips to meet mine, letting me know that she was okay with it.

"Morning," she whispered, her voice raspy from sleep.

"Good morning," I replied, moving my lips up to her jaw and then cheek again before looking into her tired but big, hazel eyes.

She had one leg wrapped around me and I stayed leaned over her while my left arm was propped up next to her head.

"Did you have a good night?" I asked, eyeing her carefully.

"Yes, you?"

Her left hand moved to my cheek where her thumb then brushed along my skin in the sweetest way possible.

I nodded, licking my lips and leaning in to place a kiss to the corner of her mouth.

"Are you hungry?" I asked, staying close to her lips with mine.

"A little. I'm still tired," she whispered, closing her eyes and cupping the back of my head with one hand.

I wasn't ready to get out of bed yet either, and the way she pulled me in wouldn't let me move away from her.

So the only thing there was for us to do was enjoy the time we still had to ourselves before I'd have to pick up Ira.

It was her initiating the kiss but it was me who deepened it shortly after.

Kissing her was another reason why she was perfect for me.

It came easy and felt so damn right.

As if her lips were made for me.

Our kiss turned into exploring each other's wants and needs, and as if the kiss couldn't get any more passionate, she took over and pushed me back to straddle my hips while keeping her lips on mine.

I didn't mind her taking over for a while, but to handle my dick and its own brain, I had to make sure I was on top again soon.

For now, it felt nice feeling her warmth covering my shaft, and I had easier access to her ass which was a bonus.

I loved to touch her, and I knew she liked being touched as well.

As our tongues moved with each other, she started to circle her hips on top of me to create even more sparks between our bodies and the soft noises she was making didn't make it a lot easier for me and my friend down there.

She was driving me crazy by that simple movement of her hips, but it did so damn much to me.

I squeezed her perfectly round ass and pressed her against me to make her feel more of me while she showed me just how good of a kisser she was.

It was interesting watching her personality turn from sweet and loving to passionate and sexy in just a few seconds.

"If we keep going, I might not be able to hold back, Rooney," I mumbled into the kiss, and after a few seconds, she broke the kiss to look into my eyes.

There was lust in hers, but I could also make out the slight embarrassment in them.

"What's wrong?" I asked, pushing myself up to sit up straight and lean against the headboard while she slipped down into my lap.

I cupped her face and made her look at me as her gaze dropped, and when she finally met my eyes, she sighed.

"I'm a virgin. I wouldn't know what to do," she whispered.

There was something telling me that she hadn't had sex before, but the way she moved her hips on top of me I thought I could've also been very wrong.

Either way, she was perfect, and her being inexperienced showed me that she trusted me with her innocence.

"I wouldn't do anything you wouldn't want me to, Rooney. But we have to stop because I might explode in any second."

She was still pressed against me, but as long as she didn't move it was all right.

"We'll take things slow. I told you before, love. I'm not pushing you to do things you're not ready for. Including sex."

"Okay," she said, smiling. "So you want me to get off you?"

I chuckled and kissed her cheek before nodding. "Better if you do unless you want me to embarrass myself."

Rooney

We spent the morning together until Ira facetimed Wells to tell him he wanted to be picked up from Grandma's house.

It was almost eleven when that happened, so I said goodbye to him and decided to let him spend the rest of the afternoon with Ira to get some alone time while I started working on Ira's birthday present.

I didn't tell Wells about the idea I had, and since Ira was turning four soon, I wanted to surprise him with something he most definitely would love.

Plus, he'd have one of a kind.

I had a massive canvas under my bed which I never used ever since college started, so I decided to pull it out of there and paint a massive painting with all of Ira's favorite superheroes on it.

I started sketching it with a pencil, and I thought it would look good if Hulk was breaking through a wall right in the center of the canvas and all the other superheroes surrounding him.

He'll love it.

I sat on my bedroom floor while I kept sketching what I had envisioned, and I liked how it was turning out so far.

After lunch, I turned on some music to get me in the mood to paint, and I quickly spent the whole afternoon painting the first layer.

That usually didn't take me too long, even on a bigger canvas, as I would go over it a few more times with more colors and details so there was no need for me to spend a lot of time on the first layer.

Sometime in the evening, Evie came home from a day at the country club with her parents, and as annoyed as she was, I knew she'd spend the evening on the couch with some takeout food and a movie she watched a few times already.

I joined her as I was done painting for the day, but as much as I tried to free my mind and just relax, Wells popped up in my head every once in a while, making my heart ache and wish I could just go down there and see him and Ira again.

But I didn't wanna be too intrusive, also because we both had to make sure we wouldn't rush things.

"AJ was at the club today. Had Dana clinging to his arm all day long, and surprisingly, he looked fine with it."

I turned my head to look at Evie, and while I stared at her with a raised brow, she kept looking at the screen.

"Why are you telling me this?" I asked, confused.

She shrugged. "Thought you'd wanna know."

"Why?"

"Hell, I don't know! You two had a thing and then fought last night. Can't I gossip about him?" she asked, seemingly annoyed with me.

Luckily, her strange mood swings didn't bother me anymore, so I simply pushed them aside.

"I'd like to never talk about him again unless it's very, very important. I'm happy, and I don't want him to ruin this happiness for me."

Evie nodded and lifted her hands to defend herself. "Fine."

Good.

That was settled.

Now all that was left to do was get Wells out of my mind unless I wanted to have a wet dream.

I could still feel his cock pressed against my middle, and as little experience as I had, I couldn't stop thinking about the first time getting closer to him.

Without any clothes on, next time.

Chapter Twenty-One

Wells

A few days went by and work took over most of my time again.

I had lots to do, and the only free time I had was after work when I picked up Ira from my mother's house to make him dinner and play with him before putting him to bed and getting back to work.

I hadn't seen Rooney in the past five days, but since we were getting closer to the weekend again, I was hoping to head upstairs and knock on her door to ask if she was free on Saturday.

Which was tomorrow.

I had a little something planned for her, but also for Ira as he loved nature and running around where no one could tell him not to.

Playgrounds were limited, so I thought about taking them both on a little trip to a big, beautiful field in the middle of nowhere to have a picnic and enjoy some quiet time.

I was sure she would say yes, I just hoped I wouldn't be too late and she didn't already make plans.

But before I could go to her place and ask, I had to take Ira to the children's hospital to check on his insulin levels and general health.

We arrived and I helped Ira out of the car, and because hospitals were a little frightening for a little boy, I was more than happy to carry and calm him.

I kissed his cheek before walking through the parking lot to get to the entrance, and when we entered, he immediately started to suck on his thumb and twirl his hair around his finger the way he so often did to make himself relax.

It wasn't much of a sucking he did, but just having his thumb in his mouth most likely brought him back to when he was even younger and needed something to calm down with.

I didn't mind, as long as he'd someday get rid of the habit and wouldn't walk around as a teenager with his thumb in his mouth.

Funny thing was, I did the same thing when I was little.

At least that's what Mom told me but I couldn't remember.

"Hi, what can I help you with today?" the woman behind the front desk asked, smiling at me and then at Ira.

"We're here for a checkup with Dr. Cole."

"I'm Ira," he called out before I could say any more, pointing at himself to make sure she knew who he was talking about.

"Ah, yes. I got your name right here on the list. He's still in a meeting but Dr. Cole will be right with you. Please take a seat in the waiting area," she offered.

"Thank you," I replied, smiling back and then carrying Ira to the waiting room.

"Can I play?" he asked, pointing to the corner with a little desk and colored pencils on it and a chest with books and toys next to it.

"Of course. Go see if they have any new toys in there," I told him as I sat down and let him run free.

"Wow!"

I watched as he pulled out a book, which first of all was no surprise that he wanted to read instead of playing, then he ran back to me to show me what he found.

"It's me!" he said, his eyes wide and filled with joy.

On the cover of the children's book there was a little blond boy holding a little action figure, and while he pulled up his shirt, he revealed he had an insulin pump as well.

"Oh, wow, Ira! It's a book about a diabetic just like you are," I told him, not sugarcoating anything because he knew the truth.

"Can you read it to me, Daddy?" he asked, fascinated about his new find.

"Of course. Come sit next to me."

He climbed up onto the chair to my left as I turned the first page.

I started reading to him as he looked at the pictures and pointed to everything I was mentioning to show me that he knew exactly what I was talking about.

"He has a pump too!" Ira pointed out, showing off his own just like the little boy in the book did.

"That's right! And you also know how it works, hm?"

"That's a great book," a deep voice said, and I turned my head to look at Dr. Cole.

"How are you doing, Ira?" he asked, and with a little bit of hesitation, Ira nodded at him and then waved.

"I'm ready, please follow me," he told us.

As he turned his back, I pulled out my phone and took a picture of the book so I wouldn't forget its title and author.

"We'll go buy this book at the bookstore right after Dr. Cole is done with the checkup, okay, buddy?"

Ira nodded and hopped down off the chair while I put the book back, then I grabbed his hand and walked with him into Dr. Cole's patient room.

"How are things going?" he asked as I sat down on the chair on the other side of his desk with Ira on my lap.

"Good. Nothing to complain about. Ira has adjusted well to the pump and we never had any trouble with the dosage. Ira's feeling healthy and is very active."

"That's good to hear. I would like to do a blood test then talk about something new we're working on. It's another insulin pump, specialized for children under twelve. It's not much different when it comes to the usage of it, but the technology has improved. We're just gonna see if it could be a fit for Ira or not."

"Okay, sounds good."

Whatever Dr. Cole thought would help with my son's health, I'd be okay with Ira having the newest and best devices needed for his diabetes.

Rooney

My week had been so busy that I didn't even get a chance to get the mail from downstairs for three days.

Once again, I hadn't left my apartment in days, and let Evie do all the grocery shopping to keep me alive.

I was busy with studying, classes, and painting Ira's birthday present which was coming along nicely.

Only a few more details and it would be ready.

It was almost six p.m. when I finally decided to push everything aside and be done for the week.

I had earned my weekend, and I hoped to spend it with Wells and Ira.

I was walking down the stairs to get the mail Evie never brought upstairs for whatever reason, probably to avoid all the bills she had to pay with her parent's money, and as I opened the entrance door, I saw Wells's car park in front of the building.

I smiled, not able to keep my excitement to see him and Ira again inside of me, and the second his car door opened and he stepped out, he smiled brightly at me.

"Hey there, gorgeous," he said, looking handsome as ever.

"Hi," I greeted back, chewing on my bottom lip.

"Weird how we live this close but don't see each other for days, huh?" he joked, and I laughed at his true words.

"Yeah, it's weird."

I walked down the steps to get to his car as he helped Ira out who came running toward me with a book in his hands.

"Look, Rooney! It's me!"

I squatted down to get a better look at the book, and when I noticed what it was about, I smiled and nodded.

"That really is you! Where did you find this amazing book?" I asked.

"At the hospital," he told me.

"He had a checkup and there was this book in the waiting room. I thought it was very informative and sweet, so we went to the bookstore and bought it, right buddy?"

"Yes! And more books!"

I smiled and got back up to wrap my arms around Wells's neck, and since it's been too long, I kissed him softly.

He placed his hand on my lower back while his other was holding the bag of books Ira was talking about.

"I missed you," I whispered against his lips, and he smiled before breaking the kiss to look back into my eyes.

"I missed you too. How was your week?"

"Stressful, but I finished everything that needed to be done and now I'm free the whole weekend. I was hoping we could spend it together."

His nod came quick, and I had a feeling that he had been hoping to spend it with me too.

"I have a little something planned, actually. How about a picnic tomorrow? I know a nice, quiet place," he suggested.

"Sounds good to me."

"Wanna come have dinner with us tonight?" he then asked, making the start of the weekend even better.

"I'd love to. I just need to take a shower, then I'll be right down."

"Perfect." He leaned in again to kiss me, and after a quick dip of his tongue, he moved back again.

"I'll see you later then," he told me, taking a step back to let me walk to the door.

"See you soon," I told them both, and after Ira waved at me, I grabbed the mail and headed back upstairs.

***

"Look, Rooney!"

I moved my gaze from the steak in the pan to Ira sitting at the kitchen table with the books Wells got for him all spread open.

"It's a dragon!"

He pointed to a dark purple, pretty scary-looking dragon covering two pages, but he was rather fascinated by it than afraid.

It was a children's book after all.

"That's a big one, huh? Do you like dragons?"

Wells was taking a shower and I told him to take his time and not stress about dinner for once.

I had it all under control, and Ira seemed to be okay with me watching him while his dad was in the other room.

"Yes, but they are not real. I didn't see one at the zoo," he pointed out.

True.

"They would need a very tall and big enclosure," I explained.

"Because they can fly," he added, holding up his pointer finger like a little professor.

"That's right," I replied with a chuckle.

He was such a little charmer, just like his father.

Safe to say Wells wasn't the only one stealing pieces of my heart, but this little guy knew exactly how to win someone over.

I was already in too deep, and I knew that if something were to happen between Wells and me, I'd have a hard time not being close to Ira.

"What are you two talking about?" Wells asked as he entered the kitchen, interrupting my deep thoughts and making me look back up from the meat.

"Dragons!" Ira announced.

"Dragons are great. You okay?" he asked me, stepping behind me and placing his hands on my waist while kissing the back of my head.

"Everything's perfect. Dinner's almost finished," I told him, leaning back against him.

"I'll set the table."

When he stepped away from me, he told Ira to put away the books and help him set the table, which he did without making a big fuss about it.

Tonight was going to be perfect, and I couldn't wait for the picnic Wells had planned.

"Do we need to cook something for the picnic tomorrow?" I asked, arranging the meat and veggies on each of our plates.

"There's a new place right outside of town where they make healthy meals to take out and they also have many sugar free options. I've always wanted to try their things out, and it's perfect for Ira."

"Oh, you mean *Divine*?"

"Yeah, I think that's what it's called. Have you been before?" he asked.

We sat down at the table and Wells cut up the meat for Ira.

"Yes, actually. A few months ago. It was delicious," I told him.

"Perfect. Then I guess our date is set for tomorrow. Did they have sweets too?"

I nodded, remembering all the amazing-smelling baked goods. "They have this insanely good cinnamon roll. It was low carb and sugar free, and I think I ate two of them. But there are so many more things to choose from. You'll love it."

"I can't wait. I'm happy to have you here with us again," Wells said, smiling and reaching for my hand to squeeze it before we both started to eat.

The warmth in my chest never left ever since I saw him earlier in the parking lot, and I knew that feeling wouldn't leave until we'd be apart again.

Chapter Twenty-Two

Wells

"Wow!" Ira exclaimed as he ran toward the beautiful scenery ahead of us.

After last night, I couldn't stop thinking about today, and to spend the day with Ira and Rooney was the right distraction I needed after a hard week at work and an even harder one ahead of me.

"It's beautiful here," Rooney said, her eyes wide with fascination.

"It is. Perfect for a picnic," I replied, waving Ira back to us as he turned around.

"Come here, bud. Let's eat first, then we can explore, okay?"

He ran back to us and immediately reached for the blanket I brought to sit on.

There was a flower field to our left and a big mountain with trees surrounding it, their leaves red, orange, and yellow.

Fall really was beautiful in Wyoming, and this little place would be one I'd keep at the back of my mind to take them both here again someday.

"Please help me, Rooney," Ira told her, and she smiled at him as he tried to pull the blanket straight on the grass.

She helped him set the blanket and he quickly sat down to wait for me to pull out all the food we got at *Divine*.

"Oh, look! There's even a little pond down there," Rooney said, pointing to it to show Ira.

"Maybe there are fish!"

"Could be, yeah. If we have some left over crumbs, we can feed them," I suggested, knowing he would enjoy it just like he did at the zoo.

"Have you been here before?" Rooney asked while she helped me place a little bit of everything we got into the plates.

"I drove by it a few times, and I've seen it on maps I had to work with for some projects. I've also googled it and there are more people here in spring and summer, but I figured it would be much prettier in fall."

"It definitely is. I love it here," she told me, smiling sweetly.

She wouldn't mind me taking her here more often then.

"Let's eat!" Ira announced, holding up the kid's fork and knife I brought from home.

We chuckled and watched as he went straight for the gluten free pasta salad with fresh tomatoes, and while he chewed, I could tell he liked it as he immediately fell into this absent state where he was focused solemnly on the food in front of him.

"Guess you now know where you can go if you're ever too lazy to cook or don't have any more ideas," Rooney said with a grin.

"I'm never too lazy to cook," I replied, nudging her side with my elbow.

We started to eat as well, and every once in a while, Ira looked up at us with a questioning look, holding up his fork with a type of food he has never had before.

He had to make sure he knew what it was before he put it into his mouth, but once I told him, he ate it without hesitation.

"Are you really not gonna tell me what you'll get Ira for his birthday?" I asked, wanting to know.

"If you're gonna tell him, no. If you can keep a secret...sure."

I chuckled and leaned closer to her to kiss her cheek, then I whispered. "I can keep secrets."

She squirmed and gently pushed me away by lifting her shoulder, and with a big smile, she whispered, "I'm painting a massive picture of Ira's favorite superheroes which he can hang up on his bedroom wall."

"Really?" I asked, surprised that she would actually go out of her way and take the time to do something like that.

No, I was more amazed than surprised.

"He's gonna love it, Rooney. That's amazing," I said with a chuckle, still not comprehending it. "How long have you been working on it already?" I asked.

We could openly talk about it without being afraid of Ira listening as he was focused on making his Hulk figure eat some of the food.

Sharing is caring, but I was glad Hulk couldn't eat or else Ira wouldn't get his needed nutrition for the day.

"I started last Sunday after you went to pick him up, and I've been working on it every day for about three to four hours. It's been fun. I haven't painted such a colorful painting yet."

"You're incredible. He's gonna freak out. Does that mean you're gonna spend the day and night with us on his birthday? I have already sent out the invitations to his friends' parents, and some have already gotten back to me to let me know that their kids would love to sleep over at Ira's."

"How many has he invited?" she asked.

"I think ten or eleven. Six have already said yes."

"That's a lot of kids," she pointed out. "Are those all kids he met at the park?"

"Most of them, yeah. But there is one mother who hosts get-togethers at her house just so parents and kids around town can get to know each other. Also to make sure the kids are safe, and if anything ever happens, we know who to trust or call for help."

"That's very sweet. So he won't be lost when he starts kindergarten but already knows a few faces," she said.

"Exactly. That's very important to me. Ira is quick to trust anyone who's kind to him, some more than others, but meeting with these other kids and parents is teaching him that it's okay to say hi to the people he already knows, but not strangers he has never seen before."

"I understand. Kids don't see any danger or bad in people. It's sweet, but dangerous."

I nodded, finishing my lunch and placing the empty plate next to me.

"But he would've never accepted anyone in his life the way he accepted you. He knows you're different, and he can feel there's more to you than just a girl his father hangs out with."

She smiled up at me but couldn't contain a grin. "So we're not just spending time together to make out and eat together?"

I chuckled and shook my head. "Fuck no," I muttered.

"Daddy! That's a bad, bad word!" Ira exclaimed, looking at me with a deep frown and worried eyes.

Why did kids have to hear the worst things that came out of people's mouths?

Rooney laughed softly and nodded to agree with Ira. "He's right. That's a very naughty word."

"I'm sorry, bud. I won't say it again. I promise," I told him, brushing through his blond locks.

"Pinky promise?" Ira held out his pinky to me and I curled mine around it.

"Pinky promise. Oh, Hulk too?"

He nodded as he held Hulk's hand to my pinky, and I promised his little friend the same.

"All done!" Ira then said, pushing himself up onto his feet. "Can we explore now?"

"Yeah, we can."

I got up as well and took Ira by the hand while Rooney put all the plates together and back into the basket.

"Thank you," I told her once she was up on her feet too, and with a sweet smile, she kissed my cheek.

"Anytime. Let's go check out the pond," she suggested, and Ira quickly took off, pulling me with him.

I loved how attentive and helpful she was and she had all the right intentions.

"Do you see fish in there, Ira?" I asked, standing close to the edge of the pond and holding him close to me so he wouldn't fall in.

He eyed the water carefully, then shook his head.

"I don't see any fish," he told us, turning his head to look at us.

"Yeah, I don't think there are any in there," Rooney said, puckering up her lips.

God, the more I looked at her, the more intense my dick twitched.

I couldn't focus on her though, seeing as Ira was right here with us and I didn't wanna take any of my attention from him.

But anything Rooney did or said, even if it was the littlest gesture or movement, I wanted to pull her to me and kiss her deeper than I ever had.

She was slowly taking over my mind, but, hell...I did not fucking care.

We spent the rest of the afternoon in that beautiful place without anyone bothering us, and when Ira told me he was getting tired, it was time for us to pack our things and go.

When we arrived home, Rooney told me that she'd be right back to get some of her things to sleep at my place while I gave Ira a quick bath and put on his pajamas.

"Splash! Now you're wet, Daddy!" Ira grinned, pointing at my shirt.

I laughed and shook my head. "It's you who needs a bath, buddy, not me. Come on, turn around so I can wash your hair."

I used a little bit of his shampoo and massaged it into his hair gently while he let his two action figures fall into the water by holding them high up in the air.

"Do you remember what Dr. Cole said yesterday about the new pump, Ira?" I asked.

"No," he replied.

I didn't expect him to though.

"Dr. Cole said that they'll soon have a new pump which will be a little bit bigger than the one you have now."

"Bigger?" he asked, scrunching up his nose and turning his head to look at me.

"Yes, just a little bit. And since it's new, you'll be one of the first to try it," I explained.

His lips were parted as he took everything in that I said.

It was easy for him to understand things, but he took a while to make sure he would now remember what I was telling him.

"But as I said, it's a little bigger than the one you have now, so it might be a little heavier and you'd have to get used to it while playing and running around," I told him.

He nodded to let me know he understood, but soon after he shook his head. "I don't want a new pump," he said.

"Are you sure? Dr. Cole said you can test it out for a few days and then you can decide. How about you try it and then you decide?"

He thought about it for a while, then nodded. "Okay."

At least he was up to test things before he pushed them away forever.

"Good, then I'll call Dr. Cole on Monday to let him know."

I washed the shampoo out of his hair and then dried it with a towel to make it stop dripping before wrapping him into the towel to dry off.

"Can I dress myself?" he asked.

"You've been dressing yourself every morning and night, Ira. Of course you can," I told him proudly.

He was getting so damn big, and I already missed the times he was still a baby.

I loved to cuddle him all night long, have him sleep next to me or on my chest, and watch TV until late into the night just to make sure I wouldn't miss anything.

Like his first word.

Ira was one of those weird kids who could fully walk at only nine months, but only started to talk when he was one.

Weird as in he would tun around and show you things, but couldn't communicate other than by pointing his finger and tapping on things.

I liked him that way, but he was even more fun now that I could have full conversations with him.

His first word was daddadda, which in my dictionary for baby language translated to daddy.

Safe to say he knew who I was back then, and I hated the thought of him growing up and starting to use dad instead of daddy.

Shit, I had to stop thinking about it before I pulled out all his baby pictures I put in an album.

"This way?" he asked, holding up his undies.

"Yes, that's correct, buddy."

I waited for him to put it on, followed by his pajama pants and long-sleeved shirt which of course had another superhero on it.

"Let us check your insulin level, then you can play a little until you're ready for bed, okay?"

"Can I watch Ninja Turtles?" he asked.

I figured as he never spent much time in front of the TV that it would be okay.

"Of course. First, can you tell me what number this is?" I asked, turning the little device toward him so he could see the display clearly.

He studied it for a while, then held up his hands with his fingers spread out to show me the number written on the display.

"And how many fingers are those?" I asked, testing him.

"Eight," he told me.

"That's right! And the second one?" I asked, pointing at the number next to the eight.

He made a fist and I nodded, smiling proudly again.

"Correct! That's a zero. And together that number is called eighty."

"Eighty. Eighty is good, right?" he asked, frowning and looking back down at his pump.

"Yes, eighty is perfect. If you wanna eat a little something while watching TV, I can make you a little snack. How does that sound?"

"Okay," he simply replied.

I went into the living room with him to let him cuddle up on the couch with a blanket and turned on the TV to put the Ninja Turtles on.

"Daddy's gonna put away a few things, okay? Let me know when you want your snack."

He gave me a quick nod, and before I started to clean out the basket with all of our picnic things in it, I brought him a glass of water.

I heard the front door open after a soft knock, and as I got back to the kitchen, I looked around the corner to see Rooney standing there in her sleepwear.

"Come in," I told her with a smile.

She locked the door and walked over to me, and as she reached me, I pulled her to me and kissed her lips.

I couldn't wait to have her to myself all night long, and by the sweet perfume she was wearing, I knew she had something in mind for tonight.

Whatever it was, I'd take it slow with her, go at her own pace and see how far she wanted to take things.

Chapter Twenty-Three

Rooney

Ira had fallen asleep on the couch after eating his snack while watching TV, and as Wells picked him up to put him to bed, I waited on him in the kitchen where I was still drinking the glass of red wine he had poured me.

Something about tonight was making me nervous, but not in a bad way.

Maybe it was the wine, but I was still on my first glass and normally I didn't start feeling the alcohol until after two glasses.

I breathed in deeply and tried to calm myself, but when Wells walked back into the kitchen, my heartbeat picked up speed.

It felt as if it was going to explode in my chest.

"Everything okay?" he asked as he noticed me staring at him.

"Yes, everything's perfect. Is he asleep?"

"Yeah, he woke up for a short moment but he won't wake up until tomorrow morning. Running around that flower field this afternoon wore him out."

He stepped in front of me and placed his hands on either side of me on the counter, making me lean against it with no escape in sight.

"Deep thoughts?" he asked, his eyes wandering all over my face and studying me closely.

"Yeah, I...I was just thinking about us," I told him quietly, reaching out with one hand to place it on his shoulder.

"Is that so? And what kind of things are flashing through your mind about us?"

He grabbed the glass out of my hand and placed it on the counter, then he put both hands on my waist to lift me up and stand between my legs.

I wrapped them around him and placed both hands on his shoulders now, smiling at him.

Even with me sitting on the counter, he was still taller than me and had to tilt his head to look into my eyes.

As much as I wanted to tell him what my thoughts were, I couldn't.

Not because I didn't want to.

"Please don't make me do this," I whispered, looking at his lips and then letting my gaze drop to his chest where my fingers started to pick at his shirt.

"Make you do what, Rooney?"

His voice was low and raspy, and of course it had to sound so damn sexy.

"Tell you what I feel or think. I'm not good at it, and I don't wanna mess things up."

I was scared to rush things.

As much as he showed me that he wanted me too, I couldn't be the first to open up about my feelings to him.

I was too afraid to get hurt, even if I knew that was part of seeing someone.

Just because things seemed to go well between us, that didn't mean we would end up together.

"Then show me how you feel in a different way," he suggested.

My eyes were back on his.

Maybe if we keep things to ourselves, we'd have more time to think about it all.

Who are you fooling, stupid girl?

But as always, speaking from the heart was never my strength, and I knew I'd sooner or later regret not opening up to him in that very moment.

I leaned in to kiss him, holding his face in my hands now and letting his wander all over my body.

Here's to mistakes and a potential—no, *predictable*—heartbreak.

Maybe I was feeling the alcohol already.

His tongue brushed along my bottom lip as his hips pressed against me, letting me feel his already hardening shaft.

That's what I wanted, even though I was still unsure about the whole me being a virgin thing.

But, hell...it's not like sex scared me.

I pushed my hands into his hair and tugged on it gently as he deepened the kiss, pushing his tongue into my mouth and letting it dance with mine without being too pushy.

I liked when he kissed me, and I liked it even more when he used his hands to run them over my body the way he was doing right now.

One hand stopped at my hips while the other pushed up my shirt to touch my skin, making me shiver and smile.

Safe to say he knew how to use each of his body parts to make me feel good, and no matter what tonight would bring, I'd enjoy every second of it.

He moved his hand up along my spine, making me shiver all over again and squeeze my thighs against his hips.

The familiar pulsating and stinging between my legs started to become more intense as he continued to kiss me passionately, and my panties soaked up the wetness I was releasing down there all thanks to him.

A soft moan escaped me as his hand reached the underside of my right breast, making my breath hitch but arch my back to silently tell him that I wanted more.

He understood, and his hand cupped my breast gently before giving it a squeeze.

AJ had done this to me before, but again, nothing he ever did made me feel the way Wells did.

As if Wells had a magical power to make me feel so much more.

"Fuck," he growled against my lips before breaking the kiss and looking back into my eyes.

Lust was filling his, and I knew mine looked the same.

He started to pinch my nipple between his two fingers as his other hand moved up to cup my other breast, massaging it while he kept his eyes on me.

"I don't think I have to tell you again that if you want me to stop, you have to let me know, hm?"

I nodded, my lips parted and hips pushing even more against his now hard cock.

"I don't want you to stop," I breathed, pulling at his hair and then letting my hands fall to the waistband of his sweatpants.

A grin tugged at his lips, then he pushed my shirt further up to get a better look at my breasts.

"You're so damn gorgeous, Rooney," he whispered, keeping his hands right there and leaning in to kiss the top of one breast.

I couldn't close my eyes.

I wanted to see everything he did to my body and I didn't wanna miss a thing while he made me feel so good.

My plan was to get rid of his shirt first, then his sweatpants, and maybe later his boxer briefs.

Heck, I wasn't even that nervous anymore.

He trailed kisses around my left nipple first, then the right, and after taking another good look at both my breasts, he pulled one nipple into his mouth and sucked on it while his tongue circled around the little nub.

I moaned softly, trying not to make too much noise as I knew Ira's bedroom door wasn't fully closed.

Every flick of his tongue against my nipple sent sparks directly to my clit, which I then realized was where all the pounding and stinging came from.

It wanted Wells's attention too, but I enjoyed him playing with my tits and didn't want to interrupt him.

I was feeling very brave in that moment as all those sparks exploded in my lower belly, so I pushed my hand into his pants to cup his cock, feeling just how big it actually was.

I could feel the tip tucked between his lower stomach and waistband, and I wondered if that was comfortable.

But instead of asking, I started to move my hand along his length, feeling his tip peek out every time I moved along it.

Low growls made his chest vibrate, and after he was done with my other nipple, he looked up and grabbed my wrist to stop my hand from rubbing against his cock.

"Are you sure you want this?"

I frowned at him, unhappy with him keeping me from exploring his body.

"You said I'd have to stop you if you're going too far. I haven't said a word ever since you started kissing my breasts," I told him, my voice stern and my words surprisingly direct.

That got a chuckle out of him, and to show me that he understood I wanted more, he leaned in once again to pull one nipple into his mouth only to let go of it again and pull me off the counter to carry me into his bedroom.

My heart was pounding with excitement, and as quickly as he moved over me when I was on the bed, I reached back down to continue stroking his cock through his boxer briefs.

Wells

She wasn't as timid about this as she was before.

Well, at least that's how I interpreted it as she told me she was a virgin and wouldn't know what to do if we had kept going that one night making out right here in my bed.

But the way her hand rubbed my dick felt incredible.

The drop of precum was already rubbed into my stomach, and since I haven't had sex in a long time, my dick had gotten used to hands.

My hands, to be specific.

But there was no shame in making myself come every once in a while, when I had an almost four-year-old to take care of daily and work which was often times a pain in the ass.

But since other women didn't really appeal to me, I was happy it was Rooney touching me right now while I kissed her lips.

No idea how far we'd go tonight, but I knew I couldn't let her stop before I came.

I've always told myself to never let a girl this close without exactly knowing how I felt about her, but I was already in too deep with her, my heart beating like crazy because of her.

I wasn't in love with her yet, *I think*, but I sure as fuck knew that she wouldn't get rid of me anytime soon.

As much as I hated to admit it, she was carrying around the same damn issues I had, which was pushing aside what we really felt to not get hurt.

I knew she wouldn't tell me first, but to not get hurt myself, I had to be selfish.

It's gonna hurt like hell if it all goes wrong.

Her left hand moved under my shirt to let her fingers run along every single one of my muscles before they stopped at the waistband of my boxer briefs.

I had to take my clothes off, but once I did, I was determined to take hers off too.

I pushed myself off her and stood at the side of the bed looking down at her while I pulled my shirt over my head and pushed my sweatpants down my hips.

Her eyes were glued to my stomach at first, then she noticed the tip of my dick peeking out of my boxer's waistband and that's all she could see from that moment on.

I grinned, knowing from the look on her face that she liked what she was seeing, so I placed my hand over my dick and rubbed it slowly while keeping my boxers on.

"You're teasing me," she whispered, making me grin wider.

"Am I?"

"Yes, and I don't think I like it," she told me with a frown and her bottom lip pushed out.

I chuckled and reached for her hand to make her sit up right in front of me, and by placing her hand on my dick, she continued to rub it while looking at it closely.

As little experience she had, she definitely wasn't afraid to show her interest in a man's body.

I liked that, yet I couldn't just turn her around onto her stomach and fuck her from behind the way I'd like to.

Fuck.

My inner caveman was trying to escape, but I couldn't let him.

Not yet.

"Can I..." she asked, looking up at me and tugging at my boxer briefs.

I nodded, then let her push it down to free my hardness and give it more space.

I kept watching her closely as she wrapped her hand around it, slowly moving it along my length.

The muscles in my body tensed, and I reached around her to grab a fistful of her hair while my other hand played with her tits again.

I wanted her to explore without having to tell her what to do, and to my surprise, she leaned in placed a soft kiss to the tip of my dick.

To take it a step further, she wrapped her lips around it carefully, sucking on it as if it were a lollipop.

"Ah, fuck..." I muttered, letting her know that what she was doing felt good, and to encourage her to keep going.

I held on tight to her hair but didn't move her head closer so she wouldn't feel pressured, but then, she didn't seem to want to stop and kept taking my dick deeper into her mouth.

It seemed as if girls didn't have too much trouble finding out what a man liked, as us men had far more problems figuring a woman's body out.

"Feels so fucking good," I told her.

I liked it rough, but with that sweet innocence of hers it made the sensation she was creating with her lips just as intense as when a more experienced girl would suck my dick.

She was doing everything right, and I loved watching her trust herself with what she was doing without asking for approval.

"Just like that, love. Your lips feel amazing around my dick," I whispered.

I should've locked the door as kids were known to run into situations they'd rather not see, but I didn't wanna move or stop her from what she was doing.

I felt an orgasm build inside of me, but I was able to push it aside for a little while longer before I had to take a step back from her.

I leaned in to kiss her lips by cupping her jaw and tilting her head back, and as much as I didn't want to push her, I had to know where she wanted this to go.

"Tell me, love. What do you want?" I asked against her lips, placing another kiss to it and then looking into her eyes again.

It took a moment for her to reply, but her response was not what I had expected, and it made my fucking dick twitch more than once.

"I want to make you come. And I want you to do the same to me."

Turned out sweet Rooney knew how to say what's on her mind after all.

Chapter Twenty-Four

Rooney

My body was relaxed, but my mind had never been this tense.

Everything I said to Wells was what I really wanted, but strangely enough, it was my mind telling me to stop instead of my heart which I guessed was how it was meant to be.

Having my lips around his cock felt weird at first, but the taste of his precum wasn't bad at all, and my will to explore a little more of his body grew bigger with every slide of my mouth along his shaft.

I felt good about what I was doing, and he more than once told me that it felt good, which definitely pushed me to try and take in more of his length.

Wells was standing in front of me with his hand wrapped around his cock, stroking it while letting his eyes move from my face down to my breasts.

It was clear that we wouldn't stick to just foreplay, and I was glad we didn't. I wanted more of him.

His tongue came out to lick his bottom lip, then he smiled and tilted his head. "Are you on birth control?" he asked.

Important question, and luckily, I was.

"I am," I told him, enjoying the way he was admiring my body.

"I'm clean. I was tested a few months ago. And I gotta be honest...I don't enjoy sex with condoms. Besides, I haven't had sex in years."

I wouldn't know how it feels, so I didn't care either way.

As long as he was gentle.

And was that how Ira was conceived?

Him having sex with Leah without protection?

Those were questions for another day. I had to focus on us now.

"Wanna take off your pants for me, love?" he asked, keeping his voice low and his eyes on me.

I nodded and lifted my bottom off the bed to push my pants and panties down my legs, then I sat back down to take them off complete, followed by my socks.

His eyes wandered downward, stopping at my breasts once again before they took in that one part of my body that no man has ever touched with their hands.

I didn't feel uncomfortable with him observing my body inch by inch, but the cool air around us was making it hard for me not to squirm and push my legs together.

"Come here," he whispered, holding out his hand.

I placed mine in his and let him pull me up on my feet so I would stand in front of him, looking up into his eyes.

Both his hands cupped my face, and the tip of his cock touched my belly.

"You look worried," he told me, studying my face closely.

I wasn't worried or else I would've felt that way, right?

"I'm not," I replied, my hands finding their way to his muscular stomach and chest.

"Are you sure?" he asked, brushing his thumbs along my cheekbones. "I can tell you want this, and I promise you I'll do whatever it takes to make your first time unforgettable, but if there's anything you're worried about or wanna talk about first, now is the right time to do that."

I eyed him for a moment, then smiled at him and shook my head. "I'm okay. I want you, but I'm getting really impatient," I said, laughing softly.

He chuckled and shook his head, leaning down to kiss my forehead before he took a few steps to make me get back onto the bed.

"You've enjoyed sucking my dick, huh?" he asked, teasing and grinning.

I loved when he talked without filtering his words.

Showed me a different side of him from when Ira's around.

I nodded at his statement, and to make me wait even more, he leaned in to kiss my lips passionately.

He held himself up with both hands next to my head while he pushed my legs apart to settle between them.

His tongue moved against mine, leaving me breathless.

I could feel the heat between my legs rise, which he must've noticed as well, as he moved his right hand down to my pussy, gently covering it with his palm.

Two of his fingers moved along my folds, feeling the wetness and then circling that sensitive little nub I played with before.

I didn't get anywhere with just my fingers, but on my eighteenth birthday, Evie thought it was a fun idea to let me open her present in front of everyone else and embarrass me with a box filled with sex toys.

Not that I didn't like the present, I just wished I didn't have to open it with all of our new friends from college staring at me.

They must've thought I was a sex fiend or something.

I was the total opposite.

Hence me using those sex toys by myself, without sharing them with my partner.

Anyway, my point was that I only ever reached a climax with the little vibrator that came in Evie's present, which was also the only toy I used frequently.

Wells's fingers were warm and gentle, and they kept circling my clit to stimulate that tingling sensation in my lower belly.

He wasn't teasing me on purpose, but it sure as hell felt that way.

A soft moan left me as he broke the kiss to look back into my eyes, and from that moment on, words weren't necessarily needed.

He lifted his hand and held his fingers right in front of my lips, and I quickly understood what he wanted me to do.

I opened my mouth and pulled his two fingers in, sucking and wetting them the way I did with his cock before.

While I did, his eyes moved to my lips to not miss it, and the way his own lips parted told me that he was enjoying this just as much as everything else we had done so far tonight.

"You're such a good girl," he whispered, his voice hoarse and low.

Before pulling his fingers out, he pushed down on my tongue to get the saliva that had built on it, wetting his fingers even more.

Then, to not let my saliva drip onto me, he quickly placed his fingers back on my clit and started circling it again.

"I'll make you come first," he told me, placing a kiss to my lips and looking back into my eyes shortly after.

My mouth was parted, and as stinging around my clit got more intense, I asked, "What about you?"

A smug grin tugged at the corner of his mouth. "I'll come inside this sweet pussy. God, Rooney, I can smell you from up here and I promise you I've never smelled anything this sweet before."

His words not only warmed my heart, but also made it pound hard.

I enjoyed seeing him like this, but I love his daddy-side just as much.

To not feel useless or selfish, I reached between us to wrap my hand around his shaft again, but when I noticed it was dry again after my blow job, I figured I would wet my hand as well before rubbing him.

Would probably feel better, right?

I lifted my hand again, and with his eyes on mine, I licked the palm of my hand and fingers before reaching back down and rubbing along his length.

"You sure you never did any of this before?" he asked, chuckling.

I shook my head and smiled.

Nice compliment.

"Just keep doing what you're doing. Feels so fucking good," he murmured as I brushed my thumb over his tip, the most sensitive spot.

I was trying my best not to close my eyes because I didn't wanna miss a thing that was happening, but as he moved his fingers faster, the tension inside of me built.

"Relax, Rooney. Can't make you come if you're all tense," he told me.

That was easy for him to say, but I knew once I relaxed, I'd get to my needed relief much quicker.

My breathing hitched as he stopped moving his fingers, and I looked at him with a deep frown, wondering why he would stop at that exact moment.

"Please don't stop, Wells," I begged, bucking my hips and trying to get his finger on my clit again.

But instead of doing what I asked for, he moved his hand away from my pussy.

A whine escaped me.

"I change my mind. I want to taste your sweetness when you come," he growled, moving down and between my legs, spreading them wider apart and immediately letting his tongue flick through my folds.

"Ah! Oh, God!" I moaned, grabbing fistfuls of his hair in my hands and pulling him closer to that sensitive spot.

I could feel him grin for a second, then he continued to pleasure me but with his tongue this time.

That felt *so* much better, and he sure knew how to do it right.

"Wells," I breathed, keeping my eyes on him before they forced themselves closed.

Darkness surrounded me, but the closer he pushed me to that climax, the more sparks were visible.

My hips started moving again, directing him to the exact spot on my clit which would make me spiral right out of control.

I was still trying to hold on to the intense feeling creeping up on me, starting from my toes which I so often felt when I made myself come, and shortly after, fireworks exploded all around me.

Wells

The taste of her pussy coming made me realize what I've been missing all these years.

Then again, I was a hundred percent sure there was no other woman out there who tasted as sweet as Rooney.

Her fluids flowed down between her folds mixed with my saliva, and I swallowed as much of it as possible, not getting enough of her.

When I moved up to look at her face, her eyes were still closed and her lips parted while trying to catch her breath.

I couldn't help myself, and with a cocky grin I said, "If this took your breath away, then I can't imagine what will happen when I fuck you."

As her eyes opened, her cheeks turned red immediately.

"This was the first time a man ever..."

"I know," I said, kissing the tip of her nose. "And I'm happy I'm your first."

I rubbed my dick while I adjusted between her spread legs, but before I could place my tip at her entrance, I decided it would be easier if she'd lie differently.

"Turn on your side, sweetheart," I told her, lifting her right leg and pulling it to the other side so her hips were sideways, but her back still flush against the mattress.

She didn't need to ask why, as her eyes already handled it for her.

"It'll be easier for me, and probably less uncomfortable for you this way," I said, brushing along her waist and hip, then moving my hand further down to cover her ass.

"You're beautiful, Rooney."

Her eyes were filled with the type of lust that just couldn't be ignored, and I would make it my goal to show her just how good it could feel, having me inside of her.

No idea how I managed to go without sex for almost four years, but it didn't feel right to sleep with random women I knew I wouldn't see a second time.

I was focused on being a dad, and Ira was my number one priority.

Always.

But as important as Ira was, I could already tell that this thing between Rooney and me would last longer than expected.

Well, I didn't expect much at first, thinking she was just my new neighbor who was sweet and kind to Ira and me.

Little did I know she would break that wall of security around my little family, nestle herself right next to my son and me, and close that wall back up again.

I wouldn't push her out, not while I kept feeling this desire for her inside of me.

Still unsure what it really was, so undisclosed was a very fitting word for Rooney's and my relationship.

I brushed my tip along her folds, wetting it to make it slide better and make it easier to push inside of her.

I looked up to see her hooded eyes on my hand, observing everything closely.

"I'll go slow. I want to make it feel good, so tell me to stop if I need to."

She gave me a quick nod, but it seemed as if she hadn't actually listened to what I said.

Her mind was set on having sex with me tonight.

Since she was ready, I pushed my tip against her entrance and it easily slid in slightly thanks to her wetness.

I stopped to not hit the thin barrier inside of her already, but as she moved her hips to adjust, my dick slid in further but stopped again as her tight walls stopped me from sliding in deeper.

A small frown appeared on her face, and I squeezed her hip gently with one hand while still holding on to the base of my dick.

"You okay?" I asked.

"Yes, it feels good," she said, her voice unsure at first. "Keep going," she then added with more determination this time.

I looked down again, thinking how amazing it felt to have her pussy wrapped around my dick, and with a quick, swift move, I pushed inside of her to break through the barrier.

A soft cry left her chest, but as I started to move to ease the pain or tension she was feeling from me burying myself deep inside of her, she relaxed again and smiled before letting her head fall back into the pillow.

"Fuck..." I growled, cupping her ass with one hand again and placing the other on her flat stomach.

"Feel good?" I asked to get the affirmation that I needed to move a little faster.

She nodded, smiling up at me and fully relaxing at last.

"It feels amazing," she replied, and that was enough for me to move my hips faster and fuck her rougher.

It wasn't everything I had to offer, but this was enough for now.

Leaning over her, I kept thrusting my hips while taking her lips again, kissing her deeply but keeping the focus on our bodies.

Her soft moans got louder as she had gotten used to my length burying deep inside of her, and I kept kissing her to ensure Ira wouldn't wake up from his dad and neighbor doing something strange in the bedroom.

Last thing I wanted was for him to be weirded out, but luckily, there was no sign of him awaking because of our moans and groans yet.

He'd call out to me first, so the chance of him walking in on us was low.

"Just like that, love. Keep squeezing me with that tight pussy," I muttered against her lips.

Not sure she realized she was doing that, but shortly after I said it, the squeezing stopped for a second only for her pussy to start pulsating.

I could feel she was close, so I kept fucking her fast and deep.

And from that moment on, it didn't take too long for my dick to start throbbing in the same rhythm as her pussy clenching around it.

That was it.

It was time for me to stop holding back and release myself inside of her the way I promised her.

Breaking the kiss but staying close to her face, I looked into her eyes and wrapped my fingers around her throat as the muscles in my body weakened just before my cum filled her pussy.

Uncontrollably at first, but I quickly got a hold of the orgasms' power to push the orgasm further and release more of what wanted to come out.

A low groan vibrated in my chest as I tried to keep quiet for Ira's sake, but it was hard controlling my body while the most beautiful girl in the world stared back at me, wide-eyed and pleased with what just happened.

And to make things even better, she started to circle her hips, silently trying to make me keep fucking her.

I chuckled at her enthusiastic need for more.

"Ready for round two already?" I asked, smirking.

She nodded, but just as I expected her to, she was out of breath.

"Fill your pretty lungs with oxygen first, love, and if you're not sore in a few minutes, we can go for round two," I told her.

She didn't reply, which was enough evidence that she was either trying to catch her breath or feeling sore already.

I leaned in to kiss her lips, then the tip of her nose and then her forehead.

"Let me clean you up. This won't be our last time."

"Promise?" she breathed.

The fact that she needed reassurance hit hard, but then, I would've felt the same if she hadn't already showed me that she wanted more.

"I promise, Rooney. Don't think I can ever say no to being buried deep inside of you again."

Chapter Twenty-Five

Rooney

As much as I enjoyed my first time with Wells, I was glad we didn't go for round two.

As I opened my eyes the next morning, I felt the soreness he was talking about last night, and every move of my legs made my pussy ache.

It felt good, but having him fuck me again would definitely hurt.

I stretched underneath the covers and yawned as I reached out behind me to find out if Wells was still in bed with me or not.

Ira woke up early, at least that's what he told me, and I'm sure Wells would be up whenever he was too.

I didn't know what time it was though, and the rain outside hid the sun and made it hard for me to guess how long I've slept.

Wells was still next to me, yet he was lying there with his back turned to me.

That was unusual for us, as he would always cuddle me and still hold me the way he did when we fell asleep.

Not this morning though.

I turned around to look at him, and I soon found out why his arms weren't around me.

Ira had crawled into bed next to him, and to ensure him not falling off, Wells held him close to his chest.

They were both asleep, so I decided not to wake them and let them rest while I cleaned up what we had left standing around in the kitchen last night and maybe start on breakfast.

I carefully got out of bed and put on my sweatpants before walking around the bed to get to the door where I stopped to look at the two of them again.

Ira was lying on his back with his face buried in Wells's chest, and Wells had one arm above Ira's head while the other was wrapped around his body.

They looked adorable all cuddled up, so I pushed the door open to get out of the bedroom and walk down the hall to the bathroom.

After freshening up a little, I headed to the kitchen and brewed coffee, then cleaned up around the kitchen and living room, just so Wells wouldn't have to deal with it later.

He had cleaned up after himself and Ira too many times already.

I had left my phone on the kitchen counter last night, and when I picked it up to check who had messaged me, AJ's name was the only one I saw.

I sighed and rolled my eyes even before reading his messages, but after what happened that night in my room, I knew it wasn't just to check in with me and ask how I was doing.

I tapped on the message he sent first and opened it to read it, and it was already leaving a bad taste in my mouth without ever having to say it.

I'm fucking Dana because I can't have you.

At least she's into guys her age.

I hope it's worth fucking that older guy.

The messages were sent last night at three fifty-six a.m., and all I could think of was, *he must've been very, very drunk.*

I sighed again, this time much heavier than before, and because I couldn't let this slip like a normal person, I replied to those three very offensive messages.

That's not very kind, Aiden. Even when you're drunk.

I put my phone away and poured myself a cup of coffee, then sat down on the couch and pulled my legs close to my body to get some comfort after reading those horrible things.

How dare he?

We were done a long time ago, he made a mistake to come close to me without my permission, and now he was trying to make me jealous or whatever it was he was doing by sending me shit like that.

Not acceptable.

I took a few sips of my coffee and tried to get my mind off AJ, and to my luck, Ira walked around the corner and into the kitchen with his bare feet and Superman pajamas.

"Good morning, little man. You're up early," I said, keeping my voice low.

He nodded and rubbed his eyes with both fists, then came over to the couch to stand in front of me.

"Is daddy still asleep?" I asked, brushing my hand through his blond locks to tame them.

It didn't work, but I liked his wild look.

Just like Wells's.

He nodded again.

He wasn't much of a talker early in the morning, but then, I didn't blame him.

It was almost seven-thirty.

His eyes moved to my coffee cup, and I smiled as he kept them there with his lips parted.

"Would you like to drink something?" I asked, not trusting myself with food around him because I wasn't sure what he could and couldn't have.

"Water please?"

"All right. Let me get you a cup." I smiled at him and got up from the couch to put my coffee down, and as I walked over to the kitchen, he climbed onto the couch and stared at the black TV screen.

Not sure if he wanted to watch something, but I thought I'd ask.

"Would you like to watch something on TV or play with your toys until daddy wakes up?"

I brought the cup of water back to him and he took it out of my hands to drink a few sips.

"I wanna watch TV," he said, his little voice soft and sweet.

"Do you have a favorite cartoon you like to watch?"

I sat back next to him and grabbed the remote to turn on the TV as he shook his head and shrugged.

"Hm, we'll find something," I promised him, and sure enough, cartoons I watched when I was his age popped up on the screen.

"Looney Tunes! Do you know them?" I asked, looking at him as he was already fully focused.

He gave me a quick nod, then pointed at the screen and said, "It's Bugs Bunny!"

"Yeah, that is him!" I replied, smiling and somewhat proud that a kid these days still knew who Bugs Bunny was.

I grabbed my coffee again and took a few sips to finish it, then placed the cup back on the coffee table again to get more comfortable on the couch.

Then, Ira did the sweetest thing which surprised me but warmed my heart.

He moved closer to me, pushed his thumb into his mouth and rested his head on my lap before pushing his other hand into his hair to twirl his locks around his fingers.

I've seen him do this before, but he was looking for comfort while comforting himself, and I thought that was the most adorable thing ever.

I smiled and placed my hand on his side, letting him cuddle up to me without having to ask me for permission.

This little boy could do whatever he wanted and I would allow him into my personal space.

It was the best feeling knowing that he trusted me even without Wells around, and I knew Wells trusted me around Ira too.

So, without having to worry about anything, we watched cartoons, talking to each other occasionally.

Conversations with kids were never forced, and should never be, so it was okay for Ira to be silent more than not.

Wells

Seeing them cuddled up on the couch watching cartoons with each other was the most adorable sight I had seen in a long time.

It was always clear to me that Ira liked Rooney, but I would've never imagined them being this close this soon.

More because of Ira, but he didn't seem to have a problem spending time alone with Rooney.

I smiled as I observed them from the kitchen, and when I walked up to them, Rooney turned her head to look up at me with a smile.

"Good morning," she greeted me. "Sleep well?"

"Yeah, a little too well. You should've woken me," I told her, leaning down to kiss her forehead.

Ira was still focusing on the TV, and I smiled knowing he was okay and enjoying this slow morning.

"Hey, buddy," I said as I sat down next to Rooney, and when he finally tore his gaze off the screen, he pushed himself up and crawled over her lap to get to me.

"We're watching Looney Tunes," he told me, pointing at the screen and sitting on my lap facing the TV.

"I see that. Have you had a nice morning with Rooney?"

He nodded, and I kissed the back of his head before looking at her with a smile.

"Have you guys been up for long?"

"About an hour. I was up first, then he walked in and asked to watch something on TV. I hope that's okay," she said.

"Of course. I'm sorry about him sneaking into my bed. I'm still trying to find a way to get him to sleep in his own bed through the night."

"Oh, no, don't worry about that, Wells," she said with a smile, lifting her arm and placing it behind me on the back of the couch, then she pushed her fingers into my hair gently.

Good.

Because I didn't think I was ready to walk Ira back to his own bed after he crawls into mine.

"How are you feeling?" I asked, looking down at her thighs before meeting her eyes again.

She sucked in her cheeks, then smiled and shrugged. "A little sore. Last night was amazing."

"No regrets?"

"Not a single one," she replied, leaning in and kissing my lips quickly. "I made coffee. Would you like a cup?"

"Sounds good. I'll make breakfast a little later. You're not hungry yet, right, bud?"

Ira turned his head to look up at me and shake his head at my question. "But can I have my Hulk juice, please?" he requested in the most mannerly way possible.

"Of course you can."

I picked him up and sat him down on the couch next to me so I could get up with Rooney, and when we both reached the kitchen, she filled two cups with coffee while I pulled out all the fruits and veggies I always used for the juice.

"Would you like some too? I think I'm gonna make some for me as well," I told her.

"Thank you, but I'll stick to the coffee for now. Did you plan anything for today?" she asked, leaning against the counter next to me and watching me slice the veggies small enough to fit in the blender.

"I was hoping to take Ira to the park, but it's raining, and I thought we'd go to the indoor playground. Would you like to come?" I asked, hoping she would say yes.

"I told you I wanted to spend the weekend with you two. Of course I'm gonna come," she replied with a smile.

"Perfect. I might ask Ira if he wants to invite his little friend. Probably more fun that way," I said.

She nodded as she took a sip of her coffee, and after I put everything into the blender and she had placed her cup on the counter, I leaned over to kiss her lips.

I deepened the kiss quickly after and placed my hand on her cheek to pull her closer, and she came willingly with her hands on my naked chest.

It felt good seeing her still here after last night, but it wasn't like I was scared of her leaving in the morning.

She wasn't a one-night stand, and the promise I made about last night not being the last time we had sex was one I would keep.

As the blender stopped, I broke the kiss to look at her. "I love having you here with us."

Those were simple words, but they meant so much to me.

To her as well, as her eyes brightened and her smile got bigger.

"I love being here with you," she whispered, brushing along my chest with her thumb and then stepped away to let me get to the blender.

I'd keep her here forever if I could, but it was too early.

Though, she had already brought her second toothbrush to keep next to mine in my bathroom, which I thought was cute.

"Let's cuddle up for a little while longer on the couch, then we can decide if we wanna have breakfast before heading out, okay?"

She nodded, grabbing both coffee cups as I held Ira's and my smoothie to take to the living room.

Today would be a fun day, even if it rained outside.

Chapter Twenty-Six

Rooney

"Ah, there they are," Wells said as a man with his toddler walked toward us.

We had already entered the indoor playground and waited for Ira's little friend to arrive by the parents' seating area.

Wells had called the boy's father to invite them here, and he happily agreed to bring his son to play.

I liked knowing Wells wasn't completely alone, but he has his mother close and other parents around who he could rely on.

"Benny!" Ira called out as he saw his friend, and as if they couldn't get any cuter, they ran toward each other and hugged.

It was slightly awkward, but they were small, so what would you expect?

"Hey, man," Wells said, greeting the guy with a handshake. "Rooney, this is Grant," he said, stepping aside to let me say hi to Grant.

"Hi, nice to meet you," I said with a smile, holding out my hand.

He shook it and nodded, looking rather serious but also a little stressed. "Nice to meet you too, Rooney. I'm guessing you're not Ira's babysitter," he said with a smug grin.

I chuckled and shook my head, but it was Wells who replied. "Don't mess with her," he told Grant jokingly, then he looked at Ira and his friend.

"Ira, say hello to Grant."

He turned around to look up at him, and after a quick wave, Benny did the same to greet us.

We said hello back, but it was clear that neither of them were up to talk any more.

"You two play nice, all right? No pushing other kids and always be kind. And stay together," Grant told Ira and Benny, and both nodded while they held each other's hand, ready to run out onto the playground together.

There were students working here to make sure no kid got hurt, so we could sit here and observe from afar while they took care of the children.

Wells got down on eye-level with Ira and pulled up his shirt to check on his pump which he had around his neck instead of clipped to the waistband of his pants, making it easier and more comfortable for Ira to run around.

"Remember to come take a sip of water every once in a while, okay, buddy? We'll be right here."

Wells was more the protective type of dad, while Grant couldn't seem to wait until they ran off so he could have a little quiet time.

It was amusing, but I didn't let him notice.

"Okay. Can we play now?" Ira asked, pushing his dad off but in the sweetest way possible.

He chuckled, kissed his forehead and nodded. "Go have fun."

Their first destination was the double slide with the ball pit on the end, and we stood there for a second just to make sure they made it up safely, then we sat down at a table.

"You're still in college," Grant said as his dark eyes studied my face.

He was handsome, probably Wells's age, but the total opposite when it came to his looks.

He had jet black hair, which Benny had too, and his beard was thicker than Wells's stubble which made Grant look more mysterious than he already seemed.

"Yes, I'm an art student and in my junior year at Central College," I told him. "What do you do?"

I wanted to know more about him just to prove that he wasn't as strict and serious as he seemed to be.

"I'm a firefighter," he said, keeping his answer short and direct.

"That's amazing," I told him with a smile.

Wells must've noticed me trying to keep this conversation going as he placed his hand on my thigh and squeezed gently.

"Yeah, it is. But it's fucking stressful. Wish I could go a damn day without feeling this way. Still don't know shit about what it's like to have a calm and fulfilling life."

His grumpiness was somewhat intriguing.

I didn't blame him for the way that he was, because we all had our own problems to deal with, but as hard as I was trying to enjoy his presence, his darkness was making it difficult for me.

I had only just met him, so there was still time for me to warm up to him.

"Grant's a single dad too. His ex, Benny's mother, has him every other weekend," Wells explained.

"And let me tell you, to this day, I have no fucking clue how he does it, working and being a father twenty-four seven."

I smiled.

I knew how hard Wells worked, and the way he cared for Ira was incredible.

"He's great," I said, looking at Wells with a smile.

"Grant's just making his life sound worse than it actually is. Don't believe every word he says," he told me with a wink.

Grant let out a harsh laugh and shook his head, leaning back against the chair and getting more comfortable.

"You two are a thing, huh? Never thought I'd see him date again. How did you meet?"

"I moved in with my best friend who happens to live an apartment above Wells," I explained, and Grant raised a brow.

"That girl still living in there? Thought she'd be out of there quicker with all that money her parents have."

Understandable, and also interesting that he knew who Evie was.

"Do you know her?" I asked.

"I know her parents. Been invited to one of their country club galas a while ago after we managed to stop a fire from destroying one of their new apartment complexes. It was still a construction site, but some teenagers thought it'd be funny to start a fire one night."

"I see. Well, their galas are nice, aren't they?"

"Sure, lots of free booze and hot chicks in tight dresses, but still not a scene I would wanna hang around for more than one night," he told me.

A waitress came up to our table and smiled with a notepad in her hand, asking what we'd like to drink.

Since it was a kid-friendly place, they didn't serve any alcohol, so they both ordered a Coke and two glasses of water for the kids, and I asked for a homemade iced tea, as everything else was too sugary.

We continued to talk, but it soon turned into Wells and Grant talking about work and all kinds of things I didn't know much about.

I found out that they met in college and met again years later in this town, even though neither of them lived here before.

It was a coincidence, and although they didn't hang out much, Ira and Benny brought them closer together again.

"Did Chastity send you the invite to her next get together?" Grant asked.

Wells's hand was still on my thigh, and I had placed mine over his, brushing over it to show him affection.

The way I did it best.

"Yeah, I got her message. Not sure Ira and I will attend yet. He's getting a new pump soon, and I want him to adjust to it before he goes wild."

"Let me know if you decide to go," Grant said, taking a sip of his Coke and moving his eyes to mine. "Have you always been into older guys?" he asked.

He was straight forward, which wasn't a problem at all, but I did feel my cheeks heat up a little thanks to his very alpha-like attitude.

"Uh, I never really had a type, so I guess age was never something that mattered," I told him.

He nodded, grinning at Wells and shaking his head. "Lucky bastard."

"Yeah, I definitely am," Wells said, grinning at me.

I laughed softly and squeezed his hand, thinking I was just as lucky.

"Daddy!" Benny was running toward us with a big grin on his face, resembling his father's quite a bit.

"What's up?" Grant asked as Benny reached him. "I went on the big slide and it went down like this!" he exclaimed, holding up his hand and gesturing how steep the slide was.

"I don't believe you," Grant said sarcastically, smiling at his son. "That steep?"

Benny looked at him with wide eyes. "Yes! Ira did it too!"

Wells frowned at that, looking like he knew Ira wouldn't usually go for a slide like that.

He looked around to see if he could see Ira anywhere, then he turned to look at Benny.

"Where is Ira?"

"I don't know," Benny shrugged.

"We told you to stay together and not run away from each other, Benny," Grant said, sighing and shooting Wells an apologetic look.

Benny was the wild one in the friendship, that's for sure.

Wells got up and let go of my hand. "I'll go see if I can find him," he said, and I immediately got up to go with him and help while Grant continued to explain the rules to Benny again.

"I'm sure he's okay," I told him, keeping my voice soft and calm.

"Yeah, but I hate knowing he's wandering around here somewhere all by himself."

Totally understandable.

We walked past the slides and monkey bars, checking every single corner until we stopped by an archway with stickers of all kinds of fictional characters around it.

Inside, there was a room with tables and chairs for kids to sit at and play with Legos and playdough, and in the far left corner, there was Ira sitting all by himself with his back turned to us.

A relieved sigh escaped Wells, and after smiling up at him, we walked toward Ira to check on him.

"Hey, buddy. What are you doing here all by yourself?" Wells asked, squatting down to be closer to him.

Ira turned his head, and after taking one look at him, it was clear that he had been crying.

"Oh, bud. What happened?"

Wells pulled him into his arms and Ira let go of the two little Lego figures to hug his dad.

I watched Wells rub Ira's back to comfort him, and although he still looked sad, he didn't cry again.

"Benny said you went on the big slide. Is that why you're sad? Did it scare you a little?" he asked.

Ira nodded and pouted, picking at Wells's sweatshirt with his little fingers.

"You know you don't have to go on things that you aren't sure about, hm?" He put both hands on Ira's waist to make him step back and look into his eyes. "But I'm proud of you for trying and sliding down the slide. That's very brave of you, Ira."

I loved the way Wells talked to him.

So gentle and kind, not too harsh but still in a way that would make Ira listen.

"It was the green slide," Ira told him.

"Wanna show me which one and then we can go drink and eat something?" Wells suggested.

"Yes, please!"

"All right, come here." He picked him up to carry him, and before we started walking, Ira smiled at me sweetly.

"It's a fun place, huh? There's so much to see here," I said, rubbing his arm.

"I saw a dinosaur!" he announced, the sadness in his eyes gone already.

"You did? Was it big?" I asked enthusiastically.

"That big!" He held his hand above Wells's head to show how tall the dinosaur was, and we chuckled at his wide-eyed expression.

We walked out of the Lego area and walked past the dinosaur, then the green slide he went down on.

"You can be so proud of yourself for sliding down there, Ira. You've been very brave," Wells told him, kissing his cheek.

"But I was sad," he replied, pouting again and looking at his dad.

"And that's okay. But after you feel sad, you can feel happy for what you've done. Next time, don't cry but smile and say *I did it!* to yourself."

Ira thought about it for a while, then he nodded and threw his fist in the air. "I did it!"

Wells grinned and nodded. "Yeah, you did! You can do anything and don't let anyone tell you any differently, okay? And remember that it's okay to say no to things if you're unsure about them."

"Okay."

Pleased with Ira's response, we walked back to the table to sit down with Grant and Benny again, and while Ira drank his water, we looked at the menu to see if there was anything that sounded good.

Wells checked Ira's pump to figure out if he could eat something sugary.

Since he had been running around the past hour, I was positive that he could use some of the energy that could be found in sweets.

"Ira, would you like carrot cake or apple pie?" Wells asked.

That was a very hard decision for him to make as he didn't often get to eat dessert.

After a while, he still couldn't decide, so Wells suggested to take a slice of both to share.

That was a great idea.

"What would you like?" he asked me, placing his hand on my thigh again.

"I think I'll have some apple pie as well," I told him.

He gave me a quick nod and leaned in to kiss my temple before lifting his hand to get the waitress's attention.

While he told her our order, I moved my gaze to Grant who had been watching me closely, and I smiled at him to hopefully get him to stop.

It wasn't bothering me, but it was starting to get too intense for me that I had to look away.

Not sure what he wanted from me, but it was clear that he had a thing for girls my age as he also checked out the waitress as she walked away.

Well, I wasn't on the market anymore, but even if, I didn't think Grant and I were a match anyway.

Chapter Twenty-Seven

Wells

I didn't miss the looks Grant shot in Rooney's direction, as if he was ready to strip her down and show her a good time the way he did with other women he barely knew.

In the dictionary, under the word womanizer, you'd find a picture of Grant's face.

But it was clear that Rooney didn't give him one second of her time after noticing his looks too, and she kept smiling at me to assure me she wasn't going to fall for Grant's *whatever he was doing*.

It was getting late in the afternoon and Ira was already tired, ready to head back home.

Although he was a kid with lots of energy, Benny was far more active, so Grant decided to stay for a while longer until his son was worn out.

We said goodbye to them, and as Grant hugged Rooney, I kept my eyes on his hands to make sure he wouldn't move them further down from where they were on her lower back.

Luckily for him, he didn't try and make a move and let go of her quickly.

He'll find his next girl to fuck and send home the next morning.

I was sure of that.

On the car ride home, Ira fell asleep in his car seat and I carried him upstairs while Rooney walked behind me holding his Hulk figures Ira took with him on the car ride.

"I'll have to wake him soon for dinner. You'll eat with us, right?" I asked her as we stopped in front of my door.

She nodded and took the keys out of my hand to unlock the door for me. "I'll go change upstairs and then be right back."

She stood on her tiptoes to kiss my cheek, then she pushed open the door to make it easier for me to head inside, and once I did, I smiled at her.

"Don't be too long," I said before she walked upstairs.

Once inside, I walked into Ira's bedroom and put him down carefully.

I checked his insulin pump to check what kind of food he needed, then I headed back outside and into the kitchen.

Weekends with Rooney were starting to become a habit, something I couldn't say no to anymore, even if weekends were usually just for Ira and me to spend time together.

But how could I not let Rooney in if she was taking up most of my thoughts every day?

I was starting to really like her, and after last night, there was no way I could ever push her away from me.

Though, the thought of being in a relationship was scaring the shit out of me.

I didn't want to commit to something if there was the possibility of losing or hurting her, and I had to keep Ira in mind as well.

If he'd get even more attached, and things didn't work out the way I wished it would, it wouldn't be easy for him to let go of Rooney.

His heart needed protection, especially because of him never having a motherly figure in his life.

The other thing that was starting to come up in my head more often was the day he'd finally ask about his mommy.

Until now, he never questioned why his friends had moms but he didn't.

The older he got, the harder it would be to make him understand what happened at his birth, but telling an almost four-year-old that his mother died after giving birth to him didn't sound like something any kid that age would take well.

Making up a story wasn't an option either.

I'd find a way to explain it all to him, as soon as he was ready and asked about it.

I started on dinner and only half an hour later, Rooney walked into the apartment.

"My mom called me. She asked if I wanted to go visit them on the ranch in two weeks over the weekend," she told me, leaning next to me against the counter.

"Sounds fun," I said, smiling at her.

"Yeah, so I told her I would bring someone to meet her and dad."

She pressed her lips into a thin line to keep a grin from spreading across her face, and I raised a brow before realizing where she was going with this.

"You wanna introduce me to your parents?" I asked.

"Yes. Now that I met your mom, I think it's only fair to let you meet mine. If you're okay with it," she said, puckering her lips now. "Is it a bad idea?"

"No, I think it's sweet you want me to meet your parents. I'd love to come," I told her, smiling.

"Really?"

I chuckled. "You look surprised."

"Well, I didn't think you'd agree this quickly," she told me with a shrug. "Thought you'd have to think about it first."

I put the wooden spoon down I was using to stir the tomato sauce for the pasta and turned to look at her.

"Rooney, haven't I made it clear last night that I want you?" I asked, not able to stop myself from grinning.

"You did. The soreness between my legs reminds me of it every time I take a step."

"Then you shouldn't be surprised to find out that I wanna meet your family. Besides, Ira loves animals, so I know he'll love the ranch."

She smiled brightly and put both arms around my neck to come closer, and I held her tight to my body with my hands on her lower back.

"You'll both love it. I'm not a country girl, but I do enjoy nature, and the ranch has so much to offer. Mom and Dad hired two people to do tours of all the animals they have, and I'm sure they'll have one when we're there."

"Can't wait," I whispered, leaning in to kiss her lips.

Her hands moved into my hair, gripping them gently and deepening the kiss as I opened up to her.

Her tongue brushed against mine, and I let her explore my mouth until I had to turn my attention back to the pot so nothing would start to burn.

"We'll have plenty of time to kiss after dinner. Save your energy for later," I told her with a grin.

She laughed softly and stepped away from me. "Got enough of that."

"Good. Don't think I will hold back tonight," I promised with a wink.

Her cheeks turned red and she quickly turned away to start setting the table.

She wasn't a virgin anymore, but my choice of words made her squirm and shudder every damn time.

It was the sweetest thing ever, and I hoped the more times we had sex it wouldn't disappear.

I felt my dick twitch in my pants while I did the simple task of cooking pasta, but her presence was what teased me without her even saying a word.

I needed to take a quick break before we started to eat, and I told her I would go wake up Ira to have dinner with us.

When I walked into his bedroom, he was already awake but still lying in bed with his arms covering his face.

"Hey, buddy. Did you have a good nap?" I asked, sitting down at the edge of his bed.

He moved his arms to look up at me, then he nodded and reached for me with both hands.

I pulled him to me, making him sit up and wrap his arms around my neck, and I put my arms around him as well to cuddle him and kiss his head.

"Daddy made dinner. Wanna come eat with Rooney and me?" I asked.

"Okay."

I got up with him still in my arms as he wrapped his legs around me to hold himself up, and as we walked toward the kitchen, I started to tell him about the weekend we would spend at a ranch.

"Rooney's mom and dad have a ranch with lots of animals, and we're gonna see them soon. How does that sound?" I asked, kissing his cheek before entering the kitchen.

"I like animals," he told me, still sleepy from the short nap.

"Hello, little guy," Rooney greeted him with a smile and Ira looked at her and waved.

"I like animals," he repeated to make sure Rooney heard him, then he proceeded to reach for his water once he was sitting in his chair.

"Oh, I know you do. The zoo was fun, huh? We have different animals at the ranch, like cows and horses," Rooney told him.

Ira's eyes widened. "Can we ride the horses?"

"Sure! And you can also feed and brush them. It's gonna be lots of fun," she promised.

I smiled at her and filled our plates with pasta and sauce, then I sat down myself to start eating.

Yes, Rooney definitely wasn't going to leave my side for a long while.

Rooney

Last night, after Ira went back to bed, there wasn't much talking that Wells and I did.

After doing the dishes and heading straight to bed, our second time having sex was even hotter than our first, but the stinging in my pussy as he thrusted in and out of me did hurt more than the first time.

It wasn't painful, but I had to get used to the burning sensation before I could fully enjoy his hard way of fucking.

He really didn't show mercy in bed, which of course was okay with me.

I was starting to like having sex, and I was excited for the next time we'd see each other again.

I left his apartment a few minutes ago as I had to finish up Ira's painting and make sure I had everything ready for my classes next week, so after saying hi to Evie, I went into my room to finish my work.

It was eight p.m. and since I had dinner at Wells's, I could focus on my things for the rest of the evening.

If only AJ wouldn't have interrupted my plans.

"Hello, Rooney," he said, startling me.

He hadn't said anything about coming by, and Evie didn't mention it either, so I shot him a dirty look when I turned to look up at him.

"Why are you here?" I asked, my brows raised.

He shrugged. "Wanted to come visit Evie. Thought I'd make sure you know I'm here," he said, sounding cockier than usual.

I didn't like this side of him, and I was still not sure where it had come from.

"Okay, thanks."

I turned back around to continue drawing Ira's birthday present which I thought looked amazing but was missing a few details.

"Marvel fan now?" he asked, coming closer and basically invading my privacy.

"It's a present," I muttered, trying to stay calm and kind. "And it's not just Marvel," I pointed out as there were superheroes on here from different universes.

"Right. I guess I deserve the way you are toward me after those texts I sent you."

No shit.

"They were unnecessary. But you were drunk, so I guess it's okay to blame it on the alcohol," I said, rolling my eyes but not looking back at him.

"Never blamed it on the alcohol. It was stupid and I admit it. But I still think this between us could've turned out differently. Seeing as you are still dating that guy."

His words were slowly making me lose my patience, which I'd rather keep or else I couldn't finish this detailing on the painting.

I set my brush down on the plastic underneath the painting to ensure my carpet wouldn't get painted on, then I turned to look at AJ with a frown.

"Do you really wanna continue to argue over this? Because I don't have the time or motivation for it. We've been over it, Aiden. More than once. So if you could just let me be, I'd be very thankful."

He stood there with his arms crossed over his chest and his eyes set on mine.

"What if I don't feel as if we have talked this out?"

"Then you didn't listen the first time and agreed on us being friends without meaning it. Besides, it looks like you've moved on from me, since you've been hanging out with Dana for the past few weeks. Or are you just using her to make me jealous?"

He laughed and shook his head. "I don't need to make you jealous."

"Then why are you rubbing your relationship or whatever you have with her in my face? I don't care about her, but you obviously feel like you need to keep harassing me with your toxic behavior."

I might've been a little harsh there, but that's how I felt and I didn't wanna spend more time on him if it didn't get any better.

"Have you ever liked me, Rooney?" he asked, his voice lower and softer now.

Jesus, was he on something?

"If you can't answer that question yourself, then you might wanna rethink this whole thing you're doing, whatever it is. You wouldn't be here if you knew the answer."

"Then why are you getting mad if I wanna talk to you about us?"

"Because I don't see a point in talking, AJ! We broke things off, I moved on, and then met someone new. Why can't you accept that we will never be a thing again? We tried, we didn't feel things were going somewhere, and that's still the way I feel."

We were both quiet for a while, but he still didn't look like he was done here. So before he spoke, I got up from the floor and stepped closer to him to place my hand on his upper arm.

"You're a really nice guy, Aiden. You're kind and smart, and this isn't you. I've said this before but if you need to hear it once more, I'll tell you again," I said, letting out a heavy sigh. "We can't be more than friends."

He studied my face while I hoped to finally get it into his mind that we were nothing more than friends.

In the end, I really liked him, and it would be a shame to lose him.

"God, why can't you two just stop fighting? I told you not to go in there," Evie said, her voice annoyed.

I looked past AJ to see her standing by the door, then I took a step back and looked at Aiden again.

"We're not fighting. Just talking things out," he said.

Wait, did he finally realize how ridiculous his messages and words were?

"We're friends," he added.

I smiled at him, and a heavy weight lifted from my shoulders.

"I don't care what you are as long as you stop arguing. It's annoying, and I asked you here to help me with the light fixture in my room, not to come bother Rooney."

"Friends," I said to him, and he nodded with a smile.

Although he agreed, I knew it still bothered him that he didn't get anything more out of this.

But my heart was slowly opening up to someone, and I had to take care of it to not get hurt.

Men.

They only ever complicate things.

Chapter Twenty-Eight

Wells

Kids birthday parties were insanely wild, and not even students at college parties could get to the level of excitement these kids were feeling right now.

Ira was four, and he was having the time of his life with almost all of his friends tonight.

Out of the eleven kids invited, only one couldn't make it due to having the flu, but other than that, all six boys and five girls were playing together, sharing toys, dancing and laughing with each other.

I went to check on them in the living room where I had pushed the couch back against the wall to give them more space, then put all of Ira's toys he wanted to play with from his room in the middle of the living room for everyone to enjoy.

I squatted down next to Ira who was playing with Sia and Waylon and tapped his shoulder to get his attention.

"Are you having fun with your friends, bud?" I asked, brushing through his thick, blond locks.

He smiled brightly at me and nodded.

"That's good! How about you tell everyone to come sit at the table? Your birthday cake is ready. You can blow out the candles," I told him, almost not able to keep in my emotions because my boy was getting so damn big.

"Cake!" he called out, then told Sia and Waylon first before getting up and running to his next friends.

I chuckled and let Sia take my hand. She was a little shy as her family had moved here only a few weeks ago and she still had to get to know everyone, but she was determined to sleep over like everyone else.

"Do you like carrot cake, Sia?" I asked as I helped her up onto a chair.

I had expanded the kitchen table so all eleven kids would fit. They had already eaten lunch together, which went pretty smoothly also thanks to Rooney talking and helping the kids.

"Yes," she responded quietly.

"You're gonna get a big slice then," Rooney told her, turning her head to look at her and smile.

I watched as more and more kids came to the table to sit down, and once everyone was seated, I dimmed the lights and started to sing Happy Birthday to Ira.

Rooney and soon all the kids started singing with me, and I stood behind Ira while Rooney placed the cake with four candles on it in front of him.

She had found a recipe which was sugar free, but still ended up sweet for the kids to enjoy.

It was Ira's choice to get a carrot cake for his birthday, but since we had eleven kids hoping for chocolate and other sweets, I went to Divine to get a few muffins and brownies.

They were sugar free as well, but I had to make sure Ira wouldn't eat too much.

Poor bud.

Can't even enjoy all the food he wants on his birthday.

But Ira wasn't bothered by it.

"*Happy Birthday to you!*" we sang in unison, and I kissed Ira's temple and whispered, "Make a wish, buddy!"

He scrunched up his nose and thought about his wish before blowing out the candles.

"That's a pretty cake," I heard one of the girls say.

I looked up to see Bethy, the oldest out of the bunch who was already six, stare at the cake wide-eyed.

"It is, huh? Rooney made it."

Bethy looked at Rooney with excitement dancing in her eyes. "Can you give the recipe to my mom?" she asked, making us both chuckle.

She sounded like a teenager already, but she was very sweet with the younger kids.

"Of course! I'll write it down and give it to her tomorrow morning," Rooney told her.

Once every kid had a slice, they ate and kept talking about this and that and making plans about what they would play with next.

"They're loving it," I told Rooney as I stepped next to her and leaned against the counter.

"I'm glad they do! They're all adorable. I thought that this many kids would mean trouble, but they're all playing nicely with each other.

Luckily.

"They're all having a good time. Thank you for helping me out," I said.

"Of course! It's fun, and I couldn't have let you do this on your own. You deserve a break sometime, you know?"

I laughed and reached for her hand to pull it up and kiss the back of it before locking our fingers. "Yeah, I know. But it's hard to look away when Ira experiences new things. I love seeing the joy in his eyes."

She nodded and leaned against me for a moment before she let go of my hand and turned around to cut another slice of cake.

"Here, you gotta try some too."

I took the plate from her and took a bite of it. "It's delicious, Rooney. Thanks for taking the time to bake and everything. I know how busy you've been the past week."

"It's fine, really. I'm done with all of my assignments and I have no tests next week."

I nodded and took another bite. "That's good. Ira is just as excited as I am to go to the ranch. It's still on, right?" I asked.

"Of course! If you get off work early we can head there Friday afternoon. It's a one hour drive to the ranch," she told me.

"I'll make sure I'm home by four."

"Wells?" Sia was walking up to us with her empty plate in her hands.

"Yes, darling?" I bent down to hear her clearer over the sound of the other kids and took the plate out of her hands.

"I have to pee," she said, her voice quiet and soft.

I smiled, then pointed at Rooney as I thought she'd be more fitted for this in case she didn't feel too comfortable with me helping her to the toilet.

"Rooney will show you to the bathroom, okay?"

Sia nodded and reached for Rooney's hand, and just at the sight of her holding a little girl's hand made my heart melt all over again.

I could see her being a mother.

It came naturally to her, but I had to stop thinking so far ahead.

I had yet to meet her parents, and although not much time had passed ever since we first met, I could tell that this weekend on the ranch would only push us closer together.

"Anyone want some more iced tea?" I asked the kids as I stepped up to the table, and a few of them called out to me for more.

I filled their cups, then walked over to Ira to check in on him.

"Did you enjoy the cake?"

"Yes, it was good," he replied, looking up at me with joyful eyes.

"When can I open my presents, Daddy?"

"Let's wait until Sia is back from the bathroom and then you can start opening your gifts, okay?"

He nodded and got down from the chair before running back into the living room.

His friends followed him, and while we waited for Rooney to get back with Sia, I started to put all the presents onto the coffee table in front of the pushed back couch.

"Ira can sit on the throne," Bethy suggested as she helped me get all the presents without me having to ask her for help onto the coffee table.

"That's right! Opening presents is fun, huh?"

"Yes, and I got to open mine already because my birthday was in April."

I knew that, as Ira was invited to her birthday this year.

"Ira, you can sit here!" she then called out, pointing at the couch.

He came running toward us and crawled up on the couch, then he smiled at me and said, "Can I open Rooney's first? It's the biggest!"

"No, you have to save that for last, Ira! It's gonna be more fun that way!" Bethy suggested, making Ira quickly change his mind.

I chuckled and handed him the first one as Rooney walked back into the room with Sia.

Rooney

Ira was opening his presents while all the kids sat in front of him, excitedly watching what he got.

Every toy was fun and different, making Ira smile at each one of them, but I was positive that none were as great as the gift Wells gave him to open this morning.

A Hulk costume.

A full-body one, I might add.

He had worn it all morning, but before his friends started to arrive, he took it off because it was getting too hot inside.

Once all the presents were opened, Wells helped me put the painting I made on the ground, and all the kids sat around it as Ira ripped the wrapping paper to shreds.

"Woah!" one kid said as the others admired the colorful work of art in front of them.

"Holy shit," Wells whispered, letting out a laugh afterward. "You actually painted this?"

"Yeah, looks good, huh?"

I was proud of myself as I spent hours perfecting it for Ira, and Wells nodded with his eyes glued on the canvas.

"It's incredible, love! Look at Ira, he's mesmerized," he said with a chuckle.

Ira's lips were parted and his finger carefully brushed along the painted surface.

"Do you like it, buddy?" Wells asked, and he quickly nodded, still not able to talk.

"Did you paint it?" Bethy asked, seeing as she was the most talkative kid around here.

"I did, yes. Do you like to draw and paint?"

"Not really, but my mom likes to. Maybe you can be her friend," she suggested.

I laughed softly and rubbed her back. "Sounds great, Bethy."

Ira got up while some kids already turned to play with something else and others kept admiring my work and pointing at the superheroes they recognized.

I sat down on the couch and let him hug me tightly. "Thank you, Rooney," he said, his manners never lacking.

"You're so welcome, Ira. We can hang it up in your room tomorrow, okay?"

He looked at me and nodded, then turned his head to gaze up at Wells and pointed at the painting.

"I got all superheroes!" he announced.

"It's amazing, huh? Rooney's a great artist," he said, brushing the back of my head.

God, these two held my heart.

How could I ever stay away from them?

The rest of the afternoon and evening was spent watching a movie of Ira's choice, eating dinner, and then listening to a story I read them to fall asleep.

Wells and I were sitting on Ira's bed, Wells cuddling him while all the other kids were wrapped up in the sleeping bags they brought to sleep in tonight.

The carpet was soft enough, but we gave them more pillows from the living room to make sure they were comfortable enough, but none of them seemed to be bothered by the floor as this was a sleepover after all.

It was fun, and they enjoyed the story I was reading them.

A few had already fallen asleep, including Ira, and the rest were trying to keep their eyes open while I finished the last few pages of the book.

"Now, sleep tight, and tomorrow morning we'll have a delicious breakfast waiting for you," I told them quietly.

Some of them said good night, and once Wells tucked Ira in and kissed his head, we walked out of the bedroom, leaving the door open a crack.

"I hope none of them get home sick. But they all looked happy and relaxed."

I nodded, wrapping my hands around Wells's arm and leaning against him. "Today has really been fun and all the kids were great. I think they'll be fine. Even Sia."

She was the first to fall asleep, and it was sweet to see Bethy holding her hand to let her know she wasn't alone.

We entered the kitchen and looked around it and the living room, thinking the same thing.

This had to be cleaned up before they woke up in the morning so we could have a nice breakfast and the kids would then get picked up around lunch time.

So, without having to say a thing, we started to clean up and put everything away, and once the dishwasher was going, we finally were ready to go to bed ourselves.

I yawned, letting Wells pull me to him and place his hands at my lower back.

"Don't think I will let you sleep yet. I'm only just getting you to myself," he whispered close to my ear before kissing the soft spot underneath it.

I smiled and moved my hands up his arms to wrap them around his neck. "Are you sure you're not too tired for this?" I asked, knowing his answer already.

"Never too tired to fuck you," he rasped.

Shivers moved down my spine, making me press my thighs together and ease the stinging between them.

There was no time for me to stop him as he picked me up and carried me into the bedroom, locking the door behind us just in case one of the eleven kids in Ira's room—which was big enough for them, by the way—decided to walk in on us.

He sat down on the bed and made me straddle his lap while his hands moved from my ass to my hips, pushing my shirt up and breaking the kiss to pull it over my head.

Words weren't needed, and I opened my bra at the back to let him cup my breasts and pull one nipple into his mouth.

I started to move on top of him, circling my hips against his and rubbing my crotch against his hardening shaft.

My hands were back in his hair where they so often were because I couldn't get enough of it, and I tugged and pulled gently, knowing he liked it when I did that.

He sucked on my nipple and circled his tongue around it, then he did the same thing to the other one, wanting to give them the same attention.

I wanted to touch him too, so I moved one hand down his chest and to his stomach where I pulled his shirt up to get rid of it, and once he let go of my breasts, he pulled his shirt over his head and threw it on the ground to dispose of it.

His lips were back on mine, and his hands squeezed and pulled at my nipples, making my pussy clench the way it always did when he was inside of me.

I couldn't wait to feel him again, but it's been a while since I've tasted him, so I broke the kiss and got off his lap to kneel between his legs.

I looked up at him, grinning like a fool and opening his pants.

His pants were off as quick as our shirts were, and when his boxer briefs were gone too, I wrapped both hands around his shaft and rubbed it before putting my mouth on it.

His hand moved into my hair, grabbing it tightly and pushing my head against him so I had to take him in deeper.

I liked this more than I had anticipated, but the way he looked at me, and the low, raspy noises he made while I sucked his cock made my pussy wetter every time.

"You're so fucking beautiful, love. Just like that..." he panted, moving my head with his hand but letting me have control over it.

I took him in deeper until his tip touched the back of my throat, and the first time I sucked him, I didn't think my gag reflex was this *unfazed* by his length.

Guess it's a good thing as he always tried to keep me there for a few seconds before letting me catch my breath again.

"Don't stop, baby. Fuck, keep circling that tongue around my tip," he said, his voice raspy and low.

I tried to smile because knowing I was making him happy, made me happy as well.

I kept going, moving one hand along the base of his cock while I placed my other one at his balls.

I knew he liked it when I played with them, but they made him come so much faster, and I didn't want that before he fucked me.

So I teased him a little, making sure he wouldn't release his cum inside my mouth and kept sucking his cock while he said things to me I wished I could've recorded and listened to whenever I pleased myself and he wasn't around.

"You really want me to come in your pretty mouth, love?" he asked, his muscles on his upper body all tensed and sexy.

I released his cock from my mouth and shook my head, but to keep teasing him, I pushed his shaft up against his stomach to take one of his balls into my mouth.

"Ah, fuck!" he growled, gripping my hair tighter and then jerking my head back.

"I'll skip fucking you tonight if you don't stop teasing me," he said in a warning tone.

He was serious, and God...could he get any hotter?

He was already handsome as hell, but acting all bossy?

Fuck. Me.

I bit my bottom lip and brushed away the drop of precum mixed with my saliva dripping down my chin, then licked my thumb and shook my head.

"I want you to fuck me," I told him in a sweet voice.

A grin appeared on his serious face, then he nodded next to him on the bed.

"Lie on your stomach," he demanded, standing up and rubbing his cock while I got on the bed the way he wanted me to.

Once I was comfortable, he stepped between my legs, pulled my pants down to then push my legs apart.

His tip brushed along my folds from behind while he grabbed one ass cheek and pushed it out to get better access to my entrance.

"Will you tease me again next time?" he asked, squeezing my ass tightly.

I wanted to shrug at first, but I knew that was a bad idea.

So I shook my head and turned my head as far as I could to look up at him.

He was looking at me with a raised brow, and I shook my head again with a smile.

"I won't, I promise."

Maybe.

I would, probably.

"Good girl," he growled, and in one swift move he was deep inside of me, stretching my walls and taking my breath away.

I closed my eyes and opened my mouth, moaning but trying to keep it low.

"Told you I won't be nice tonight."

But his words only excited me.

I loved this side of him, and the harder he squeezed my ass with both hands now, the more heat rose from my pussy.

"Wells, please," I begged, wanting him to move and wiggling my ass.

A chuckle came from him, now him being the one to tease me.

But it didn't take long for him to finally thrust into me, fast and hard and with no mercy.

"So fucking tight," he rasped, his cock pulsating inside of me.

I could already feel my body tensing, and the faster he fucked me, the more intense those sensations got, ready to explode inside of me.

This felt so much different, and the way he took control over my body felt just as good.

With every thrust, he pushed deeper inside of me while we moved closer to the light waiting at the end of this hot and steamy fuck.

One of his hands moved into my hair to grip it tightly and push my head into the mattress harshly.

He wasn't hurting me, and I was slowly but very surely turning into an addict of hard fucking.

Wells knew exactly how he had to move to make me come, and although I've only ever been close to coming without him touching my clit, I felt as if this time it would happen.

I relaxed my body and let him keep fucking me the way he liked to and didn't think about reaching my climax too much because I knew it would only mess things up.

"I'm gonna come deep in your wet pussy. Fuck, you feel so fucking good, love," he hissed, out of breath.

I kept my eyes closed and felt the orgasm building inside my lower belly, slowly creeping up on me.

"Come with me, Rooney. I want you to clench that pussy and milk me while I come," he growled.

How could I ever say no to that?

And with a few more thrusts he stopped as he was buried deep inside of me, releasing his cum and groaning as I was sent spiraling out of control.

This.

This is what I want from now on until forever.

And I was certain there was even more inside of him that he couldn't let out because of all the kids sleeping in the room next to his.

Chapter Twenty-Nine

Wells

Rooney couldn't stop grinning at me the next morning while the kids ate breakfast.

Some were still sleepy, but they were all up and already dressed, ready to get picked up by their parents in a few hours.

Our night was different, but not in a bad way.

Never had I imagined sweet and innocent Rooney would enjoy getting fucked roughly, but I was glad she did.

We were eating while standing up since all the kids occupied the whole table, and every once in a while, Rooney leaned against me and I pressed a kiss to her head to show her some affection too.

Things were going great between us, even without ever talking about what we were, or what we wanted to be.

I guess it wasn't the right time to talk about it, but I knew that I wanted to keep her around.

Maybe we didn't need to talk about it.

It was perfect the way it was.

I was happy, Rooney was happy, and most importantly, Ira was too.

"Wells?" Bethy called out with her hand raised as if she was in school and had to ask for permission to talk.

I looked at her, but as I moved my gaze to Sia sitting next to her, I knew what she wanted to tell me.

"Oh, sweetheart," Rooney said, putting her plate down on the counter and walking over to her.

I watched her pick Sia up as she was silently crying.

"She said she misses her mommy," Bethy told Rooney.

"Mommy's coming to pick you up in just an hour, sweetie, okay?" she said, rubbing Sia's back and trying to cheer her up.

Sia hiccupped as she tried to keep in her cries inside, but when she realized it was okay to cry, she hugged Rooney tightly and let all her emotions run free.

When she stopped next to me, I brushed along the back of Sia's head to calm her, not able to stop thinking about how great of a mother Rooney would be.

Shit.

Not now, man. You're too old to have another kid, and she's too young to have her first.

"Should we call your mommy and see if she can come pick you up earlier?" I asked, getting a quick nod from her.

"All right. Let's call her together."

Rooney let me take her so she could watch the other kids, and for a split second, it felt as if we ran a daycare.

"Sit right here," I told Sia as I sat her down on the counter, and I grabbed my phone to call Frieda, her mother.

"Do you wanna talk to her?" I asked, brushing back a strand of her blonde hair.

She shook her head but kept her eyes on my phone.

Only a few seconds of ringing, Frieda picked up.

"Is everything okay?" were her first words.

"Hey, yes. Sia's been asking for you. Think she's a little homesick," I told her, looking into Sia's sad face.

A sigh escaped Frieda, but not an annoyed one.

"Well, at least she made it through the night, hm? I'll pick her up in ten," she said.

"All right. See you then."

We hung up and I smiled at Sia. "Your mommy's coming in ten minutes. Do you wanna go play a little until she's here?" I asked.

"I can play with her."

As sweet as Bethy was, she had to stop creeping up on me like that.

"Sound good?" I asked Sia, and she nodded, trusting Bethy.

I lifted her from the counter and let them walk together to the living room where they sat down at Ira's little table where he often drew and painted.

I moved my gaze to Rooney who was looking at me with a smile, and I gave her quick nod to let her know everything was okay.

As much as I loved seeing Ira all happy and enjoying being with his friends, I was ready to see them all leave so I had time for my son and Rooney again.

***

Later in the afternoon, my mother and George decided to come by and give Ira his birthday present.

I told them to not come by on his birthday, as we would have all the kids over and there wouldn't be much time to sit down and have a cup of coffee.

"Look, Ira. George and I got you a little something," Mom said, holding out a present for him to take.

"What is it?" Ira asked, sounding as if he had enough of presents since yesterday.

He got spoiled with so many amazing gifts, but I could proudly say that the Hulk costume he was wearing again was definitely his favorite.

Well, that and Rooney's painting we already hung up in his room.

"Well, open it up and find out," Mom said.

We watched Ira rip the wrapping paper open, and I already had an idea of what it might be.

"It's a comic book!" Ira called out.

I knew he would soon ask to start learning to read, and comics were a great way to do so.

I loved comics when I was a kid, so I'd have fun reading them to him until he could read them himself.

"Yes, but there's something else on there," Mom said, reaching for the card stuck to the front.

"This is a subscription for these comics, and you'll get a new one in the mail every week to collect," she explained.

"Woah!" Ira said, his eyes wide.

"That's nice of you, Mom. Thank you," I told her.

"I have to spend my money somehow, right? I told them to send the bill each month to my house and the comics here."

I nodded, smiling as Ira already started looking into the comic book.

"So, Rooney," my mother started, making Rooney look at her. "You've helped him take care of the kids and birthday party?"

"Yes, it was fun. The kids were amazing and Ira had a really good time. We still have some carrot cake left, if you'd like to try some," she offered.

Mom was so intrigued by Rooney that everything she said or did was fascinating.

"That sounds wonderful, Rooney. George, would you like some too?"

He nodded, and Rooney quickly got up but stopped to brush her hand through the back of my hair.

"Want a slice too?"

"Yeah, sure. Wait, I'll help you."

I knew if I sat there I would get bombarded with my mother's questions about Rooney and me, and I wasn't ready to tell her what I haven't even told Rooney before.

"You look tense," she said as we got to the kitchen.

"I just can't wait to be alone with you and Ira again," I told her, kissing her cheek and then grabbing a few plates from the cupboard.

"We'll have plenty of time when they're gone," she told me with a smile.

She cut the cake and placed a slice on each plate, and I told her to make Ira's a little smaller as I planned on cooking dinner later.

When we headed back into the living room, my mother looked worried all of a sudden, and I raised a brow to silently ask her what's wrong.

"I called your father to ask if he'd come back to Riverton to see his grandson on his fourth birthday, but he wasn't interested. I wish he would take being a grandfather more seriously than sleeping around with random girls in Vegas."

I rolled my eyes.

I didn't expect much else from my father, hence why I didn't invite him in the first place.

He never called on my birthdays either once he left Mom.

"It's fine. Ira had a fun birthday with his friends, and you guys are here."

"But it's not difficult to pick up his phone and call and say happy birthday," she said, sighing heavily.

I didn't wanna talk about my father, so I changed the subject.

"Rooney is taking Ira and me to her parent's ranch next weekend. They have lots of animals and Ira's already very excited, right bud?"

He nodded and took a bite of the cake. "I can ride on a horse!" he announced.

Mom wasn't happy about me changing the subject, but for Ira's sake, she smiled and asked more questions.

I needed this afternoon to be over quick to finally be alone with the two that meant the most to me.

Sure, I loved my mother, but that was different.

So much different.

Chapter Thirty

Rooney

The week couldn't have passed any quicker and we were already on my parent's ranch.

We had taken Wells's car to drive here because of Ira's car seat and due to the bigger space in the back for our bags.

We'd spend a whole weekend here, and we would get dirty walking around, so we had to have clothes to change into.

"I see horses!" Ira called out as Wells stopped the car next to dad's in front of their house.

It was a typical house you'd find on the country side, and it fulfilled every single cliché about living on a ranch or farm.

"They're pretty, huh? We can go see them up close later," I suggested and stepped out of the car.

Once Wells got Ira out, my parents walked out of the house to greet us.

Luckily, they weren't wearing clown costumes today.

I hugged my mother first, then my dad, then I turned around to introduce them to Wells and Ira.

"It's so nice to meet you two. Rooney has told us a lot about you," Mom said, and I wondered if that was true.

All I ever said was that I was seeing someone, and that someone had a son.

"Nice to meet you too, Louise," Wells said, then he held out his hand to my dad. "Devon," he said, and Wells nodded. "Nice to meet you. This is Ira."

Ira was a little unsure at first, but more because my dad was a little scary looking.

He had that full-beard going on, covering half of his face, but once he smiled, Ira waved at them and said hi.

"I see you got your boots on already! All you need is a cowboy hat and you're ready to ride!" Dad told Ira, making him smile and giggle.

"You're funny," he said, making us all laugh.

"Come inside! I prepared you guys two bedrooms. Don't care who sleeps in which room, but you have the whole second floor to yourselves for the weekend."

I nodded, letting Ira take my hand while Wells and Dad took our bags out of the car.

"I saw horses!" Ira told mom, and I smiled, knowing her heart already melted for the sweetest little boy ever.

"Have you ever been close to one before? If you want, we can go ride on one later," she suggested.

"Yes, please!"

Ira's excitement grew with every minute that passed, and once we were inside the house, his eyes widened as he saw all the western decorations my parents had.

It was as if you walked into a saloon, with wood and leather everywhere.

"This place is amazing, huh, bud?" Wells asked.

"It's a cow on the wall!" he called out, pointing at the stuffed head above the fireplace.

"That's a bison," Mom explained. "We have a few of those too, and they are very, very big!"

"Bigger than a cow?" Ira asked, amazed by his surroundings.

"Much bigger! Wanna touch this one?"

Ira nodded and Wells picked Ira up to let him caress the soft coat of the bison.

"It's a little scary," Ira said, but he bravely kept touching and admiring the animal.

"They're very sweet, you know? You can even feed one if you want to," Mom said.

This weekend was definitely for Ira, but I loved seeing the love and same excitement in Wells's eyes as his son explored new things.

"Rooney, your father and I have to drive into town to get a few things, but Alexis and Kira are outside with a group of visitors giving them a tour of the ranch, so why don't you guys tag along and we'll have dinner later on?"

"Yeah, sounds good." I looked at Wells who nodded.

"Sounds great. Thank you for having us this weekend," he added.

"Oh, of course! We're happy to have you. We'll see you later."

Ira couldn't take his eyes off the bisons grazing on the big field behind the shed, and while Kira and Alexis took the group over to the horses, we stopped and kept looking at them from afar.

"We didn't see bisons at the zoo," Ira pointed out ad Wells picked him up so he could sit on the wooden fence.

"Right, we didn't see them at the zoo," Wells said.

I smiled at them and let Wells pull me closer to him with his arm around my shoulders and the other around Ira to make sure he wouldn't fall.

"I think they're coming over to say hi," I said, pointing at two of the bisons coming closer.

"Should I be worried?" Wells asked closer to my ear, and I quickly shook my head.

"They're very calm and gentle." I've been around these animals when I was younger, and I've learnt a lot about their behavior.

As long as you stayed calm and fed them, they would stand there and let you pet them.

"Here, I brought some apples. They mostly eat grass, but they love apples," I told them, taking the apples out of the bucket I filled with veggies and fruits before heading out and handing each an apple. "Just hold your hand out flat like this and put the apple on it so they can easily grab it," I told Ira, helping him hold his hand out as one bison stopped in front of him.

He was a little hesitant at first, but once the bison ate the apple, he clapped his hands and giggled happily. "I did it!"

"Good job, buddy!" Wells said proudly.

"You can give him a little pet while he's eating," I told him, reaching out my hand to touch the bison's head.

Ira did the same, petting him and then pulling both hands tightly against his chest to show his happiness.

"He's soft!"

"He is, hm? Wanna give him another apple?" I asked.

"You do it, Daddy," Ira demanded, and Wells chuckled.

"All right. Let's see if the other one wants an apple too," he said, holding his hand out for the bison closer to him.

"There we go," he said once the bison ate the apple.

I was already having the best time of my life, and I couldn't wait for Ira and also Wells to see more amazing things on my parents' ranch.

My parents were back late in the afternoon right on time after we've done a tour of the whole ranch and all the other guests left again.

We walked into the house to greet my parents, and as nervous as I was for them to meet Wells, it wasn't as big of a deal like I had thought.

In the end, my parents were closer to Wells's age then I was, but they weren't judging us because of our age difference.

"I'm starting with dinner. Would you like to help me, Rooney?" Mom asked, smiling at me.

"Oh, yes. You remembered what I texted you last night, right? About Ira having diabetes?"

"Of course I remembered. You like vegetables, right, sweetie?" she asked Ira.

"Yes, and I eat a lot of fruit and sometimes I can eat something sweet."

Ira was limited to eat certain things, but nowadays, there were enough food companies selling foods with less sugar in them, made for diabetics.

Still, I knew Wells liked to feed Ira healthy things.

"That's wonderful! Would you like to help cut some of the veggies?" Mom asked.

Ira looked up at Wells to ask for permission, and he nodded with a smile, then brushed through his hair.

"Of course you can. Daddy's gonna go to the bathroom and then I'll be right back, okay?"

"Okay," Ira replied, reaching for my hand and already pulling me toward the kitchen.

Wells smiled at me when he saw how relaxed and happy Ira was, and I smiled back at him to assure him everything was fine.

Things were great, but I wondered when the day would come when we finally had to speak up about what this thing between him and I actually was.

Wells

When I came back from the bathroom, Rooney's dad stopped me before I could head into the kitchen.

He was sitting on the couch and pointing at the seat next to him for me to sit down.

"Rooney told me you're a civil engineer, is that right?" he asked.

I nodded, but before sitting down, I looked into the kitchen to make sure everything was okay.

Ira was standing on a chair next to Rooney and her mother, carefully cutting a cucumber with a dull knife.

Looked like they had everything under control, and I was ready to have a talk with Devon.

"Yeah, I am."

I had to admit that it was strange sitting here with him, only being a few years apart in age, yet I was fucking his daughter.

"I've thought about studying to become one myself, but I guess life had other plans for me. Met Louise and found myself buying a damn clown costume a few months later," he said with a chuckle.

I laughed softly. "She was definitely the one then," I said.

It was strange.

We were around the same age and we were both dads, yet being around him made me feel as if I didn't know shit about being a father.

Maybe it was the thought of him having raised the girl I was seeing, which weirdly made him much older in my mind then he actually was.

I had to keep my mind straight.

Not overthink things.

Who knows? Maybe him and I could become friends.

"Most definitely. I knew from the moment I saw her the first time that she would mess with my head and steal my damn heart. And we got so damn lucky when Rooney was born."

I smiled, thinking they did a good job of raising such a sweet and down-to-earth girl.

"Ira's your only kid?" he asked. "Do you care for him all the time?"

I nodded. "His mother isn't around anymore and I took him in when he was six months old. He made my life so much better, and I'm lucky to have him," I told Devon.

He studied me for a moment and when I thought he'd ask another question about me being a father, he changed the subject without a warning.

"My Rooney is only twenty, but I think you're aware of that," he said.

"Of course. But age hasn't been much of a problem for us."

"For now. But what about in a few years?"

His brow was raised and I had to think about the answer before replying.

"I have to be honest...I haven't thought that far ahead. I like Rooney, and Ira does too. We're still figuring things out, but I know for sure that my intentions aren't to hurt her. She's amazing, and she's been so sweet with Ira that I don't think he would ever wanna let her go."

He studied me closely before nodding.

"That's your view. But what about hers?"

Good fucking question, because the last time we talked about us she said we were friends.

Okay, that was weeks ago, and things have clearly changed between us.

Still, there was no conversation about it after we started to come closer to each other.

Maybe I should start a conversation about it.

"That's for her to tell. I can only say how I see it."

That seemed to have been enough for him, but before he could say more, Ira called out to me.

"Look, Daddy! It's a pumpkin!"

I turned to look at him and smiled, standing up and walking toward them after giving Devon a look to excuse myself.

"Are you carving it?" I asked, standing behind him and kissing the back of his head.

"Yes, and then we eat the inside!" he announced.

"We're making pumpkin soup as well as chicken breasts and veggies. Sounds delicious, hm?" Rooney said to Ira, then she looked at me with a bright smile.

"It does. I can't wait to try it all. Do you guys need some help?"

I asked more so to not get bombarded with new questions by Devon, and luckily, Rooney nodded and pointed to the table.

"I'll help you set the table."

And so we did while Devon stayed on the couch to continue reading something on his phone while Louise helped Ira take everything edible out of the pumpkin.

"Did Dad ask any weird questions?" she asked, worry filling her eyes now.

"No, not really. But there's something I wanna talk to you about. But not right now."

Her brows furrowed, and I realized I made it sound more serious than I wanted it to.

There was nothing she had to worry about, but she'd have to try and be honest and open with me the same way I would have to be.

God, I'm not ready for that talk.

Chapter Thirty-One

Rooney

Dinner was a success but I didn't want it to end.

Wells looked serious when he told me he wanted to talk to me about something, and my heart had been racing the whole damn time while we ate the delicious food Ira helped us prepare.

I had an idea about what he wanted to talk about, but I wasn't ready for that.

I wanted to enjoy this weekend, have fun on the ranch, and have a good time with Ira and Wells.

This brought us even closer together, and I loved how much Ira trusted me, but also my parents, whenever Wells wasn't around for a few minutes.

Maybe that's what he was lacking.

More adults around him who treated him like a prince and adored him just as much as his father did.

Not that Wells wasn't enough for Ira, but it was nice seeing Ira bloom into an even more open and talkative little boy.

He wouldn't stop asking questions about the animals on the ranch, and Dad promised to let him help feed them tomorrow morning.

For that, we'd have to get up very early, so Mom told us to go to bed so we would get enough sleep and not be tired in the morning.

Wells and Ira had already said goodnight to my parents, and I told him I would be right up.

We didn't talk about who sleeps in which bedroom, but I would be okay with Wells sleeping with Ira and me in the other guest room.

"What's that frown for, darling?" Dad asked as he sat back down at the table while I helped Mom put all the dishes into the dishwasher.

"Oh, it's nothing. I was just thinking," I told him, smiling and turning to look at him.

"You sure about that? Ever since dinner you've been acting strange."

Leave it to him to figure me out in less than a second.

I sighed and shook my head. "It's nothing you have to worry about, Dad. I'm happy you guys welcomed Wells and Ira here. They're loving it so far."

"But there is something bothering you, sweetie," Mom said.

"Yeah, there might be something, but it's nothing I need you two to help me with. I'm fine, okay?"

They both looked at me, trying to decide if they wanted to keep pushing me to tell them, or if they'd rather leave me alone.

Whatever Wells wanted to talk about, it wasn't my parents' business, and as much as I loved them, this wasn't something they had to worry about.

Besides, I didn't think Wells would start an argument here and now.

"I'm going to bed," I told them, my voice calm as I was close to getting annoyed with them.

"I love you. I'll see you in the morning," I added, hugging Mom and then Dad before heading upstairs.

As I reached the second floor, Wells walked out of one the guestrooms, leaving the door open a crack.

"He's already asleep. Guess the afternoon was exhausting," he said, keeping his voice low.

I smiled and gave him a quick nod. "So...you wanted to talk?"

He looked at me for a while before reaching for my hand and pulling me to him.

I placed my hands on his chest, keeping my eyes on him to not miss a single emotion in his eyes.

"Let's get into bed first."

His eyes wandered all over my face while his hands were placed at my lower back, holding me close to him.

If he was holding me so close, could he possibly be mad at me?

Unless he was trying to lead me on.

God, Rooney! Stop manipulating your own damn thoughts.

"Okay," I whispered.

Something felt off, yet he had this effect on me to make me feel as if nothing was wrong.

He was messing with my mind, and half of it was me doing it to myself.

Wells lifted one hand and placed it on my cheek, then he leaned in to kiss my lips, now definitely making me overthink every little thing.

He wanted to talk, sounded serious saying it, and now he's kissing me in a way that felt calming and assuring.

Ah, what the heck.

I gripped his shirt tightly with my fists and deepened the kiss, making him lean over me more and pull me even closer against his body.

I didn't wanna let go now, knowing that if I did, I'd have to face whatever was coming my way when we got into bed.

But instead of letting my brain think about every possible reason why he wanted to talk, I focused on our bodies and let him know how much I wanted him.

Maybe he'll change his mind?

Our tongues touched, and his hand moved to the back of my head to grab a fistful of my hair, making me sigh as he tightened his grip.

My hands were still on his chest, but I didn't dare move as this kiss was getting more intense by the second.

A low growl escaped him, and just as I thought this kiss would never end, he moved back and broke it, looking back into my eyes.

Lust was filling his, but I knew mine looked the exact same.

He eyed me for a moment, then smiled and let go of my hair to grab my hand. "Come on," he whispered, leading me into the bedroom where we first got ready for bed before we got under the covers.

"Is it serious?" I asked, needing some kind of hint about what he wanted to talk about.

He sat back against the headboard and pulled me closer to him, but instead of lying down with him, I pushed myself up to sit next to him, needing to be eye to eye for this.

He held my hands tightly in his lap, brushing his thumbs along my skin softly and taking a deep breath before nodding. "As serious as it can get."

That wasn't a joke, and my heart started racing again.

"I think we both know there's some communication lacking between us when it comes to a certain topic," he said, keeping his eyes on mine while I tried my best not to look away.

So it's *that* talk.

I was already uncomfortable, because talking about my feelings never ended well.

It frustrated me when my heart and mind battled against each other, both seeing it differently and manipulating each other until I couldn't take it any more and started to cry.

At least that's what happened when I first opened up about what I really felt for AJ, and it wasn't even him I talked about it to.

No, it was Evie, and the quickly annoyed person that she was, she couldn't really help me get over it before I had to get over it myself and finally talk to AJ.

I couldn't cry in front of Wells, so I tried my best to keep my breathing steady and calm, and for now, I thought it was working.

"Before this turned into something more, you told me we were friends. I know it's hard for you to talk about this, but all I need you to say is if you still see me as a friend or a person you just hang out with to have some fun with."

Normally, that's exactly why I would avoid meeting guys, but for some stupid reason, here I was again.

Wells wasn't just a guy I hung out with to get whatever out of it. I liked him. And Ira too.

So tell him!

That was my heart speaking, but as expected, my mind wouldn't stay out of this conversation.

Let him tell you first so you don't look weak if he's just using you for fun.

Yes. That.

Exactly that.

How could I know that once I told him I liked him, he wouldn't break me by telling me he doesn't like me back in that way?

Also, why hasn't he mentioned anything about a third possibility of us going into the direction of becoming a couple?

Because he doesn't want a relationship, dummy.

"What do you think we are?" I asked back, listening to my mind instead of my poor heart.

He raised a brow at me and chuckled. "Guess you're still unsure if you have to answer me with another question."

I furrowed my brows.

I hated this conversation, and all I wanted to do was turn away from him and sleep instead of having to deal with this again.

If you just open up to him, you'll feel better. No matter what his response is, my heart told me, knowing it was telling the truth.

How the hell did I get to the point where I started to have conversations with my damn organs?

"So are you if you can't answer my question either," I pointed out, feeling like an idiot already.

Wells sighed and ran his hand over his face, obviously not in the mood to argue either.

"How can we ever talk about this without you overthinking and questioning everything?"

Woah! Did he just say it's my fault?

No, he's trying to find reasons, not accusing you.

My emotions were running wild, but I tried my best not to let them explode and show.

I had to calm down—*no,* my mind needed to calm down, because my heart knew exactly what to do and I'd rather have it control me instead of my brain.

"I'm not asking much of you, Rooney. You're suffering, and I hate to see you like this, so why can't we just have a normal conversation about this?"

I looked down at our hands which were still in his lap, trying to find an answer to his question.

How can I not open up about my feelings if I know exactly how I feel about us?

But just as I was about to collect all my strength and answer him, a little voice interrupted me, and it wasn't my mind stopping me from finally opening up.

Wells

"Daddy?" Ira stood by the door with one hand in his hair and the other on the doorknob, looking unsure and worried.

I squeezed Rooney's hand to let her know that I saw her determination to speak up about her feelings, but that we'd have to move this conversation to another time.

I was being a dick to her just moments before, trying to push her to answer me while I protected myself from whatever it was she was feeling.

I was positive we felt the same, wanting to be with each other and maybe go a step further and call what we've been doing in the past weeks dating, but it was clear that she still needed time, and I wouldn't push her if it made her feel upset.

"What's up, buddy?" I asked, reaching out my hand to him.

He quickly walked over to my side of the bed while Rooney moved over, knowing he would be spending the night with us.

"Can't sleep?" I asked, and he nodded.

Must be the fact that he was alone in a bedroom he had never been in before.

"All right, come here," I said, helping him up onto the bed and letting him get comfortable on my chest the way he used to when he was a baby.

I glanced over at Rooney who was smiling gently at Ira, and without having to say a word, I pulled her to me and kissed the top of her head as she cuddled up to my side.

She was close to Ira with her head on my shoulder and her body pressed against my side while he nestled his face into my neck.

This felt nice, having both of them cuddled up to me.

But there was still something bothering the both of us that we'd soon have to talk about again.

I turned my head after kissing Ira's forehead to look at Rooney, and when she looked up at me, I smiled to assure her that everything would turn out right.

"We'll be okay, Rooney. It's just a small bump in the road," I whispered.

Chapter Thirty-Two

Rooney

The first sight when I woke up the next morning was of Wells and Ira cuddled up next to me, with Ira not on his chest but between the two of us on the mattress now.

I noticed my hand on Ira's back was covered by Wells's, and when I looked at it, my heart stung without a warning.

Something felt so right, but after last night, I still had an unsure feeling inside of me.

We hadn't talked it out yet, but for Ira's sake, we couldn't continue our argument.

A smile tugged at my lips as Wells's hand squeezed mine and his fingers slid through mine, making it feel as if nothing was wrong at all.

"Good morning," he whispered in a raspy voice, making me look up into his face again.

"Good morning," I whispered back.

His other arm was underneath my neck, keeping me close while his hand cupped my head and his fingers pushed into my hair.

"How are you feeling?" he asked, studying me closely.

"Good, I think. You?"

He nodded, looking down at Ira who was now moving next to us. Though, he didn't wake up.

"I'm sorry about last night, Rooney. I shouldn't have pushed you. I think we both still need to reflect on things," he said, keeping his voice low.

I nodded, agreeing with him.

"But that doesn't mean anything bad, you know?"

No, it didn't. But opening up about our feelings was so damn hard that it started to bother me the more I mentioned it.

"I guess we both struggle with the same problem," I told him, pressing my lips into a thin line.

"Yeah, we do. But we'll figure it out, all right? Maybe not now, but we can't keep this up for much longer," he said.

I agreed, so I nodded and leaned closer to him to kiss his lips without getting in Ira's way.

Wells lifted his hand from mine to my cheek and kissed me back gently before he broke it again to look into my eyes again.

"Let's push those thoughts aside and have a great weekend. Ira's loving it here, and I don't wanna ruin it for him."

"I know," I said, smiling at him and looking back down to see Ira move again.

He didn't need to ask me if I was okay with Ira sleeping with us because this was a step closer to knowing that he kept trusting me around his son, and Ira was comfortable enough to sleep next to me.

The thoughts from last night came back again, making me wonder that if Wells didn't want anything serious, why would he let it go as far as letting Ira sleep in one bed with us?

Something didn't make a lot of sense, but, hell...I had to stop overthinking.

I was confusing myself.

"Good morning, buddy. Did you have a good night?" Wells asked as Ira rubbed his eyes with his fists, and I smiled as he looked even cuter than usual.

Ira nodded and then stretched before turning onto his back. "Can we feed the animals?" he asked, his little voice soft.

Wells chuckled and brushed through Ira's hair. "We'll have to eat breakfast first, hm?"

"Okay. Hi, Rooney," he then said as he turned his head to look at me.

I smiled and couldn't help a soft laugh. "Hey, little man. Are you excited for today?" I asked.

Safe to say he was comfortable between Wells and me.

"Yes, I am. Can we ride on the horses too?"

"Sounds like a good idea. I know a nice place where the horses like to go as well," I told him. "We might even see clowns riding on bulls today," I added, knowing Mom and Dad did a show for their guests every Saturday.

Wells chuckled, and I frowned at him. "Please don't make fun of it," I said in a serious tone, but he knew I didn't mean it.

Sure, seeing my parents dressed as clowns wasn't something I was proud of, but that way he got to know my parents and how they really were.

Dad wasn't as stern as he seemed last night, and he put on a façade to come off like a bad guy to scare off Wells.

Luckily, Wells dealt with him better than expected.

"Are they good clowns?" Ira asked, worry filling his eyes.

"Of course they are, buddy," Wells assured him, then he looked at me to explain why he thought they'd be bad clowns.

"He accidentally saw the news at my mother's one time where they talked about those...*killer clowns.*" He said the last two words in a whisper, almost without making a sound.

"Oh, right," I chuckled, looking back at Ira. "These clowns are very funny-looking and mischievous. They'll make us all laugh," I told him, not wanting him to have the wrong idea of clowns riding bulls.

"Can we go now? Can we eat breakfast?" he asked, looking back at Wells and crawling over his chest.

"Hmmm, I might sleep a little more," Wells said jokingly.

"No, Daddy! We have to feed the animals!"

I laughed and watched as Wells started tickling Ira, careful not to hurt him where his pump was and making him giggle in the sweetest way possible.

Yes, I was one thousand percent sure that Wells didn't have bad intentions last night, but it was me who ruined it all by not being able to answer a simple question.

He clearly wanted me around, with or without Ira, and now I couldn't wait for this weekend to be over so we could talk it out.

After a quick breakfast, Dad took us to the horses where we helped him feed them and get them ready for the guests later on, but before they'd arrive at around one, I told Dad that I would take two of the horses out on a little walk to the place I told Ira and Wells about.

He was okay with that, so we continued to help out around the ranch and let Ira explore a little more.

Every now and then, and whenever we didn't have to carry or lift something, Wells grabbed my hand or pulled me closer, kissing my head and smiling at me.

It soothed me a little, knowing that he wanted to keep me close, and surprisingly, it helped me get rid of all the negative thoughts I had last night.

No way he wanted to be just friends.

No way there wasn't more he was feeling for me, the same I was feeling for him.

I leaned against him as we watched my dad help Ira get the freshly laid eggs from the chickens, and the sweet kid he was, Ira placed them gently into the basket filled with hay, making sure they wouldn't break.

"Maybe I should get him a pet," Wells said, wrapping his arms around my shoulders as he stood behind me.

I smiled, placing both hands on his arms and tilting my head to the side while keeping my eyes on Ira.

"What kind of pet are you thinking of?" I asked.

"I don't know. A dog's too much work, and a cat can be quite exhausting. Maybe...a hamster. Something small that fits in a cage."

I puckered my lips and thought about pets that were easy to take care of for kids.

"How about a little turtle?" I suggested. "He loves the Ninja Turtles."

He thought about it for a while before kissing the back of my head and nodding. "Might be a good first pet. I'll have to get more information about keeping a pet turtle first," he said.

Good thing he wouldn't just go into a pet store.

"Look, Daddy! We got eleven eggs!" Ira announced, then he came running toward us with the basket in his hands.

Wells let go of me and squatted down in front of him to let Ira show him the eggs he found, and I smiled before looking up at Dad who seemed pleased with what he was seeing.

"And he got them all out by himself. Think I'm gonna hire you to come work on the ranch, Ira," Dad said.

I smiled, seeing Ira's eyes light up although he might not have understood what Dad meant.

But that's okay, because all that mattered was knowing that Ira was happy, and it was written all over his face.

"You can take these home tomorrow. I'll let your mother pack some of our home grown salads and veggies too."

"Thank you, Dad," I said, smiling at him.

"That's kind, Devon. Thank you," Wells added, standing back up.

Dad nodded and looked back at Ira. "You can give me the basket so you can go ride on a horse."

Ira immediately let go of the basket, then he jumped up excitedly and started running for the horses.

"Slow down, buddy!" Wells called out, but Ira was too focused on getting to the horses and Wells had to run after him.

That was the first time Ira didn't listen, but hey...there were horses waiting on him.

I wouldn't listen either.

"Have fun, and be careful," Dad told me.

"I will. I'll see you later."

When I reached the stable, Wells was carrying Ira back to the entrance, shaking his head.

"He would've run straight into a horse's personal space if I hadn't caught him," he said, chuckling.

"That would've been dangerous," I told Ira, placing my hand at his back. "Next time, wait on daddy, okay?"

Ira looked at me and tried to understand what would've been so dangerous, but then he nodded. "Okay."

"Are you ready to ride on a horse?" I asked, smiling again.

"Yes!" he called out, pointing at one of them. "I want that one."

I looked behind me to see one of the older horses.

I knew which ones were a better fit to go on a calm and slow walk, and the one Ira chose was actually a good fit.

"That's Jigsaw. He's gentle and kind," I said, wanting them to know the horse before they got on it to feel more comfortable.

They were already saddled, as Alexis and Kira prepared them every morning before the guests arrived.

"Have you ever been on a horse?" I asked Wells.

"Uh, when I was younger, yes. Can't say I remember much of it though."

"That's okay. You can ride with Ira and I'll hold Jigsaw's reins. He's used to having people ride on him, so you'll be fine."

Wells nodded and looked at Jigsaw before he let Ira down again to hold his hand.

He admired Jigsaw as I walked him outside where he stopped and waited.

Mom and Dad trained these horses right, so I had no doubt nothing would happen.

After I got Molly out, I made sure the saddles were tightened right, and turned to Wells to let him know Jigsaw was ready for him and Ira.

"You get on him first and I'll help Ira up afterward."

To my surprise, Wells mounting Jigsaw was more graceful than I had thought it would be, and he looked good sitting on that midnight black horse.

God, he looked like Prince Charming.

I had to shake that thought away before picking up Ira and letting Wells pull him up to sit in front of him.

"Is that comfortable for you, Ira?" I asked, watching him adjust himself on the saddle.

"Yes, thank you!"

I couldn't with this kid.

Wells definitely raised him right.

"All right! Let's go!"

I mounted Molly and reached back to grab Jigsaw's reins, and once both horses started walking, I smiled back at Wells and Ira who were already enjoying themselves.

Maybe words weren't needed at this time, so I turned back around and led the horses to the place I spent most time at when I came to visit my parents.

It's been a while, but I knew no matter what time of the year I came here, that one place would always look beautiful.

It didn't take us long to get there, and at first I wanted to get down and sit in the grass with Wells and Ira, surrounded by the pretty colored leaves of fall and just watch the mountains towering in front of us.

"It's beautiful here, huh?" I heard Wells say to Ira, and I smiled just listening to their conversation while I enjoyed the nature surrounding us.

"Can we come here again sometime?" Ira asked, making me turn to look at him, then Wells.

If he'd say yes, I promised myself to stop thinking negatively about what we might become.

Or not become, for that matter.

"Of course we can. As long as Rooney's okay with that," Wells said, looking at me with intense eyes.

I smiled.

"I'd love to take you here again soon," I said to Ira, getting a happy squeal in return.

So...that was enough of a confirmation, right?

Chapter Thirty-Three

Wells

All good things had to come to an end, and this weekend really went by faster than expected.

We had a wonderful two days at her parents' ranch, but after that much fun, even I was exhausted.

After we said goodbye to Louise and Devon, and having one last serious talk with him alone, we got into the car and drove back home.

Ira kept talking about his favorite things he had done on the ranch, and he wasn't as stunned by the clowns as much as the other kids at the show were.

He said they were *trying to be funny but they just weren't*, which made us all laugh at the dinner table before we said goodbye.

Safe to say Ira was a harsh critic, but at least none of the animals disappointed him.

He fell asleep halfway through the drive, and Rooney and I weren't as talkative as we usually were.

I blamed it on us being tired, and I was glad when we finally arrived back home.

"Would you like to come spend the rest of the evening with me before you go to bed?" I asked as I got Ira out of his seat.

He was fast asleep, and Rooney and I had to finish our talk.

She nodded after grabbing the basket with the eggs and the bag with the veggies out of the back.

"Yeah, of course," she replied with a tired smile.

We walked upstairs and she helped me open the door so I wouldn't struggle with Ira in my arms, and once he was tucked into bed, I walked out of his room to see Rooney standing in the kitchen drinking some water.

"I'll get my bags later. Did you pack everything?" I asked.

She had put her bag outside my door to then bring upstairs once we were done talking.

"Yes. I told Mom if we forgot anything that she can just bring it whenever she comes to visit me."

I nodded, leaning against the counter next to her and eyeing her face closely before deciding to continue our conversation we had two nights ago.

"Have you been thinking about my question?" I asked.

I sure did, and I wished I had asked her a different question, because mentioning it made her frown at me again.

"You asked me if I still see you as a friend or just someone I wanna have fun with, but there wasn't a third option," she said.

Valid point.

"Is that what made you upset?" I asked.

Her brows furrowed even more, silently telling me how much of an idiot I was.

"Right...sorry," I said, sighing and running a hand through my hair.

"I should've been clearer about it."

She nodded, studying me and crossing her arms loosely in front of her stomach.

Maybe it was too early to talk about this.

No, I should just rephrase my question.

"Do you still see me as a friend, or is there more that you feel for me?"

That question didn't seem to be satisfying enough either, seeing as her body tensed before she answered.

"If there wouldn't be more, I don't think we would've gone as far as sleeping together. Or you letting Ira sleep with us in one bed for the weekend."

"That's true, but that's not what I asked, Rooney."

God, I was being a dick again, but all because I wanted to protect my heart from getting hurt.

Same fucking thing she probably was thinking.

"Why are you pushing me to answer that question when you clearly are unsure yourself?" she asked, trying to keep her voice low so Ira wouldn't wake up.

"I'm not pushing you, Rooney. I'm trying to figure things out with you, and that only works if we talk and open up to each other."

She had major issues regarding bottling up her feelings, which obviously wasn't just her issue.

But my stubbornness wasn't letting go of this.

"Why don't you open up first then?"

I had never seen her this determined and frustrated, and it made me feel the same, knowing I was the one making her feel that way.

"Because I not only have myself to protect, but also Ira. He's my life, and if you're not willing to commit, which obviously is what you struggle with the most, then I'm not fucking ready to commit either."

There.

That should've been enough to make her talk about how she saw things now.

She looked at me for a while and shook her head before letting out a laugh.

"But you'd be ready to just let me hang around him and fuck me whenever you want to without us ever being more than friends?"

Good fucking question, and I had no answer to that.

"Right, that's what I thought," she whispered after a few seconds of silence. "Maybe you should find out what you want first before pushing me to tell you things you wanna hear."

Her eyes were watery, tears ready to roll down her cheeks.

I sighed, running my hand through my hair again. "Why are you saying this now, Rooney?"

"Because even if I'd say I wanted to be with you, you'd still be unsure about us."

"So now I'm the problem?" I asked as she walked past me and down the hall to get to the front door.

I followed her, hoping I could stop her from leaving when we were still arguing.

"No, Wells," she rasped, turning to me with her hand already on the door handle. "We're both the problem, and if we don't *figure this out soon*, we'll break ourselves before we can break each other."

Her words hit hard because I knew damn well they were true.

"So what now?" I asked, feeling like the weaker man in that moment.

"I'll give you time to think. I'll need it too, and once we're at peace with ourselves, we can talk about us again. Right now...I think we both have to work on ourselves, Wells."

And I knew she was right.

Us together...we weren't the problem.

I kept my eyes on her and there was still hope inside of me, but I knew this was where we had to take a step away from each other and find ourselves—our truths—first.

"Promise me this isn't goodbye forever," I whispered.

Jesus fucking Christ, Wells! Now you really sound like the biggest fucking idiot on earth.

Rooney laughed softly, sadness still lingering in her eyes. "No, silly. Just for a little while."

Rooney

The last thing I needed was to see AJ in my apartment after telling Wells that we needed to take a step back from each other.

My heart was breaking, but I knew it was necessary so I could fix myself and finally be able to love the man who had shown me so much in the past few weeks.

Love.

Not a word I liked to use that often, but I had to stop lying to myself and just be honest.

I loved that man, and my damn mind could go fuck itself because I wouldn't continue to deny it.

My heart was right all along, and I damn well knew it.

And now it was my turn to fix myself, fix my stupid issues, before telling him just how I felt.

I turned the corner into the kitchen and ignored Evie and AJ's stares while they sat on the couch.

I needed something strong.

Maybe a shot of vodka or two. Just something to give me enough of a kick to finally start dealing with my own shit before I bothered anyone else.

I was waiting on a sarcastic comment coming out of Evie's mouth, but to my surprise, it was anything but sarcastic.

"Wanna talk about it?" she asked, standing in the doorway with her head tilted to the side and her arms crossed over her chest.

Did I wanna talk about it?

Hell, I was feeling as if I was slowly going crazy.

"Why's AJ here?" I asked, looking at her and then at Aiden who didn't take his eyes off me.

"He came by with Jonathan earlier. Do you want me to kick him out?" she asked.

I looked back at Evie, then shook my head and sighed. "I need to clear my head before I can talk about it."

I grabbed the bottle of vodka and poured some into a glass, and after taking two shots, I scrunched up my nose and looked at Evie again.

"This was needed," I told her.

"Of course." She laughed softly, then pulled me into a tight hug.

"If you need anything, just call out to me, okay?"

I closed my eyes and hugged her back before nodding and stepping away from her again.

"Before you go...do I need to beat him up?" she asked.

I smiled, knowing she'd break a guy's neck if they ever hurt me, but this wasn't the case.

"He did nothing wrong. We both have our demons, that's all."

Evie studied my face to make sure I wasn't making anything up, but out of all the people I knew, she had to be the first to know how much I struggled with opening up.

She gave me a tight smile and rubbed my arm before I headed out of the kitchen without giving AJ another look.

I didn't have time or space for him right now.

I got into bed and curled up into a ball underneath the covers, staring at the wall in the dim moonlight.

I'd have to start from the beginning.

Was there a time that made me become the person I was today? Had anyone said something to me to make me protect myself from getting hurt?

Or was it just me?

I've never thought about being in a relationship, and when puberty hit, I wasn't as interested in men as much as Evie was.

There was a time I thought I wasn't capable of dating or giving someone else my love, but I soon found out that it wasn't the case.

I had love in me which I couldn't keep inside of me forever, and the second I realized Ira and Wells were more special to me than I had anticipated, I knew they would be the ones I wanted to give my love to.

Why are you like this, Rooney?

Now it was up to me to prove to myself that committing to something wasn't a bad thing.

Though, that took time and I didn't wanna let Wells wait for too long.

I missed him already.

Chapter Thirty-Four

Wells

Every time Ira asked me where Rooney was I had to make up some kind of lie and assure him that we'd see her again soon.

It hadn't even been one day since she told me we'd both need space, and to be fairly honest, it was a good decision, even if it took me a little while to realize that.

Once I dropped Ira off at my mother's this morning, I headed straight to work and started working on my latest project to get my mind off Rooney.

She told me to reflect on myself rather than us, but it was hard not thinking of her when she had already stolen my heart.

It was clear that I wanted our relationship to be a serious one. Well, at least it was clear to me.

So after my realization that Rooney was the one I wanted, I had to push myself to better myself.

She was right when she told me that we were both causing problems, but how on earth would we be able to solve it if she pushed me away to deal with it herself and letting me do the same?

My mind was messy and it didn't feel right being apart from her, but what else was I supposed to do?

I leaned back against my chair and sighed heavily, brushing my hands through my hair and tugging at the ends while looking at the clock.

It was five minutes to three, and I could leave early today to bring Ira to the hospital to get his new pump.

Maybe that would make me stop thinking of her.

I finished what I was working on and saved everything to shut my computer down, then I grabbed my phone and headed outside to get to my car.

My nerves started to show, this time not because of Rooney but because of Ira.

The new pump would be better, but heavier, and I hoped he'd adjust to it quickly.

When I got to my mother's house, Ira was already waiting on the porch with her and waving at me as he saw me pull into the driveway.

I smiled, waving back and getting out of the car once I parked it.

"Hey, bud!" I said as he came running toward me with his arms wide open.

My heart warmed immediately, and I picked him up as he reached me.

"Hi, Daddy!"

His arms hugged me tight around the neck and I pressed him against me while kissing his head gently.

"Did you have a fun day at Grandma's?" I asked, letting him lean back so he could look at me.

"Yes! We played and painted and saw ducks."

"You did? Did you go to the park then?" I asked, not able to stop kissing his sweet face.

God, I was the luckiest guy on earth to have this little guy as my son.

"Yes," he said, already squirming in my arms to make me put him back down. I looked up at my mother who was smiling at us, and I smiled back to not show her how I was really feeling on the inside.

"He hadn't had anything to eat since lunch, just like you said," she told me.

"That's good. Thank you. I'll let you know about tomorrow. I might have to stay a little longer," I told her, helping Ira into the car already.

"Okay, I don't mind keeping him for dinner if you wanna take a little time to yourself after work. Or maybe to spend it with Rooney," she said.

The mention of her name set all the feels off inside of me, making me shiver which is something I definitely never felt.

"Can we see Rooney?" Ira asked, listening to everything that was being said.

"Uh, no, buddy. Not today."

"Something happen?" Mom asked, already knowing something was off.

"Everything's fine, Mom. She's just busy with college, that's all," I lied.

"Well, if you ever wanna invite her to have dinner with us, just let me know. Have a good night," she then said, waving at Ira and getting a wave back before his focus was back on one of the books we bought a while back.

"Bye, Mom," I said, kissing her cheek and then getting into the car.

"Are we going to the hospital?" Ira asked.

"Yes, to get your new pump. Are you excited?"

"Will it hurt?"

"No, it won't. It's just like the pump you have right now. Dr. Cole will only change the device but the rest stays the same, okay?"

"Okay. Can we go to the bookstore after?"

Heck, why not?

He's been brave all his life, and if books were what he wanted, then I'd spoil him until he was old enough to buy them himself.

"Of course we can. Is there a special book you'd like to read?" I asked, looking at him through the rearview mirror.

He had his eyes on the book in his lap but was able to have this conversation with me.

"I think I want a book about mommies and daddies."

That almost made me slam on the brakes.

Shit, where did that come from?

I stopped at a red light and turned to look at him, but he didn't seem too fazed by his answer.

"Has Grandma talked to you about mommies and daddies today?" I asked.

He had never mentioned his mother, but then, I never thought he knew he had one.

One who sadly wasn't around to see him grow.

Ira shook his head, then he pointed into the book. "This girl has a mommy."

I looked at the picture and nodded, sighing softly. "Yeah, she does."

"Does she have a daddy too?"

I was a hundred percent sure he didn't get the concept of parents, as he mostly saw his friends with either their mom or dad, but not both at the same time.

"Probably, yeah." I was having issues with this.

First of all, talking about this in a car was a little inconvenient, and secondly...how the fuck would I tell my son that his mother died during his birth?

"I want a book about mommies."

And that was final because he didn't say another word about it.

How come every time I had something to deal with, other things piled up on top of that and made everything even harder?

Guess luck wasn't on my side these days, but I surely wouldn't ignore Ira's need to talk about mothers.

I owed this to him, and the sooner he learned about what happened, the easier it would be to deal with it.

At least that's what I hoped for.

"Here we are. Ready to meet Dr. Cole?" I asked as I helped him out of the car.

Ira gave me a quick nod and reached up to let me pick him up once I closed the car door, and together we walked inside to get to the front desk.

"Hi, I'm Ira and I get my new pump today!" he said, filled with excitement.

The woman sitting behind the desk smiled at us and nodded. "Dr. Cole has been waiting on you, Ira. You can go straight to his office."

"Thank you," I smiled and walked down the hall to get to Dr. Cole's office, and once we were there, I knocked on the open door to get his attention.

"Come in. I heard someone's getting a new pump today!"

"I do! A bigger one!" Ira announced.

"That's right! Just a little bigger, but it's much better and also very new," he explained.

I sat Ira down on the bed and stood by him to assure him I was right there with him while Dr. Cole prepared a few things.

"What did you do today, Ira?" he asked, starting a conversation to calm him a little.

Ira knew he could trust him, yet he was still nervous which was okay.

"I was at my grandma's house and we painted and went to the park!" he told the doc.

"That sounds like a lot of fun. What's your favorite thing to do at the park?"

"I liked the monkey bars!"

I smiled, remembering how frustrated he was earlier this year when he couldn't even hold on to the bars without me helping him.

He managed to go across it on his own a few months ago, and he was really getting better at keeping himself up there.

"You're a strong one then, hm?"

Ira nodded, agreeing with his doctor.

"All right. See? This is your new pump. It looks about the same, but it has a few different buttons to regulate the insulin," he explained, talking to me now.

I looked closely to make sure not to miss any information that was important for me to know, and Ira just stared at the pump and watched Dr. Cole to make sure he wouldn't do anything that could hurt him.

I rubbed his back gently to let him know that there would be nothing to hurt him, and he leaned against me as he pushed his hand into his hair to twirl it around his fingers.

"The only button you need to know is the on and off button, plus this one where you can check the insulin level. Just press the button for three seconds and the numbers will appear."

He held it toward me so I could try it, and once it worked, Ira wanted to try too.

"It's easy, huh? And it works just like your old pump. You change it every week, but since this is only a test run, you can leave it on him until Friday and we'll see how well it worked, and if he got along with it."

I was glad Ira had the choice after trying the new pump because even if this one was better, as Dr. Cole said, I wanted it to be more comfortable for Ira.

It didn't take long to switch the pumps, and only twenty minutes later, Ira and I were out of the hospital again, ready to go.

"Still wanna go to the bookstore?" I asked as I strapped him into his car seat.

"Yes, please!"

How could I say no to that?

"All right, and maybe after we can grab a delicious dinner at Divine. Remember? The place we got the yummy pasta and cinnamon rolls from."

Ira nodded. "When we went on a picnic with Rooney. Can we go picnic with her again?"

He had no idea how much I wanted that, but I still had to deal with my own shit, and that could take a while.

"Soon, buddy."

We spent almost an hour at the bookstore and looked at books that would potentially make it onto Ira's bookshelf.

There were a few books I had to take from Ira and put on a worker's cart so they could get back on the shelves where they belonged as they weren't very kid friendly.

Luckily, Ira couldn't read yet, and the two drawn people on the Kama Sutra didn't catch his eyes like they would older kids.

"This one?" he asked, running back to me with a book that had a family tree on the cover, and I pressed my lips into a thin line to prepare myself for what was coming next.

"There is a grandma and grandpa, and a mommy and daddy, and that's me," he said, pointing at the little boy pictured on the lower end of the tree branches.

I studied the book cover before looking at Ira with a gentle smile. "You're wondering where your mommy is, huh?"

I kept my voice low, trying not to look too sad in front of him.

I didn't want him to think it was a sad thing that his mother wasn't around, but I wanted him to understand that it wasn't an easy situation.

He didn't reply at first and went on to open the book.

After a little bit of silence, he talked again. "When can I see my mommy?" he asked, breaking my damn heart into millions of pieces.

I cupped the back of his head and pulled him between my legs, making it easy to be on his level while sitting on the kiddie couch.

I pressed my lips against his forehead and closed my eyes, trying my best not to lose a few tears.

"I'll tell you all about your mommy tonight before you go to bed, okay, bud?"

"Is it a happy story?"

Leave it to him to notice something was off.

I smiled at him, brushing back his hair and kissing his cheek. "I can promise you will love the story," I told him in a gentle voice.

And I will tell him how beautiful you were inside and out, Leah.

Chapter Thirty-Five

Wells

We were just about to enter our apartment complex after getting dinner at Divine as Grant pulled up with his car in the parking lot.

Ira immediately recognized the car as his best friend's, and waited patiently for him to get out.

"What are you doing here?" I asked Grant as he stepped out of the car.

"Was hoping to get a beer. Bad timing?" he asked, opening Benny's door and letting him out so the two little ones could say hi to each other.

"Uh, no. Ira and I just have to eat dinner."

"That's fine," he said, locking the car and looking at our sons. "Benny has been asking for Ira all day, and I know he won't go down easy tonight if he doesn't see him."

Understandable.

My son was a real nice little guy.

"I got a new pump!" Ira announced, showing it off to his best friend and then Grant.

"Looks great, Ira. Gonna take good care of it, hm?"

"Yes, I will," Ira replied with a nod, then he reached for Benny's hand to pull him up the stairs and to the entrance.

"He doing okay?"

"Yeah, he doesn't seem to be bothered much by the new pump," I told him.

"My kid would've already ripped that shit off him. You're damn lucky that he's so well behaved. Been trying to get Benny to a doc who can tell me if he's got ADHD, but his mother said he's never this hyperactive when he's with her. I call bullshit on that. This kid never stops, and she's just trying to avoid therapy sessions with us."

I was no doctor, but even a blind person could tell that Benny had too much energy for his age.

"Don't give up, man. Besides, I don't think a kid like mine would fit you. You're too rough, too annoyed with life to have one like Ira. He'd bore the shit outta you," I said with a grin, not meaning it in a rude way toward Ira.

I loved how calm and sweet he was, and I didn't think I could ever deal with a kid like Benny.

We were both lucky in different ways, he just had to realize that.

When we got upstairs, I made Ira sit at the table while Benny was already playing with his toys.

"That's my favorite Hulk, Benny. You can play with him until I can play too, okay?"

"Eat up, bud. But don't hurry or else your belly will hurt later," I told him, putting his dinner on a plate and handing him a fork.

I sat down next to him and started to eat as well while Grant sat down on the couch to keep an eye on Benny.

"So? Any more dates with your neighbor?" Grant asked as he leaned back and turned his head to look at me.

"Uh, no. None in sight," I replied, trying not to mention her name so Ira wouldn't ask about her. "We spent the weekend together, but things didn't end very well."

"Jesus, already? What's the problem?" he asked.

"We need to figure some things out before deciding what we want."

"She not okay with your kid? I thought she liked him, and she seemed like a girl who likes kids."

God, no.

Her love for Ira and vice-versa was not the problem.

"She does, and that's not the issue. She's still young, and although she knows what she wants, she's struggling to open up and commit. But I struggle with the same shit," I said.

"Bad word, Daddy!" Ira frowned at me.

"I'm sorry, buddy. I won't say it again," I promised him.

"You're kidding, right? You two already looked like a couple, and all of a sudden you're both unsure about what you are or wanna be? Jesus, man. If it were up to me, I'd already marry her."

Sure he would, after all the time he spent staring at her while we were at the indoor playground.

"I'm telling you, man. If you don't want her, I'll gladly ask her out. She's upstairs, right?"

That got Ira's attention. "Is Rooney home?"

I sighed and nodded. "Yes, probably. But she's got a lot to do for college, you know? We'll see her soon though."

"So I can paint and play with her again," Ira added.

"That's right," I said with a smile, then glared at Grant.

"Don't you dare go talk to her. I know I want her, I just have to man up and get my sh—" I stopped myself before Ira heard another bad word come out of my mouth.

"I need to assure myself that being in a relationship isn't a bad thing."

Grant studied me for a while before nodding. "If you feel like she's the right one, don't make her wait for too long. Girls are crazy, and their minds can change in a split second. So be sure not to play with her head too much."

Rooney wasn't the crazy type, but he was right about one thing.

I couldn't mess with her head the way I messed with her heart.

But then, my heart was messed with the same way, and quite frankly, we did it to ourselves.

"All done!" Ira called out, already getting out of his chair to tell me that he was ready to go play.

I looked at his plate and decided he ate enough, but I pointed at his water to make him drink a little more before he'd enjoy a nice little playdate with Benny.

"A few more sips and you're good to go," I told him, and he didn't hesitate to drink his water.

Once he was done, I got up and helped him up to the sink to wash his hands, and after that, he was free to go play.

"How about a night at the bar? It's been a while, and it might help you clear your head before you make your final decision."

I looked at him as I started to clean the table.

Guess I could ask my mother if she'd take Ira for another night this week.

"Thursday okay?" I asked, and he shrugged.

"Sure," he said, getting up from the couch and walking over to me. "As long as you promise to loosen up a bit and take that fucking stick out of your ass."

***

They left after an hour or so, and I finally got to put Ira to bed and read him one of the new books we got.

He cuddled up to me on my bed, because even if I wanted him to sleep in his own, I knew tonight wouldn't be easy for either of us.

He had chosen the family tree book, and once we were both comfortable, I opened the book and started reading it to him.

He listened carefully and looked at the pictures while I waited for the moment where he'd ask about mothers again.

I was reading the part about grandparents, and how they were related to the little boy pictures on every page, and shortly after reading that one paragraph, Ira pointed at the grandmother and said, "Grandma is your mommy."

I nodded, kissing the top of his head. "That's right. Grandma is my mom."

"And this is Freddie's mommy?" he asked, pointing at the woman holding Freddie's hand on the picture.

"Exactly." And instead of making him ask about his mother again, I decided to just go for it.

Better now than when it's too late.

He's four, and talking to him about this was inevitable.

"Remember how Freddie here explained how babies are born?"

Ira nodded, turning his head to look up at me with wide eyes.

He was a little confused as to why kids needed a mother to be born, as he never saw his mom.

"Well, you were born the exact same way."

Shit, this is difficult.

Maybe pictures would help.

I reached over to the nightstand and opened the drawer to get out a stack of photographs I kept from Leah.

I looked at them for a second before holding one of them closer to Ira so he could look at it.

"Is this my mommy?" he asked, keeping his eyes fixed on Leah sitting on a couch with me next to her.

"Yes, that's her. And you know who this one is next to her?" I asked, smiling.

"No."

"That's me. I look a little strange with almost no hair, hm?"

He scrunched up his nose and giggled. "You look funny on the picture. Your hair got longer," he pointed out.

"Yeah, much longer. This was six years ago. Your mom and I were really close, you know?"

And now comes the hard part.

Shit, I couldn't cry.

I told him this wasn't going to be a sad story.

"Where is she now? Can I see her and play with her?"

I wish you could, buddy.

Luckily, it wasn't the first time we had the conversation about angels in heaven.

"Remember when you couldn't go to Grandma's because she was saying goodbye to a friend of hers?"

"Yes, Grandma said she said goodbye to her angel friend who is now in heaven."

Thank God he remembered.

I wasn't ready to explain it all to him again.

"Well, when you were born four years ago, your mommy became an angel too."

His lips were parted and his eyes a little unsure at first, then he said, "So mommy's in heaven too?"

Incredible how smart and understanding this little boy was. He listened and let everything sink in that I told him, which made it all so much easier.

For both of us.

"That's right. Mommy's in heaven. See how beautiful she is?" I asked, pointing at Leah in the picture, then showing him another one where she sat on an elephant on her trip to India.

"I was on an elephant too just like mommy!" he said happily.

"That's cool, huh? You know, your mom loved animals just as much as you do, and she wanted to protect and save them so no one could harm them. She was something like a superhero, saving animals," I said, thinking pulling superheroes into this conversation would be a good thing to keep this story a happy one.

"Wow! I wanna be a superhero too when I grow up!"

I smiled and pulled him closer, kissing his temple and closing my eyes.

The urge to cry was near, but I couldn't cry in front of him. I wanted him to know that it wasn't a negative thing that Leah was gone.

I wanted him to know how great she was, and that no matter what, she'd always be his mother.

"You already are one, bud."

I let him look at the other pictures too, and after a while, I thought it would be a good idea to let him know that we could still visit his mother.

"If you want to, we can go say hi to mommy someday. There's a special place where every angel has its home, other than in heaven."

"Where?" he asked, his eyes widening with excitement again.

"It's a place called the cemetery. It's where we can go visit our angels on earth and bring them flowers and little presents," I told him.

"Can I bring mommy flowers and Hulk?"

I smiled. "I know she'll love him. Whenever you're ready to go, buddy, we'll go visit her, okay? Just tell me when and I'll take you to her."

Ira nodded, still looking at the pictures, keeping his thoughts to himself.

I wanted to give him the time he needed to fully comprehend everything, so while he looked at the pictures, I brushed through his blond locks and enjoyed having him close to me.

Without Leah, Ira wouldn't be with me now, and I had to thank Henry for bringing him to me, the guy she had been with while she gave birth to Ira.

I was so damn grateful to have him, and like I had imagined, I wasn't able to keep my tears from rolling down my cheeks.

Hell, knowing your son would grow up without a mother was hard for me too, but I had so much love to give to him, and I would never stop loving him.

Not even when he was ready to move out for college.

I'd be one of those annoying dads who had to check in on their kids twenty-four-seven.

"Daddy? You said this is a happy story," Ira said, worry filling his eyes.

I smiled, brushing my tears away and nodding. "It is, bud. It's a beautiful story and it's okay to cry when something's very beautiful," I explained.

"So...did you cry when you saw Rooney? Because she is beautiful just like mommy."

I couldn't help but chuckle at his comment, and there was no way I could deny that.

"I didn't cry, but I was close," I told him, grinning.

Leave it to Ira to make a conversation light and fun.

"I love you, Ira," I whispered against his head, hugging him tightly as he leaned into me more.

"I love you, Daddy. And I love Mommy too."

Chapter Thirty-Six

Wells

Ira was excited to sleep at Grandma's house and he was already waiting by the door for me to finish packing his bag.

I had told him that I was meeting Grant for the night, and when he asked why he couldn't come with us to the bar, I had to explain that bars weren't where four-year-old boys were allowed.

He tried to bribe me saying he would behave and not talk about his favorite superheroes, but I had to disappoint him.

Though, most of the adults there would definitely love to talk about things like that.

"Can we go now?" he asked, holding on to the doorhandle while looking at me with his head tilted to the side.

I walked over to him and nodded, holding his backpack filled with toys toward him so he could hang it over his shoulders.

While he did, I put on my shoes and coat. "You're starting to get a little impatient, huh? How about we take things slow? We got time, you know, buddy?"

He frowned at me and reached for the doorhandle again.

"I'm four," he stated, as if that would justify the fact that he was more impatient than ever.

I chuckled as I grabbed the little duffle bag and nodded at the door. "Let's go. I can tell you don't mind being away from me tonight."

He didn't answer while he opened the door and stepped out, but once he reached the stairs, he turned and looked at me with a gentle smile. "But I will only sleep once at Grandma's, Daddy. Don't be sad."

This kid.

His character was changing right in front of my eyes and I loved every second of it, even though I wanted him to stay the same forever.

"I'll try not to be," I said with a grin, locking the door behind me.

As we got downstairs, Ira was about to push open the door when Rooney pulled at it from the outside.

We were both taken aback from seeing each other after last Sunday night, and neither of us said a word but kept staring at each other.

"Rooney!" Ira called out, hugging her legs.

It took her a moment to greet him back, but once she tore her eyes off mine, she looked down and placed a hand at the back of Ira's head with a smile.

"Hey, little man. Going out tonight?" she asked, squatting down to talk to him after he let go of her.

"I'm going to Grandma's so Daddy can go to the bar."

"That's fun! Did you pack enough toys to play with?" she asked, smiling at him.

"Yes, all of them! And a puzzle. Did you know I have a new pump?"

Ira was still a little unsure about the pump, but he liked to flaunt it.

I would too, honestly.

"I heard about that, yeah. What's the new pump like?"

Her way of talking to my son was soothing, and I knew how much Ira wanted to see her the past few days.

God, seeing them together again felt so damn good.

"It's bigger," Ira replied with a shrug.

"As long as it doesn't bother you, hm? That's great, Ira."

"Can you come play with me maybe tomorrow? I'm not at Grandma's tomorrow," he explained.

Rooney's eyes moved from Ira to me, and I let out a sigh, knowing that put her in a little bit of a weird situation.

"Rooney has things to do for college, you know? I'm sure she'll find a time to come and play soon," I said, keeping my eyes on hers.

She pressed her lips into a thin line, then looked at Ira again with a soft smile. "We'll find a time to play and paint together soon, okay? I promise it won't take too long," she told him.

I knew she would keep that promise, but it wasn't easy knowing she was still struggling to figure out if committing to us, Ira and me, was what she really wanted.

I had already made up my mind, and now seeing her again only strengthened that decision.

Rooney was the one I wanted.

"Okay. Daddy said I'm impatient so maybe don't make me wait for too long."

She laughed softly and I chuckled, thinking he *did* understand what impatient meant.

"Pinky promise," Rooney said, holding out her pinky to make him hook his around it.

She hugged him before getting back up, and when she looked at me, I couldn't let her go without knowing if she was okay.

"How are you doing?"

She shrugged, nervously playing with her fingers.

"Good," she replied.

I studied her face for a second and didn't quite believe her.

"How are you really feeling, Rooney?"

I couldn't be the only one to hate this silence between us, and although I was okay with giving her all the time she needed to think this through, I couldn't wait for too long to finally hold her again.

She took a deep breath and shrugged again, but instead of a simple answer, she said, "I'm getting there. This isn't easy, you know?"

"I know. I don't wanna push you." I looked down at Ira who noticed the situation wasn't as relaxed as he first thought.

"I'm just gonna get a drink with Grant. We're home this weekend, in case you wanna..."

"Okay," she said, looking at Ira again and smiling. "I'll see you soon, Ira, all right?"

She reached out to brush through his hair, and Ira nodded and waved at her. "See you."

I gave her one last look before she headed upstairs, letting that heavy weight push down on me again the second she was out of my sight.

Things felt easier with her around, but as long as she wasn't ready, I couldn't tell her that.

After dropping off Ira at my mother's house, I drove to the bar Grant told me to meet him and walked inside only to find a crowded bar.

Wasn't really my scene, but I already said I'd meet him here.

I saw him sitting at a booth which he probably couldn't reserve for just us as two women sat right across from him.

I wasn't really into talking about my issues with strangers eavesdropping, but I could also just not talk about my problems.

"Hey, man," I said as I reached the booth, and when he looked up at me, he grinned.

"There he is. Hope you don't mind these two beautiful ladies sitting with us. They didn't have any other place to sit so I invited them here."

I looked at both of them, taking in their pretty faces covered in makeup.

Well, these two weren't too bad, but I knew it was exactly what Grant would go for.

"Dreya and Mel," Grant said, surprising me that he knew their names.

"Wells," I said, nodding and then sitting down next to Grant.

Before I could start conversing with them, I lifted my hand as a waitress walked by to order a beer, then I looked back at the girls to find both of them looking at me with wide smiles.

"Grant told us you're a single dad too. We think that's totally sweet."

We think?

Didn't they have their own mouths to talk and own opinions to tell?

"Uh, yeah, I have a four-year-old boy."

"What's his name?" one of them asked, and I already wanted to leave.

"Ira."

"Aw, that's the sweetest name ever! And Grant also said your sons play together all the time?" the blonde one said.

I shot a glare at Grant for pulling me into this even though he knew I didn't like talking to random girls at bars.

"He's not in a very good mood lately. Maybe let's focus more on me than him," Grant said.

His dick-behavior didn't bother me today, as long as these two would stop asking me questions about my personal life when this was the first and last time we'd ever see each other.

Besides, I could use some quiet time with a beer in hand.

Ignoring the two women was the least of my problems right now.

Rooney

I was on my fifth unfinished painting ever since Wells and I decided to take time away from each other, and every new canvas I ruined made me angrier at myself for not being able to handle my feelings and needs as quick as Wells could.

I saw it in his eyes.

He knew exactly what he wanted and made a decision, only to now wait for me to do the same.

Well, I had my feelings under control, actually.

I knew I wanted to be with him, and I knew the stinging in my heart today when I had to lie to Ira and tell him that I was busy with school was something I never wanted to experience ever again.

That little boy held a piece of my heart in his hands, while his dad held the other.

So, what was my issue?

Commitment.

Because relationships weren't always fun and games, and they often ended badly, which was the biggest part of it all I definitely wanted to avoid.

Still, just because I was afraid of getting hurt, why would I ever lock myself up when I damn well knew there was a handsome, loving, and charismatic man waiting on me?

I shook my head at myself and let the paintbrush fall onto the canvas with probably the worst artwork I had ever created on it.

My mind was all over the place, which was probably why I couldn't focus on just one color scheme, but had to mix and use the worst colors ever on the canvas.

I leaned back against the stool I rarely sat on as the floor was much more comfortable to sit and paint.

My reflection in the mirror caught my attention, and I stared at myself, wishing it would tell me something.

Something I could grab onto and finally pull myself to where my heart had always wanted to be ever since I met him.

Next to Wells.

And close to Ira.

I had to get out of this situation.

I couldn't even read myself anymore, but I had to find a way back to myself again.

I knew myself better than anyone else did, which was fairly obvious, so why couldn't I just stop overthinking when it was the best thing I could do in this situation?

This isn't you, Rooney.

"Wanna get takeout and watch a movie and drink wine?" Evie asked as she stepped into my room without knocking or announcing herself.

I looked up at her with raised brows, then I sighed and shrugged.

"Sure. No Jonathan tonight?" I asked, pushing the canvas and paint aside to get up.

While she talked, I took off the sweater I wore to paint, which already had stains all over it, and changed into a clean sweater to be just as comfortable.

"He's out of town visiting his cousin," she explained with a raised brow.

I laughed at her expression. "You don't think he really is visiting his cousin?"

"No, I don't. Which I shouldn't be jealous about because I have no idea if it's a girl or boy cousin, and also, I don't like him that like that anyway."

"Right. You like him to sleep with you whenever he has the time to," I pointed out, not believing a word she said.

"Exactly. What about your man—"

"Nope," I interrupted her, letting her know that I wasn't up to talk about Wells.

I was on the right track, though I still needed time.

"Jeez, okay. No more guy-talk. What movie do you wanna watch?" she asked, walking out of my room and heading to the kitchen.

"I don't care. No rom-coms. No dramas."

I sat down on the couch and pulled the blanket over my legs to stay warm.

"Not sure I know movies outside of those two genres," she said, walking back to me with the menu for all the places we could order takeout from.

"Then maybe it's time to change that," I told her. "And I'm craving sushi."

As much as my heart was aching for Wells and Ira, this girls night would make me think of other things and maybe even lock my decision into place so it wouldn't take more than two days until I could knock on Well's door and tell him exactly what I wanted from him.

His love, and in exchange, he'd get mine.

Chapter Thirty-Seven

Wells

"If you're gonna propose another night at the bar, I won't let you in," I said to Grant as he stood in front of my door with Benny holding his hand.

"Still mad about that? Jesus, man. You could've taken part in that conversation."

Never.

Not with two women I already forgot about.

"Can I play with Ira?" Benny asked, and if it weren't for him, I wouldn't have let them in.

"Of course, Benny. Ira's in his room playing," I told him, stepping aside so he could run inside.

"Shoes, Ben!" Grant called out, and he stopped in the middle of the hallway to take off his shoes and then run into Ira's room.

Ira hadn't been feeling well since last night, but as today was Sunday, he had been recovering from feeling tired and sick all day long.

I heard them giggle as they saw each other, wondering how those two boys would turn out when they were older.

Well, I was certain that Benny would still cause havoc wherever he'd go, but I was still unsure about Ira.

He was calm and serene now, but that could soon change, as he already is starting to become a little more sarcastic and outspoken.

"Still on a break or whatever you call it?" Grant asked as we walked into the kitchen.

"Saw her on Thursday before dropping Ira off at my mother's. She looked sad and unsure, so I guess she still needs time to realize that she wants to be with me."

I grabbed two beers out of the fridge and gave one to him, then we sat down on the couch.

"And I'm guessing that's how you feel about her too? Haven't seen you with a girl in years."

Yeah, that was probably why it took me a while to realize I needed her by my side.

"She's young, and our age difference is something that could get in the way of many things, but I need to take this chance on her."

"Yeah, you do. You're miserable," Grant said with a grin.

I rolled my eyes at his comment and shook my head. "I'm doing just fine, but I'm missing something. Someone. Someone who shows me that I'm not just here on earth to be a hard-working father. I love Ira, but all the love I give to him leaves a void in my damn heart. And Rooney already started to fill it with her affection."

Grant eyed me carefully while I spoke, and after both of us were silent for a minute, he raised a brow and nodded.

"Let's hope she sees what she's doing to you then. Don't think she's heartless and would just push aside everything you two have already gone through. She seemed like a sweet girl."

And I was lucky he wasn't going after her when he found out we were taking some time apart.

As big of an asshole as Grant was, he would never take a girl away from me.

But then, I wasn't sure Rooney liked him that much when she first met him.

"She's the sweetest, which makes this even harder. I know how much she's hurting and struggling right now, and all I wanna do is head upstairs and hold her."

Grant raised a brow at me and sighed. "In a situation like this...that's probably the only right thing to do, man."

Yeah, it was. But I promised myself to let her come to me instead of me pushing her to do so.

"A few more days," I whispered, sighing and running my hand through my hair.

Neither of us spoke for another minute, sipping on our beers and listening to our sons play in Ira's room.

Maybe the less I thought about her, the sooner she'd be back in my arms.

"Go on. Tell me all about your night with those girls," I said, leaning back and looking at him.

A grin spread across his face and he got ready to tell me every single detail about his threesome.

It was clear that after I left the bar, that he'd take both of them home.

He must've thought I'd take one with me to clear my mind and have some fun, but to not disappoint the girl that was meant to be mine for the night, he took both of them home.

Like a real gentleman, of course.

"First of all...it was a good thing I went home with both because one wouldn't have been enough. They were both good at different things."

"Right," I muttered, amused but at the same time slightly weirded out. "When are you gonna find a woman that's worth being the only one in your life? You're getting old too, you know?"

"Forty-five isn't old, fucker. And I'm good with just hookups. It's easier," he explained.

Sure. Whatever suited him.

"Daddy, can I have a sleepover with Benny tonight?" Ira asked as he walked into the living room a little later.

I looked at him and puckered my lips.

He still looked a little weak and tired, but before answering Ira's question myself, I looked at Grant to see what he thought of that.

It was Sunday night, but I wouldn't have minded taking Benny to his mother's house as Grant would have to work.

"Not tonight, Ira. Benny's visiting his mom tomorrow morning, so we gotta get up early," Grant explained.

I turned back to Ira and brushed along his hair at the back of his head. "Another time, hm? Maybe it's best as you haven't been feeling good this weekend."

Ira pouted for a second, which he rarely ever did, but then he nodded to let us know he understood. "Okay. Another time," he repeated, letting us know that he wouldn't forget about this.

When he left to get back to his bedroom, Grant chuckled and shook his head. "My kid would've thrown a damn tantrum by now. Teach me your ways, Daddy," he said, grinning like an idiot.

I rolled my eyes at him and laughed out loud. "Go to hell," I muttered, standing up and carrying my empty beer bottle into the kitchen.

"I wish." He drained his beer and got up himself, walking over to me and placing his bottle next to mine.

"Time to put the kid to bed if I don't want him to make a fuss about not letting him sleep tomorrow morning. And then his mother will be pissed at me because he's grumpy all day from getting too little sleep."

Problems I was somewhat lucky not to have with Ira, but was also missing from being a parent.

Ira made life easier than anything else, which was a real blessing.

"Benny, let's go," Grant called out, and seconds later, his son came running from Ira's bedroom with one of his action figures in hand.

"Ira said I can take this home to play," he told us, holding The Flash up into the air.

"Yes, but I want him back," Ira added, stopping by the kitchen archway.

"That's nice of you, Ira. Did you say thank you, Ben?"

Benny nodded and turned to Ira, promising him he will bring The Flash back next time.

I could already see them taking each other's footballs or even cars when they're older, sharing everything ever since they were little.

At least I hoped they'd stay friends forever.

We walked Benny and Grant to the door and said goodbye, and after locking the door, I turned to Ira and asked what he wanted to do for the rest of the evening.

It wasn't too late, and he didn't seem tired yet, so another hour or so would surely make him want to go to bed.

"I want to watch TV."

This thing of suddenly wanting to sit in front of the TV more often wasn't bothering me as much as I thought it would in the beginning, as it was mostly only a few times a week for half an hour, as he wouldn't be able to keep his eyes open any longer than that.

Besides, I loved watching TV when I was his age and wasn't feeling well.

"How about a movie? There's not much to watch on TV at this time of the day for kids," I told him.

He already got comfortable on the couch while I filled his bottle with water.

"Okay," he simply replied, waiting patiently for me to sit with him.

"Here, bud."

I held the bottle to him and sat down next to him, then I turned on the TV and leaned back, changing to Netflix and going through the kid's channel to find a good fit for tonight.

"That one!" he called out, pointing at the screen. "The one with the funny hat."

"*Charlie and the Chocolate Factory?*" I puckered my lips and tried to remember if there were any scenes I thought weren't very kid friendly.

But, heck...it's a damn kid's movie.

"Are you sure? Or do you wanna see if there's another one you like?"

"No."

Clear enough.

I pressed play and set the remote down next to me, then let Ira cuddle up to me as I covered him with a blanket.

"Can we go visit Mommy soon?" he asked out of the blue, but it made me smile as he hasn't forgotten about me offering to take him to the cemetery.

I brushed through his hair and thought about it for a minute, then nodded and kissed the top of his head.

"We can go tomorrow if you'd like."

"And can we buy her flowers and bring a present?" he asked, keeping his eyes on the screen while having this conversation with me.

Guess he got the multitasking ability from me.

"Of course we can. We'll buy the prettiest flowers, deal?"

Ira nodded. "Deal."

It would take us an hour to go visit Leah's grave since her parents wanted her close and in her hometown, but Ira would finally get to be close to her.

At least that's what I thought.

***

His cries woke me up in the middle of the night, and at first it felt like a dream.

But when his usual soft voice turned into a croaking roar for help, I jumped out of bed and ran into his bedroom.

Ira was curled up into a ball in his bed, his hair sticking to his sweaty forehead while the smell of vomit slowly filled my nose.

"Oh, bud," I whispered, turning on the light to see him better than with just the night light on, and when I looked back to him, I saw his face, bed and floor covered in vomit.

How can a little body like his release so much fluid at once?

"Daddy!" Ira cried, tears streaming down his face.

"I'm here, buddy. You'll be fine. I promise," I told him, trying to calm him and at the same time figure out what was happening.

I felt helpless at first, unsure what to do or if I could touch him without hurting him more.

"What is it, Ira? What's hurting? Your belly?"

He couldn't answer as more tears followed and his body jerked at the heavy and intense hiccups overcoming him.

Shit, what the fuck do I do?

"Shhh, buddy, you'll be fine, okay? Daddy's gonna take good care of you," I promised him, brushing his hair back and looking around the room to find something to grab onto and make this all better.

Rooney was the first person that came to mind, but I didn't have her number to call her, and shouting her name wasn't gonna help me either.

I pulled the blanket over Ira's body to keep him warm, then I picked him up and headed out to the hallway to put on my shoes.

Luckily, I went to bed with a shirt and sweatpants on after being too tired to change, so I quickly slipped on my shoes and unlocked the door.

"Daddy!" Ira cried, nestling his face into my chest.

I hated seeing him like this.

He had been sick in the past, but never had he cried this hysterically and helplessly.

Something was really wrong, and if I didn't get to the hospital soon, this would only become worse than it already was.

My heart was pounding as I took the keys from the table next to the door and headed outside without grabbing a coat for myself.

That didn't matter right now, because all I was set to do was take Ira to the children's hospital and make sure he was okay.

"You'll be fine," I kept whispering as we reached the door to get to my car, and once I unlocked it, I was unsure if leaving him alone on the backseat was really a good idea.

"Shit," I muttered, looking up at the building in the hopes someone was still awake.

It was after four a.m., and there was no one who could help me get my son to the hospital to make his pain go away.

Rooney

His cries were what woke me, and for a second I wondered if I had ever heard of another kid living in this apartment complex.

Then it hit me, and I quickly got out of bed as the cries quieted down in the hallway but continued outside in the parking lot.

I turned on my nightstand lamp and walked over to the window to look outside, and when I saw a distressed Wells with a very agitated Ira in his arms, I grabbed my sweater and pulled it over my head, then headed out of my room to put on my shoes and run downstairs.

Something must've been terribly wrong.

I could feel it, and I couldn't imagine how horrible that feeling must've been for Wells.

"What happened?" I asked as I stepped outside into the cold fall night, and when Wells saw me, I could see some kind of relief in his eyes.

"I don't know what's wrong, but he can't stop crying. He threw up. I don't know what it is," he told me as I stepped closer to them.

"Oh, sweet boy," I whispered, caressing his head before grabbing the car key out of Wells's hand.

"I'll drive you to the hospital," I told him, already walking over to the driver's side.

"Thank you, Rooney. God, I wanted to call you but I don't have your number. I was helpless," he told me.

I smiled at the thought of him thinking of me in this situation, and when he was sitting in the back with Ira in his lap, I looked back through the rearview mirror to get one more look at the two people that I could never let go through this on their own.

Ira's cries got quieter throughout the drive, but instead of that being a good thing, I felt Wells's nervousness grow as he tried to speak to his son.

"Ira! Ira, buddy, stay awake, okay? We'll be at the hospital soon. Don't fall asleep, bud," he begged, making my heart race like crazy.

I needed to hurry up, and luckily, there were no cars around in the middle of the night.

"Ira, don't sleep, buddy. Please keep your eyes open," he continued to tell him, but Ira's hiccups and cries got quieter with every second that passed.

The panic in Wells's voice was not to miss, and I cursed myself for pushing him away almost a week ago.

I should've been there for him when Ira was starting to feel sick, and maybe we would've been here earlier without him having to frantically stand outside and wonder how to get his son to the hospital all by himself.

"We're here, Ira. Stay awake, bud. We're here," he repeated as I stepped out of the car and helped him get out with Ira still in his arms.

His face was pale and his mouth all dry.

The sight of little Ira like this was horrifying, and it was something no parent would ever wish for their children to go through.

"I checked his pump. I should've checked it earlier. His insulin level is too damn high," he croaked out with a shaky voice.

"Let's go inside," I told him, rubbing his arm before heading to the entrance.

To our luck, the lady at the front desk recognized Wells and Ira and immediately called someone.

I had no clue how hospitals worked, and I didn't want to assume things that weren't true, so I kept quiet while the lady pointed us down the hall where a doctor already walked toward us.

"He's not responding. His insulin level is too high. Please, help my boy, Dr. Cole," Wells begged desperately.

I was glad he knew the doctor, and once Ira was in the safe hands of doctors and nurses, I pulled Wells to me and hugged him tight as he cried into the crook of my neck, his arms tightly around my body.

"He'll be okay. They're gonna take good care of him, Wells," I whispered, caressing the back of his head and letting him know that he's not alone.

Chapter Thirty-Eight

Wells

It's been an hour since they took Ira into a separate room, and while we waited in the waiting room, Rooney held my hand and assured me that they would know exactly what to do to help Ira get back on his feet.

I was grateful to have her with me, because at least then one of us was calm.

If I had called my mother, she'd be more hysterical than me, and that would've only made me more nervous.

Rooney was a source of serenity and security I didn't wanna let go of, but when the door to Ira's room finally opened, I pushed myself off the chair and walked toward Dr. Cole.

"Is he okay? Can I see him?" I asked, looking past him to try and get a glance of my boy.

"Ira is awake and well. He suffered from hyperglycemia. He lapsed into a diabetic coma, but we got him all the fluids his body needed and he's already feeling much better."

All I could hear were the words *awake and well* and *feeling much better.*

"How did that happen? Didn't he just get the new insulin pump?" I said, confused and a little angry.

That thing was supposed to make life easier for him.

Make him play like a normal kid and not have him poke his damn finger every time to check his blood. And to avoid those fucking insulin shots which I knew hurt him every damn time I had to give one to him.

"Yes, and that's where I have to apologize to you. The new pump must've had a malfunction. We've looked into it and found what the problem was. We'll have to call back the nine other patients we gave a new pump to as well, just in case theirs have issues too. I'm very sorry this happened, but I can promise you that he's doing better," he said with an apologetic look.

He was a doctor, and there was no reason for me to be mad at him.

He didn't create that pump, and if anything, I'd have to sue the damn company that manufactured them.

I gave him a quick nod and looked past him again. "Can I see him now?" I asked quietly, slowly losing my patience.

"Of course. Take all the time you need. If you intend on sleeping here, there's a second bed for you. We'll be back to check on him in the morning."

I quickly walked into the room to see Ira sitting on the bed with an infusion of some fluid hooked to his hand in which he was holding a banana, eating it slowly.

"Hey, bud. How are you feeling?" I said, sitting down on the side of his bed and brushing through his wild hair while tears stung my eyes.

Before he could reply, the nurse checking the monitor next to his bed smiled at us and said, "He's been very brave, just like his favorite superheroes," she said.

I wanted to smile, but it didn't turn out as I wanted it to.

Of course he had told them all about his favorite superheroes already. "Has he been up for long?" I asked.

"About forty minutes now. As he lapsed into the diabetic coma, we had to improve his fluid levels in his body. He's getting phosphate into his body to raise that level as well, and the banana is great to help with his low potassium level," she explained, telling me much more than Dr. Cole had.

He probably felt like shit letting a four-year-old try out a new pump.

I nodded at her, then looked back at Ira who still looked a little weak, but that must've been the tiredness.

"Are you feeling okay?" I asked again, holding his other hand and squeezing it gently.

"I'm okay," he said, unfazed by the fact that he was at the hospital.

Maybe it didn't hit him yet.

"Will he still get a pump?" I asked, unsure if I'd want him to get the old one back in case the same shit happened.

Insulin pumps were supposed to take care of the blood sugar, not make a damn mess and put my kid into a diabetic coma.

"Dr. Cole will talk to you about this later today. For now, we gave him the needed insulin and will check in on him every hour to see where it's at," the nurse said.

She must've been around my age, and the way she looked at us told me that she had kids of her own, knowing what it feels like to worry about your child.

"Patients who lapse into a diabetic coma are quickly back on their feet the moment their bodies get what they need. Don't worry, he'll be out of here no later than lunch time."

I smiled at her, this time managing a real one that met my eyes.

"That's good news. Thank you," I said, looking back at Ira as she left the room.

"I was so worried, buddy. But you were so strong and brave," I praised, caressing his cheek and letting out a relieved sigh.

"Does your belly still hurt?" I asked, but he shook his head and took another bite of his banana.

"Rooney!" he called out, and I turned around to see her standing there with her arms loosely crossed in front of her, and a soft, gentle smile on her face.

"Hey, little man. How are you feeling?" she asked.

"I'm okay," he said, holding up his banana. "They gave me a banana."

"Is it good?" she asked, and the kind, sweet boy he was, he held the banana out for her to take a bite.

"Oh, no. You eat it, so you can get out of here quickly, hm?"

He nodded, and although I felt the awkwardness between us, I nodded to silently tell her she should come closer.

She closed the door behind her and walked over to the bed, stopping right next to me and reaching out her hand to brush along Ira's hair. "I'm happy you're okay, Ira. You were so very brave," she praised, but it didn't bother me one bit.

If anything, I wanted her to show him this much affection every damn day from now on.

I placed my hand on her lower back to thank her for being here, and helping me get Ira to the hospital in time, but instead of having to say those words, she understood without me ever speaking.

She smiled at me and wrapped her arm around my shoulders while turning her head back to Ira who was done with the banana, and I took the peel and placed it on the table next to me to dispose of it.

"Maybe you should get a little bit of sleep, buddy. How does that sound?" I asked.

It was already five-thirty, but to me, sleep didn't appeal much. Same with Ira.

"I'm not tired. Can I watch TV?" he asked, making me chuckle. "This early in the morning?"

"I don't have my toys," he pointed out.

"Fair point," Rooney mumbled, not able to hide a grin.

"All right, TV it is then."

There probably was some kid's show starting this early, at least that was the case when I was his age, and sure enough, we found some cartoons.

"You should get back home," I told Rooney, knowing she'd have classes starting at nine like every Monday morning.

She studied my face for a while to try and decide if leaving was what she wanted to do, but eventually gave up and nodded. "I have a presentation, but after that, I'd like to come back here," she said.

Her love and care for Ira warmed my heart, yet there was this unpleasant feeling still lingering between us with no exit in sight.

"Okay, I'm sure we'll still be here by then."

Rooney nodded, squeezing my shoulder tightly before turning and looking at Ira. "Bye, Ira. I'll see you in a few hours, okay?" And to show just how much she cared about him, she leaned in to kiss his forehead with both her hands cupping his face softly.

"Where are you going?" he asked, already longing for her.

It's been days since he's been wanting to have her close, and the moment he does, she has to leave again so soon.

"I have to go to class and hold a presentation, but after that, I'll come back."

"Pinky promise?" he asked, holding his pinky up and giving her a serious look.

She laughed softly, hooking her pinky with his and nodding. "Pinky promise."

She turned back to me and gave me a quick smile, and with her hand on my cheek, she brushed her thumb along my skin gently.

I could tell there was something in her eyes wanting to tell me everything she was feeling in that exact moment, but this was not the time or place for it.

"Here, take my car," I told her. "I won't leave anyway."

She nodded, placing her hand at her sweater's front pocket to indicate my keys were in there, and after another sweet smile, she left.

"Will she keep her promise, Daddy?" Ira asked, his voice hopeful.

I smiled at him after watching Rooney leave, and as sure as I could ever be, I nodded.

"Yes, buddy. She'll keep her promise."

Rooney

During the presentation in front of my art history class I couldn't stop thinking about Ira, wishing I could've stayed with them at the hospital.

Although he was doing much better, I knew Wells was still overwhelmed about what happened early this morning.

But despite the shock he got, he handled it well.

I decided to drive to a toy store and get Ira a little get well present before heading back to the hospital, but on my way to Wells's car parked in the college's parking lot, AJ called out to me and made me turn to look back at him.

Class was over sooner than expected, and I knew Ira wouldn't be released from the hospital before noon.

"Driving his car now?" he asked as he reached me, and I pressed my lips into a tight smile, hoping this wasn't going to be one of his jealousy attacks.

"I had to borrow it," I simply said, not wanting to tell him what really happened or why I wasn't driving my car.

He didn't need to know everything.

"I see. So...how are things going?" he asked, pushing his hands into his front pockets and tilting his head to the side.

"Good. College is great," I replied. "You?"

"The usual," he said, shrugging. "There's a gala I have to attend tonight at the country club. Didn't Evie tell you about it?" he asked.

"Uh, no, she didn't. But I haven't seen her in two days, I think. She hung out with Jonathan a lot the past few days," I told him.

"So you're not going?"

I shook my head and puckered my lips. "No, sorry. But I'm sure you'll have fun."

He chuckled and shrugged. "Probably. Hey, we're cool, right? I'm sorry for last time. I didn't wanna hurt you or anything. I guess I'm finally realizing that sometimes I have to let go of things that aren't meant for me."

I studied his face for a while before nodding, then I smiled. "I might not be meant for you as your girlfriend, Aiden, but I've always told you that you're my friend. You're a nice guy, and I'd hate to give up on you. We can still talk, you know?"

"Will your boyfriend be okay with that? I heard older men can be just as jealous as college guys."

I laughed at that whole-heartedly. "I think he'll be okay with it."

Hey, you didn't deny him being your boyfriend, my mind said, making me smile brightly like a fool.

Well, technically, Wells wasn't my boyfriend. Yet.

"Listen, AJ." I placed my hand at his upper arm and squeezed it gently. "I have to go, but we'll talk, okay? Thank you for stopping and talking to me."

Instead of waiting on his goodbye, I turned on my heels and walked toward Wells's car with quick steps, pulling the door open and hopping in to drive to the toy store.

My heart was racing and it luckily didn't take me too long to find the perfect present for Ira, and I was already back on the road to drive to the hospital.

Once I got there and parked, I pulled out the bag with the hulk hands and went inside to finally see them again, but as I turned the corner to get to Ira's room, Wells walked out of it.

As he noticed me walking toward him in a rather confident and fast walk, he tilted his head to question why I looked so determined.

There was no time to explain as an overwhelming feeling of love and gratitude washed over me, and when I reached him, I let the bag fall down to my feet before wrapping my arms around his neck, kissing him with no hesitation.

He was surprised and didn't kiss me back at first, but when he realized what was going on, he eased against me and put both arms around my back to pull me even closer.

Was I moving too fast?

Hell no!

We've done far more than kissing before, and it was time to let him know just how much I wanted to be his.

I felt tears stinging my eyes as his fingers curled around my hips, and his tongue brushed over my bottom lip to request entrance.

I parted my lips, letting him dip his tongue into my mouth and move along mine as my hands made their way into his thick locks.

Maybe this wasn't the right place to have a full-on make out session, but I couldn't wait any longer.

I couldn't torture myself any more, and I knew he felt the same.

There were so many thoughts running through my mind, some telling me that this was wrong, but the majority of them rooted for me to finally let him in the way I should've a long time ago.

My heart was wide open for him and Ira, and no matter what may come our way in the future, I didn't care.

As long as I had them right next to me.

"What was that for?" Wells asked, chuckling softly after he broke the kiss but stayed close to me with his forehead leaning against mine.

I caught my breath after that long, passionate and much needed kiss, then I smiled and tugged at his hair gently. "I need to get this out. I love you, and I'm sorry if this is the least romantic place and time for me to tell you, but I love you so damn much,

Wells. I want you. I want to be with you. And I want Ira close. God, I love him too," I told him.

It was hard to admit all this, knowing only a few hours earlier I still had no clue if committing to a relationship was the right thing to do, but this eye-opening realization that this man loved me back and would push his own demons aside to let me in came crashing in just minutes before.

"You're the one I want, Wells," I whispered, needing him to hear it one more time.

His eyes wandered all over my face to find answers to the questions floating in his eyes, and I could only imagine how strange this must've been for him.

He smiled, cupping my cheek with one hand while keeping me close with his other on my lower back.

"And you're sure about what you just said, Rooney?" he asked.

Where'd he get the nerve to ask me that?

I laughed softly, my happiness spreading from my chest into my whole body. "I've never been this sure about anything in my life, Wells," I promised him.

His eyes kept wandering over my face before he finally realized that I was being one hundred percent honest.

"I love you too, Rooney," he said, his voice low and raspy.

He must've been up ever since I left as he sounded tired.

I smiled at his response and kissed him again, sealing our words with our lips.

This time our kiss didn't last too long as we heard footsteps get closer and we were pretty much standing right in the middle of the hallway.

I stepped away from him involuntarily and grabbed the bag with the present in it from the floor.

"I'll be right with you," he whispered close to my ear and kissing my temple before heading toward the bathrooms.

I watched him leave, then stepped aside to let the nurses pass, getting an annoyed look from one of them before I opened the door to Ira's room and entered it.

He was laying on his side with his back turned to me but his head facing the TV which had been moved to the side so he was a little more comfortable.

I smiled, and when I reached his bed, I saw his eyes closed.

Good thing he was getting some sleep after a scary night like this, but it was Wells who could've used sleep instead of Ira.

I set the present down at the end of the bed where it wouldn't bother him as his feet only reached half of it, then I took off my coat and walked over to the table where two balloons and a big, fluffy teddy bear was sitting.

Wells was back quickly, and after closing the door behind him, he smiled at me and nodded at the teddy bear.

"Mom and George were here earlier this morning, but Ira has been sleeping through the whole visit. He's exhausted from staying up until seven-thirty and watching TV," he explained.

I nodded and walked over to him as he sat down on the bed which was meant for him and stopped in front of him to place my hand at his neck.

"Did you sleep?"

"Not really. I laid down with him, but I barely closed my eyes. The horror of hearing him call out for me wouldn't let me fall asleep."

I felt sorry for him as he definitely would be having trouble falling asleep from now on.

"You did everything right, just know that, okay?" I said quietly, letting him pull me between his legs with his hands at the back of my thighs.

"I know. But we got here thanks to you. How did you..."

"I heard him cry," was my simple explanation, and he gave me a quick nod before wrapping his arms around me and leaning into me with his head against my chest.

"Thank you. I wouldn't have made it without you, Rooney," he whispered.

I pushed my hands back into his hair and leaned down to kiss his head. "There's nothing to thank me for, Wells. I'm glad I could help, and that he's doing better now."

I'd do anything for them.

That's clear to me now.

Chapter Thirty-Nine

Wells

"Can I open it?" Ira asked the second he saw Rooney's present at the end of his bed, and I smiled at his excited expression as Rooney walked over to him with a nod.

"Of course you can. Are you feeling much better now that you got some sleep?" she asked, sitting down next to him on the bed and pulling out the wrapped present from the bag.

"Yes, I'm okay," Ira replied with a smile, his eyes widening at the colorful wrapping paper.

She didn't have to get him a present, but I knew if I had stopped her from doing so, she'd get more than one just to tease me.

I loved how caring she was, not just with Ira, but with everyone around her.

Even though we said that we loved each other, we still had to talk about things when we got the chance to, but right now, watching Ira all happy and healthy was what we needed to do.

"What could it be?" I asked, standing up from the guest bed and standing next to Rooney while Ira ripped the paper to reveal what was inside.

"Woah! Hulk hands!"

Rooney had gotten him gloves resembling Hulk's fists which he could put on like gloves and reenact all the scenes from the movies.

"Those are awesome, aren't they? I saw them and immediately thought of you so you can wear them with the costume Daddy got you for your birthday," Rooney suggested.

Genius.

"That's what was missing from the costume, huh?" I said with a grin.

"Yes, they're awesome! Can I put them on?" he asked, trying to get them out of the packaging.

"We'll do one hand, okay? You still have the infusion in your left one," I pointed out, not wanting to accidentally rip it out.

"Okay," he agreed, holding out his right hand and waiting for Rooney to pull the glove over it.

"Just make sure you won't go full-on havoc around this place and destroy everything," I warned in a joking tone, and Ira held his hand out with a grumpy frown on his face, showing off his Hulk-resembling facial expression.

"Maybe I should go back and exchange these for that dinosaur I saw at the store," Rooney said sarcastically, making Ira's frown turn into a pout.

"No!" he whined, but Rooney was quick to assure him that she was only joking.

"I won't take them back. These suit you and they go well with your costume, huh?"

"Yes, and when we go home I can put it on and play Hulk," he told us determinedly.

"Sounds like a plan," Rooney agreed.

The door swung open and Dr. Cole walked inside, noticing the new gloves first thing as he looked at us.

"Are you a big Hulk fan?" he asked, checking his board and then walking around the bed to get to the IV.

"Yes, he's my favorite superhero," Ira said proudly, showing off his new gloves.

"He's great, huh? Wanna know who my favorite superhero is?"

Ira stared up at him with wide eyes, amazed that an adult also liked superheroes.

"My favorite is Hellboy."

Ira pushed his eyebrows into a frown, looking up at me with a questioning look.

He had no clue who Hellboy was, but I was glad he didn't as it was probably the most scary-looking out of all the superheroes ever created.

"That's one from a different type of comic, bud," I told him, then looked up at Dr. Cole. "He only knows Marvel and DC comics," I explained.

"I see. Well, should we check your insulin level one last time before you can head home, Ira?" Dr. Cole asked, and he nodded enthusiastically.

Doc turned to look at the monitor where Ira's pulse, temperature and other things were showing that I quite frankly had no idea about what I was seeing on the screen.

"His blood sugar is right where it's supposed to be, and overall he's got no red lights lighting up that we have to worry about. Now, about the pump. We left the sensor on his belly but took out the infusion set which is attached to the pump. It's up to you what you wanna do, but even if it's hard for you to accept it, the old pump he had might be a better resolution than measuring his insulin level every time by taking blood from his finger."

I knew the old pump never caused any problems, and making Ira take a shot every time he needed insulin wasn't what I wanted for him.

I looked at Rooney who was watching me closely while I made my decision. "If the old pump decides to ruin shit again, I can't promise you I'll be back at this hospital again," I told him, being somewhat serious about it.

"Daddy, you said a bad word again," Ira said frustrated, and I brushed over his head to apologize.

"I'm sorry, buddy. It won't happen again," I told him, looking back at Dr. Cole again.

"I can promise you the old pump won't have any issues. It hasn't had any ever since we started hooking patients up with it, and I'm sorry once again for what happened."

After all these apologies, I was starting to feel bad that I was attacking him instead of the company that made those new pumps.

Rooney got up from the bed while Dr. Cole put a new infusion set onto Ira's belly and then he attached the tube and pump so the insulin could start flowing into his body whenever it was needed again.

"All set. Ready to go home, Ira?" he asked, and Ira quickly nodded with a wide smile.

"Have a nice day then, and I'll see you very soon for a checkup, okay?"

"Okay, thank you."

I smiled at my well-behaved son and said goodbye to Dr. Cole, and once he was out of the room, I let Rooney help Ira get dressed while I grabbed all the gifts and balloons to take back home.

"Are you hungry, buddy?" I asked, looking down at him as we walked down the hall, him holding Rooney's hand.

"Yes," he replied.

He hadn't had anything other than water and a smoothie from the hospital since early this morning, so I thought a drive to Divine for some delicious pasta and maybe even a dessert was much needed.

***

The afternoon went by fast, and in a blink of an eye, Ira was back in bed with his favorite Hulk next to him.

"Sure you don't wanna sleep in my bed tonight?" I asked.

If it were up to me, I'd keep him right next to me until he's eighteen, but the brave little boy he was, he shook his head and said, "I wanna sleep in my bed with Hulk."

"All right. If you need anything, you know where to find me."

I leaned in to kiss his forehead, then let Rooney who was sitting on the edge of the bed with me give Ira a goodnight kiss as well before we both got up.

"Sleep tight," Rooney whispered, and Ira waved at us before we went out of his room.

"I'll be checking in on him every half an hour," I muttered, walking into the kitchen with Rooney.

"He's okay, Wells. You need to relax a little bit and take deep breaths. You're agitated," she said, rubbing my arm to show her affection.

God, I loved this woman so much, but despite that, I still felt there were things we needed to discuss.

I pulled her to me and cupped her face in both hands, making her look into my eyes and stay close to me with her body pressed against mine.

"Wanna go to bed and talk? There wasn't much talking going on between us today," I said.

"Yeah, sounds good," she replied, knowing this couldn't be avoided.

I smiled, hoping to show her that I wasn't too miserable, and after leaning in and kissing the tip of her nose gently, I nodded toward the hallway. "Come on."

I took her hand and let my fingers move through hers to hold onto her, and when we got to the bedroom, we both took off our clothes and hopped into bed.

After getting comfortable and all cuddled up, I turned my head to look at her, brushing her long hair back to see her face in the moonlight.

We looked at each other for a while before I finally started talking.

"How long have you known you loved me?" I asked, needing to know to not boost my ego, but to find out if this silence between us could've been avoided.

It wasn't only her though.

I was dealing with the same shit, and if I had only slapped myself in the face, I would've realized sooner that I wanted to be with her.

"That evening we met in the hallway, when you went to drop off Ira at your mother's...later that night I slowly started to see things clearly," she whispered.

So I had read her right that day.

She was close on making a decision, yet we weren't able to make a fucking move.

"I could've been holding you for the last four days," I replied, keeping my voice low.

A smile appeared on her beautiful, natural face, and I cupped her jaw to hold her head in place while I leaned in and kissed the corner of her mouth.

She didn't ask me the same question which only showed how much she lived in the present and didn't like to think back to what has been.

That was okay, because she damn well knew I've loved her already at the time.

"Promise me we'll be open about our feelings and thoughts from now on. I don't wanna second guess every little thing because I can't read your mind. I promise you I'll be honest. You're mine, Rooney," I whispered close to her lips.

"I promise you, Wells."

I'd remember those words now and forever, and she had nothing to worry or overthink about because I promised her the same.

I kissed her lips before either of us could say another word, and I immediately deepened the kiss to get more of her.

Tasting her sweetness and feeling her tongue dance with mine so gently yet passionately.

I kept my hand on her neck to take control, leaning over her to push her back into the pillow and deepening the kiss.

Soft moans left her lips while I moved my tongue against hers gently, and she gripped my shoulders as if she needed something to hold on to.

She was safe in my arms and I wanted her to know that.

No matter our age difference, no matter where we stood in life at this moment, we knew we belonged together and would make this work.

For us, including Ira.

If Rooney wouldn't have been so caring toward my son, I wouldn't have taken this step. Just a single disagreement from Ira and I wouldn't have taken a chance on Rooney.

It didn't sound right, but if Ira wouldn't be okay with this, I didn't feel like having a new woman by my side.

I tilted my head more to the side to push my tongue even deeper into her mouth, making her let out another one of those sweet sounds, and my fingers around her throat tightened before she pulled at my hair tightly.

My dick needed attention, but since it wasn't as easy being intimate with a little boy who also had to adjust to the fact that a new woman was now in his life, I had to quickly get rid of my hardness as I heard his footsteps come closer.

I broke the kiss, giving Rooney an apologetic look right before Ira pushed my bedroom door open, standing there in his pajamas and his fingers twirled around his hair.

"Changed your mind, bud?" I asked, knowing it wouldn't be as easy falling asleep tonight.

But kudos to him for trying.

Ira shook his head and took in the scene in front of him, his eyes hooded and shiny from being tired.

"Come here," I told him, reaching out my hand and shifting on the bed to get a little more space between Rooney and me.

Ira walked up to the end of the bed and crawled up, then he nestled himself right in the middle of us.

"Is this okay?" I asked Rooney.

She smiled at me and nodded, pulling the covers over our bodies and making sure Ira was comfortable and tucked in.

"This is perfect," she whispered, placing a hand on Ira's side as he turned to look at me.

I smiled at them, loving everything I was seeing.

Leah might not have been here with us, and Ira now knew his mother was in heaven, but I was happy to see them be this close.

I wasn't expecting Rooney to be Ira's new mom. She's young and in college and still had time to figure out if she'd one day wanna become a mother herself, but for now, I was glad they found each other this way.

I lied down next to Ira and placed my hand on the side of his head, and after leaning in and kissing his forehead, I looked back up to Rooney as she kept smiling at me with that sweet, gentle smile.

"Is this okay for you?" she asked back.

I couldn't have nodded any quicker. "This is perfect," I said, repeating her own answer.

We looked at each other for a while, thinking this couldn't get any better.

"I love you," I whispered, but before she could reply, Ira had something to say as well.

"We didn't visit Mommy," he said, looking up at me and then turning his head to look at Rooney.

"My mommy's an angel," he explained, making my damn heart squeeze tightly.

Rooney smiled down at him and nodded. "She is, hm?"

"Yes, and Daddy said we can visit her at the...uhm, I don't remember what's it called," he said with a frown.

"The cemetery. I'm staying home with you tomorrow and we can go visit Mommy, okay?" I suggested.

"Okay."

As much as it wouldn't have bothered me, I didn't want Rooney to come along. Ira meeting his mother for the first time was something I wanted to keep as a memory for only the two of us.

A special memory, and I knew Rooney understood.

"And when we get back home, we're gonna take Rooney on a special date," I whispered to Ira.

His eyes widened. "Okay! It's a surprise," he whispered a little too loudly, but Rooney had already heard my plan anyway.

She laughed softly, caressing Ira's arm as I winked at her.

I was right about her nestling herself right next to my son and me, even though it didn't take as long as I thought it would.

I was happy, and Ira was too.

And seeing Rooney content and serene instead of having all those worries swirling around in her head made me feel the same.

Chapter Forty

Rooney

"I'm ready!" Ira called out as he came running out of his bedroom and into the kitchen.

I was helping Wells clean up the table after eating together, and since I had to get to class soon, he was nice enough to get up early to prepare breakfast for us.

"You look amazing, Ira!" I told him, watching him show off the outfit he put together by himself without Wells's offered help.

"I like the elephants on the sweater," I said, smiling.

"Mommy likes elephants because she saved them in India!" he told me enthusiastically.

"She'll love it, buddy," Wells said, then he looked at me to explain more. "Leah was part of an animal rescue organization. He's seen pictures of her riding an elephant in India."

"That's amazing. She'll be over the moon to find out you love animals just as much as she does," I said to Ira.

"Yes, and she will love the flowers we buy for her."

He was the sweetest, and I was excited for him to finally get to be close to Leah. Wells told me about their talk and how he carefully explained to him that his mother wasn't with us anymore, and he took it pretty well, although I was sure he'd soon ask more about her and how it actually happened.

He was too young to be told that she died from complications at his birth, but whenever he was ready, Wells would surely tell him all about it.

"Did you clip the pump to your pants?" Wells asked, reaching down to check, but Ira shook his head and pulled his sweater up further.

"I put it around my neck, see?"

"Is that more comfortable for you?" Wells asked. Ira shrugged.

"Probably, huh? You can always change it back if you want to. Go put on your shoes so we can go visit Mommy," he said, and Ira was off to get his shoes on.

"You sure you don't want me to drive you to class?" Wells asked as he turned to look at me.

I shook my head while drying my hands with a towel, then I wrapped my arms around his neck and smiled.

"I need to get a few paintings to class and back, but thank you."

His arms moved around my back to hold me close to his body, and after eyeing me for a while, he leaned in to kiss my lips.

"Be ready by six tonight, all right?"

I nodded, excited to see where he and Ira would take me. "Can't wait."

"I'm ready!" Ira called out again, making us smile and let go of each other.

We walked into the hallway to see Ira stand up from the floor, and when I reached him, I squatted down and placed both hands at his sides.

"Have a wonderful day visiting your mommy, and tell her all about your favorite toys and animals."

Ira studied my face for a while before tilting his head to the side with a questioning look. "Do you think she likes Hulk too?"

"I *know* she does. Hulk's the coolest," I said with a grin, then I pulled him into a hug while he wrapped his arms around my neck.

"I'll see you tonight."

"Okay," he replied, and once he let go of me, I pressed a kiss to his temple before standing back up and turning to look at Wells.

"Drive safe. Text me if there's anything you need."

"I will. Have a good day," he told me, kissing me and then opening the door for me.

"Bye," I said, smiling at them and then heading upstairs to get ready for class.

My heart was full, and it wouldn't stop pounding ever since last night.

There was nothing left for us to discuss or go over. We knew we were meant to be together, and I couldn't stay away from them any longer.

When I got inside my apartment, I heard Evie talking to someone, but as no one responded while she was quiet, I figured she was on the phone.

I decided to leave her alone and take a quick shower before bothering her with my new-found happiness, but when I heard her say Michail's name, she caught my attention.

I walked over to the kitchen and saw Evie sitting there at the table with what looked like a contract in front of her, her thumb clicking the pen nervously.

"I know it's still early for us, but I promise you and your wife that your investment in us was worth every single cent."

Sounded serious, and I had never seen her like this before.

Sure, she came from a family that knew how business was done, but she's only ever wanted to party instead of following in her parents' footsteps.

"Yes, she knows all about it and we will be ready for the grand opening in one month. Great, thank you so much, Michail. And tell Morgana I said hi!"

She hung up the phone and grinned at me, but I was suspicious and unsure to find out what kind of promise she made him.

With my arms crossed over my chest, I raised a brow waiting for her to explain it all.

"Okay, don't freak out...but we'll open the gallery in one month and Michail already sent some pictures of our paintings to potential clients who want to come check them out soon."

My jaw dropped. "Evie...that building isn't even close to being renovated. How on earth are we going to present our paintings in only one month?"

"Relax, Rooney. My parents have everything under control. I sent them the pictures of how we want the interior to look, and they have already hired people to start working on it tomorrow. We can finally sell our paintings and make money," she said in a sing-song tone of voice.

Wasn't complaining about that, but I wasn't sure we could get everything up and running in just one month.

"Stop worrying, Rooney. God, they have everything under control and all we have to do is get our paintings to the gallery when it's done."

"It's the lack of clients that's worrying me, Evie."

We didn't have many connections other than people who liked art but would never buy them, and Michail's connections first had to decide whether they wanted our art or not.

Nothing was sure as of yet.

"People talk, and before we know it, we have a line forming outside the building with people wanting to buy our paintings. I promise you."

I took a deep breath and hoped for the best.

I'd have to send Michail a message to say thank you for everything he and his wife were doing for us.

I just hoped he didn't expect much in return, because there's wasn't a lot I could offer.

Wells

There were quite a few people at the cemetery when I parked my car near the front gate.

I unbuckled my seatbelt and turned in my seat to look at Ira who was already taking in the few headstones he could see from afar.

"It looks scary," he said.

"Well, it's not a scary place, buddy. This is where all the angels are, and see how many people are visiting them?"

"Yes, there are people visiting their angels," he said, suddenly feeling much better about the fact that we weren't here all alone.

"Another thing, Ira. We have to be very quiet to not bother anyone, okay? We can talk to Mommy when we get to her."

"Okay. I'll be very quiet," he promised me, whispering and holding his finger up to his lips.

"Now, do you have Hulk and the flowers?" I asked.

He wanted to hold them on our drive here, making sure they would stay pretty for his mom.

"Here," he said, starting to unbuckle his seatbelt.

I got out of the car and helped him out, and with the flowers and Hulk in his arms, we started to walk along the graveled path to get to Leah.

I was starting to get emotional, not only because I would be close to Leah again, but because of Ira and his determination to meet her for the first time.

He was still young, but I was starting to think he really understood what all of this was.

We turned left where colored leaves covered the path, and Ira smiled as he stepped on them to make them crackle underneath his feet.

"It's pretty here," he whispered, and I nodded to agree with him.

"Here, Ira," I said, stopping in front of Leah's headstone, and Ira turned to look at the picture on it, smiling as he recognized her.

"Hi, Mommy!" he said in a loud whisper, waving at her and immediately making my eyes tear up.

Fuck...I knew I would get emotional, but not this soon.

I squatted down and pulled him between my legs, both facing the headstone and looking at it.

"This is my favorite superhero. His name is Hulk and he smashes a lot of things!" he explained.

It was crazy how he just accepted the fact that his mother wasn't physically with us anymore, but he talked to her as if she were.

It warmed my heart, and I caressed his sides while he continued to talk to Leah in the sweetest way ever.

"And we bought flowers because Daddy said you like flowers. They are very beautiful," he told her, and I smiled at the little boy we created.

Although he wasn't planned, he was so, so loved and I would've made the biggest mistake not to take him in the day her ex brought him to me.

"Wanna put the flowers on there?" I said, pointing next to the other flowers I knew Leah's parents or friends must've brought.

"And Hulk too?" he asked, looking at me and frowning as he saw my face. "Daddy, you don't have to cry, okay?"

That was so much easier said than done, but for him, I'd do anything.

"Okay, bud. I'll stop crying," I said quietly, kissing his cheek. "You can place Hulk next to the flowers, yes."

I watched him put both things carefully in front of the headstone, and after a little bit of hesitation, he looked at me with question in his eyes. "Can I give her a kiss?"

"Of course you can. Do it like this," I said, as the headstone could've been dirty.

I was sure Leah's parents made sure it was clean at all times, still I didn't want Ira to press his lips against the stone itself.

I lifted my hand to my lips to kiss my fingertips and then press them against Leah's picture.

Ira watched me and then did the same, smiling.

"Hey, you know what else Mommy liked that you like as well?" I asked, pulling him closer to me again.

"No, what?" he asked excitedly.

"Hulk juice! She drank one almost every day to stay strong and healthy, just like you."

Well, it wasn't Hulk juice per se, but a smoothie she always told me to drink as well because it helped with our immune system.

"Woah, really? Maybe we can bring her one next time," he suggested.

"Sounds like a great idea. I'm sure she'll love it."

Seeing Ira like this, and knowing he wasn't sad assured me that taking him here was the right thing to do.

We spent another hour right there with Leah, talking about everything Ira wanted to talk about.

I didn't push him to leave, and if he'd wanted to, we'd even stay here the whole day.

But to change things up a bit, yet stay close to Leah, I suggested to go on a little walk into town and get something to eat before heading back to her and saying goodbye for today.

He promised Leah that we'd be back soon, and he made me pinky-promise to take him here every day.

Since that would be a bit of a problem as I had to work and it was a one-hour drive, I promised him to take him once a month.

He agreed to that, and after waving at Leah's headstone one last time, we got into the car to drive back to Riverton.

"That was nice, hm?" I asked, looking back at him through the rearview mirror.

"Yes, it was so much fun with Mommy," he said, smiling brightly and then turning his attention back to one of the books he had brought with him.

Leah was still with us, and I knew Ira would be thinking about her every day from now on.

Chapter Forty-One

Rooney

"Rooney!" Ira called out my name as he saw me come down the stairs.

Wells had texted me that they were ready to leave to go eat dinner, and I had already been home for almost two hours, dressed and ready for them to come back from visiting Leah.

I smiled at him and picked him up as he reached me, holding his arms out to me and then wrapping them around my neck to hug me.

"Hey, little guy. How was your day?" I asked, kissing his head before looking at him.

"It was so much fun! I talked to Mommy and I gave her flowers and Hulk," he told me, his eyes happy and wide.

"That's wonderful. And what did you talk to her about?" I asked.

He obviously loved talking about Leah, and I wouldn't stop him from doing so if that's what he needed and wanted.

"About superheroes and Hulk and animals!"

"That sounds amazing. I'm glad you had a great day," I told him, letting him down again and looking up as Wells walked out of the apartment.

"Hey, gorgeous," he said with a swoon-worthy smile.

"Hello, handsome," I replied, grinning and placing a hand at the side of his neck as he came closer to kiss me.

I missed them so much today, and I was excited to spend the evening with them.

"Hungry? Ira and I are taking you to a nice little place we're sure you'll love," he said, his hand on my waist.

"Very hungry," I replied.

"We're going to the Mexican restaurant," Ira said, and I looked back down at him with a smile.

"Oh, I love Mexican food! What about you?"

"I love tacos."

Simple, but a very, very important fact.

"I totally agree, buddy," I said, grinning, and then realizing that I had called him by Wells's nickname for him.

Neither of them seemed to mind though, and together we walked down the stairs to get to his car.

Once we were driving, we listened to Ira tell us all about the book he was reading, and we all learned a few more things about the Middle Ages.

It was a sound book, so instead of having to read it, which Ira wasn't able to yet, we listened to the man speaking about knights, medieval clothes and other things.

I liked how wide his span of interests was, and for once he wasn't talking about superheroes.

Not that he bothered anyone with that, but he was a smart kid and kept so much information in his brain after listening to something new.

"All right, bud. You can take one of the other books with you, but you won't be able to hear anything in there with the medieval book," Wells said.

"Okay, I take this one," he said, showing us his book about reptiles.

I wondered if Wells had already decided on what kind of pet to get him, as it would be a nice Christmas present for Ira.

Once we got inside and sat down at the table, we already ordered something to drink and then looked at the menu to figure out what we wanted to eat.

"I've checked on their website to see if they have some sort of nutrition board for their food items, and luckily they did," Wells explained, looking up from the menu.

I nodded and looked at Ira as he held up his finger to let us know he was about to talk.

"I can eat a beef taco and a vegetable taco," he told me.

Wells was very careful with what Ira eats, and although it might be too much supervising, I thought it was a good thing that he monitored his son's diet.

"That sounds really delicious. Maybe I'll have a beef taco as well," I said, smiling at him.

It didn't take us long to choose our dinner, and to our surprise, it came quicker than expected.

"So, tell me. How was class today?" Wells asked as he pulled Ira closer to the table on his chair.

"It was fun. We got to see all the other students' paintings they worked on for the past few weeks, and it was nice seeing the different styles and inspirations on the canvases."

"You need to show me all of your paintings one day. I'm sure you have some sort of picture gallery on your phone, hm?"

"Actually, I take a polaroid of every painting and put the picture in a box. Ira's is in there too," I said with a smile.

"Bring that box with you sometime. I wanna see the pictures."

I nodded and took a bite of my taco, then I remembered what happened this morning and sighed.

"Remember how I told you about that couple wanting to invest in Evie and me? Well, they bought the building and want it to be ready in a month. Evie's parents have put money into the renovations, but I don't know how Evie and I could run a gallery while we're still in college," I said, starting to freak out a little bit.

"Well, it's just a gallery, right? Be there whenever you have time to. Or need to. I don't think it's necessary for an art gallery to be open twenty-four-seven if the artists aren't available at that time."

I nodded at his statement, puckering my lips and thinking about it before replying. "Besides...Evie and I wanted to work there once we've graduated. Take commissions and maybe hold a few events to show off our art."

"Sounds like a good idea to me. You're still in college. You'll have enough time to figure things out, but I think it's great that you already found someone who wants to help you in the future."

I agreed, though it was still a little overwhelming.

"Can we paint again soon?" Ira asked, and I looked at him and nodded.

"Of course we can. I can bring paint and brushes with me on Friday, so we can paint all night, okay?"

He nodded before taking a bite of his taco.

"Maybe we can get Daddy to paint too this time, what do you think?"

"Yes!" he said, wide-eyed.

Wells chuckled and took a sip of his Coke. "I'll try my best. I'm not nearly as good as you two are at it."

"We'll teach you, Daddy. It's not difficult at all," Ira assured him, making us both laugh.

"We'll see about that, bud," he said, chuckling and then looking back at me.

Without saying another word for a while, we enjoyed our food and each other's company, with our hearts filled with gratitude and love.

Wells

I had to have Rooney to myself for the rest of the night, so to her surprise, but Ira's knowing, we dropped him off at my mother's house so he could spend the night and the next day with her.

I had to get back to work in the morning anyway, and spending one night alone with Rooney was exactly what I needed.

As we arrived back at my apartment, I gave her a few seconds to take off her coat and shoes before I pushed her up against the wall in the hallway and kissed her lips while my hands moved from her hips to her ass.

A smile spread across her lips, and I deepened the kiss right after to show her how serious I was.

My hands squeezed her ass tightly, then I lifted her up to make her wrap her legs around my hips to hold herself up while her hands moved into my hair.

"I need to be inside you," I mumbled against her lips, feeling as her body shivered in response.

And that was all I needed.

I carried her into the bedroom and let her down on the bed so she was sitting on the edge of it while I kept kissing her with my hands cupping her cheeks now.

I pushed my tongue inside her mouth and played with hers as her hands moved up and underneath my sweatshirt.

She knew exactly where this was heading, and without hesitating, she unbuckled my belt and then opened the button and zipper of my pants to then push them down, followed by my boxer briefs.

When my dick was out, it was already hard and ready for her touch, and sure enough, Rooney wrapped her hand around the base and leaned in to kiss the tip before her lips moved over it.

I cupped the back of her head with one hand and pushed her closer to me, but I let her take control right after.

Her hand and mouth moved along my shaft, making me clench my jaw and fist her hair tightly.

"Fuck...just like that, love. Keep that pretty mouth around my dick," I rasped, watching her every move to not miss a thing.

She was so goddamn good at this, and I never wanted her to stop.

But before I knew it, the tension inside of me started to rise quickly, making my body tense up as she sucked harder.

"You're so damn beautiful, Rooney," I whispered, brushing her hair back with my other hand as her eyes looked up at me, glowing and filled with mischief.

She knew she didn't have to do much to make me hard, but I didn't wanna come in her mouth.

"You're teasing me again. Fuck, love. You really wanna play this game with me tonight?" I asked, reaching for her throat and cupping it gently.

Her eyes flashed with some type of naughtiness, and although I liked that look on her, I really didn't want to shoot my load in her mouth.

I took a small step back so she had to release my dick from her mouth, and before she could say anything, I turned her onto her stomach with her legs dangling down the edge of the bed and pulling her pants down to reveal her round ass.

I gave a gentle smack to her ass before pushing her legs apart and positioning myself between them, and after pulling down her panties as well, I grabbed my shaft and brushed the tip along her folds before sliding into her wetness easily.

She'd already gotten used to my size, but her soft cry made me stop deep inside of her to let her adjust herself a little before I started to thrust in and out of her.

Fast and hard.

Just how we both liked it.

I gripped her hips tightly and pulled her back against me with each thrust to bury myself deeper inside of her, and every time I hit that wall inside of her, a moan left her lips, making my dick harder.

"Please," I heard her beg, reaching back with one hand to grip my wrist. "Harder," she then breathed.

She didn't have to tell me twice.

I continued to thrust into her and reached to her head to grip her hair again, pushing the side of her face against the mattress.

That way I still had a good view of her face while pleasure washed over her, and to make her feel even more, I reached around her hips between the mattress and her body to rub my fingers over her pounding clit.

Her moans got louder, and she tried to muffle them by covering her mouth with her hand, but the harder I fucked her, the louder she became.

I loved her like this.

Carefree and needy.

"Keep squeezing my dick with your sweet pussy and I'll come deep inside of you, love," I encouraged, knowing that's exactly what she wanted.

Her walls were warm and wet around me, and the way her pussy pulsated made my dick throb harder after each thrust.

I couldn't hold it in any longer, and only seconds after she moaned my name, I followed close behind, letting my cum fill her until it flowed out of her and down my length.

We both had to get our breathing under control, so talking wasn't really happening in that moment.

But the longer we stayed silent, the stronger the love between us got.

She was my girl, and there was no way I could ever leave her.

Chapter Forty-Two

Rooney

One month later

They really managed to pull it off.

The gallery was renovated, and in only thirty minutes, people would come inside to see what Evie's parents have done to this old building.

It looked incredible, and it exceeded all of my expectations for sure, but I had never been this nervous in my life before.

My palms were sweaty and the dress I was wearing was way too tight, making it even harder for me to breathe.

All of our finished paintings were hanging on the bourbon brick walls, and others were displayed on easels to go with the rustic look of the whole building.

"I can smell your nervousness from up here," Evie called out, and I turned to look up at her, standing on the large, spiral staircase leading to our new studio where we have put most of our supplies already.

I was still painting at home, as I didn't wanna leave the apartment after coming home from college.

There was no need for us to paint at the studio, but it was nice knowing we were set for after graduation.

At least I hoped that was gonna be the case.

"What if they won't like our paintings?"

"One more of those idiotic questions and I will throw my favorite work of yours at your head," she warned, coming down the stairs as graceful as ever.

She looked amazing, but then, she always did.

I had to convince myself that I didn't look like a potato in this dress, and after staring at myself in the mirror for a while, I decided that I didn't look as bad as my mind told me I did.

"It's gonna be great, Rooney. Michail promised that there will be many of his friends coming tonight, and who knows...maybe we'll already get some new interested buyers."

I hoped so.

What was the point of having a gallery, and talent, if no one would buy our art?

I took a deep breath and nodded, biting down on my bottom lip.

"Okay, it'll be fun," I said, trying to convince myself.

"Great, then let's open the doors and let them in early. There's already a line building outside," she said, making my eyes widen.

"What?"

Evie grinned and turned to the catering staff waiting behind the round table for people to stand and drink and eat something. "Get ready, people. These are very important guests."

The staff was the same from her parents' country club, so she didn't hold back on being bossy.

They all picked up their treys filled with either champagne, orange juice, or canapés for the guests to enjoy.

"Relax, look good, and talk about your art. That's all you need to do tonight."

Another deep breath, and Evie opened the large front door to reveal our guests standing outside, all dressed appropriately for an art gallery.

I let my eyes wander over their excited faces, which already calmed me down a little, but then I saw Wells holding Ira's hand, both dressed in black jeans, a navy blue sweater and a white-collared shirt underneath.

God, they both looked handsome, and when Ira saw me, he waved and pulled Wells toward me with a big smile.

"Hello, handsome man," I said, caressing his cheek and leaning down to kiss his forehead.

"Wow, you two look incredible! Did Daddy do your hair today?" I asked, and he quickly nodded.

They both had their hair slicked back with gel, resembling each other even more than usual.

"I like it," I told Ira, then I looked up at Wells who was eyeing my dress. "You look gorgeous, love," he told me, placing his hand on my waist and kissing me gently.

"Thank you," I whispered against his lips before taking a step back and grabbing his hand.

"I'm glad you're here. You took all my nervousness from me. Though, I think it will be back again soon," I said, laughing softly.

"You'll be fine, love. This is a great opportunity to get to know new people and potential buyers. Make the best out of it."

"I will. You two just take a look around, okay? There's even a little painting station in the back for the kids," I said.

I wanted that solemnly for Ira, so he could have some fun instead of staring at pictures which probably didn't really interest him much, but as I looked around, I saw more kids than expected coming in with their parents.

"That's great. Go network. We'll be fine," Wells told me, kissing me once more before taking Ira's hand again. "Let's go explore, hm?"

"Okay. Bye, Rooney!"

"Bye, buddy. Have fun!"

I watched them disappear in the crowd, and I turned to look for Evie.

She was standing by the entrance, talking to Michail and Morgana, and I thought I'd better go say hello too, as this wasn't just Evie's gallery now.

"Ah, there she is. Rooney, hope you're doing well," Michail said in his thick accent.

I shook his hand, then Morgana's, and with a smile I replied, "I'm wonderful, thank you. This is amazing. I'm still processing it all, but Evie and I are so, so grateful. Thank you for everything you've done for us," I said, unable to keep my gratitude on the downlow.

"We see potential in both of you. This evening is for you to enjoy, so have fun and talk to people about your art. Make them interested, all right?"

Evie and I both nodded, and once we said goodbye, we were both off to greet some of our guests.

It wasn't as bad as I thought it would be, and sure enough, I was walking up to strangers to tell them all about my paintings.

Wells

"We haven't been at an art gallery in a while, huh?"

Ira nodded, staring up one of Rooney's paintings of a woman holding flowers, which were almost dead though.

It was beautiful, and I loved the pastel pinks complimenting the light yellows in the canvas.

Rooney knew exactly what she was doing to people with art like that. It calmed them, made them reflect on every single thing that came to mind when they looked at the paintings.

"This is pretty," Ira said, tilting his head to the side.

"Yeah, it really is," I agreed. "Remember when you were little and I took you to the museum to look at art?"

"No, I don't remember," he said. Well, of course. He was only about a year at the time.

I smiled and squatted down next to him, placing my hand at his lower back. "I held you up to the paintings so you could see them better, and then I explained to you what was painted on those canvases."

Ira chuckled and scrunched up his nose. "That's silly, Daddy," he said, leaning against me.

"Why's that silly?"

"Because when I was a baby I didn't understand English," he pointed out.

Touché.

I laughed and stood back up. "Wanna check out the kid's area?"

"Yes."

We headed over there, and while Ira chose the colors he wanted to use, I picked up the oversized, already painted on shirt Rooney placed on the kid's chairs so their clothes wouldn't get dirty.

Great idea, I thought.

"Here, put this on, bud."

I helped him get the shirt on, then I let him start painting while I reached over to the round table to grab a glass of champagne for me.

As a waitress walked by, I stopped her with my hand on her arm. "Could I please get a glass of water for my son?"

"Oh, of course. I'll be right back," she replied, smiling.

I had to give it to Evie and her parents.

They knew how to host events.

"What are you painting, Ira?" I asked, sitting down next to him on a kid's chair.

No one else was here, so I wasn't taking up any space.

"It's a woman with flowers," he said.

I smiled, watching him copy Rooney's art. Maybe I should get a painting for my apartment, as Ira already had his superheroes hanging on his bedroom wall.

"Here you go, sir," the waitress said, holding her tray with the water on it toward me.

"Thank you." I took the glass and placed it in front of Ira, telling him to take a few sips every now and then.

"If there's anything you need, I'll be around here somewhere."

Her flirtatious voice had been ignored by me immediately, but I smiled at her and said thank you again before she left.

No need for her to flirt.

I had my girl, and I wanted her to be mine forever.

"Wells, so good to see you here," a familiar voice then said shortly after, and I turned to look up at Rooney's parents, looking a whole lot different in a dress and suit.

"Hello, Louise," I greeted, standing up and taking her hand. "You too. Rooney didn't tell me you two would be here tonight."

I shook Devon's hand as well with a nod. "We wouldn't miss this. We're surprised this building is so big," he said.

"Yeah, it's incredible. Hey, bud? Look who's here," I said, making him snap out of his focus.

"Hi!" he said, standing up on his chair and reaching his hand out for Devon.

He definitely took a liking to Rooney's dad, which I found incredibly sweet.

"Hello, Ira. Wow, you look good tonight! Did Daddy help you get dressed or did you choose this outfit on your own?"

Ira looked at me for a second, then he pointed at me and said, "Daddy did. Rooney said I look handsome."

"Oh, you do, sweetie," Louise told him with a smile, then she placed a hand at my upper arm. "Rooney told us a little bit about what happened between you two after driving back home from the ranch. We've noticed both of you being a little tense, but I'm happy you talked it out."

I nodded. "She's the one for me. We both had our struggles, but we're happy," I told her, taking another look at Devon still holding Ira.

"We know you'll take good care of her. Not that she needs to be looked after, but I'm glad she has someone to lean on. Someone other than Evie," he said, not meaning it in a negative way.

Evie was just a little...wild. And Rooney needed someone she could slow down with. Take a breath and just let go every now and then.

"Daddy loves Rooney," Ira assured her parents.

"Oh, we know he does. And she loves him right back," Louise said with a wink.

She looked back at me and smiled. "I'm sure you've talked to her already tonight? She looks gorgeous, doesn't she? It's been a while since I've seen her in a dress like that."

I looked at the crowd and found Rooney standing there, talking to an elderly couple.

Her smile lit up the whole room, making me smile as well. "She looks incredible," I said in a hoarse voice.

While I watched her, I could see her eyes light up, and after she shook both their hands, she stood there in shock for a second before looking around to find a familiar face.

Evie walked over to her, her eyes wide and their hands holding each other's tightly.

Something must've happened that made them try their hardest not to freak out in the middle of the room, and when Evie's dad walked up to them with a small note in his hand, they couldn't contain their excitement anymore.

"Ohmygod!" Evie said, and Rooney added something I couldn't quite understand.

"Can I have everyone's attention, please?" Evie's dad, Dan, said loudly.

Rooney looked our way before Dan continued to talk, and her smile brightened even more as the room quieted down.

"Thank you all for coming tonight. First off, I wanted to say thank you to Michail and Morgana for making this possible for my daughter, Evie, and her best friend, Rooney. They both had a dream ever since they were little, and it seemed as if painting was the only thing keeping them close. Their special friendship helped each other to become better at what they were doing, pushing each other to give their all and become the best versions of themselves. Their art is just as special as their friendship, and I know they will do great things in the future."

Rooney's cheeks were turning bright red as all eyes were on her and Evie, but she smiled at us and gave Ira who was still in her dad's arms a little wave.

"And they have proven that their art is already loved. Mr. and Mrs. Andersson bought one of Evie's, and one of Rooney's paintings tonight at their grand opening!"

The crowed clapped and cheered, and the happiness in Rooney's eyes made my whole body warm.

"That's incredible," Louise said in awe, waiting for her daughter to reach us and then hugging her tight.

"That's fantastic, my dear. You sold your very first painting!"

Tears rolled down Rooney's face as she let her mother hold her, and when Louise let go, she turned to her dad and hugged him too, letting Ira in on it as well.

"So happy for you, darling," Devon said, letting go of her again to let it be my turn now.

I pulled her closer with my hands on her waist, kissing her lips before hugging her tight. "I'm so proud of you, love. I knew it would work out," I told her, letting her nestle her face into the crook of my neck.

"I'm so happy. I love you," she whispered.

"I love you too," I replied quietly before letting go of her and cupping her cheeks to brush away her tears.

"Are you sad?" Ira asked, worry in his voice.

Rooney laughed softly and shook her head, then she rubbed his back to assure him she wasn't crying because she was sad.

"I'm very happy. That's why I'm shedding some tears, you know?" she explained.

Ira studied her face for a while and tried to figure out if she was being honest or not, but after a few seconds he smiled. "I'm happy too."

We laughed, and I caressed the back of his head. "We all are, buddy."

Epilogue

Rooney

My senior year in college wasn't as bad as I thought it would be.

The stress other people anticipated wasn't really there for me, and ever since we made that first sale at our gallery's opening, people have been interested in our art and calling or emailing us daily.

It worked out better than we imagined, and in only one month, Evie and I would work full-time at the gallery, painting, holding exhibitions, and selling our art.

Life was perfect, and with nothing else standing in our way, we could relax and live a little.

It's been almost a year since the opening, and I've never been happier in my life.

I parked the car in front of the apartment complex after a long day at the gallery and walked inside to head up the stairs and stop in front of Wells's door.

He gave me a key a while ago, so I could come and go whenever I pleased. He had asked me to move in with him last month, but I told him that I wasn't ready for that yet, or to make a decision.

Deep down I knew I wanted to move in with him and Ira, seeing as I was already spending every night here with them.

Though, that would mean I'd leave Evie alone, and that could result in her throwing parties again.

She hasn't changed a bit, and we even had a few fights and disagreements when it came to our art, but we were all good now.

Our friendship was stronger than her outbursts of anger when something didn't go her way.

"Anybody home?" I called out as I entered the apartment, and sure enough, Ira ran down the hall to greet me.

He had grown quite a bit in the past months, just like his blond locks, but he was still the sweetest little boy ever.

"Hey, buddy!" I said, hugging him tight as he wrapped his arms around my hips.

"Look what we got!"

He held up a brochure about turtles, and I already had an idea where they've been today.

"No way! Did you go get the turtle we've been visiting?" I asked, my eyes full of excitement.

"Yes! He's swimming! Come on!"

It was hard seeing him grow, and thinking about his fifth birthday coming up was making me sad but happy at the same time.

I let him pull me into the living room where we had already placed a tank on a steady stand.

It was a semi-aquatic tank where the turtle could go for a swim but also climb onto rocks to sunbathe.

We had set up the interior of the tank already, so the only thing that was left to do was place a turtle inside.

"Look!" Ira said, stopping right in front of the tank to admire the little turtle which would double in size eventually.

"Aw, he's adorable! Did you give him a name yet?" I asked.

"Yes, his name is Donatello because of the Ninja Turtles, but I call him Donny."

"I was hoping he'd get a Ninja Turtles name," I said with a grin, turning to him and kissing his head.

"We'll take good care of Donny. He'll have the best life ever," I promised.

"Yeah!"

"I see you met Donny already." Wells's voice made me turn around and look at him, standing there in only his jeans as his wet hair dripped all over the floor.

"He's a nice turtle," I said, grinning and walking over to him to kiss him.

"I missed you today," he whispered against my lips, placing both hands on my lower back.

"I missed you too."

"Okay if we eat dinner here tonight? I don't feel like going out," he told me, brushing his thumb along my back gently.

"Yeah, of course. Is everything okay?" I asked, worry filling my voice.

"I'm good. Just wanna spend this rainy evening with you two in here."

"Sounds good to me," I said, smiling up at him and pressing one more kiss to his lips.

"Any new commissions today?" he asked as I walked back to the hallway to take off my coat and shoes.

"Yes, one. It's a bigger project, so I won't be taking any more for the rest of the month. Might take me a while," I said.

"That's good. And did you think about my offer?"

He meant moving in with him.

I turned to look at him and sighed, knowing he wouldn't accept no for an answer. But I wanted to tease him a little before telling him my answer.

"Are you sure you want all my clothes in your closet? And all my shoes and coats taking up your beautiful, free space?" I asked.

He chuckled. "You don't have that many clothes, love."

"But what if we fight? I have nowhere to run if I accidentally piss you off," I said quietly, not wanting Ira to hear me talk like this.

"We won't fight. But if we strangely do one day, I'll just lock you up in a room with me and wait until you talk to me again. It's that easy."

I really hoped we never had a fight, because that was definitely not a way to ease the tension.

I walked over to him and wrapped my arms around his neck, his hair wetting my sleeves.

"Are you sure you want me to move in?" I asked in a whisper.

His hands moved from my hips down to my ass, cupping it gently before squeezing it.

"One hundred percent, Rooney. I want you here with me every day and every night. Officially."

I puckered my lips and studied his face for a moment, then I tilted my head to the side with a smirk. "Can't we wait another year or so?"

His hands tightened on my ass, making me squeal. "I'm getting old, woman. It's either now or never. Make a decision. Now."

His bossy voice sent shivers down my spine, but I knew he wouldn't be that mad at me if I told him no.

"Okay, I'll move in with you and Ira," I said, smiling and pushing my hand into his hair.

A smug grin spread across his face, then he kissed me as his hands now cupped my face.

It was the right thing to do, and although it took me one month to say yes, I didn't have to fight with my mind and heart about it.

Thank God.

Wells

I was already planning the day for when she moved all her things into my apartment while making dinner.

Ira was reading to Rooney, as he started kindergarten and I thought it was a good time to teach him how to read.

He loved it and read at least four strips of a comic or whatever book he was into to me and Rooney.

We loved how fast he progressed, and because of that, we let him have the pet turtle.

It was an easy pet to keep at home, but I made him promise to help clean Donny's tank whenever it was time to clean it.

Of course he didn't refuse that.

His health hadn't changed much ever since the accident with that new pump, and his diabetes was still under control.

There wasn't much complaining from Ira's side, but he was already used to the pump anyway.

"Dinner's ready," I said, placing thc platcs onto the table and looking over to the couch.

"Coming," Rooney said, brushing through Ira's hair and praising him for reading well.

"You're getting better each day. Soon you can start reading one of Daddy's books, hm?" she suggested.

I chuckled, thinking those books were a little too deep for a four-year-old.

Psychology and Philosophy...didn't think he'd enjoy it much.

We sat down at the table and I poured us all some water. "Looks delicious," Rooney told me with a smile, and I thanked her after setting down the water bottle again.

"I tried something with the spices your mother gave me last week on the ranch. I hope I didn't ruin the taste by adding too much."

"I'm sure it's delicious, Daddy," Ira said, sounding older than he was, but thanks to him still calling me *Daddy*, he assured me he was still my little boy.

"Thanks, bud. Try it," I said, taking a bite of the rice mixed with veggies.

"It's really good," Rooney said, nodding and then smiling at me.

"Yes, it's really good," Ira repeated.

Good.

I was slowly getting better at new recipes.

"Any idea what you wanna do this weekend, Ira?" I asked.

"Can we visit Mommy?" he asked.

I looked at him and nodded. We'd been just last month, but I promised him I'd take him once a month, whenever he wanted to go.

"Of course we can."

"Wanna come too, Rooney?" he asked her.

She had come with us before, but in the beginning she didn't wanna bother us while Ira visited Leah.

Out of respect, but I knew Ira didn't mind.

"Of course. I'd love to come," she told him with a smile.

It was quiet for a while as we finished our dinner, and when I got up to get some more for Rooney and me, Ira asked, "Can people have two mommies?"

I puckered my lips and shrugged. "Of course they can. Some people have two moms or two dads. Maybe even three moms," I said, shrugging again.

"So...can Rooney be my mommy too? Then I'd have one in heaven, and one here with me."

His words made me want to squeeze him tight and never let go.

God, that kid was something else.

I looked at him and smiled. "That's up to her, bud."

When I gazed at Rooney, she already had tears in her eyes, trying not to cry from Ira's words which must've hit her hard.

In a good way, of course.

Ira looked at Rooney with a questioning look. "Can you be my mommy so I can have two?" he asked.

And that sent tears into my eyes as well.

She reached out to take Ira's hand, and after giving it a soft squeeze, she nodded. "Of course I can. I'd love to, Ira."

"Are those happy tears?" he asked unsure, and when she nodded again, he smiled brightly and got up from the chair to hug her tight.

"I love you, Ira. And I'll always be here for you," she whispered, holding him tightly against her body and kissing the top of his head.

"I love you too, mommy."

And in that moment I knew this bond between them, and the love they had for each other was forever.

They were my family, my love, and I couldn't have wished for a better one.

Follow Seven

Instagram
@sevenrue

Reader's Groups on Facebook
Seven Rue's Taboo
Extremely Taboo, Shockingly Sick and Twisted 2.0

Subscribe to my newsletter!
www.authorsevenrue.com/newsletter

SCAN THIS CODE FOR MORE SEVEN RUE BOOKS